HIDDEN ECHOES

MIKE JEFFERIES was born in Kent but spent his early years in Australia. He attended the Goldsmiths School of Arts and then taught art in schools and prisons. A keen rider, he was selected in 1980 to ride for Britain in the Belgian Three Day Event. He now lives in Norfolk with his wife and three stepchildren, working full-time as a writer and illustrator.

MIKE JEFFERIES

HIDDEN ECHOES

Grafton

An Imprint of HarperCollins*Publishers*

Grafton
An Imprint of HarperCollins*Publishers*,
77–85 Fulham Palace Road,
Hammersmith, London W6 8JB

First published by Grafton 1992
This edition published by Grafton 1992

9 8 7 6 5 4 3 2 1

Copyright © Mike Jefferies 1992

The Author asserts the moral right to
be identified as the author of this work

ISBN 0 586 21679 0

Set in Linotron Garamond (Stempel) by
Wyvern Typesetting Limited

Printed in Great Britain by
HarperCollinsManufacturing Glasgow

TO MY WIFE, SHEILA,
who watched the Doorcrack open and
in the widening silence heard the
hidden echo of other worlds.

CHAPTER ONE

A Mouthful of Waycake

THOLOCUS, the Clockmaster of Eternity, slowly rose from his chair at the head of the gathering of Diviners whom he had summoned from the halls of the hours to his tower on the rim of the City of Time. He spread his hands out in a helpless gesture across the mountainous piles of parchments, manuscripts, stone tablets and papyrus scrolls that littered the huge marble table, the empty ornately carved chairs and the stone benches and had eventually spilt in untidy waves across the floor. For a moment he surveyed the Diviners' solemn impassive faces and listened to the rub of the wind against the tall crystal windows and the persistent mumbling rhythm of the millions of clocks that measured time in all the vast, echoing halls of the city. A dark spectre of chaos and devastation rose in his mind. What would come to pass if the walls of reality were to wear thin and tear apart to reveal those ancient worlds that lay parallel to the Earth? Worlds that they, in their wisdom, had so carefully hidden in the dawn of time, whose savage beasts and wild peoples they had banished into the realms of myth and fantasy.

Tholocus shuddered and pushed the thoughts aside. He had not summoned the Diviners to share such speculation. It was true that once, an age of ages ago, there had been Doorcracks – flaws and secret roads through the shrouds that hid the earth – but they had long been sealed up and the knowledge of them swallowed by obscurity. No, the dark canker of disaster that threatened would not find a way through the fabric of reality, their Paradise was safe from such an invasion. But what form would the prophecies take? He leaned forward, resting his hands upon the writings of Heraclitus and addressed the Diviners gravely.

'I fear that we stand upon the yawning brink of a catastrophe. All that we have laboured to achieve will fall into silent and everlasting shadows. I am afraid that the hour-glass of Paradise is running out.'

He paused and joined his long, thin, brittle fingertips together as he frowned, his age-worn face crinkling into a maze of thoughtful wrinkles.

'This will happen unless with all this knowledge we can unravel the mysteries and the meanings of those ancient prophecies and discover what might lie beyond the destruction of Paradise.'

'There can be nothing but black emptiness, ruin and desolation. Nostradamus wrote it clearly,' Fusca interrupted, pointing accusingly at a thick leather-bound volume in front of him.

He rose unexpectedly from his chair, a thin, stunted Diviner in robes of livid mauve, picked up the book and held it above his head. His quavering voice was full of rancour as he continued, 'Or have you forgotten, Clock-master, that we were forewarned against weaving the walls of reality and creating a world apart, a Paradise called Earth?'

'Silence!' Tholocus snapped angrily, turning his piercing azure gaze upon Fusca as he quelled all further accusations before continuing in a softer voice.

'I have gathered you all here to seek a way of protecting what we created in the dawn of time: not to riddle the dust that cloaks old arguments.'

'There is a feeling of unrest that spreads throughout the

creatures and peoples from the Crystal Swamps and the Windrows of Thorn and it has travelled far across the wild grasslands of Bendran. I fear that the prophecies of doom will touch every reality,' called out another Diviner half-rising from his chair.

'Yes,' interrupted a third also climbing to his feet, 'There are even rumours that the Asiri, the feared Lord Mauder of Bendran, searches for a place he calls Paradise. Perhaps. . .'

'Enough!' cried Tholocus crashing his fist down so hard upon the piles of scrolls and books that clouds of dust billowed up to engulf him. 'The tick of time in Paradise cannot affect the other realities. The windsprings of their lives are measured differently from those on Earth,' and he dismissed with a brief shake of his head all thoughts that the cause of or the answer to the catastrophe might lie close enough to cast a shadow across his doorstone.

The Diviner, Kyostus rose from his chair and in a quavering voice he cried out, 'If only there were prophets alive who could help us to divine the shape and form that this catastrophe will take.'

'But there are,' Illundal answered loudly from the far end of the huge table where he sat partly obscured by an enormous pile of modern manuscripts and books that he had recorded through the lens in his tower. 'Great minds have sensed the shadow of doom. Look, there are dozens here: look at the writings of Mya Capthorne, or the works of Denso Alburton who through his dreams foretold of the deluge that has swept across the Crystal Swamps. He has dreams so powerful that they penetrate the walls of reality – surely they can help us?'

The Diviners' voices rose in heated argument. Some were shouting that it would be madness to reveal their existence or lift the veils of secrets that shrouded the City of Time because they could not predict the consequences of such an action. Others insisted that they must form a Grand Council of debate gathered from the learned of every reality. Tholocus clapped his hands and brought the gathering of Diviners to order.

'We shall cast votes and if enough of you are in favour of it Waymasters and Journeymen will be sent out to try to rediscover the secret ways, whatever the consequences.'

Near Miss as Winged Monster Wrecks Jumbo

At 9.15 am local time an incoming Jumbo Jet from London was forced to take avoiding action whilst touching down at John F. Kennedy airport. A strange winged beast had suddenly materialised on the main runway.

Captain Bealy Brown, the pilot, said, 'We didn't know what hit us. One moment we were making a completely normal touchdown on a clear runway and the next a huge, misshapen creature the size of the baggage terminal was right there, straddling the tarmac.'

Captain Brown applied the emergency brakes but the right wing tip hit the creature, causing the jet to swerve violently and the undercarriage to collapse. The animal vanished moments later but not before amateur photographer Norman Hart managed to take this photograph.

The senior air controller at JFK confirmed that something did appear momentarily on the radar screen and that a full investigation is now underway. Pan Am reported that none of the passengers travelling on the Jumbo was seriously hurt but one of the air hostesses had to be treated for concussion.

It was getting too dark to read the front page of the *New York Times* again. The light was too dim to study properly the hazy amateur photograph of the monstrous winged beast.

Harry Murmers let the *Times* slip from his fingers and crumple into an untidy mess of newsprint on top of the *Daily News* that already littered his desk and he swivelled his chair so that he could look out of his office window and see the panoply of bright lights and sheer glittering towers that made up the Manhattan nightscape. He let out an envious sigh.

'Why couldn't one of my writers come up with a story like that?'

Faintly in the street below his building he could hear the hum and roar of the evening traffic flowing out of the city. He heard the mournful wail of police sirens and the hoot of the tugs on the East River. He shrugged, turned back to his desk and flicked on the switch of his desk lamp. He blinked as the pool of bright light transformed the newspapers into a relief map of mountains, covered in light and shadow. He glanced to his left and let his eyes dwell for a moment on the rows of dull grey metal filing cabinets that covered the wall and contained so many manuscripts, so many unrealised hopes and fragile dreams.

'Jesus, those hacks on the *Times* and the *News* don't have the imagination of a herd of goats between them, but look what they can come up with on a slow news day!' he muttered, addressing the filing cabinet where he kept the fantasy writers' files.

Smoothing out the crumpled newspapers he began to fold them up when his intercom suddenly crackled and Kate's voice from the outer office filled his room.

'Mr. Murmers, there's a guy out here who says he has to see you right now. Right away. I've told him you're busy and I've tried to make him an appointment for tomorrow morning but he won't leave. He's acting very strangely and he refuses to give me his name. He won't leave until he's seen you. What can I do?'

Harry heard the note of panic begin to tighten Kate's voice and he stabbed at the button on his intercom. 'Kate. Kate, don't do a thing. I'll be right out.'

He began to move while he was still talking but before he could rise from his chair the office door burst open. Harry caught his breath and froze as he stared at the wild-looking figure who filled the doorway. He had read in the news how some of the street gangs from the Bronx had attacked a building just a few blocks away, overwhelming the security before robbing and wrecking a dozen offices, and now they were here. He was staring into the face of his worst nightmare. The figure advanced a step and the light from the desk lamp illuminated the vivid mass of tattoos that disfigured his face and powerful arms. His hair was a mass of petrified waves of orange curls. His clothes were little more than the stripped and speckled rags and tatters of stinking uncured animal skins that hung from his shoulders and were held at his waist by a wide belt of scaly leather with a vicious curved dagger thrust through it.

'Murms? Murmers?' the figure growled, the sound rising harshly from deep in his throat as he curled his lips back from two rows of yellowing teeth that had been filed into needled fangs. 'Are you the guardian of Denso Alburton?'

His dark black eyes narrowed questioningly as he reached the desk. The harshness in his voice broke the spell of fear that had frozen Harry. He clawed desperately as he tried to open the desk drawer beside him. Wrenching it half open he snatched at the Smith and Wesson automatic that lay just inside. He had bought the gun years ago when he had first opened the literary agency. It had come with the furniture but he had never imagined using it. It had been an extra insurance as it lay amongst the files and the paperclips, gathering dust, until now.

The strange tattooed figure was almost upon him. It was leering as it reached across the desk, smothering him with the stench of decay. The corruption of the ghetto clung to the rags. Harry didn't dare guess at how many more of the ghetto creatures were swarming through the outer office terrorising Kate. Savagely he kicked at his desk sending his swivel chair crashing backwards and away from his attacker, rolling into the windowsill as he brought the gun up. Clumsily he worked the slide back along the barrel with his left hand to pump the first round into the chamber. He was sweating so badly the butt was slipping in his right hand.

'Get outta here you bastard!' he shouted.

He aimed the barrel at the chest of the figure towering over him at point-blank range and squeezed the trigger. Nothing happened. The trigger remained stiff and unyielding with the safety catch locked on and the harder he squeezed the more it cut painfully into the first finger of his right hand.

'Damn,' Harry hissed, blinking at the trickles of sweat that were stinging his eyes as his attacker sprang lightly up on to the desk top and jumped down in front of him. He grasped the wavering gun barrel with his left hand.

'I came in peace. I am Tholocus' messenger,' he growled again, only now his voice was harder, more brutal and demanding.

Harry scrabbled with the safety catch and somehow managed to release it. He forced the barrel of the gun upwards and pointed it towards the figure's stomach. He squeezed desperately at the trigger. It sprang back from the pressure of his finger and the hammer snapped down with a sharp metallic click on the empty chamber. The hollow sound split the silence and seemed to echo around the room.

He squeezed again and again, terror jerking and twitching his trigger finger as he stared up helplessly into the face of his attacker. The sickening ache in the pit of his stomach swelled up to drown and swallow him as he remembered that he had never loaded the clip of ammunition that came with the gun, that he had locked it away in the other desk drawer in case of accidents. His attacker's face was so close now that he could see tiny insects no bigger than pin heads crawling across the mass of tattoos and vanishing into his orange hair.

'Are you the one they call Murmers?' the figure rasped, his fetid breath making Harry gag as he helplessly nodded. The useless, empty automatic was wrenched from his twitching fingers.

'I am Orun, the Waymaster, Tholocus' messenger,' the figure repeated angrily as he squeezed and crushed the gun's barrel, twisting it with his bare hands and buckling it out of shape as easily as if it was made of dull black plasticine. He thrust it back into Harry's grasp. For a moment anger boiled in Orun's black eyes and then he sighed and stepped back.

'I have journeyed far from my home in the Crystal Swamps and have toiled through many dangers in search of you, Murmers, Guardian of Alburton.'

Harry shivered. He was trapped against the window sill, defenceless. The palms of his hands were slippery with sweat, his breaths coming in shallow, terrified gasps as he waited for the wild ghetto creature to reach out and snap his neck or hurl him through the window. He guessed he must be an acid-head, high on PCP or angel-dust or some other mind-blowing drug that caused him to rave on about Tholocus and crystal swamps: but whoever he was, Harry recognised Alburton's name in the rantings. Denso Alburton was one of the fantasy authors he looked after, but to call him Alburton's guardian was ridiculous. Nothing else the man said made any sense.

Harry remembered reading somewhere that angel-dust or PCP, he couldn't be sure which, transformed its users into violent psychopaths who would cling on to the weirdest scraps of reality and was supposed to give them bursts of incredible strength through muscle spasms. He didn't know what the madman was using but he was as sure as hell certain he was rotten with the stuff by the way he had twisted the barrel of that gun in half with his bare hands.

Orun looked down at the dark-haired figure who cowered before him and saw fear and suspicion clouding his eyes. He should have welcomed him as Tholocus' messenger. He should have broken a bitterseed waycake and offered him a cup of wasp honey nectar. It was the custom to welcome Waymasters that way. And if Murmers was the guardian whom he sought, why didn't his skin show something of his heroic task. There wasn't a single tattoo or illustration of how he had guarded Alburton. His skin was as clear, as pure and unmarked as a child's.

Orun glanced down at the mass of vivid tattoos that covered his own forearms. Rippling, moving illustrations of his long and dangerous journey along the secret pathways from the City of Time to the Doorcrack in the walls of reality. Tattoos that marked him as a highborn Waymaster. But perhaps here, this side of the Doorcrack, everything was different. The world he had stepped into was certainly terrifying with its sheer, towering buildings that brushed against the clouds, buildings honeycombed with millions of glittering lights when darkness fell. The roar of metal monsters filled its teeming streets and deafened him. Even this gloomy chamber wasn't what he had expected. He glanced quickly behind him, catching his breath as he saw rows of books that covered the far wall. To stand so close to so much knowledge unnerved him, he hadn't expected Murmers to be a Learned and fear made him more cautious. Perhaps he should offer a gift of meeting to this guardian. He delved into the leather pouch that hung from his belt, withdrew a fragment of a waycake wrapped in reeds and held it out to him but his eyes narrowed to shadowy, cautious slits as he watched and waited for Murmer's reaction.

Every nerve and sinew tensed in Harry's body as the Waymaster's hand reached towards him. He wanted to hurl the useless automatic into his hideously tattooed face, duck past him and make a run for the door but he had seen the guy's strength and the way he had leapt across his desk and he knew that he was helplessly trapped. But the instinct for survival was strong: he was staying alive, his mind racing on overtime as it sifted through everything that he could remember about the characters that Denso wrote about. The tattoos struck a chord but he wasn't sure what they meant, his head felt as if it was stuffed with rags. He tried to act naturally as he waited for the lucky break, a moment's distraction. He was frozen rock-still in his chair and a tight paper-thin smile was painted across his gaunt trembling lips.

'Take the offering!' Orun growled, thrusting the knuckles of his hand hard against Harry's chest and making his jersey buttons cut painfully into his skin through his thin cotton shirt.

Harry swallowed. He knew he had to humour this lunatic: his life depended upon it. He had to indulge whatever threads of reality he was clinging on to, take whatever was being thrust at him. He let the useless buckled automatic fall to the floor beside him, reached up and took the little bundle of reeds. Inwardly a voice was silently screaming inside his head, urging Kate to pick up the 'phone in the outer office, if she was still alive, and punch 911 for the cops.

Orun watched closely as Harry pulled open the reeds and removed the piece of crumbling unleavened cake. Inside the reeds he found a hard, greying mouldy piece of what looked like coarse bread. It was speckled with blackened grains of oval seeds with a greenish coating and there were dirty fingerprints and gnawed grooves where strange teeth had nibbled it. Harry felt his stomach tighten as he realised that he was expected to eat a piece of the disgusting offering. Lifting it from the reeds he slowly turned it over in his hands. He looked up into the intense tattooed face that overshadowed him and fought to keep his own expression blank to mask his revulsion as he brought it up to his lips. Suddenly his mind focused sharply on the tattoos. His memory came flooding back: Denso had used characters with tattoos. This guy was obviously out of his mind, fantasising, probably fixating on one of those characters. But which book was he from? Which one? Denso had written so many.

Harry chewed at the crumbling rind, somehow getting it past the knot in his throat, and a cold sweat beaded his forehead. What if this ghetto creature had fixated on a character from one of the earliest books? Jesus, most of them had been out of print for over twenty years and he could barely remember the haziest details from them. Harry blinked and dropped his gaze as he concentrated and tried to remember all the titles. One book shuffled itself to the front of his mind, *The Sea of Glass*. Slowly, scraps of it began to come back. Denso had set the story in a brutal world of shifting mud, a primitive nightmare of survival. The main character had been a hunter, or a wizard, he wasn't quite sure which, but he did remember that there had been travellers. Yes, that was it, Denso had called them Waymasters:

now it came back to him. He remembered now the liquid lunch with Denso after he had read the manuscript and it had been sold to a good publishing house. He had congratulated him on the Waymaster characters: it was a neat touch the way he had tattooed their journeys onto their skin.

Harry caught his breath as he realised that he had probably stumbled into the core of this ghetto creature's fantasy. He was acting out the role of a Waymaster. He had even had his body tattooed from head to foot just the way they had in the book. Harry shuddered. It must have been really painful having the tattooist needle in all that detail around his eyes and mouth. Even so, it was one thing knowing what the guy was fixating on but what the hell did he want in this office? What had he broken in here for? Snatches of that near-forgotten lunch-time conversation drifted back to him across the years. Denso's voice laughed and echoed faintly in his head. He glimpsed him making a face and spilling a glass of wine from the second bottle and he remembered the diners from the other tables turning around in alarm as he loudly exclaimed that he couldn't imagine anything worse than being a Waymaster from his story and having to drink wasp honey nectar and eat bitterseed cake at the end of each journey. He imagined that it must have tasted worse than horse shit.

Denso's voice faded in Harry's head and he once again heard the hum of the traffic in the street below, the tick of the office clock and the rasping, waiting breaths of his attacker. Harry's mind focused on the fragile memory of Denso's words, clutching at them as desperately as a drowning man would grasp at the line thrown to him. Bitterseed cake, wasps' honey, bitterseed cake . . . of course, this madman was imagining that he was at the end of a journey: that was why he had offered this cake wrapped in reeds. Perhaps if he offered him some of Denso's books as a gift it might distract him long enough to get past him, into the outer office and then the elevator and onto the street outside. Yes, he must offer some signed copies, pretend there were some kept in the outer office. He would give him a whole stack of Denso's later books, a gift from the guardian: they would distract him while he made a break for the door.

Harry swallowed. He hoped he was on the right track and the tattooed figures in the story were in fact Waymasters. 'I . . . I . . . I have forgotten to greet you properly as the custom demands, Waymaster. Your sudden arrival startled me and threw me off-guard. I'm afraid I don't have any bitterseed cake but I can give you copies of Denso's latest work. They are in the outer office, I'll just get a couple for you. Perhaps you would like to take a seat.'

Murmers had eaten the cake: custom dictated that he should now bring Alburton forward to meet him. He had not journeyed through the walls of reality in search of books, no matter how powerful. The Clockmaster had books enough, thousands and thousands of them.

'No!' he hissed impatiently, 'It is Denso Alburton I seek, not books. Where is he?'

His hand tightened on the hilt of his dagger and his eyes remained alert and watchful. Tholocus had warned him to tread with caution, saying that for all his searching Alburton might still elude him. Now his first nagging doubts began to crystallise into certainty. Alburton wasn't in this tower: this was not the citadel that he sought amongst so many. The figure who cowered before him was too weak to be Alburton's guardian. He, Orun, had done well to follow that first instinct of doubt, using its warning to bind and silence the woman in the outer chamber when she had tried to deny him an audience with the man who pretended to be Murmers. It had been prudent to seal off the outer doorway against escape.

24

Orun sighed wearily and loosened his dagger from his belt. He had revealed the purpose of his journey and now he must kill this feeble pretender and his door guardian to secure their silence. For the blink of an eyelid he quailed beneath the enormity of his quest. There were so many legends, so many names and signs in all the colours of the rainbow, in drawings that he did not understand amongst this Forest of Towers. Perhaps he had already passed by the one that he sought.

'Don't kill me for Chrissake!' Harry screamed. He ducked beneath the raised dagger and dashed to the right of the desk towards the bookcase. 'I've got a whole stack of Alburton's books over here. You can take the lot. Keep them. They're all signed.'

Orun snarled as Harry ducked past him and spun round angrily thrusting the blade at him. But he hesitated as he turned, his eyes widening into a startled stare, his mouth falling soundlessly open. He had been so intent upon the figure in the chair whom he had thought was the one he sought that he had not given the outer edges of the room a thought. He had glimpsed the rows of books that lay in shadow beyond the light of the lamp but he had not given them more than a cursory glance. Now he let his dagger fall from his hand and fell on his knees before the wall of books spread across the righthand side of the chamber. There were rows and rows of books of different shapes and sizes and in front of them were thousands more in towering shadowy stacks, all piled up in careless disorder before the overflowing bookshelves.

He sucked in a shallow breath and felt beads of cold sweat break out upon his forehead, making the mass of vivid tattoos shimmer and blend together. He had misjudged this Murmers: for all his signs of weakness he must be a guardian or a diviner or a master of fate to possess so many books and he dared not harm him. Only once before in his life of journeys as a Waymaster had he been so close to so many books and that had been at the threshold of this long odyssey when he stood in the high Tower of Tholocus on the rim of the City of Time, where every breath and whisper, every thought and idea, are written down. He had not dared to touch the books when he was in the high tower: they were the fountainhead of all knowledge, the wisdom of yesterday and the windows into tomorrow. Only the learned, the diviners and the masters of fate, could interpret the words. It was a gift from the gods to be able to unravel what lay hidden in the endless lines of signs and symbols that were written upon each page.

Orun gasped aloud and his hand trembled and twitched involuntarily as Murmers began pulling books from the middle of the shelves, dropping and scattering them and upsetting the tottering stacks on either side of him in his haste to find the works of Alburton.

'Here's one, *The Crystal Bowl*. Here, catch it!' Harry cried with relief tossing the hardback across the desk, sending it skimming low and fast to keep the madman away from him. He'd use the whole damn lot as missiles if he had to. 'And here's another, and another . . .' he called, stumbling over the litter of books and journals that he had upset as he headed towards the open doorway which led to the outer office and freedom.

A startled cry from the other side of the desk made him glance fearfully sideways and momentarily check his stride. He stared at the kneeling ghetto-creature. He was clutching the books that Harry had hurled across the office, holding them reverently against his chest, caressing their spines and covers, tracing the raised block lettered titles with his fingertips. His eyes were turned blindly upwards in ecstasy and his mouth uttered a continuous monosyllabic chant. He seemed oblivious to his surroundings as he knelt in the pool of light beside the desk and he ignored Harry's rush for the doorway.

Harry frowned. There was something about the way the madman was touching the words and their individual letters. His fingers were moving in an erratic sequence across the spines and jackets of the books that he held. It made him think that perhaps the guy couldn't read. Harry shook his head. No. It wasn't possible. It didn't make any sense. The guy had burst into his office living out one of Denso's characters. Harry blinked suddenly, shrugged his shoulders and made a dive for the door. What did he care if the lunatic could read or not? He had to rub shoulders with all sorts of crazy people in this business. He would get out fast and call the cops. Let them flush him out.

Harry stumbled around the door-jamb into the outer office and stopped abruptly. His mouth fell open and he strangled a scream as he stared at Kate. She was trapped in her swivel chair, the metal arms bent and twisted as though they were strands of thick rope brutally tying her arms. Her skin was bruised and bleeding where the metal had cut into her, but that wasn't what horrified him and brought his bile nauseously choking up into his throat. It was the loathsome, vividly striped, crab-like creature that was smothering her face, its glistening yellow pincers clamped into the soft skin around her mouth, pinching it into a wizened tortuous line of silence. Her eyes were wild and white with terror. He knew that he had to get the revolting thing off her before it pinched her nostrils together and suffocated her. He took a step towards her chair and reached out a trembling hand to try to snatch the throbbing creature away from her face but as his fingers touched its glistening armoured shell it changed colour to a violent purple and convulsed its body, tightening its grip around her mouth.

Red pinpoints of blood welled up around the claws and began to trickle silently down her chin. Kate pulled herself back as far as she could away from his hand and violently shook her head from side to side. Her dark auburn hair scattered in ringlets of light and shadow framing the frantic terror mirrored in her eyes as they silently implored him not to touch the monstrous thing again.

'I've got to get it off,' Harry hissed, his hand hovering inches from her face as the creature's colour dissolved back through the spectrum and it relaxed its murderous grip.

He had to do something to stop whatever that madman in his office had begun. He had to stop this nightmare developing into something worse. He stared wildly around the outer office and looked towards the door. Perhaps if he made a run for it. Perhaps he could escape and raise the alarm. But he shuddered as his eyes focussed on the mass of threads or cords that criss-crossed the doorway, forming an opaque grey barrier across it. It looked at a glance as if it was a living web or curtain crawling with thousands of tiny insects.

'Jesus Christ!' he gasped, looking back at Kate and fighting down the horror at what he had seen.

His hands were trembling and wet with sweat. The 'phone. Remember the 'phone. It was right there in front of him on Kate's desk. All he had to do was reach out. He glanced down: it looked OK. He made a fumbling grab for it. He cried out as he snatched his hand away. An ice-cold pain burned through his fingers and shot up his arm.

Harry staggered backwards clenching his jaw and grinding his teeth from the shock, nursing his numbed, tingling arm. The skin on his face and neck prickled as if he had received an electric shock – as if the telephone had been wired directly into the mains supply. Forcing himself to shut out the image of Kate trapped in her chair with that hideous creature clinging on to her face he moved hesitantly back towards the desk to take a closer look at the telephone, taking care not to touch it again.

Harry frowned. It wasn't just the 'phone that had something wrong with it, he noticed as he got closer, the whole desk top was covered, no shrouded, with a shifting fabric of darkness. It was as fine as silk and almost transparent and it clung to the contours of the 'phone, the pens and pencils and books that littered the desk. It absorbed the light, the reflections and the tones and colours of everything it covered, reducing it all to a dull, lifeless mass. Harry was sure that he would have noticed the shadowy shroud the moment he entered the outer office if his attention had not been drawn directly to Kate's plight. He had no idea what could have caused it but now he hesitated and was afraid to move, afraid of meeting new horrors whichever way he turned.

He shivered. Fear of what was happening to him knotted his guts. He hadn't a clue what was going on. One moment he had been idling, reading about the winged beast that had materialised on the main runway of JFK and the next this crazy ghetto-man had invaded his office. Harry blinked as the sweat dripped into his eyes. His train of thought stopped right there. No-one from a street gang, no ghetto-creature, could do the things that he saw now.

A noise behind him made him spin round. The Waymaster was crowding the doorway of his office. He was frowning uncertainly and beckoning, no commanding, him to walk back in. Harry knew there was no escape but he fought down his panic and stood his ground, his fists clenched at his sides.

'No!' he snarled, holding Orun's gaze, 'I'm not moving an inch until you get that monstrous thing off Kate's face and release her from her chair. And . . . and . . . you can

29

undo whatever it is you did to her desk and the outer door. *And* you can tell me who you are and what you want from me and what the hell's going on.'

He paused, giddy and breathless but to his complete surprise, Orun didn't sneer or reach out and snap his neck but strode past him and plucked the livid crab-creature from Kate's face and slipped it into a leather pouch that hung from the back of his belt. He grasped the buckled arms of her chair in both hands and twisted them roughly back into their original shape, releasing her from her painful prison.

'It was but a precaution. You must forgive me, Door Guardian.'

He bowed to Kate and spoke in a soft mumbling voice as he gathered up the night-dark gossamer fabric from the desk top and folded it into almost nothing in his powerful hands before stowing it in a smaller pouch that hung from his belt. Crossing to the door he whispered some incomprehensible chant across the mass of webs that covered it. They began to tremble and vibrate. The tiny creatures that were weaving it began to digest it, scuttling silently backward and forward, eating the living barrier they had created. Harry gasped and watched the tiny creatures swell up as they finished devouring the threads and swarm across Orun's fingers and up his arms into the cover of hard skins that he wore. Orun blinked and lifted his eyes to Harry's face as he began to speak.

'I am Orun, Waymaster from the Crystal Swamps. I command you to bring Alburton forward.'

Harry felt a cold chill in the pit of his stomach. The guy was clearly crazy wherever he came from. If any of his regular visitors had made such a demand he would have kicked them out into the street, but after what he had seen this guy do he wasn't even going to smile. His eyes narrowed and he calculated the distance from where he stood to the doorway. He had played quarterback briefly at college. He used to be quick, but that had been years ago. The voice of self-preservation whispered in his head and brought him back to reality. To make a break would be madness. His best bet was to soothe this Orun character, find out exactly why he wanted to meet Denso and then find a way to placate him. Anyway, he would be crazy to try to make a break for it when he didn't even know if the outer door was locked or if Orun had left other, more hideous, crawling creatures guarding the dimly-lit hallway and stairwell outside his suite of offices. But as sense prevailed and he overcame his urge to rush to the door an idea began to form in his mind. Perhaps Kate could escape now that she was free of the crab-creature and the buckled arm rests of her chair. If he could just draw Orun back into his office she might be able to make a run.

He turned his head towards her and managed to catch her eye and slowly and repeatedly he directed his gaze back towards the door. Kate frowned with bewilderment and dabbed gingerly at the dried itching trickles of blood that had clotted on her cheeks and around her chin. Her mouth felt as if it was swollen a foot in front of her face, as though it had been squeezed and stretched through a wringer. Her teeth were chattering uncontrollably, filling her head with noise, as she tried to work out what Harry was trying to tell her. Suddenly it clicked. She caught at the thread of his idea. Her eyes widened and she nodded, barely moving her head, masking the slight movement from the madman's watchful gaze by raking her fingers through her dishevelled hair. Harry swallowed a sigh of relief as he saw Kate nod. Now all he had to do was to draw this Orun character back into his office and keep him talking.

'Exactly what is it you want Denso Alburton to do for you?' he smiled as he tried to keep his voice light and easy while retreating into his office, picking his way through the books that he had scattered towards the window. He hoped the breathtaking panoramic view of the glittering Manhattan nightscape would distract Orun while Kate made her run for the door.

'Alburton must come,' Orun growled in reply.

'Look,' Harry continued, spreading his hands in a helpless gesture, 'it's just not possible for Denso to be here. He doesn't live in this city: he lives two thousand miles away on the West Coast. It's morning out there and he's probably in his studio. He doesn't like being disturbed when he's working. But you're welcome to take any of his books. Look, I'll gather them up for you.'

Orun hesitated in the doorway and shook his head. He was certain now that this was the Murmers he had been sent to find and not a false guardian. He had felt and seen the symbols upon the spines and covers of the books that had been thrown at him and he had traced Alburton's name with his fingertips on every one of them. So why was there still a scent of treachery and lies in this chamber? Orun's sharp eyes and ears had missed nothing of the silent whispers, the urgent gazes directed at the door that stood between them.

'You will stand with your master,' he hissed at Kate, reaching back for the bulging leather pouch that contained his pinchquiet.

Kate shuddered as she saw his tattooed fingers loosen the flap of the pouch and a vivid claw appear. She hurried forwards and squeezed past him, a look of despair on her stark white face as she crossed the office. The millions of lights in the sheer towers beyond the window looked so hopelessly far away, even the sounds of the city seemed to have faded. She blinked at the tears of terror that were blurring her eyes and sank down on the windowsill beside Harry.

'It's hopeless,' she whispered. 'He even seems to know what we're thinking. He's got us trapped and we're never going to get out of here.'

Harry gripped her hand so fiercely that for a moment it stopped his own hand from trembling. He levelled his eyes with Orun's and his fear of the madman turned to anger.

'I told you Alburton's two thousand miles away. You can take every book of his that I've got. What the hell else do you want from us?'

Orun frowned, 'I want nothing, Guardian. Tholocus will reward me for guiding Alburton to the high tower on the rim of the City of Time.'

'Towers! City of Time!' Harry retorted, his face flushed with anger, 'You can read about that sort of stuff in any of Alburton's books but it's not real. It doesn't exist beyond fantasy.'

Harry stopped as Orun took a threatening step towards him. Kate's fingernails were digging painfully into the palm of his hand, warning him that his anger had pushed Orun a little too far. But Orun laughed, then shook his head at the disbelief mirrored in Murmers' eyes.

'Has a blindness clouded your memory, Guardian?'

He frowned, causing the vivid tattoos to crumple together on his forehead, and abruptly stopped his question, swallowing the word that had gathered to the tip of his tongue. Faint echoes of Tholocus' counsel sounded coldly in his head and he remembered the words that had been said before he began the search for Alburton. Tholocus had warned him that if he found the doorcrack and broke through into twentieth century Earth that no-one would believe the things he told them. To the peoples of Earth there was no reality or existence in parallel beyond their own. He remembered protesting that he had travelled as a Waymaster through so many horizons of reality and that none he had met had been *that* ignorant, but Tholocus had drawn him close and whispered that long ago Earth had been set apart, nurtured before all others, made into a paradise. No-one but the Council of Collective Consciousness knew of its existence and it had been hidden behind veils of secrets. Each time beasts or wanderers had accidentally broken through while time was still young they were explained away with lies and half-truths that disguised the true nature of things and they had become ghosts, legends and myths.

'But Alburton had foretold of the great deluge, I have heard the Elders tell the story in the firelight.'

Tholocus had smiled and answered, 'There have always been dreamers, men and women of vision. Those who, because they did not disbelieve, have glimpsed through the veil that we wove so carefully.' Tholocus had sighed. 'But who listens to wise men? Who marks the measure of their wisdom?' He had suddenly strode across to the window in the tower and pointed out across the darkening rim of the City of Time. 'I fear that time is wearing thin, Orun. Some terrible catastrophe is creeping up upon us to spread its shadow across Paradise.'

Orun remembered how he had searched amongst the vivid tattoos upon his arms, his legs and across his stomach and chest as the Clockmaster counselled him. He was searching for a route, for a road to this Paradise, this place called Earth. If it existed it should have been painted in the brightly coloured illustrations which showed every single footstep that he had ever taken as a Waymaster. But there were none that he could find and his heart had quailed at the fear of being truly lost without a landmark to follow.

He had clutched at the hem of Tholocus' gown of runes, crumpling the history of time between his fingertips and cried out, 'How will I begin to search for this Paradise if it is beyond the furthest horizon that I have ever trodden? If this Paradise is truly a world set apart how am I ever going to find it? Surely its peoples will crush me beneath their feet for daring to seek them out?'

Tholocus had smiled and shaken his head and pointed to the walls of books that edged his chamber. 'It is a place of wisdom and great learning. Now go quickly and look for your road in all the dark and secret places where paths divide and oak weeds and brambleheads overshadow the tracks. Look where the dust of time lies thickest, where a Waymaster would shrug and turn away, for we hid the pathways and put them where none would easily journey.'

'But where ... where will I look? How will I ever find my way there?' he had protested.

Tholocus had frowned and turned back to gaze across the City of Time. 'Once it would have been so easy,' he murmured. 'Once, long ago, every thread was at my finger-tips.'

Sighing, he had crossed to a crowded bookshelf and carefully withdrawn a battered first edition copy of *The Sea of Glass*. Supporting the book's broken spine he had turned back the scarred cover and read the dedication on the fly-leaf. Then he had smiled. 'Yes. Yes, of course, that is where you must begin. The Diviners will gather here in my tower. When you journey they will concentrate their minds to open a Doorcrack in the City of Towers.'

He had turned towards the Waymaster and read aloud, 'To Harry Murmers. I dedicate this book to you for patiently guarding my dreams while I transcribed them into reality.'

Tholocus had paused and shut the book, causing a haze of fine dust to billow up and make him blink. 'Yes, you must seek out this one called Murmers for he is Alburton's guardian.'

35

Thoughtfully, he had opened the book again and scanned the opposite side of the flyleaf, reading the publishing legend, and his lips had formed the words 'New York'. He had nodded severely as he remembered about the dark unhappiness he had heard about in that place and he had warned Orun to tread with caution. He instructed him to seek the Earthian within the Forest of Towers and urged him to convince Murmers that he, Tholocus, the Clockmaster of Eternity, had great need of Alburton in the City of Time.

Orun had begun to ask how he was to find this Murmers in the Forest of Towers but the Clockmaster had silenced him, had taken his hand and taught him, by touch and sight, how to recognise the signs and symbols that made up the word Murmers. 'Search for this word carved in either brass or stone and once you are certain that the one you have found is Alburton's guardian you must convince him that the shadow of catastrophe grows daily longer across the Earth and that he must journey back with you to the Grand Council.'

Orun had shivered and pushed Tholocus' warning and his nightmare of a journey through the forest of citadels that stood shoulder to shoulder to the back of his mind. Now he looked helplessly into Harry's eyes and didn't know where to begin. How was he going to convince him of Tholocus' truth? He glanced down to the crumpled newspapers on the desk top and caught sight of the hazy photograph of a wrathwa beast.

'There! That must prove that I speak the truth! That is a wrathwa beast from Bendran!' he cried, pointing to the photograph in the *Daily News*.

Harry glanced down at the crumpled newspaper and shrugged his shoulders. It had been a long hard day and he was getting tired of being this madman's prisoner. His patience was wearing thin. 'I've never heard of a wrathwa beast. Is that something out of one of Alburton's books? That snapshot in the paper is so hazy and so out of focus that it could be almost anything you wanted it to be.'

'I think it's probably made of rubber or plastic,' Kate interrupted in a tight frantic voice that made Harry turn sharply towards her. 'Yes,' she continued before he could stop her, 'I think that thing in the newspaper was a huge inflatable model, you know, one of those things filled with gas that they use for advertising. I bet it was part of some publicity stunt for beer or something that went disastrously wrong and when that plane crashed trying to avoid it they stuck a pin in it to get rid of it quickly.'

Harry tensed, expecting Orun to swarm forwards to stifle Kate's outburst and perhaps strike out at either of them. But the madman hesitated, digesting her words, a look of confusion in his eyes.

'Yes, that's got to be the answer,' Harry added quickly trying to seize at Orun's moment of hesitation and use it to their advantage. He wanted to convince him that the whole thing was a figment of his imagination.

'One moment it was there as large as life on the main runway and the next it had vanished because someone had burst the bubble. Come on, Orun, no one's going to believe it was a wrathwa beast, are they? Look, hacks make up stories like that all the time to freshen the news on a slow day. But this is the real world where a hazy photograph doesn't make something real out of fantasy. No matter how much we want it to it doesn't give flesh and blood to creatures from our imagination. Why don't you just take the books and . . .' Harry paused and licked his lips. It was working: the cloud of confusion was deepening in Orun's eyes. '. . . and the next time Denso calls me I'll tell him that you were here and that you are really into his worlds. I'll get him to dedicate a copy of his latest book personally . . .'

'No! That will be too late!' Orun cried, violently shaking his head and clenching his fists in frustration. 'You must believe me. You must believe that it was a wrathwa beast – a carrion creature made of flesh and bones – that suddenly appeared through the cracks in reality and not some magic of your plastics that vanish when you prick them.'

He searched his mind desperately for something, anything, that would convince them and he stared down at the vivid tattoos on the backs of his hands and wrists. There were illustrations of his dark road through the walls of reality and his search amongst the City of Towers. 'Look, I can prove to you that I am Tholocus' messenger!' he cried suddenly, closing the gap between them in two giant strides.

He unbuckled his belt and threw it with its bulging leather pouches and dagger onto the desk top. He tore off his rancid jerkin and rough cut breeches and stood naked before them. Kate gasped and Harry stared in astonishment at the thousands of vivid and minute pictures covering every inch of his skin, strange and wonderful illustrations needled in the finest detail, showing weird beasts and peoples and incredible places.

'I am Orun the Waymaster from the Crystal Swamps,' he whispered proudly, stabbing a finger at a tiny picture of shimmering pools of marsh and mire, low hills and dense vivid vegetation beneath his left collarbone, 'and these drawings are the true records of every footstep I have ever taken.'

He moved his finger slowly across his chest and down his left arm, stopping above his elbow at a mass of huge halls and graceful colonnades and spires overshadowed by a ring of slender towers. 'That is the City of Time where this journey began,' he hissed, raising his arm to within inches of Harry's face and flexing the muscles of his forearm to make the dark violent pathways and hideous beasts that he had fought on his way writhe and move.

'That looks like the Statue of Liberty and the Staten Island ferry tattooed on the back of his hand,' Kate exclaimed, leaning forward, her fear momentarily forgotten as she recognised the familiar landmarks.

'How did you do that?' she began, but her words died in her throat and she shrank back away from him, pressing herself against the cold windowpane as Orun closed his fingers, then straightened them and thrust his hand closer to her face so that she could see the clear image of herself trapped in the outer office with the foul crab-creature pinching her lips together with its claws.

'It's just not possible . . .' Kate gasped, her eyes hypnotically drawn to the hideous picture of her terror etched across the knuckles of his right hand. 'This can't be happening, none of it, unless . . .' She paused, her lips tightening and trembling. Bright spots of blood broke through the drying scabs around her mouth. She reached up to touch them and felt the blood sticky on her fingertips, '. . . unless I'm dreaming. Unless I'm trapped in some terrible nightmare.'

'This is no dream,' Orun hissed urgently, crowding so close to her that their bodies touched. He pinched the soft flesh of her forearm, making her cry out and pull away from him.

'Now do you believe me, Guardian?' he rasped, thrusting the tattoo of the buckled automatic that had appeared upon his left wrist under Harry's nose. 'Now do you believe that there is more to the landscape of reality than the blind shrouds that smother this earth reveal?'

Harry swallowed, blinked and shifted uncomfortably on the windowsill. And then he silently nodded his head.

There was no escaping what he saw: the mass of vivid tattoos contained a glimpse of worlds that went far beyond the imagining of Denso Alburton or any of the other fantasy writers that he had ever read. The tattoos seemed so vital and alive, and he could have sworn that the creatures depicted on Orun's shoulders had moved while he was looking at them.

But how could he accept that the naked figure standing before them had stepped through the walls of reality? That his wild stories were true – that other times and worlds really did exist in parallel with Earth? Harry glanced anxiously over his shoulder at the soaring, glittering nightscape of Manhattan. An hour ago it had looked so solid, so impervious to anything less than a nuclear war. The picture in the *Daily News* had been a stunt. But now those slender spires looked so vulnerable, so helplessly frail beneath the shadow of things to come.

'Will you now summon Alburton into the chamber so that we can begin the journey back? Tholocus counselled me that time was running out.'

The urgency in Orun's voice cut across Harry's thoughts and made him turn sharply back to face the Waymaster. Harry frowned, trying to grasp at the bare threads of what Orun had told them. Images of all the things that might lie out there in the darkness almost overwhelmed him and he shook his head. 'Wait! Wait a minute,' Harry hesitated. 'I can't make a lot of sense out of all this in one swallow. If everything you have told me is true and all the things and places in those tattoos are real then where the hell are they? There just isn't room for them here, the world's already crowded enough. Look, before you burst in here tonight I had never seen or heard of anything so crazy except in the realms of the imagination created by Denso and the other fantasy writers.'

Orun frowned. For a moment he had thought that the tattoos had convinced Murmers but new confusion and doubt clouded his eyes again. 'These tattoos are only my humble journey lines. They are the memories of the footsteps that I have taken and they are less than a glimpse of what lies beyond the walls of reality.' He spread his arms in a gesture that encompassed everything, the office with its walls of books, the towering skyscrapers beyond the window and the bright canopy of stars in the dark void overhead. 'There are millions of threads in the tapestry, each one layered and woven with the next, appearing and disappearing through the weave of reality. They are everywhere, all around us.' He paused and stepped closer to Harry, whispering, 'Tholocus warned me that you would not believe, because this place you call Earth has been shielded, hidden in a vale of secrets, sheltered from all the other worlds that rub against it. He saw that you would not comprehend any existence beyond your own. Well, look, look again, Guardian, at the wild peoples and the ferocious beasts in these tattoos. They inhabit the worlds that I have journeyed through. Be warned, they will be quick to over-run this hidden paradise if the fabric of reality begins to crumble or they can find a way to burst through it. Alburton must journey with me. Tholocus seeks his wisdom to shape the fate of your tomorrows and prevent such a catastrophe from happening.'

Harry felt a cold shiver touch his spine as his eyes were drawn back to the vivid tattoos and he picked out the horrific details of the beasts and creatures that swarmed across Orun's chest and shoulders. 'I believe you,' he whispered, 'but what the hell could Denso do to stop monsters like those? He's only a fantasy writer.'

Orun laughed harshly, 'I am merely the messenger, the guide, but Tholocus counselled me that Alburton is a divine thinker and the Clockmaster of Eternity would not have summoned him lightly.'

Harry blinked and tore his eyes away from the brilliantly coloured tattooes. The more he stared at them the more he seemed drawn into the worlds they illustrated. 'But Denso's not here. I told you earlier, he lives three thousand miles away and there's no way he could be here before tomorrow night at the earliest, and that's assuming I can contact him on the phone now. Then I've still got to convince him to drop whatever he's doing and fly across right away, and he hates cities.'

Orun stared into Harry's eyes, searching for the truth, fearing that he still doubted, but nothing clouded the vision of reality that he glimpsed. 'You must convince him. Time is running faster than quicksand between our fingers. You are his guardian. You must know what will bring him here.'

Orun paused and stepped back and reached down to gather up the bundles of rough animal skins that he had dropped on the floor and quickly covered his nakedness. 'Tell Alburton of our meeting. Describe what you have seen in my journey-lines and tell him that our boats of straw weathered the flood.'

Harry laughed but the sound echoed harshly and without humour and it was lost in the night sounds of the city beyond the office window. 'No, there's no chance that would work. He'd just say that I'd been on the sauce or reading too many of his books. Even if I described you down to the smallest detail he wouldn't believe you are real. He'd have to see you in the flesh.'

Harry paused and studied the wild appearance of the Waymaster for a moment. 'Why don't we both fly out there? Yes, I'll 'phone him now and set it up. You can meet him face to face and he can examine those tattoos for himself.'

'No,' Orun growled forcefully, 'There is no time to fly

on the wings of those metal birds that roost where the wrathwa beast appeared. The Doorcrack through the walls of reality that we must take is here in the very heart of this Forest of Towers and I know of no other that will lead us to the City of Time. You must summon him to come to us. You must find a way.'

Harry slumped back onto the windowsill beside Kate and he raked his fingers through his dark curly hair as he thought hard. Denso wasn't the easiest of people to manipulate into doing something he didn't want to do. God knows he had enough trouble getting him to submit his finished manuscripts in time and that would have been nearly impossible if Denso hadn't needed the money. He clapped his hands together and stood up as an idea crystallised in his mind.

'Denso will do almost anything for money!' he cried. 'He'd go right around the world backwards for . . .' Harry frowned and stopped talking. Orun was staring at him blankly.

'Money. Do you know what money is?' Harry asked softly.

Orun thought for a moment and then asked slowly, 'Is it like barter? Like exchanging fish for grain or for earthenware pots?'

Harry smiled, 'Yes. But Denso wouldn't travel a yard for a handful of grain.'

'I think what Harry had in mind was more in the way of hard currency. You know, dollars, gold or silver, even diamonds, something like that,' Kate muttered, knowing Harry's train of thought.

'Dollars?' Orun frowned. 'I know nothing of such things. But gold, I know gold, I can easily get that for you.'

In one sweeping movement he reached across the desk top and gathered up his wide leather belt from where he had

43

carelessly thrown it down as he disrobed. Apart from his dagger it was strung with at least half a dozen heavily bulging leather pouches just like the one he had pushed the pinchquiet into.

Kate shuddered and clutched at Harry's arm fearing that Orun was going to release more of those foul crab-creatures as he quickly untied the leather thongs that were bound around the necks of the two pouches. He looked up and laughed, 'If it is gold that will bring our prophet out of the wilderness and into this forest of towers then offer him these trinkets.' He tipped up the two pouches and poured two shimmering pyramids of tiny golden rings and brooches, buttons and buckles onto the desk-top.

Harry and Kate stared speechlessly at the two small heaps of gold jewellery. Each piece was carved with elaborate designs inlaid with silver and set with ice white diamonds that sparkled coldly against the soft, warm, yellow glow of the gold in the light from the desk lamp. Harry took three hesitant steps from the window to the desk and bent to pick up a buckle inlaid with a design of silver flowers.

'It's beautiful. Absolutely beautiful,' he whispered, turning it over and over in his hand. He frowned before he looked up, 'Where the hell did you get all these beautiful pieces? Some of them must be thousands of years old, Egyptian or Incan designs. There must be a fortune lying here.' He paused, eyes narrowing, and hastily put the buckle down. 'You didn't break into some museum while you were searching for me? You didn't steal them, did you?'

'Waymasters do not steal,' Orun hissed angrily, his eyes hardening against the insult as he rebuckled his belt around his waist. 'What I have given to you are little more than trinkets, forgotten buckles, buttons and pledge rings.' He laughed harshly, 'Gold is plentiful in the streams and rivers that feed the swamps and if it has a value it is because it is

easy to work and does not spoil or rust. This meagre handful of trinkets would be nearly worthless, of less value than
three earthenware pots. I merely keep them as weights and
sparkle lures to use when I fish or hunt for food on my
journeys.'

'Pledge rings? Are they like wedding rings?' Kate cried
gathering up a handful of the heavy gold rings that were
inlaid with silver petals and diamond flower-heads.

Orun nodded. 'They are exchanged when families merge.
The number of petals denotes the family's wealth and position. But will these few trinkets be enough to tempt our
prophet, Alburton?' he asked as he watched them sifting
through the jewellery and examining it piece by piece.

Harry blinked and looked up. 'Oh yes, I'm sure it will.
I'll call him right away.' He reached for the telephone.

Orun retreated silently to the doorway of the office and
then paused and bowed, 'I shall return, Guardian. Tomorrow, when the darkness has fallen and the Forest of Towers
are ablaze with light I shall be here.'

Harry spun round towards the doorway. 'Hey, wait.
Wait one minute. You've got to tell me what to say about
the gold. Do you want him to have it as a gift or is it
payment in advance for accompanying you to this City of
Time? What am I meant to tell him?'

Orun smiled and gently shook his head. 'I cannot say. I
must go now and watch over the Doorcrack. Tholocus
warned me that the pathways through the walls of reality
are unpredictable and I fear in case it may squeeze shut. Use
the gold in whatever way you wish: you are Alburton's
guardian.'

And then he vanished.

Harry stared at the empty doorway for a moment, then
shrugged. If it wasn't for the pile of priceless jewellery on
the desk and the buckled automatic lying at his feet he

would already be doubting the reality of the Waymaster's visit. He punched out the area code and then Denso's number. Faintly he heard the ringing tone and he glanced down at his watch: it would be noon on the coast and Denso would be sitting in his shady courtyard hidden beneath a maze of leafy shadows and in the background there would be the eternal sighing whisper of the surf breaking on the beach. The wire crackled and he heard Denso's voice, sharp and clipped, angry at the sudden interruption.

'7230 – who is it?'

Harry sucked in a breath. 'Denso, it's Harry. Now listen and don't interrupt. I've got a king's ransom lying here on my desk as an upfront payment for you to rewrite the fabric of time. There's this guy called Orun who made the payment. He wants to meet you here tomorrow night in my office to tie up all the details. He says the offer only holds good for twenty-four hours so you had better catch the first plane across.'

CHAPTER TWO

Dragons and Demons

Low wet clouds of darkness boiled across the plains of Bendran misting the endless grasslands with glistening raindrops. Shrouds of swirling mist drifted across the higher ground turning the clumps of twisted blackthorn and mountain ash into ghostly figures whose icy fingers rattled and rubbed mournfully together. Above the trees silent black spires of bare granite rose to touch the night sky, their ridges and gullies vanishing in and out of the thickening curtain of mist.

Kote, the Journeyman of Bendran, shivered as the cold and mist enveloped him, grasped the silver-threaded reins and clung more tightly to the ridge of smooth scales that grew in front of the saddle of Lugg, the dragma. The beast lurched forward and scrabbled for a better claw hold on the steep and slippery spine of rock they were traversing and they begun to climb higher, zig-zagging across the face of the rock.

Terror of the sheer drop that lay below, hidden by the mist and darkness, clamped Kote's knees tighter into the saddle rolls and he felt the tug of the belly strap that was attached to the stirrups.

'Climb! Climb!' he hissed in a whisper through chattering teeth as he stabbed brutally with the rowels of his spurs, cutting into the creature's scaly sides.

The beast snarled and roared and scuffled upward, its breath erupting in vaporous clouds of steam, its long tail thrashing the rock face in search of better purchase.

'Quiet, you'll wake the wrathwa beasts and bring them down from their roosts!' he hissed in panic, staring anxiously across the wind-riven, glistening rockface toward the black entrances of the caves where the beasts roosted. But nothing broke the night silence except the dragma's bellowing breaths and the faint clatter and echo of the loose rocks that their climb had dislodged as they tumbled away beneath them.

Kote shook his head in despair as he blinked at the stinging beads of moisture that clung to his eyelashes. This journey was madness. He would never have dared to trespass so near to the wrathwa roosts had Tholocus not commanded it. He had protested against such a journey, stripping his arms bare to reveal the tattoos on his chest that illustrated all his journeys on the plains of Bendran, pointing to where they clearly showed the leagues of desolation that lay in the shadows of the Wrathendall rock-spires that rose to touch the sky.

He had stabbed a trembling finger at the vivid pictures of the soaring wrathwa beasts that guarded those black spires, but Tholocus had impatiently cut him short.

'You are a Journeyman. You must travel by the roads that I set you on. The Wrathendall Spires is a secret road of my making: follow it carefully and it will lead you up to the Doorcracks in the walls of reality.'

Kote had stared blankly at the Clockmaster as he had drawn a yellowing manuscript from beneath his cloak. 'Shadows of catastrophe darken Paradise, Journeyman,' he had whispered urgently, holding up the manuscript and tracing the name 'Capthorne' on its cover, 'scale the Wrathendall Spires and touch the sky of Bendran. Pass through it into a place called Earth and search out the one they call Mya Capthorne. Her writings have perceived the imminent disaster and they may hold a key to averting it.'

Lugg suddenly froze mid-stride and almost dislodged Kote from his back, scattering the images of Tholocus counselling him to bring Capthorne to the roof of the world. Kote barely had time to snatch at the silver-inlaid pommel of the saddle and stop himself from toppling backwards before the dragma, sensing danger, scrabbled sideways and hurried across the gullies and broken chimneys of rock that criss-crossed the sheer cliff-face, seeking a place for them to hide. As he moved he sent loose rocks and splinters of brittle, weathered granite cascading down into the mist and darkness below them.

Lugg slithered into one of the larger gullies, working its way down between two tall shoulders of smooth rock before it stopped. It lifted its head, snaking it backwards and forwards, searching the rock-face that it had just traversed, its scaly nostrils dilated, its reptilian tongue flickering out to touch the cold, wet stone, searching for the first vibrations of pursuit. Then Kote felt the dragma tense beneath him, its neck rising in a rippling arch of spines that splayed outwards and forwards in razor-sharp points. It crouched in the shadows of the gully statue-still, fangs bared, staring out into the shifting curtains of mist, watching and waiting for the wrathwa beast that it had almost trodden on to awake and strike.

Kote smelled and heard the beast moments before he saw it launch itself from the rock face and soar away into the darkness. The overpowering stench of decay enveloped him and the clatter of its armoured scales and leathery wings as they unfolded echoed and rumbled in their narrow hiding place. It was less than a dozen strides away. Smoke and fire from its cavernous mouth blazed across the rock face. Kote crouched, flattening himself between two ridges of Lugg's razor-edged spines as the wrathwa swept back toward them, its sulphorous yellow underbelly and armoured talons illuminated by the vaporous fire that dribbled from its jaws. Flames hissed and crackled along the edges of the gully, filling every dip and crevice, singeing Kote's orange hair as the fetid air beneath the skeletal ridges of the beast's wings was fanned into a gale. The wrathwa was stopping, hovering above them in a mass of shifting fire and shadows.

Kote glanced up fearfully, realising that the creature was descending to roost on their hiding place. Frantically he stabbed his spurs into the dragma's flanks. 'Upwards!' he cried. 'Follow the gully upwards: it's our only chance to escape before the beast crushes us to death.'

Lugg darted upwards, scrabbling with his claws at the rough, slippery sides of the gully, dislodging a cascade of loose rock and shale behind them. The wrathwa bellowed, white fire erupting from its mouth, its scaly head turning towards the noise of the falling rocks. By the light of the wrathwa's fire Kote saw that the gully they were climbing flattened out. In three more scrambling strides they would be exposed on the sheer rock-face again. Searching desperately above them he saw a hollow chimney of rock away to the right. He opened his mouth to shout to the dragma but the roar of the wrathwa's scorching breath drowned out his voice as it turned to swoop down and devour them.

Kote threw up his arms to shield his face from the tongues of fire that poured from the wrathwa's mouth toward him. Lugg screamed, thrashing his tail against the sides of the shallow gully, his back arched in convulsions as his spines began to shrivel and burn. A sudden hail of ice crystals swept over them, stinging Kote's neck and hands and covering the dragma's burning body, quenching its spines and enveloping it in clouds of hissing steam. The swallowing shadow of the wrathwa was snatched away by the sudden storm, its blazing breath hissing and crackling as it vanished. The sound of its roaring voice gradually grew muffled and far away.

Kote tried to look up but the full force of the ice storm swept down across the Wrathendall Spires and cut into his skin, making him hunch ever lower over the dragma's smouldering hide. Icicles clung to his hair and face and were heavy on his back and shoulders where they formed a brittle crust.

'There's a chimney above us to the right!' he shouted, urging the dragma forward as he remembered fireside tales of the ice storms in the Wrathendall Spires. He knew that they must find shelter before the weight of the ice that clung to them tore them away from the rock face and sent them hurtling to their deaths on the foothills below.

Within moments of the storm beginning the rock-face glistened beneath a thick layer of black ice. Lugg began to climb towards the chimney, his claws skidding and slipping on the treacherous surface. Kote held his breath as they traversed the rock and breathed again only as they edged and slithered their way into a break in the chimney wall. Inside the chimney the wind howled and shrieked and a fine shower of ice crystals swirled and eddied as they sparkled in the darkness. They were safe from the storm. Unsheathing his dagger Kote chipped away at the layer of ice that clung to them.

'We must keep going, up towards the roof of the world!' he shouted.

The ice storm abated as abruptly as it had started and the howling wind fell away to less than a whisper inside the dark, spiralling chimney of rock. Slowly, claw by claw, Lugg began to climb, twisting and turning, searching in the blinding darkness for each crumbling crevice. Nothing but the labouring rasp of his breath and the sharp crack, crack of the ice on the spires outside their refuge broke the smothering silence.

Kote shivered from the intense cold. His hands and feet burned with a numbing fire. Tholocus had not forewarned him about the cold and he wore only thin breeches and an otter skin jerkin with his rush boots. His teeth began to chatter uncontrollably in his head and ice tears welled up to trickle and freeze on his cheeks. His fingers became so numb that they began to slip from the pommel of the saddle, the coldness was draining his strength and his feet began to slip out of the stirrups. Twice he almost fell from the dragma to plunge down the chimney and eventually, in his terror of losing his grip upon the scaly beast, he lashed the reins around his waist and securely knotted them over the pommel of the saddle.

Time began to blur in the claustrophobic black funnel of rock and his mind began to wander. One moment he imagined he was back in the crowded streets of the citadel of Bendran, bartering with others as he trod the roads that led to all the places illustrated in his vivid tattoos. The next he was standing in the Clockmaster's shadow in his high tower on the rim of the City of Time, staring up at the millions and millions of books that lined the shelves. Another moment he was brought sharply back into the icy darkness of the chimney as the dragma scrabbled for a claw hold and scraped him across the wet, black rock. Kote cursed as the rocks grazed his back and shoulders, looked up into the darkness and blinked and caught his breath, for there was light above them, a faint circle of pale blue growing stronger and nearer with each scrambled movement that the dragma made.

Kote tried to laugh but the sound only cackled in his throat as the layers of hoar frost that clung around his nose and mouth cracked. He spurred the dragma ruthlessly upwards until Lugg hooked his front claws over the crumbling rim of the chimney and pulled himself cautiously up into the light. His hooded eyes blinked rapidly as he twisted his head from left to right, his long tongue flicking in and out of his mouth as he searched for any sign of danger.

Kote blinked and shaded his eyes against the harsh, white petrified landscape that stretched away in front of him and gasped as he looked out across the roof of the world. The dragma, sensing that they were safe, slithered forwards out of the dark chimney and down to the edge of the snowfield that covered the jagged summit of the Wrathendall Spires. Kote untied himself from the saddle, dismounted and walked forward only to sink to his waist in the snow. He quickly retreated back to the dragma and remounted. He had journeyed through many snowstorms on the plains of Bendran but he had never known such snow, never known it to be so deep. He looked more carefully and saw that the wind had driven it into frozen waves and icy sculptures of all shapes and sizes, in some places they towered as high as a wrathwa beast. He frowned, bit his numb lips and wrapped his jerkin more tightly about his shoulders to try to protect himself against the cold as he looked backward and forward across the endless landscape of ice and snow. It wasn't at all what he had expected: he couldn't touch the sky – it seemed to be just as far away as it had been on the plains below the Wrathendall Spires and there was no sign of a clear road for them to follow through the frozen wilderness.

Kote hesitated, undecided. He hadn't really understood Tholocus when he had talked about other worlds beyond this one, the one he knew and had travelled. Ideas about Doorcracks that led into them through the walls of reality were completely beyond his comprehension yet despite his doubts and fears he had faithfully trodden the path that Tholocus had set him upon. But now that he had reached the roof of the world he was at a loss to know in which direction to travel. The wind was beginning to howl across the petrified landscape, whipping up a haze of ice crystals that stung his face. The sky was darkening across the Wrathendall Spires and heavy snowclouds gathered.

The dragma shifted, lifting its burnt spines and turning its back to the bitter, rising wind. Kote glanced backwards as the dragma's hind claws slipped and dislodged a scattering of loose shale and he cried out, urging Lugg on and away from the edge of the sheer drop. Once Lugg had moved a pace forward Kote clutched the saddle and craned his neck to take a look back again. Stretching out below them through the broken layers of cloud he saw the plains of Bendran bathed in sunlight. They looked so far away that the sight made him dizzy. He whistled softly and looked up at the darkening sky above his head. Perhaps he was in the sky, perhaps the sky was like a mist that you could touch and pass through without feeling it. Perhaps their road was only a footstep away, hidden somewhere in those dark boiling clouds. Tholocus had counselled him to look in all the dark and forbidding places.

'Forward, Lugg!' he shouted, picking up the reins and spurring the dragma towards the centre of the darkest of the swirling clouds.

A flurry of snowflakes swept around them, stinging Kote's face and blinding him, making him lurch forward over the dragma's neck. Lugg hesitated and half-turned his head, sensing a dark, winged shape soaring down out of the sky behind them, but it vanished as the blizzard enveloped them. Lugg shook the settling snow from his spines and forged ahead into the whiteness, floundering and breasting through the deep snowdrifts. The wind hummed all around them, rattling the dragma's spines and tugging at the knots and tangles in Kote's hair as it drew them into the centre of the stormclouds. Suddenly the blizzard fell away to nothing and the wind dropped to a whisper. The clouds pressed in closer, binding and shrouding them in a stifling silence. It grew hot and airless and the snow from the blizzard melted and trickled down Kote's face.

He looked up, frowning. 'I think we must be in the eye of the storm,' he hissed.

Lugg growled and turned his head at the sound of Kote's voice only to stumble and lose his footing on the snow-covered rocks. He thrashed his tail as he tried to regain his balance and suddenly lurched forward as the frozen land-scape vanished from beneath his claws.

Kote cried out as they fell, twisting and turning, and he lost his stirrups and his seat upon the dragma. He was tumbling over and over in the darkness. Indistinct shapes, withered trees and wind-cracked rocks loomed out of the blackness on either side of him and brushed and crashed against him knocking the breath from his body. He tried to catch hold of them in an effort to break his fall but they melted and vanished away at his touch. Twice he collided with the dragma and he tried to cling on to him but his spines slipped through his fingers.

He landed with a bump and fell forwards on to his face in a thicket of tangled wet undergrowth. Lugg landed heavily beside him and lay there snarling in fright. Kote lay still for a moment, winded, and then shakily climbed to his feet. He felt sick with dizziness and his head throbbed with pain. He rubbed at his temples and looked cautiously around. They were on a hillock among a dense circle of trees. Looking out across the bleak countryside he could see a low horizon-line broken by rolling hills. He looked up at the stars sown across the night sky and he caught his breath: they were completely different to the stars in the sky of Bendran. They must have found the secret road through the wall of reality and journeyed into the place called Earth!

Kote glanced anxiously around him looking for the Doorcrack that they had just tumbled through. He had never in all his journeys travelled such a dark and unfamiliar road and he feared losing the entrance lest he be trapped in this place. He began to trample the thick undergrowth, picking up and beating at the bracken with a broken branch, working in a widening circle around the dragma and moving up toward the ring of silent oak trees that crowned the summit of the low hill. Pausing, he held up the backs of his hands and examined them in the starlight. He watched as the faint tattoo lines of his journey which began at the top of the Wrathendall Spires began to appear.

'Of course, it must be somewhere amongst the trees,' he breathed as the bare black tree-trunks with their tangle of interwoven branches began to show in vivid detail across his knuckles.

Hurrying forward he reached the edge of the circle of trees and was about to step between two of them when, with a sudden roar, a huge black shape with fire-red eyes and a gaping mouth belching vaporous flames rose up out of the ground in front of him. Stirring up a gale of mouldy leaves and broken twigs, it swept straight toward him, knocking him over and sending him sprawling in the dew-wet bracken before it swooped away between the trees.

'Wrathwa!' Kote hissed as he climbed slowly to his feet, brushing the leaves and twigs from his jerkin. The monstrous winged beast soared and turned, rising above the hillock in clouds of steam and fire.

Shuddering and keeping a watchful eye on the wrathwa, Kote retraced his footsteps up the hill and peered cautiously between the tree trunks whence the beast had appeared. A black echoing entrance, a bottomless void of moving shadows, filled the space between the trees. He moved closer, tilting his head to listen. A wind was rising in the Doorcrack: it sucked at the air around him drawing it in until it howled and shrieked along the dark road and hurried back to the top of the Wrathendall Spires.

Kote smiled as it tugged at his hair and he whispered, 'The way home.' He reached through the Doorcrack and touched the swirling darkness before he moved back.

He frowned as he stared at the ring of trees. He knew that he had to disguise the Doorcrack and keep it safe from prying eyes while he searched out the one called 'Capthorne' – but how? It was so large and it would be exposed in the daylight on the summit of the low hill. He stepped further back and studied the ring of gnarled oaks with their tracery of tangled branches, a thousand thousand withered fingers that reached down almost to touch the ground.

'Of course! I will treat it like any other door that I would conceal,' and he reached back and unclasped a heavy leather pouch that hung from his belt.

Slowly he withdrew a broken stick of draweasy – the Journeyman's crayon – a thick, fibrous, sticky black crayon blended from a secret recipe of blood, skin and bones mixed with roots and herbs and magically teased together in a membrane of boughlin skin. Kote knelt in front of the doorcrack and spat on a blade of grass as he touched it with the crayon and drew the first line of his tree, a thick black vertical line between the existing oaks. He wet another stem of grass a handspan from the first and drew the second line, rapidly blocking in the tree truck, mimicking the rough pattern of the bark. But the lines wavered and threatened to collapse as the draught being sucked into the Doorcrack drew them inwards.

Kote cursed under his breath. He had never had to conceal such a large entrance before and in desperation he drew two thin spidery branches out of the trunk, linking them and securing them amongst the lowest of the branches from the existing oaks on either side of the Doorcrack. The thin crayon branches stretched as taut as bowstrings and hummed in the wind that was swirling through the entrance but they held the drawing of the oak tree in place and Kote quickly added to them, thickening them, drawing a mass of interwoven branches, finger-fine twigs and withered winter leaves. He whistled softly to the dragma and called to him, summoning him to stand across the Doorcrack while he climbed up onto his back and added the upper forking branches.

Dawn was edging the bleak horizon line with a grey morning light before Kote had finished disguising the Doorcrack and had dismounted from the dragma's back. He slipped the worn-down stump of draweasy back into its leather pouch. Wiping his fingers on the wet bracken he stood back, hands on hips, to admire the gnarled oak tree he had created so realistically.

'No-one will be able to find . . .' he began but his words died in his throat as a fast moving shadow flowed over them. He spun round and threw himself into the undergrowth.

Lugg snarled and followed him, burrowing into the dense bank of bracken moments before the wrathwa beast swept back over the hill. It wheeled and circled as it searched the ring of oaks with its fire-hot eyes. Once, twice it almost landed where Kote and the dragma crouched in the undergrowth before it beat the cold dawn air beneath its wings and glided away, letting out a roar of sulphurous breath as it flew towards another wooded hillock, rising above the morning mist in the distance.

Kote rose slowly to his feet and watched the winged creature soar away into the strengthening daylight. He smiled at the dragma as it emerged from the bracken and shook its spines to dislodge the leaf mould and broken twigs that clung to him.

'You know, Lugg,' he whispered, 'I think I must have hidden the Doorcrack so well that even the wrathwa couldn't find it.'

Kote watched the wrathwa fly away until it became a tiny speck in the sky and then vanished before he glanced briefly up to the circle of oaks and looked at them carefully in the daylight to make sure that he would remember the pattern the trees made against the sky.

'Now we must find the one called "Capthorne",' he murmured, trying to remember every word of Tholocus' counsel through the persistent ache in his temples.

He was sure that the Clockmaster had spoken of a spire or pinnacle of rock and that he should begin his search within its shadow but as he surveyed the leagues of flat fields and water-filled dykes lined with poplar trees that spread out towards the distant horizon his heart sank. Perhaps he had stumbled into the wrong stormcloud on the top of the Wrathendall Spires. Standing in the stirrups he slowly turned his head and allowed his eyes to follow the broadest waterway west across the flat landscape until he saw that there were small square houses with angular roofs and glistening windows that reflected the low sunlight, some straggled along the top of the bank of the dyke. They looked very different from the circular reed and thatched dwellings of the people of Bendran, more forbidding, more unwelcoming. He hesitated, undecided as to whether he should ride toward them, when he glimpsed a finger of light in the sky further to the west between two low hills. He watched it carefully and realised that it must be the sunlight touching a spire or pinnacle of rock.

61

'That must be the place the Clockmaster talked of. It is the only high point in all this dreary landscape,' he muttered to the dragma, spurring him forward down the hill.

Slowly they worked their way toward the light, crossing fields full of soft, black earth rowed and ridged up into waves that oozed up between the dragma's claws and made it stumble. They slithered over hedges and rough banks and floundered in the brackish silt in the deeper dykes before finding a stony track that led them to a narrow road bordered by high banks. Now the going was easy and the dragma scuttled along, his claws casting sparks on the hard, dark surface of the road.

Suddenly, ahead of them, beyond a sharp bend in the track, they heard a roaring sound and a savage manditaur rushed towards them. Kote looked around desperately and spurred the dragma at the steep bank on the right of them in an effort to escape. But the beast was upon them before Lugg could take a stride.

Kote stared at the oncoming creature. Close to, it wasn't like a manditaur, or any other beast that he had ever seen before. It didn't have arms or legs, but was squat and rigid, with a gleaming, armoured body, and there were blazing lights and strong rows of teeth in its head. The roaring noise changed as it swerved and emitted a high-pitched screeching sound. Instead of attacking them it climbed the opposite bank and ploughed two deep furrows in the earth before toppling over on to its side and then tumbling slowly over and over and back down to the road amidst clouds of hissing steam and the sound of shattering glass before coming to rest on its side, its belly towards them.

Lugg leapt backwards away from the creature, rearing up onto his hind legs ready to attack it with his front claws, his razor spines along his neck and back prickling outwards in his aggression. Kote clung to the saddle, his dagger in his left hand, waiting for the thing to move. The roaring noise had stopped and gradually the hissing clouds of steam that had been pouring out of its belly had died away to silence. The Journeyman frowned: he had never known a beast to die so easily. He released his grip on the saddle and slid to the ground, cautiously approaching the dead creature. He stopped a stride away and scratched his head: there were four wheels joined to the underside of the beast. They were much smaller and fatter than the cart wheels the people of Bendran used and they were covered with a strange black pattern, but they were wheels. He reached out with his dagger and prodded the nearest one with the needle point of his blade. It pierced easily through the black patterns on the rim of the wheel and it caused it to make an angry hiss of air.

Kote jumped backwards. He crouched against the bank of earth fearing that he had awoken the creature, expecting it to roll over and attack them, but it lay still across the road, rigid and lifeless, and the revolving wheel gradually came to a stop.

'This is like no beast I have ever met before,' Kote whispered to himself creeping forward again, prodding and tapping with his dagger at the irregular shaped belly of the creature. It rang with a hollow sound of metal upon metal.

'Lugg,' he hissed urgently without looking back at the dragma. 'I don't understand this creature at all. Its belly is encased in metal and it runs on wheels. I'm going to have to circle around and take a look at its head to find out if it is really dead. Move in close behind me and be ready to attack if it moves.'

Cautiously Kote circled around the metal beast only to stop and stare, his mouth falling soundlessly open. The body of the creature was crushed and buckled beyond recognition. Shattered crystal was strewn across the road from its eyes and two widening pools of stinking liquid seeped from its battered head. Now he could see that the monster was really dead, he decided to look for a trophy to cut from the body and hang on his belt. Then he caught sight of a bloody figure trapped inside. For a moment he stared and then it moved.

'Lugg, look, we've killed the beast before it had time to devour its last victim. Come! Help me to free him!' he called excitedly as he reached in through the buckled windscreen.

Lugg snarled and moved in beside him, and with his powerful claws tore the front section of the roof of the car away from the buckled door-posts exposing the figure trapped inside. A bloody face stared up at them, its eyes ringed with terror. He screamed once and threw his arms up across his face, smearing the blood that had begun to congeal on a ragged gash upon his forehead. He struggled frantically and then slumped forwards, unconscious, amongst the twisted dials and levers and broken glass inside the metal creature.

'Quickly,' Kote hissed, misinterpreting what he saw, 'before the beast closes its inner mouth and bites him in half.'

Reaching in between the shards of shattered glass, he thrust his hands beneath the limp figure's armpits, roughly dragged him free of the wreckage and carried him a dozen paces along the road before lying him down on the bank. He stood back and stared down at the unconscious body. His clothes and shoes were unlike anything he had ever seen before. He wore a white undershirt of the finest silk with a flag of striped material tied around his throat. Over the top he wore a dark grey jerkin and breeches that matched exactly in colour and were woven from the finest fibres he had ever seen. But it was the shoes that fascinated him the most: they were as black as night and shone like a mirror and when he reached down to touch them they felt like glass.

The figure stirred, his eyelids flickered, and then he

opened his eyes. For a moment he stared at Kote and the dragma, his eyes slipping in and out of focus. Then his look of terror returned, his eyes widened and his forehead wrinkled, breaking the bloody crust on the gash that vanished into his hairline and sending trickles of blood into his eyes.

'Drag ... drag ... dragon!' he cried, trying to scramble backwards up the steep bank.

Kote half-glanced at the dragma who stood behind him and understood the source of the man's terror. He began to shake his head and opened his mouth to reassure the man that he had nothing to fear from Lugg when he caught the sound of another of the metal creatures approaching.

'Quickly, we must hide,' he urged, advancing towards the man and trying to scramble backwards up the bank. But the person screamed as he approached, rolled away from him and leapt to his feet. He ran towards the oncoming beast as it neared the bend in the narrow road and began to wave his arms frantically, shouting at the top of his voice for help.

Kote grasped the pommel of Lugg's saddle with his left hand and vaulted into the saddle. He was about to chase after the terrified figure but hesitated, realising that he could never reach him in time. Instead, he wheeled the dragma to the right and spurred him up the steep bank. The scaly reptile swarmed up the bank in three strides and took them into a dense thicket of thorn bushes. Kote cursed the thorns as he slipped from the saddle and crept back to the rim of the bank to watch what would happen in the road below.

The oncoming creature roared around the bend, hugging the crown of the road. Kote craned his neck and saw that it looked a little different to the one that now lay broken across the road: it was smaller, lower to the ground and it was a shiny blood-red colour. It swerved and stopped abruptly, its roaring voice changing to a high-pitched screech. Doors flew open along its sides and two figures leapt out and ran towards the person that Kote had rescued. Kote inched his way forwards, listening intently as he recognised words amongst the frantic shouts that were coming from the road.

'I tell you I came around that bend and there was a dragon. A dragon as big as a house in the road. And . . . and . . . there was a demon with orange hair riding it. It ripped open the roof of my car. It . . . it . . .'

The other voices broke in and tried to calm the frantic figure who was pointing up the steep bank to where Lugg had scrambled to safety. Kote ducked back out of sight only moments before the group in the road looked up to the hawthorn thicket on the top of the bank but he carried on listening to their excited voices. He frowned and scratched anxiously at his orange hair. He hadn't given any thought to how different this place called Earth might be from the other places that bordered on the world of Bendran. The people were the same wherever he had travelled: their customs and their languages always varied a little but he had the Journeyman's gift of tongues and he had passed freely among them. Each world had its natural dangers to avoid. There were lurkbeasts that waited submerged in the glistening pools of the Crystal Swamps, the manditaurs that roamed the Windrows of Thorn, the hovering bouglin that stooped silently out of the dark thunder skies of Krak and the wrathwa beasts, fire-eaters and scavengers of every horizon he had ever journeyed.

The voices on the road were suddenly raised, making Kote leave the cover of the thorn bushes and draw closer to the rim of the bank again to listen intently.

'No, it's better if you sit down quietly and rest on the grass until the ambulance and the police arrive. Every time you move it opens up that cut on your forehead and it's no

66

good to keep upsetting yourself with this story of a dragon. There's nothing we can do until the police arrive.'

'Dragons!' interrupted a third, slower, deeper voice, loaded with disbelief. 'All this talk of dragons and demons is nonsense. Everyone knows they don't exist outside of fairy stories and certainly not here in Cambridge. No, it's more likely that you fell asleep at the wheel of your car and dreamt of the dragon and the demon with the orange hair; you then woke up as you hit a cow or a sheep that had wandered on to the road. Next you'll be telling us that the demon had horns and pointed ears . . .'

Kote frowned as he listened. Clearly these people of Earth didn't believe that dragmas existed, yet they knew all about them and about the fairies of Cluricawn and the horned wanderers of Gavati.

'No . . . no . . . I'm telling you the truth. The dragon was as large as a house. Look! Look here at these claw marks on the roof of my car – and the devil riding him didn't have horns or pointed ears but was covered in vivid tattoos, thousands of them, all over his face and arms.'

The deep voice began to laugh when the other hushed him into silence. 'Listen, I can hear the police siren. They'll search the area on top of those banks and find out whatever caused the crash.'

Kote scrambled back into the thorn bush as he heard the approaching wail of the siren. He realised from the snatches of conversation that the sight of Lugg had caused the armoured creature to swerve and that what he had thought was a manditaur wasn't really a creature at all but a 'car', a sort of armoured cart, that was propelled along by some sort of magic. He knew then that the whole incident was his fault and that the police, or the guardians of these cars, were going to search for him and probably capture him.

'Lugg, quickly, we must find somewhere to hide,' he

hissed, crawling through the thorn bushes and staring out across the bleak open countryside.

Rich, dark ploughed fields stretched away in every direction but directly ahead, about a league distant, on slightly higher ground, he saw the eaves of a dense wood.

'Lugg, run on your toes and leave no trace of our passing,' he whispered, springing up into the saddle and gathering the reins as he spurred the dragma forwards. Lugg reared up on his hind legs and fled across the heavy ploughed earth, thrashing his long tail from side to side to brush out the claw prints that he made.

Kote clung on to the pommel of the saddle. The wind sang in his hair as the dragma rushed forwards with giant strides. He glanced back over his shoulder, holding his breath as they reached the higher ground and Lugg charged in amongst the close-grown tree trunks. He let out a sigh of relief. No-one had followed them. He reined the dragma to a halt and slid to the ground before slowly creeping back to the edge of the wood to watch for their pursuers.

Briefly, two dark uniformed figures appeared on the bank above the road. They searched in the thorn bushes and then in a widening circle across the plough before slowly returning to the road. Kote watched the rim of the bank for hours without blinking before he was satisfied that no-one was going to follow them. Wearily, he sat down on the carpet of pine needles and leaned his back against a tree as he tried to riddle out what he must do next. He had to continue his search for 'Capthorne'. Clearly he must leave Lugg hidden in the trees and somehow disguise himself if he was to journey far in this place.

He tethered Lugg to an ancient, smooth-barked beech tree, winding the black iron tether-chain twice around the thick trunk and whispering to the dragma to be silent and quench his fire until he returned. Then Kote retraced his steps to the edge of the forest and listened, straining his ears to catch at the snatches of talk that drifted up across the ploughed fields from the people who gathered around the broken metal car. He smiled with relief as he heard them finally abandon the search for a dragon and its demon rider.

He retreated amongst the trees and walked along the edge of the wood until he could see the sheer spine of rock that Tholocus' counsel had told him marked the dwelling place of Mya Capthorne. He had expected a single building or a small house and he frowned as he drew close, shading his eyes and staring at the sprawl of huge buildings – a city of houses that crowded around the rock's base. He could see hundreds of people in the streets and countless metal cars facing backwards and forwards and moving in every direction. He squatted down on his haunches, leaned against a tree-trunk and sank his head into his hands. It would take an age of days to search every building to find the one called Capthorne in such a crowded place.

'She must dwell near the tower,' he murmured, 'I will search its shadow when darkness has shrouded the countryside.'

Kote waited until he couldn't see his hand in front of his face before leaving the safety of the trees and picking his way across the frozen fields to cross three roadways and slip unseen into the maze of winding streets that surrounded the towering spire of rock. The streets were well-lit and bustled with people who dressed in long coats and hats as protection against the bitter cold. Using his skill as a Journeyman he passed as silently as a shadow amongst them, barely causing a head to turn. But the roaring metal monsters were more difficult to avoid. They would roar around corners and rush towards him, their heads blazing with light, and more than once he had to jump into narrow alleyways or press himself into dark door recesses or lose his life.

Kote paused beneath a stone archway that was only a stone's throw from the pinnacle of rock and wondered where he should begin to look. Resting his hand upon the cold brick wall inside the arch he was aware of a small oblong of raised metal set on the wall. It had the feel of polished brass and its surface was engraved with signs or symbols: letters. He moved his hand and found others above and below. He delved inside a hide pouch that hung from his belt, carefully withdrew a handful of glow-worms and balled his fist lightly around them as he held them up to illuminate the archway. Kote frowned as he saw that each brass plate was engraved with a name. He reached into his inner pocket with his free hand and took out the scrap of parchment that Tholocus had given to him with Capthorne's name inscribed upon it. Slowly he compared the symbols on the parchment with the brass plates as he tried to match them one by one. Some of the lines were similar but not enough of them to spell out journey's end.

Hiding the light of the glow-worms beneath his jerkin, he slipped from the stone archway and silently crossed an expanse of frozen grass. He soon found that there were similar brass plaques set upon the wall opposite. Bringing the glow-worms out from underneath his jerkin he teased their fat wriggling tails into glowing points of hot white light. He held them aloft to study the names etched into the brass plaques. Suddenly he gave a cry of delight and lent closer to the bottom oblong of brass on the right hand side. He traced and compared the symbols with those on his scrap of parchment. It matched exactly letter for letter. He spelt out the name MYA CAPTHORNE. Moving stealthily along the stone-flagged passageway into the building, he quickly found her door with her name written upon it. He tried the handle and found that it was securely locked. He retraced his steps, carefully counting them as he did so, and left the building, working his way along the outside until he came to a lighted window.

Kote gently parted the ivy leaves that obscured the window and looked into the small low beamed room. A fire flickered in an iron grate, casting its soft light across a clutter of chairs and a low couch piled high with blankets. The walls were crowded with books and bright pictures. Close to the hearth there was a table littered with open books and sheaves of papers. He saw that some of the papers had spilled onto the floor and lay scattered close to the window but as he was about to crouch and look more closely at them he noticed a figure slumped asleep in a high-backed chair in the shadows behind the table. Kneeling, he quickly compared the symbols on his scrap of parchment with those that headed the sheets of paper closest to the window and sighed softly with relief. He was sure now that he had found Mya Capthorne's dwelling place.

IIe looked back at the figure sleeping in the shadows and was undecided about what to do. The people of this place who had seen him had called him a demon. He wasn't sure if he should tap on the window or call out his purpose when a clock struck five chimes somewhere in the darkness behind him. Instinctively he stepped back into the shadows and watched as Mya stirred in her chair and sat up brushing at a strand of fire-gold hair that had fallen across her forehead. She then appeared to touch a lamp upon the table and flood the room with bright light.

Kote stared at Mya. He had never for a moment expected to be staring into the hazel-dark eyes of a beautiful young woman. Tholocus had not warned him, or prepared him, for such an encounter.

CHAPTER THREE

Kidnapped in the Dark

MYA CAPTHORNE blinked and awoke with a jolt as the heavy environmental report she had been compiling slipped through her fingers and fell, scattering untidily across her desk.

'Damn!' she muttered straightening up in her chair and brushing at the stray strands of copper-dark hair that had escaped from her hair-band to fall across her forehead and into her eyes. The failing afternoon light had drawn long shadows across her study and the log fire had died away to glowing embers in the grate.

She yawned and reached forwards to switch on the desk-lamp, glancing through the narrow french windows as she did so and looking out at the darkening winter sky. The wind was getting up: she could hear it moaning through the bare branches of the oaks that bordered the lawns of Cathedral Close. It was tugging at the brittle ivy twigs that grew around the window, making them whisper and scratch against the panes of glass. She shivered and drew her cardigan closer around her shoulders. There was a smell of fresh snow in the air.

Across the Close the Cathedral clock struck five. Mya looked at her watch and realised that she had to deliver her lecture in less than two hours. She rose from her chair and rebuilt the fire into a roaring blaze.

Returning to her desk, she reluctantly began to gather up the report and put it back into numerical order. 'A couple of hundred years ago they would probably have called me a heretic and burned me at the stake for compiling this,' she frowned, pushing the report to one side and sitting down again. 'Now they'll only dismiss it as a collection of old wives' tales, folklore and superstition. Nobody will take it seriously. At the worst I could lose my job if I submit it.'

At twenty-four years old she was the youngest environmental research lecturer in the university and already, in this, her first year, her head of department had cautioned her to concentrate her efforts on the job in hand and not to lead the students under her tuition into the realms of mediaeval fantasy. Mya sighed and drummed her fingers on the report. She wasn't sure that she had the courage to follow in Nostradamus' footsteps, well, not tonight anyway. In less than two hours' time could she publicly reinforce his prophecies that the world was rapidly drawing to an end in her first open lecture? Could she stand in the great hall of Masters' College and say this to an audience of fellow colleagues and undergraduates?

She hesitated, opened the top drawer of her desk and withdrew the conventional report that her head of department had insisted that she compile, the one that her audience were expecting her to deliver on the well-worn environmental issues of global warming, industrial pollution and acid rain. She glanced at the introduction, scanned the close-typed paragraphs of dry statistics and then dropped it in disgust onto the desk. She rummaged in the other drawer and found her battered scrapbook, the flesh and bones of her real report, and then carried it to the desk-top. She opened it at random and carefully smoothed out the mass of yellowing press cuttings trapped between the pages and began to read through them.

DEWSBURY, YORKSHIRE, *September 20th*
The Devil's knell, the main bell in the parish church, rang continuously of its own accord for twelve hours. The last time the bell rang continuously was in 1349 to warn of the approach of the bubonic plague. The church council is holding an investigation.

FOULA, SHETLAND ISLES, *December 8th*
Villagers were startled to see dozens of white hares gathering in the fields. They continued to collect together all evening and through the night but by morning they had disappeared. A spokesman for the NFU admitted that although such a large gathering was unusual it was probably due to the particularly light sky caused by the full moon.

Mya frowned and shuffled through the press cuttings. She stopped at another heading.

MARPLE, CHESHIRE, *May 16th*
The village of Marple was overrun by a sudden plague of mice yesterday. The emergency services were at full stretch fumigating the village and extra pest control officers have been drafted into the area. A spokesman for the council said that the plague was due to the unusually hot weather.

LLANARTH, CARDIGAN, *July 12th*
Late night travellers were temporarily prevented from completing their journeys in the area due to clouds of Gatekeeper butterflies settling on their cars. Local naturalists are making an extensive study of the butterflies' unusual night-flying behaviour.

Mya shrugged helplessly and shuffled the cuttings back together as she slowly turned the pages of her scrapbook. Separately, to the untrained eye, they might appear to be no more than a collection of reports on bizarre happenings or supernatural phenomena from remote parts of the country, but, from her research, she was sure that they held hidden echoes, warnings of some impending disaster. She had tried to bring her findings to Professor Baudrey's attention. She had shown him the cuttings on the failure of the silk-worm crop in China and its similarity to their own common-garden and zebra-spiders' inability to spin webs during the last autumn. The newspaper reports from countless villages telling of flocks of crows and rooks feeding in the streets, of packs of dogs gathering to howl ceaselessly at the moon, and the naturalists' reports that told how almost every species of animal that they were monitoring had shown a huge increase in female births and a decline in male births. The list of Nature's forewarnings seemed endless and she had been about to strengthen her argument with her discovery that there appeared to be a greater than usual discrepancy between astrological startime and clock-time, a peculiarity that she had already begun studying, when her head of department's face had darkened with anger and his voice had exploded with rage.

'We don't deal in old wives' tales here, girl, we leave folklore and fairy tales to the history department. It's facts, scientific facts, that you are paid to compile: the strain of algae that is spoiling the river Severn, the chlorine factor needed in the treatment plant at the Davington reservoir.'

Mya had tried in vain to defend her findings, pointing to the naturalists' reports, arguing that they were scientific data and not a collection of wild rumours, but her arguments only drove Professor Baudrey into a deeper rage.

'I am not disputing the validity of your findings: the dogs can bark all night long as far as I'm concerned; and parliaments of crows can gather wherever people say they do: it's your interpretation of the information that disturbs me. It is this . . . this . . . headlong rush to indulge in old wives' tales rather than explore the scientific facts before forming your conclusions that appals me.'

Mya sighed and snapped the scrapbook closed as she remembered how the professor had dismissed her research before turning on his heel and striding out of the department without giving her a moment to reply, to expand her theory. She believed that almost every folk tale, or 'old wives' story' as the professor had so dismissively called them, contained enough truth for modern day society to take notice of their warnings, especially if the bases of their stories began to recur. Mya still doubted a large part of her findings: some of it was just too bizarre to swallow, and she couldn't just publish without seeking advice. She knew her work wasn't in line with the department's policy on environmental research but she couldn't turn her back on what she had unearthed, having pieced together some disturbing facts from those early mediaeval manuscripts in the university's library.

She had never really intended to follow this line of research. It had started quite accidentally in the summer of her first year as a student. She had been reading fairy stories to her sister's youngest child when she had noticed recurring behaviour patterns in the animals in the stories. It had made her visit the university library to search for other similarities and the more she delved through those early folk tales the more she uncovered a common thread of animal behaviour that echoed throughout the length and breadth of history – precise behaviour patterns that had time and again forewarned of floods, earthquakes, plagues, pestilence and impending disasters. It had made fantastic reading and she had decided to write her doctorate on the implications of animal behaviour and unnatural phenomena in relation to known historical disasters. She believed they had prior knowledge and that was when she had started collecting the press cuttings on odd animal behaviour and quite unwittingly had begun compiling the doom report that now lay in front of her.

She hadn't expected the wealth of material that flooded through her letter box from the cuttings agencies, nor at first had she grasped the seriousness of the many and varied patterns of behaviour that were being repeated throughout the natural world. Bizarre rather than unnatural would have been a better description of them. 'Nature Gone Mad', and 'Supernatural Nonsense' were just two of the countless newspaper headlines that reported on the sudden rash of neat circular mole-hill patterns that appeared overnight around villages scattered far and wide from Scotland to the Austrian Alps. And there were armies of toads and tiny lizards that invaded motorway junctions and railway stations across Europe bringing everything to a standstill until the emergency services could clear them away. There were stories of millions of bees that swarmed out of their hives to plague villages and force their inhabitants to lock themselves indoors. Even the oceans gave their warnings of impending disaster when shoals of whistler fish clogged the crab and lobster pots across the eastern seaboard of America. The ghosts of headless horsemen had begun to reappear in long-forgotten haunts. Church bells started to ring spontaneously and doors and windows to lock and unlock themselves without keys or latches being touched. Old weather patterns were repeating themselves to forecast war, famine, pestilence and plague. The whole world was going crazy, shouting its warnings everywhere, yet nobody seemed to be taking a blind bit of notice.

Mya shivered and glanced up, her train of thought broken by a movement, a shape or shadow in the darkness beyond the french windows. She froze, a cry strangled in her throat as she saw a face loom closer, press its nose against the glass and stare directly at her through the ivy leaves. She gasped, breathing in a shallow breath of terror, and threw her left hand up as if to protect herself from its penetrating gaze. The eyes held her still as they hunted her face. Momentarily the light from her desk lamp illuminated the face as it pressed against the window, etching it into her memory, imprinting the high cheekbones with their vivid tattoos and the sunken inky shadows around those piercing eyes and the full-blooded lips that tightened into a snarling leer to reveal needle-sharp teeth before they moulded themselves around her name and whispered it through the glass.

Mya cried out and the face vanished, leaving only the slightest breath of condensation on the windowpane between the ivy leaves that scratched and tapped on the cold glass. She blinked and stared out into the darkness as she watched the beads of condensation melt away. She glanced anxiously around her small study, then reached for the telephone that sat on her desk, intending to report the prowler to old Henderson the night porter who lived in the gate lodge at the entrance to the Close. She frowned and glanced back to the window as she listened to the ringing tone. It hadn't been any ordinary face pressed against her window, and it wasn't only the brightly-coloured tattoos depicting monsters and demons that covered it or the mass of orange hair that hung down around it that made it so different. It was a face, or part of a face, that she had seen a thousand times staring out at her from the earliest illuminated manuscripts that she had studied so often.

The line crackled and Henderson's paper dry voice brusquely asked her what she wanted.

'There's a prowler in the Close,' she answered, breathlessly fighting to keep her voice level. 'He's a thin young

81

man, I think, with bright red hair and tattoos on his cheeks and forehead. He was staring in at me through the french windows a moment ago.'

Henderson's rasping breaths quickened. She heard him call to one of the other porters in the gate lodge as he told him to telephone the police. He warned her to keep her door firmly locked while they searched the Close and the surrounding buildings.

'But . . . but . . .' interrupted Mya, 'I've got a lecture to deliver on the environment in the Masters' Hall in just over half an hour. Do you think you could escort me to the entrance before you begin your search? It won't take a moment, I'm afraid to cross the Close on my own.'

Henderson coughed and after a short pause reluctantly agreed to escort her, but she heard him muttering to himself that the prowler would probably get clear away in all this coming and going before he replaced the receiver.

Mya shivered, gathered up her top coat and pulled it on before looking down at the two environmental reports that lay on her desk. Her hand hovered between them. The appearance of that face at the window was too much of a coincidence, too much of a warning, to go unheeded. It must have been a sign, a sign that she should deliver the doom report. She laughed softly but without a trace of humour as she imagined what Professor Baudrey would say about her pursuit of logic.

A light knock on her door followed by Henderson's dry rasping voice made her look up sharply. She quickly gathered up the report and crossed to the door. Low clouds shrouded the Close in darkness. A flurry of snowflakes stung her face as she stepped out from beneath the archway that led to her study. She turned her collar up against the bitterly cold wind and kept close to the old porter as he trudged along the gravelled walkway and then unexpectedly turned onto the lawn and headed directly towards a small gate arch that lay in deepest shadow.

'That isn't the quickest way to Masters' Hall!' she called, hesitating to follow him.

Now she was alone and the shadows seemed to crowd in close around her. 'Damn!' she muttered, afraid of being left. She hurried after him, clutching her report tightly under her arm.

The frozen grass crackled beneath her shoes. She was aware of the wind rattling the icy twig-fingers of the oak trees that peopled the lawns and the rustle of dead autumn leaves in the gutterings of the buildings that bordered the Close. Suddenly someone close called to her from the darkness. A voice whispered her name, repeating it twice.

'Mya Capthorne. Mya Capthorne.'

'Henderson – wait!' she called. 'That prowler's following us across the lawn.'

She ran forward and caught up with the old porter and reached out to grasp his arm. 'Henders . . .' she cried, the word dying in her mouth as the arm and sleeve crumpled to nothing between her fingertips. The figure of the old porter was nothing more than a mass of lines, a shifting, translucent, scribbled silhouette that barely showed against the scurrying snowclouds. She opened her mouth to scream. She wanted to run away from this apparition but she was paralysed with terror. The silhouette of the old porter continued to collapse, the writhing lines melting into one another. The empty face sighed and folded into a vacant smile, the neck wrinkled into the shoulders and the lean, cruel face that had looked in at her window appeared through the dissolving figure and smiled at her, exposing his razor-sharp teeth.

'Capthorne? Mya Capthorne?' he asked quietly, pushing aside the last of the melting lines and stepping towards her.

He hesitated as he saw her mouth begin to tighten into a scream and her hands clench up in terror of him.

'You have nothing to fear from me!' he cried, spreading out his empty hands towards her, palms upwards to show her that he was unarmed. His voice made her blink and broke the spell of her paralysing fear.

She stumbled backwards and screamed at him, 'Get back! Get away from me. Help! Help me, someone!'

Lights sprang on in the buildings that bordered the lawns. Doors slammed and voices called out in the darkness. Kote looked about him in desperation. He could see figures silhouetted against the lighted windows and hear running footsteps on the gravel walkways. Taking giant strides towards her he closed his left hand over her mouth, silencing her screams at once. He pinched her lips shut with his first finger and thumb and grabbed her around the waist with his other hand, then picked her up roughly and began to run toward the small gate arch on the far side of the lawns.

Mya kicked and struggled violently against his tightening grip. 'Be still!' he hissed fiercely into her ear, 'I mean you no harm. I am Kote the Journeyman. Tholocus, Clockmaster of Eternity, sent me to guide you to his high tower on the rim of the City of Time.'

Mya barely heard his words as she tried to bite savagely at the suffocating hand clamped over her mouth. They were fast disappearing beneath the gateway as Kote growled at her, 'Our journey is long. If you struggle I will be forced to bind you, to truss you up as securely as a live kapiget ready for roasting.'

Mya was helpless as her captor carried her through the evening crowds. She could not believe that no-one tried to stop him: it was as though they were invisible. Vainly she tried to kick out at those closest to them but they were always just beyond her reach.

'It is useless to struggle,' Kote whispered to her. 'No-one can see us. It is part of my craft as a Journeyman to travel unnoticed through crowded places. Be still, it will make the journey easier.'

Mya went limp and tears of helpless frustration welled up in her eyes. The streets were darker and emptier now that they were away from the cathedral and the university and she saw flat, empty fields and distant clumps of black winter trees stark against the night sky between the last of the straggling houses. In panic she wondered where the hell he was taking her, why he hadn't already bundled her into the boot of his car? Fresh snowflakes began to sting her face. Managing to twist her head, she looked back the way they had come and saw the clear trail of her captor's footprints.

She knew that her scream had brought people out in the Close: she had seen and heard them converging on the lawn. Her only hope of rescue lay in the fact that they would probably follow her attacker's footprints. But her hopes evaporated moments later as the snow-flurries deepened into a real blizzard. The surrounding houses vanished from sight in the driving snow and the trail of footprints was quickly smoothed away.

Kote shifted her weight beneath his arm and watched the last road crossing for a moment, satisfying himself that none of the metal monsters was close at hand before he quickly crossed and then began the long shallow climb up across the frozen fields. Reaching the dark eaves of the wood he put Mya down, drew a thin silken cord from one of the pouches that hung from his belt and bound it lightly around her right wrist.

'If you try to escape the knot will tighten. If you call out for help from your people I will seal your mouth until journey's end,' he hissed forcefully.

'What do you want from me? Why have you kidnapped

86

me?' Mya sobbed, her tears blurring the sight of the strange tattooed figure who stood in front of her in the shadows.

Kote tried a smile of reassurance and stepped another pace away from her. 'I will not harm you, Mya Capthorne. I knew of no other way to make you begin this journey . . .' He paused, searching for the words to explain and saw a flash of anger in her eyes.

Mya sensed his indecision, opened her mouth to curse him, but hesitated, remembering a lecture that she had attended some years ago given by a police psychologist about the victims of kidnap and rape. Snatches of it came back to her. It would be better to humour her attacker, not to antagonise him, to strike up a conversation, open lines of communication, try and use it to win him over and persuade him to let her go.

'My name is Kote,' he began slowly, pointing to his chest. 'I have journeyed far through a Doorcrack in the walls of reality to find you and I am to be your guide and lead you to the high tower on the rim of the City of Time. Tholocus, Clockmaster of Eternity, has commanded this.'

Mya stared at him. Her resolve to try to communicate with her kidnapper melted away as cold shivers of fear ran up and down her spine. She realised that she was dealing with a madman who had probably escaped from the secure mental institution in Hollerton, twenty miles away.

'How . . . how . . . how do we get to this City of Time?' she asked, fighting to keep the hysteria out of her voice, trying to conceal her growing terror.

The blizzard had blotted out the lights of the town below and surrounded the spire of the cathedral with swirling darkness. Icy snowflakes were settling on her hair and neck and she knew that she was utterly alone and beyond rescue.

'Lugg, my dragma, is tethered close by in this forest,'

Kote answered her. 'He will carry us both through the Doorcrack in the walls of reality. Come, we must hurry.'

Mya hesitated as the thin silken cord tightened painfully around her wrist. Kote turned and frowned impatiently before giving the cord a tug. 'Come, Tholocus counselled me to hurry. There is no time to lose.'

'But . . . but . . .' Mya stuttered, desperately searching for the words, the phrases, anything that would stop the madman dragging her into the dark woods. 'I'm afraid of the dark,' she blurted out. 'Can't you just tie me to this tree here on the edge of the wood and bring your dragma out. I promise I won't try to escape.'

Kote smiled and she saw his sharp teeth flash in the shadows. 'If it is the dark you fear, Mya, you shall have light. Give me your hand.'

He held her open hand palm upwards and delved into the flat leather pouch that hung from his belt and withdrew a handful of the glow-worms. He teased them into glowing points of white light, gently laid them in the palm of her hand and closed her fingers over them.

'Keep your hand closed lightly around them or they will escape, but do not squeeze them too tightly or they will burst,' he whispered, watching her eyes widen in surprise as she stared down at the light that burned between her fingers.

She stood still, enchanted, for a moment. 'Ugh, I can feel them wriggling,' she gasped. She opened her hand in disgust and the glow-worms scattered at her feet.

'You fool,' Kote hissed falling on to his knees and chasing them with quick fingers as they burrowed into the snow. He gathered them up in his clenched fist, counting them twice before he spoke, 'If they escape and are exposed to daylight, they will then metamorphose into glow-wasps and those harmless lights will become lethal stings.'

88

Mya shuddered and retreated a step, shaking her head as he once more offered her the glow-worms.

'Take them,' he insisted, thrusting them into her hand. 'They are quite harmless if you keep your fingers closed lightly around them and the warmth of your hand will make them glow and light your path through the forest.'

Mya fought to swallow her revulsion as she took them back. 'Wait,' she called, holding them above her head to see Kote more clearly as he turned away from her and began to stride through the wood.

There were now doubts crowding at the edges of her reason. Perhaps he wasn't an escapee from Hollerton after all. Perhaps he *was* some sort of messenger. She couldn't imagine where he wanted to take her or what it was all about: she was sure that all his talk about a City of Time and a Clockmaster of Eternity was nonsense, but there *was* something about him. Something about his face had struck a chord when he had stared into her study window, something that had seemed so different, as if it echoed or mirrored the ancient worlds that she had glimpsed in those fairy stories. And there was the way he had disguised himself as Henderson, the old porter, that had been more like magic than anything she had ever seen. And now he had given her a strange handful of worms that gave off more light than a powerful torch.

'Wait!' she called again, but she was almost pulled onto her knees as Kote gave another more violent tug at the silken cord.

'Quickly, follow in my footsteps,' he urged. 'There will be time to talk once our journey has begun.'

Mya had no choice but to stumble after him as the cord tightened. She blinked and brushed at the swirling snow-flakes that danced around her head and threaded her way between the tree trunks that loomed out of the darkness on either side of her and moved into her circle of light. Brittle icy fingers scratched and pulled at her hair and she tripped over hidden tree roots and rabbit burrows beneath the thickening carpet of snow.

'Can't you slow down and wait for me?' she cried, almost colliding with him as she reached the edge of a clearing where he had stopped.

Catching her breath, she looked past him and let out a gasp of terror as she saw a huge reptilian creature begin to rise out of the shadows a yard in front of her. It snarled, dribbling smoke and fire, and its armoured scales glistened and rippled in the trembling light of the glow-worms that she held in her hand. Slowly the creature turned its head in her direction, blinking its hooded eyes and enveloping her in clouds of vaporous steam.

'Jesus Christ!' she cried, choking on the fetid vapour and stumbling backwards as she tried to turn and run for her life. Kote's strong hand gripped her arm and drew her step by step into the clearing.

'Do not be afraid. This is Lugg, my dragma, my beast of burden. He will carry us to the City of Time.'

Mya felt the ground shake beneath her feet as the monster moved away from her. She looked from its curved claws and its armoured flanks to the thick leather girth entwined with silver and the high-backed saddle that sat behind its shoulders amongst the spines and humps that ran from the top of its head to the end of its long tail.

'It's a dragon,' she breathed in awe. 'Just like the ones from the mediaeval stories.'

Kote's ears pricked at the word 'dragon'. He had heard it twice now since he had travelled through the walls of reality. He unshackled the black iron tether-chain and commanded the dragma to crouch on its haunches for them to mount. As it lowered its belly closer to the ground he gathered up the reins and turned thoughtfully to face Mya.

'There is nothing to fear, Lugg will not hurt you. Surely you have dragmas, or dragons as you call them, here on earth: do you not ride them as you please?'

Mya shook her head firmly, reluctant to move closer to the huge creature. 'No, dragons are the beasts of myth and legends. There is no creature on earth that can breathe smoke and fire like Lugg. The nearest animal we have to a dragon is the giant lizard that inhabits a few remote South Sea islands, and that is only about one tenth of his size.' She paused, letting her gaze wander up over his glistening scales. 'But no-one could ever tame those giant lizards for riding: they are wild, carnivorous creatures.'

Kote laughed and swarmed up the dragma's foreleg before springing lightly into the saddle. 'Well, dragmas are beasts of burden where I come from and would not singe a hair upon your head. Come on, climb up Lugg's foreleg, but be careful of the upper edges of his scales, they are very sharp when you reach his shoulder. Catch hold of my hand.'

Mya took a reluctant step forward and touched the dragma's armoured leg. The scales felt hot and as smooth and hard as glass. Reaching out she almost dropped her treatise on the environment that she had managed to keep tucked under her arm during her capture. A wild thought crossed her mind as she stuffed the bulky document into her inside coat pocket, perhaps if she let it fall and scatter on the snow, it would leave a trail, something for the Police to follow. The idea of rescue buoyed her up briefly but reluctantly she pushed the treatise further into her pocket. It was too valuable to cast into the snow like that. She dug deeply in to her other pockets for something, anything, to drop and leave as a marker in the clearing. Her fingers closed around a scrap of flimsy, crumpled paper – it was the stub of a theatre ticket that she remembered pushing into her pocket a couple of days ago as she left the Aldwych Theatre in the Strand. Beneath it she felt her handkerchief and she pushed the ticket well into its folds before pulling it out and blowing her nose. Then, as casually as she could, she dropped it at her feet and walked over it, crushing it into the trampled snow to hide it from the Journeyman's watching gaze. Reaching out with her free hand she began to clamber awkwardly up onto the claws of the dragma's foreleg.

'Wait,' Kote called, scrambling down and jumping to the ground. He bent and retrieved her handkerchief from the snow, smiling as he pressed it back into her hand. 'You accidentally dropped this silken cloth, Mya Capthorne.'

He carefully opened the fingers of her other hand and took back the mass of wriggling glow-worms, counting them back into his flat leather pouch. 'It would be dangerous to light our road and show the way to watching eyes: some may wish to follow us, and it will make the climb up into the saddle easier now that you can use both hands. Quickly follow.'

Mya glared at his back. 'Damn you,' she muttered silently, shaking the handkerchief out fiercely. She got a moment's satisfaction out of watching the crumpled theatre ticket flutter down in the darkness to land somewhere beneath the huge dragma. She stuffed the handkerchief back into her coat pocket and began to climb up across the dragma's shoulder. Kote's hand reached down and as she clasped it she felt herself lifted up into the saddle behind him.

'Lugg's scales are painfully hot, almost too hot to touch,' she muttered, blowing on the palms of her hand as if to cool them.

Kote commanded the dragma to go forward, spurring him to his feet, but frowned as the dragma surged ahead. He half-turned in the saddle to answer her, 'Dragmas are cold-blooded creatures: normally their scales feel ice-cold to the touch, and they never breathe fire, only vaporous steam. I don't understand what has happened to Lugg.'

Mya was about to reply but the dragma lurched forward breaking off twigs and branches as it cut a straight line towards the edge of the wood and Mya had to throw up her arms to protect her face from being scratched. A pace beyond the trees and the full force of the blizzard struck them.

'Put your arms around my waist and lock your fingers together. Hold on tight!' Kote shouted over his shoulder against the wind as he lurched forward and gripped the pommel of the saddle.

'Where are we going?' Mya tried to shout, but the wind sucked the words out of her mouth as the dragma forged his way through the storm.

They descended the hidden ploughed fields and crossed the narrow snow-choked road. Lugg had begun to retrace his earlier route, following by instinct and the faint scent of his own world the shortest route toward the distant circle of dark trees that crowned the summit of the low hill where the Doorcrack in the wall of reality stood ajar. Soon the blizzard began to lessen and trees and hedgerows moulded into magical, sculptured shapes by the drifting snow appeared all around them out of the swirling darkness. Just ahead Mya could make out the ring of black trees, their branches etched white, making their finest detail stand out against the darkness. She was about to ask Kote where they were when a roaring sound filled her ears, the air around her was whipped into a gale of snowflakes and a black shape darkened the sky as it swooped over them. The stench of its sulphurous fumes made her gag and choke.

'Look out, it's a wrathwa!' Kote shouted, kicking his feet free of the stirrups as Lugg collapsed to his knees and then rolled onto his side to burrow in the deep snow and flatten himself against the ground.

Kote grabbed at Mya's wrist as he kicked himself away from the collapsing dragma. He landed lightly on his feet, already searching for somewhere to hide by the time Mya fell beside him. She stumbled and would have sprawled forwards close to Lugg but Kote dragged her back towards the deepest snowdrift he could see.

'Down,' he hissed. 'Get down and lie as flat as you can.'

He forced her down beside him, almost burying her in the cold, soft snow only moments before the dark shape that had just flown over them began to beat its way back toward where they lay.

'What the hell is that?' Mya gasped, as the dark shape began to materialise into a monstrous flying dragon as large as a row of terraced houses.

It was flying erratically, low to the ground, beating its massive leathery wingtips against the snow. Its eyes burned like hot coals: it roared and sheets of fire poured out of its cavernous mouth to light up the darkness. It was almost above them now and in the lurid light of the flames that flowed out of its jaws she saw its huge claws and yellow underbelly which receded into a vicious armoured tail as thick as a tree-trunk. The air about them grew suffocatingly hot and stank of sulphur. As it passed over where they lay the snow began to melt and clouds of steam rose to envelop the beast. Suddenly the wrathwa lurched to one side and began to beat its wings frantically to gain height. It roared and snarled, its mouth full of white-hot fire, and it stirred up a gale of snowflakes as it floundered and crashed onto its side lower down the hill.

Kote rose to his knees, Mya close beside him. They both stared down at the stricken creature that lay thrashing its head from side to side. A column of flames sixty feet long poured continuously out of its mouth melting the snow and lighting all the trees, grass and hedges that lay in its path. Lugg slowly rose from his hiding place, the spines along his crest prickled out defensively and turned his head to watch the stricken wrathwa beast.

'Keep still, do not attract its attention,' Kote whispered to the dragma.

The huge creature tried to rise, clawing at the melting snow and earth packed beneath its body. It beat its wings forlornly, churning the snow to slush, its head falling lower and lower. Suddenly it took a gulp of air and snapped its jaws shut, extinguishing the column of fire. Darkness smothered the hillside but Kote and Mya could still just make out the huge bulky shape of the wrathwa below them, black and hideous against the night sky.

'It's moving towards us,' Mya whispered, gripping Kote's arm.

Kote rose to his feet pulling her with him, ready to make a run for the Doorcrack which was hidden amongst the trees but he paused and stared down at the creature. 'No,' he whispered. 'It's swelling, it's getting bigger and bigger. Look . . .'

Before he could utter another word the carcass of the wrathwa beast burst into flames with a crack as loud as a thundercrack. Hissing, crackling sheets of blue and gold leapt hundreds of feet into the air, completely enveloping the body. Ribbons of sparks spiralled and danced upward into the darkness.

'Never, never in all my journeys have I witnessed the death of a wrathwa,' Kote gasped.

Mya watched the raging flames devour the carcass from end to end. At first its complete body was silhouetted within the fire, its armoured scales buckling and bending, spitting with the intense heat. Then layer by layer, its flesh was burned away revealing a mass of blackened bones, its spine, rib cage and the skeletal framework of its wings gradually appearing through the fire. It raised its head with one last bellowing scream, its jaws became a ball of fire; then it crashed back to earth in a blaze of sparks.

'Wrathwas are ageless fire-eaters,' Kote said, his voice slow and thoughtful. 'They never die. They cannot be consumed by the fire they create: what we have just witnessed is impossible.'

Mya followed his troubled gaze back to the burning carcass and shielded her face from the heat of the flames before saying quietly, 'Before tonight I would have said that anything like that monstrous creature didn't and couldn't exist anywhere on earth. I wouldn't have believed you or anybody if you had tried to convince me. But now . . .'

'It didn't live here,' Kote interrupted her bleakly, 'it followed us through the Doorcrack. I think it was searching for a way back to the land of Bendran when it crashed into this hillside and burst into flames.'

Mya turned her head and looked out across the snowy landscape. Seeing this dragon had reinforced the idea that there just might be some truth in this Journeyman's words. 'You mean the doorway you keep talking about is near here?'

Kote nodded and pointed up the hill toward the crown of dark trees that crowded the summit and called Lugg to crouch for them to mount.

'We have watched the wrathwa's funeral pyre long enough. Come now, let us ride to the high tower on the rim of the City of Time.'

CHAPTER FOUR

Tumbling through the Walls of Reality

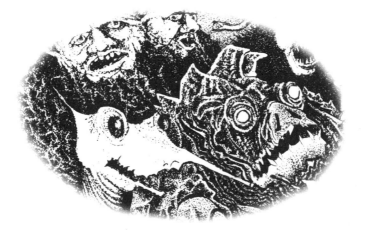

HARRY MURMERS felt as though he had paced a hundred restless miles backward and forward in the cramped space between his desk and the window. He hadn't been able to settle to anything constructive since Orun, the Waymaster, the wild man covered in tattoos, had burst into his office the previous evening demanding that he guide Denso Alburton on some fantastic journey to some place called the City of Time.

Harry had repeatedly shaken his head as he paced his office during the slow daylight hours. Doubts had crowded his mind and at times he had wondered if he was losing his grip on reality but each time he paused and glanced down at the buckled Smith and Wesson automatic that lay on his desk, untouched since Orun had left it, almost twisted in half with his bare hands. And then there was the neat pile of golden trinkets, a king's ransom, lying beside the gun to lure Denso to come to New York. He knew he hadn't dreamt it.

Harry glanced anxiously at his watch. Darkness was deepening the January shadows: Denso should have arrived hours ago. He crossed the room and leaned heavily on the windowsill to stare down at the hurrying crowds that thronged Fifth Avenue. He let his eyes wander over the sea of yellow cabs that crawled sluggishly, bumper to bumper, stretching away into the gloom. He knew that Denso hated cab rides and he searched for his large distinctive figure threading his way through the late afternoon traffic.

A noise behind him made him start and spin round to see Kate, his secretary, hovering in the doorway of his office. Her face looked pale and tense, there were dark shadows around her eyes and she rubbed her hands anxiously together.

'Do you want me to stay until . . .?' Her voice faltered and trailed away as she swallowed nervously. She reached up to touch the pinpricks of dried blood that were just visible beneath the makeup around her mouth.

Harry shuddered as he remembered her ordeal in the outer office. 'No, Kate, you had better go now before either of them arrive. I think you went through enough yesterday, don't you?' He smiled softly.

Harry returned to the window as he heard the outer door click shut and peered down at the shifting crowds, hunting through them for a glimpse of either Denso or the Waymaster. Once he thought he caught sight of Orun's shock of orange hair: he followed it along the sidewalk until it vanished beneath the front entrance of the building and then waited with bated breath for the sound of the outer door as it swung open, but the lengthening silence made him realise that he must have been mistaken.

Suddenly the telephone rang. Harry jumped and swore under his breath as he reached across his desk for the receiver.

'The bloody plane was delayed,' Denso's voice brusquely announced. 'Keep that Waymaster with you. Tell him I'll be there in half an hour.'

He disconnected before Harry could utter a word. He let the receiver fall back into its cradle: this whole business had wound his nerves tighter than a piano wire. Twenty-nine minutes later Denso flung open the outer door and strode in.

'No, he hasn't shown up. Not a word, not a whisper.' Harry spoke quickly, spreading his hands in an empty gesture.

Denso frowned, irritation showing in his dark eyes as he glanced at Harry's face before looking past him into the untidy room. 'You didn't make all this up, did you?' Denso began to ask, inhaling the words in a stifled gasp as his gaze fell on the shimmering pyramid of tiny golden rings, brooches and buckles that lay beside the twisted automatic on Harry's desk.

In two long strides he was past Harry and bending over the desk gathering up a handful of the gold. He muttered quietly to himself as he sifted it through his hands. Pausing he chose a buckle inlaid with ice-blue diamonds and held it up to examine it in the lamplight.

A smile hovered on Harry's lips as he watched Denso. He had barely changed at all in the year since his last visit. His tall, thin, angular frame was still disguised beneath a loose tweed jacket and baggy corduroy trousers although there were now slight edges of grey in his dark brown hair that gave away the passing of the years. But his gaze was just as sharp and piercing as ever as it flashed from beneath those bushy eyebrows and his shy smile still surprised you with its boyish charm. They were unlikely friends, brought together by literature, but they stayed close despite their differences.

'It's uncanny,' Denso mused, his whole manner beginning to change. 'The floral designs, the colour of the diamonds, everything about these pieces, right down to the finest details, they are exactly as I described them in *The Sea of Glass*.'

He paused, holding the trinkets: they were beginning to unnerve him and he hastily returned them to the desk-top before wiping the palms of his hands forcefully together as if to rub away the feel of them. He hadn't believed all the nonsense on the phone about a Waymaster bursting into Harry's office – he thought that Harry had probably landed him a fat advance from some new publisher who wanted him to write another trilogy and that he had come to New York to cement the deal: these people sometimes made strange demands and he wasn't about to argue if there was money in it. But obviously Harry hadn't been kidding.

'No, it's crazy,' he muttered shaking his head and turning towards Harry. 'Waymasters, Crystal Swamps, none of it existed before my book and I should know that better than anyone. I created it. It's a fantasy place, a figment of my imagination, something I dreamed up. Jesus, Harry, where did you get this stuff?'

'I told you,' Harry replied, an edge of exasperation creeping into his voice, 'one of the Waymasters from your story just burst in here as large as life, no, larger – and wilder, more like a ferocious ghetto creature – and demanded that I summon you, so I did.'

Denso turned back to the desk, picked up the buckled automatic and slowly turned it over in his hands, examining it closely before he looked up. 'Nobody could do this. Nobody on earth could twist a metal object and distort it this much without it fracturing, or at least showing a pattern of stress marks. The Waymasters that I wrote about never had superhuman strength so who was it who burst in here?'

Harry laughed harshly, his voice trembling with barely-concealed fear, and he spoke in strangled whispers without taking his eyes off the outer office door. 'How the hell should I know? I don't invent the characters you write about: it was you he wanted not me. He just burst in here with his wild demands, snatched that gun out of my hands when I tried to defend myself and twisted it out of shape with his bare hands. He did it so easily you would have thought it was made of soft black plasticine. Jesus, do you think I made this whole thing up?'

'No, no, I don't,' Denso answered quickly, tossing the useless automatic down beside the pile of golden objects on the desk-top. He had never seen Harry so tense or strung out with fear. He settled his lean frame into Harry's swivel chair and pushed it away from the desk, pivoting it toward the door.

'I think you had better tell me everything this Waymaster said and did from the moment he burst in here.'

Denso shivered in the lengthening silence after Harry had finished relating the events of the previous evening. Some of the details of the Crystal Swamps were too realistic and too far developed beyond the story he had written to be mere fiction. It was macabre and nerve chilling to hear of characters and places from his imagination coming so vividly to life.

'What time did he say he would return today?' he asked, glancing at his watch as he rose to his feet and paced to the window to look out over Manhattan.

'Early evening,' Harry replied. 'He disappeared in quite a hurry yesterday saying he had to watch over some Doorcrack in case it closed.'

'Well, he's late. He's probably trapped in that Doorcrack of his,' Denso growled, crossing to Harry's cocktail cabinet and sorting through the empty bottles until he found the one he was looking for. 'Is that all the bourbon you've got?' he muttered in disgust, emptying the dregs from the bottle into a glass.

'That's all you left on your last visit. I haven't got round to replacing it: you're the only person I know who drinks that particular brand of poison,' Harry replied flatly, keeping half an eye on the outer door.

Denso laughed as he drained the whiskey and slapped the glass down on the windowsill. He licked his lips: the taste of that golden nectar had whetted his appetite. 'I'm not waiting here any longer for this Waymaster to appear. I'm going over to Pete's Tavern. Are you coming?'

'You must wait!' Harry cried as Denso strode past him. 'What about the gold? What if he turns up the moment we've left?'

Denso paused, his large, strong hand resting momentarily on the door-handle, disappointment and relief in his eyes. 'It's not my fault he didn't keep the appointment, is it? Put the gold in your safe, lock it away and leave a note pinned to the door. He can come and find us if he turns up – Pete's Tavern is only a couple of blocks away and I've got a terrible thirst on me.'

'But . . . but . . . I don't know if he can read . . .' Harry's protest was cut short by the sharp click of the outer door shutting. 'Denso, one day you'll be the death of both of us,' he muttered, snatching up his top coat and scribbling a note and pinning it to the door before he hurried out after him. He was just in time to squeeze through the closing elevator doors and he ignored Denso's grinning face as he struggled with his coat buttons.

There was no sign of the Waymaster in the front entrance hall or on the steps outside. The January wind bit savagely at them as they left the protection of the building, stinging their faces with a blizzard of horizontal snow flakes. Harry turned his collar up and hunched against the bitter weather, keeping close to Denso's shoulder as they crossed Fifth Avenue. The thickening snow danced in the headlights of the slow moving traffic.

'We could take a cab,' Harry called against the wind but

Denso laughed, relieved to be out of the office at last. He tilted his head back and opened his mouth to suck in the swirling snowflakes.

'What's the matter, don't you like the elements, the touch of nature?' And he strode past the end of Madison Square Gardens and into the shadows of 23rd Street towards the lights of Park Avenue.

Harry hesitated – it wasn't only the weather – he would have avoided walking this way after dark: there were too many narrow alleyways and overshadowed doorways for his liking and tonight Harry had a feeling in the pit of his stomach that something awful was about to happen.

He had felt uneasy from the moment they had left the bright lights of the entrance hall of his building. He had sensed that someone was stalking them, shadowing their footsteps on the crowded sidewalks. He had seen it in the half-turned heads and brief looks of surprise all around them. The second echo of footsteps behind them sounded as if it was getting closer and closer, there was a face at the edge of his vision, blurred and distorted, that vanished if he turned. Now there was someone at his elbow: he could feel them brushing against him, touching him.

'Denso,' he hissed running to catch up, clutching at his arm, 'this Waymaster, I think he's following us.'

Denso stopped abruptly and looked around anxiously, his gaze sweeping across the empty sidewalk behind them. He looked further to the straggle of forlorn overcoated figures he could see in the lamplight of Park Avenue where they struggled against the worsening storm.

'Harry, you're jumping at shadows. There's no-one even close to us, no-one is on our tail. Jesus, this Waymaster's really got to you, hasn't he? Now, come on, keep close and remember we'd just about be able to see Pete's by now if it wasn't for this damn blizzard,' Denso answered crossly. They turned into Lexington and he strode off towards Gramercy Park.

'But I felt someone touch, no, almost grasp, my right arm, I'm quite sure of it,' Harry grumbled hurrying to keep pace as they passed the dim lights from the foyer of the Gramercy Park Hotel and crossed 21st Street.

'You're imagining it,' Denso flung the words back across his shoulder as he mounted the snowy sidewalk and, surprised to see the gate ahead of him open, passed through into the shadowy darkness of the park.

Harry put his left foot on to the grass and tried to lift his right foot from the sidewalk but nothing happened: it refused to follow. The blizzard was stinging his cheeks, its cold wetness prickling his bare forehead. He couldn't understand what was happening to him: he couldn't move – a numbing paralysis was creeping through him, spreading out from his right elbow, as if invisible ropes were being wound tightly around him. He struggled in vain to cry out, to shout to Denso as he vanished into the swirling snowstorm, but as he tried to open his mouth tiny creatures swarmed across his face, spinning thin, white, translucent tendrils of silence across his mouth. His eyes bulged with terror, panic hammering the inside of his chest as he fought violently to break free of whatever had trapped him.

A face of vivid tattoos loomed in front of him, filling his vision. It was framed by a mass of bright orange hair. The reek of Orun, the Waymaster, choked his senses. There was anger and rage in Orun's eyes as he hissed, 'You betrayed me, Guardian. You tried to thwart the counsel of Tholocus by stealing Alburton away into the night. The Clockmaster must stand in judgement over you for such treachery. Your sentence shall be pronounced in the City of Time.'

At this Orun picked Harry up roughly, flung him across

his shoulder and strode away into the darkness of the park to follow Denso.

The blizzard was smothering everything beneath its frozen shroud, sculpting the trees and shrubs that bordered the walkways in the park into new, grotesque and unfamiliar shapes. Denso caught sight of the faint glow of the street lamps in Irving Place and lengthened his stride. He was about to shout to Harry across his shoulder, urging him to hurry, when a strange sound broke the snowy silence. A low, mournful hum that seemed to stretch across the pathway right in front of him forming a barrier.

'Jesus! What the hell is this?' He stopped abruptly and tried to peer through the swirling darkness.

There seemed to be nothing unusual, only the white border of the pathway looked slightly darker, as if the snow had melted a little, and the bare branches of the hawthorns that edged the way seemed to shimmer and sway. He cursed under his breath and took another step forward. The noise grew louder, rising and falling. It sounded as if the east wind was blowing through miles of telegraph wires.

He stepped back and turned to shout at the figure emerging from the darkness behind him, 'Harry, there's something really weird here . . .'

The words died in his throat and his mouth fell silently open with shock and surprise. The figure he had thought was Harry drew closer and Denso found himself staring into the vividly tattooed face of Orun, the Waymaster. He blinked his gaze away from the mass of tattoos framed by the wild mane of orange hair and stared speechlessly at Harry's apparently lifeless body slung across the Waymaster's shoulders.

'Oh no, no . . .' Denso stuttered, finding his voice and raising it angrily. 'I never created Waymasters for murder. You can't be who you say you are, you can't be a part of my

107

imagination. What have you done to Harry, you madman?'

Orun's eyes widened with surprise. He hadn't expected the same anger and disbelief in Denso Alburton that he had encountered in Murmers, his guardian. He let Harry's limp body slip from his shoulder and sprawl in the snow at his feet. Cautiously he stepped over him and advanced towards Denso, his hand outstretched in a gesture of peace. 'Tholocus, the Clockmaster of Eternity has sent me to guide you!' he cried. He paused, watching the doubt around Denso's eyes and stabbed a finger back to where Harry lay. 'I am no common murderer. Waymasters do not kill wantonly or for pleasure. Your guardian is merely bound securely until he can be judged for his treacheries in the high tower on the rim of the City of Time.'

Denso felt a tingle of fear chill his spine. He hadn't been totally convinced by Harry's account of the Waymaster. The pile of gold trinkets, the buckled automatic lying on the desk, both could possibly be explained away, but now that he had come face to face with this wild man it had sent his mind into a turmoil. This Waymaster was real – and dangerous. A voice of survival from inside his head warned Denso to handle him with care and he began to probe gently for answers.

'Treachery? What treachery has Harry ever done to you?' he asked holding the Waymaster's gaze.

'A bargain was struck,' the man answered fiercely. 'He was to summon you to his tower for me this night, but he was stealing you away into the darkness. I saw and I followed.'

'Are you mad? We were in his office, he did exactly as you asked him,' Alburton interrupted. 'We were there kicking our heels and waiting for you, only you didn't show and I grew impatient for a drink. It's a long way from California to New York. Anyway, we left you a note pinned to the door telling you that we'd be in Pete's Tavern. Jesus Christ it's only a footstep away across the park, what do you think we were trying to do, escape or something?'

Orun frowned, 'But . . . but the chamber was empty. I caught sight of you leaving, I thought . . .' His words trailed off and he took out the crumpled sheet of paper he had torn from the outer door of the office and held it up.

'That's the note! Didn't you read it?' Denso paused, remembering that in *The Sea of Glass* the Waymasters were illiterate. 'Can't you read?' he asked in a quieter voice.

Orun shook his head, 'It is a gift of the Gods to be able to unravel the written word. I took the page in anger when I found the chamber empty.'

'I think you had better untie Harry and tell me what this is all about, don't you?'

'I have already told your guardian that I am Tholocus' messenger. He has sent me through a Doorcrack in the walls of reality to find you and to guide you to the High Tower on the rim of the City of Time . . .' Orun began, kneeling beside Harry and loosening the bindings on his arms.

'What the hell is a Doorcrack in the walls of reality?' Denso asked, raising his eyebrows with curiosity and stepping back, forgetting the low humming sound that had made him stop.

His foot touched the slightly darkened border of the pathway. There was nothing there but an empty chasm. The hawthorns on either side of the path rustled violently and he felt momentarily a mesh of threads or ropes crossing his path: they touched his shoulders, the small of his back, his thighs and calves. They felt soft and spongy and gave easily beneath his weight. He overbalanced, stumbling backwards, and he felt himself falling, spinning and tumbling.

The low hum of the wind being sucked into the Doorcrack drew him downward. He had the sensation of touching and rebounding from unseen objects in the darkness, of almost floating rather than falling. Suddenly he came to an abrupt halt in an avalanche of crumbling dry earth on a steep stone ledge that dropped away to his right. He lay there, the breath knocked out of his body, unable to move. Shrieks of sound, echoes and fragments of half-formed voices swept all around him and then melted away into the oppressive blackness that seemed almost thick enough to eat.

Gradually his breath came back to him in short gasps and he sat up, pressing his hands into the crumbling earth. He blinked and listened to the silence, wondering what the hell had happened.

'I must have fallen down a sewer vent,' he muttered to himself and heard his own voice echo back as he cursed whoever had left the vent uncovered.

He remembered before the echo had a chance to die away the stories he had heard about the sewers in New York and how they were infested with alligators and vermin the size of large dogs. He would have to get out of there fast. He was about to rummage in his coat pocket for his cigar lighter when he realised that the crumbling earth that had broken his fall was shifting beneath him. Gradually it started to carry him down the slope, and where his hand had been resting on the soil hundreds of wriggling creatures were crawling over his skin.

Denso screamed and snatched his hand away. He jumped to his feet shuddering with revulsion, imagining that his clothes must be alive, crawling with cockroaches, centipedes or worms. He burrowed frantically in his pockets and found his squat oblong lighter and snapped it open. He clicked it alight with trembling fingers, the small flame guttering and swaying and in the moment before the persistent draught extinguished the flame Denso glimpsed a kaleidoscope of raw colours, shapes and shadows that the utter darkness had obscured. Above his head shadows leapt amongst a tangled mass of roots and jagged splinters of rock. Black earth clung to layers of brittle bleached bones and stalagmites of limestone that reached up into the darkness. All around him the rough rock walls shimmered with the colours of torbernite, corundum and sapphires. There were veins of pure aquamarine and graphite so tightly pressed that their colours oozed with a phosphorescent wetness.

Something moved across his foot. Denso stared down an instant before the flame died away. He gasped, paralysed with terror. There was nothing on earth that looked like the monstrous worms that were swarming all over the floor at his feet. He knew he had to do something: he couldn't just stand there and wait for them to devour him, he had to find a way out of there. He re-ignited the flame and this time shielded and steadied it with the other hand. Swallowing his revulsion he looked down at the seething mass of white bodies that were wriggling over his shoes and away into the darkness beyond the flickering circle of light. At that first glimpse he had thought they were giant worms but now he saw they were not worms at all: worms didn't grow to the size of large rats or have skins of white armoured scales, neither did they have twofingered tendrils to pull themselves along with.

He shuddered and instinctively moved his left foot as one of them began to climb up his trouser leg gripping the thick corduroy fabric between its rows of tentacles. He swept his hands downward and thrust the flame at the creature's head. It became rigid, released its grip on the cloth and fell backward, landing on the ground between his feet. He tensed, expecting it to attack, but it arched its spine in one tortuous spasm, drew its tentacles in beneath its brittle shell and contracted into a tight ball before rolling slowly away from him down the steep slope.

The mass of monstrous white worms began to do the same, turning their blind heads up towards the flickering light. Red bulbous cyclop eyes momentarily blinked open and then snapped shut and one by one the creatures contracted into their armoured shells and slowly rolled away out of the circle of light.

Curiosity forced Denso to bend down and reach out to tentatively touch one of the last of them as it began to move. It felt as hard and as sharp as flint, and as cold as ice. Frowning, he straightened up and held the guttering flame aloft. As the weak circle of light reflected from the shimmering wall of rock and spread further away from him he saw that the floor was alive with dozens of different creatures. None of them looked like anything he had ever seen before. Cold panic made his hands tremble. This wasn't any ordinary New York sewer that he had accidentally fallen into. It was more like a fracture in the earth's surface. He began to move forward, to follow the slope of the floor upward. Overwhelming fear began to tighten in his chest: he felt desperate to get out.

The persistent draught suddenly rose, making the flame twist and flatten across his fingers so that he cursed and almost dropped his lighter. As the flame went out he saw the walls close in on either side of him, the rocks groaning and creaking as they ground together, and earth, splinters of bone and fibrous fingers of root cascaded down on his head. The floor beneath his feet buckled and shifted into sharp ridges.

Denso screamed. Then he began to run. Unseen objects caused him to fall and stumble onto his knees. He was sobbing uncontrollably as the terror of being crushed alive overwhelmed him.

A soft light flooded the blackness ahead of him. Voices were calling out his name, rising above the grinding creak of the rocks. He looked up and saw Harry's coat-tail flying out behind him and the Waymaster running headlong towards them through a haze of falling debris in the narrow corridor of shifting rocks.

'We must run. The Doorcrack is closing,' Orun shouted as he reached the place where Denso had fallen.

Searching the floor, the Waymaster gathered up one of the white creatures, now contracted into a tight armoured sphere and thrust it towards Denso as he scrambled to his feet.

'Quickly. Take this glowbright to show you the way,' he urged, glancing anxiously up to the swaying tangle of roots and trembling rocks above their heads.

Denso shuddered and backed away, 'No, I don't want to touch it. I've seen what those things turn into,' he cried, turning and shaking his head fiercely.

'Take it,' Harry insisted. 'It won't hurt you. Look, all you have to do is tap it firmly against the rock and it glows.'

He took the glowbright and with outstretched hands he tapped it sharply against the wall once and it began to glow.

'I don't believe it,' Denso gasped, slipping his lighter into his pocket and gingerly taking the sphere from Harry.

The outer shell felt warm now and the inner light source revealed a beautiful interlocking pattern of blue and white scales.

'Come on, we must run before we are trapped,' Orun urged, tugging at their arms.

Denso stared wildly around him. 'Where the hell . . . ?'

'There's no time to explain. Run as fast as you can. Quickly, follow me.'

Orun fled in lengthening strides away into the darkness.

'Jesus Christ, let's get out of here!' Denso cried as the rock walls began to rumble and grind together, and in racing footsteps they followed Orun's vanishing light.

Their flight through the Doorcrack in the walls of reality was a claustrophobic scramble, an endless rush through a closing tunnel of nightmares. The wind rose to a shrieking howl that sucked at the skin on their hands and faces and tore at their clothes and hair. They were jostled and clawed by a thousand half-seen monsters that loomed out of the shifting darkness. Denso was falling behind the other two, his lungs burning with each gasping breath and his legs as heavy as lead. He was stumbling, his footsteps becoming erratic. The brittle sphere of light slipped through his fingers and fell, shattering into a million bright fragments at his feet and was immediately swallowed by the darkness that swept over him. He cried out in despair: he couldn't go on. He couldn't take another step. Rage and anger at his own weakness swept over him and he sank to his knees, scrabbling to retrieve the vanished light.

Faintly he heard Harry's voice calling to him, urging him to follow, to come and look at something. He looked up and saw that there was light ahead, a strong yellow-green light that glowed beyond a bend in the grumbling rocks. He climbed to his feet and painfully hurried forward. Blinking and rubbing his eyes he reached the entrance and came to a shambling halt beside the other two on a narrow ledge of rock beyond the mouth of a tunnel. He stared out across the most incredible landscape he had ever seen.

'It's the Crystal Swamps!' Denso whispered in awe. 'Only they're more beautiful, more detailed, than I could have ever imagined.'

'It's a transparent landscape!' Harry exclaimed. 'Look, I can see villages, a forest and distant hills beneath the surface. It's unreal. Look at the sunset, it's not possible!'

Orun laughed softly and swept his hand out toward the setting sun. 'Tholocus told me it would be beyond your understanding.'

Denso looked down. 'The colours are so rich, so vivid. Look at the way the surface of the swamps shimmer in the evening light, blending these deep turquoise, azure and cobalt pools with those stagnant yellow marshy areas. Look at those bilious lime-green gas-bubbles bursting on the edges of those giant bullrush stems. I'd hate to fall in there.'

'Orun,' Harry hissed anxiously touching and then gripping the Waymaster's arm, 'what kind of monsters are those?'

He pointed down across the darkening marsh pools to where dozens of huge, hideously misshapen heads and long sinuous necks the colour of burnt orange were beginning to break through the viscous surface, sending out sluggish iridescent ripples as they rose. Marsh-slime dripped from the ridges and furrows of loose skin that hung beneath their powerful jowls in droplets of livid emerald and dark aquamarine. They shook their heads, scattering the droplets, and barked, sending the sound echoing across the marshes before it died away. Plumes of bilious green slime erupted through tall slender blowholes on the tops of their heads. They rose with a volcanic hiss, then splattered into the pools all around them.

'Lurkbeasts,' Denso whispered, more to himself than to the other two. They were exactly like the grazing marsh-creatures that he had written about in *Swamps of Glass*, in every detail except their colour. He found it uncanny to watch a world coming to life complete with all its creatures, a world that he had painstakingly created in his imagination, one that he thought had no existence except in his dreams. It was worse than waking up in the middle of a nightmare because once awake reason and logic and the touch of the real world forced the nightmare to diminish.

'They are harmless grazing creatures . . .' Denso began confidently, before Orun cut him short.

'No, no, beware of them, Denso. One bite and their jaws will slice you in half. They are wild, implacable beasts that lurk beneath the surface of the swamps close to the raised pathways. They rise up and drag you down beneath the surface to wait for you to drown.'

Harry took a step backward at Orun's words only to leap forward again as the narrow entrance behind him ground shut with a rumble of thunder, covering them with clouds of gritty black dust. A second clap of thunder split the air above their heads and Denso and Harry both spun around to see a dark crack appear in the bare rock only a yard above where they stood amongst the thousands of cave entrances that pock-marked the steep hillside. Stale air hissed out of the gap and wafted down over them and Harry was sure that he caught the faint sounds of birdsong and the sounds of the countryside, not the hum and roar of traffic, the blare of horns and the shouts of voices of New York that they had just left. Gone were the tramp of millions of feet, the hot, rich smell of food, the East River, smoke and exhaust fumes blending with the winter air.

The crack grew wide enough to walk into and the breath of stale air became a shrieking wind that tore briefly at the oakweeds and brambleheads growing on the ledge. Orun pulled them in close to the rock-face until the wind died away to a low humming whisper. He watched the new Doorcrack for a moment before he spoke.

'Tholocus warned me that the Doorcracks were dangerous roads to travel. He said they were unpredictable and none could tell when they would open or snap shut or where they would lead to.'

'You mean that the new opening could lead anywhere?' Denso suddenly cried, staring up at the rough rock wall above them. 'How the hell will we ever get back now?'

Orun shrugged. 'I do not know where the new way through the walls of reality will journey to.'

'But that's no good!' Denso cried. 'We'll want to go back after this meeting with this Clockmaster for Chrissake!'

Harry's laughter cut across Denso's panic and made him twist his head towards him.

'What's the hurry to get back, Denso? We've only just got here, wherever "here" is. You ought to be taking notes, there's so much material here.'

'I like to have all my adventures worked out before I start and not go jumping in with both feet before I know the temperature of the water,' Denso answered firmly, shaking his head. 'By my reckoning we haven't run far enough to reach the Staten Island ferry terminal through that black tunnel; the East River should be on our left not that endless waste of swamp and marshland swarming with savage creatures.'

'You are wrong,' Orun interrupted fiercely, sweeping his hand across the horizon-line.

'To the east stretch the grasslands of Bendran and the dark mass that lies in the shadows of those thunderheads is the Citadel of Krak. Beyond it the grasslands rise and fall in bleak hills until they reach the Wrathendall Spires, the sheer mountains of granite that rim the world and reach up to touch the sky.'

'What lies to the west beyond those shadowy shrouds of mist?' Denso asked, his interest gradually awakening as he followed the Waymaster's hand.

Orun slowly turned and shaded his eyes against the last rays of sunlight, a smile touching his lips as he said quietly, 'That, Denso, is the way to the City of Time where Tholocus, Clockmaster of Eternity, eagerly awaits you.'

Denso stared out across the shimmering swamps in silence. Harry was right: there was so much here that his imagination hadn't even begun to accept, so much he wanted to see and experience. But he couldn't see how the hell they were going to get across these swamps without being eaten alive.

'We will travel with the new dawn,' Orun answered breaking into his train of thought and bending to gather up an armful of dead oakweed branches for a fire. 'It is too dangerous to cross these marshes during the hours of darkness when the Lurkbeasts roam. We will use a straw boat for the journey in the morning, when there will be nothing dangerous out there.'

Orun watched a shadow of apprehension cross Denso's eyes and grinned at him before adding, 'Well, nothing that is except the gliding shadow of the Wrathwa beast hunting the marshes for easy prey or . . .'

He fell silent and busied himself building the fire, drawing out a tinderbox and selecting a sharpflint to light it. He didn't understand the ways of these Earthians and their endless questions and he didn't altogether trust Murmers or believe his story about the symbols scribbled on the scrap of paper he found pinned to the door, but he would bide his time until Tholocus' judgement.

'Here, let me light those twigs for you,' Denso's voice made him start and look up sharply. Denso was crouching on his haunches opposite him, hand thrust down toward the pile of kindling and a long thin pale blue flame danced between his fingertips.

Orun let out a gasp of surprise as he scrambled backwards. His expelled breath made the flame twist and waver as it ignited the pieces of wood.

'There is magic in your fingertips.'

Denso laughed easily and shook his head. He closed the lighter with a sharp snap and then tossed it casually across the crackling fire into the Waymaster's open hands. 'Here, catch!' he called smiling as he watched Orun reach out and catch the flat oblong metal case and cautiously turn it over and over in his hands. He traced the design of flowers and leaves etched into its smooth sides, feeling it with his fingertips. He squeezed and pressed it, his eyebrows creasing into a troubled frown. 'There must be a magic word or something to make the flame,' he muttered.

Denso reached across, took the lighter back and flicked open the top, depressing the mechanism in one easy movement. The flame reappeared. 'Magic is a relative word,' he smiled, extinguishing the flame and passing the lighter back to the Waymaster.

Orun flicked the flame on and off, smiling to himself as he played with it.

'In our world,' continued Denso, 'those tattoos of your journeys, your strength, the crablike creature that silenced Kate, even the webs you used to block the doorway of Harry's office could be called magic, or supernatural powers.'

Harry nodded in agreement, crouched down and held his hands out towards the crackling fire. It was getting bitterly cold now that the sun had disappeared and the night shadows were growing deeper. There were noises in the darkness, strange howls and whistling grunts that made him glance anxiously over his shoulders and crowd closer to the other two.

'Are you really sure we're safe here?' he asked Orun in a forceful whisper.

Orun stiffened and half rose as he listened to the night sounds. 'Quiet, keep low and smother the fire. There are gradaurs prowling in the rocks.' Orun kicked loose earth and stones over the flames and leapt to his feet, dagger unsheathed. In three silent strides he vanished into the thickening darkness.

Denso and Harry glanced anxiously around, searching

the shadows that surrounded them, listening to the growing volume of weird inhuman shrieks and howls. They were drawing nearer, pressing into the edges of the tiny pool of firelight.

'Jesus, this place is giving me the creeps,' Denso muttered to himself, huddling in closer to the dying fire. Ignoring Orun's warning he began to fan the embers and feed the flames with the withered twigs and branches that the Waymaster had gathered. 'Whole armies live and die on the top of my desk. Savage creatures loom up and then I fold them tidily away between the pages of my manuscript and go to lunch. We must be crazy to have wandered so readily into this living wilderness; and it's utter madness to stay here,' he mumbled.

Suddenly a huge moth the size of a sparrow whirred past his head and flew straight into the fire, exploding in a ball of brilliant sparks.

'Did you see that?' Denso cried out. 'Did you see the size of that thing before it hurled itself into the flames?'

Harry brushed furiously at the sparks that still clung to the front of his coat but Denso hissed him into silence. 'Listen,' he frowned, bringing a finger to his lips. 'Can you hear a sort of clattering sound mixed in with all those other noises? Listen, out there, can you hear? I think it's getting louder: whatever's making the noise is getting closer.'

Harry turned his head, straining his ears. He could hear it now, the persistent scraping and clattering sound. It was at its loudest amongst the oakweeds and brambleheads directly behind them. He could hear the branches creaking and in the firelight he could see them swaying without the help of a wind. The shadows on the ground between the spindly tree trunks were moving, crowding towards them.

'Jesus Christ!' he cried, staggering backwards and treading through the fire, scattering hot embers in every direction. He clutched at Denso's arm. 'There's thousands of giant blue and orange crab-things. Look! Just look at them, they're clinging onto branches and swarming across the ground towards us!'

At that moment globes of bright white lights appeared to be hanging from the steep slope above the ledge. From somewhere amongst them they heard the Waymaster's voice shouting, repeatedly chanting, 'Gradaur! Gradaur! Gradaur!'

The swarming crustaceans hesitated, their open claws raised, their bulbous stalky eyes swaying and turning between the dying flames of fire, the sound of Orun's voice and the lights on the rock-face. Suddenly they began to move, shuffling sideways and charging in a clatter of snapping claws towards the lights on the steep rocky slope.

Denso let a sigh of relief escape between his lips and began to whisper, 'It must have been the light from our fire that attracted . . .' when he saw the bright orbs above them begin to fade and go out one by one.

The scrape of clawed feet grew suddenly louder as the mass of creatures turned and began to advance across the ledge, moving menacingly toward where they stood beside the scattered ashes of the fire.

'Quick, kick the burning embers as far as you can,' Harry hissed frantically.

They both kicked violently at the burning branches, scattering them across the ledge. They watched transfixed with horror as hundreds of the brilliantly coloured creatures turned and scurried after them, crawling on top of each other, a mass of snapping writhing claws as they fought to reach the crackling flames.

'Look out, there's more behind you!' Harry cried, kicking desperately at the last of the embers, sending up a shower of bright sparks as he tried to pull Denso clear of their snapping claws.

Orun suddenly burst in between them, cursing under his breath and expertly stamping and treading on the heads of the giant crustaceans, crushing their slender antennae so that they snapped their claws blindly at his feet.

'Quickly, follow me,' he hissed, leading them in a zig-zag scramble over the writhing armoured creatures until they reached safety on the dark rocky slope above the ledge.

'Fools! Stupid fools! You were moments from death down there,' Orun muttered angrily, adding furiously, 'I warned you that gradaurs were scouring the rocks before I went to set glowbright lines to draw them away but you ignored my warning and rekindled the fire.'

'Are we safe here?' Harry asked in a hushed whisper as he looked down at the swarming mass of crustaceans that now completely obscured the ledge and the last remaining embers of their fire.

'It is not safe to stay here too long,' Orun whispered and without another word led them up a twisting track across the rock face to a higher ledge.

'Those are glowbrights aren't they?' Harry whispered as he stared down at the dozens of small spherical globes that he could just make out in the starlight as they lay scattered all along the ledge.

Orun nodded silently and with his fingertips he began to roll them carefully, one by one, to the edge of the ledge. Wherever his fingers touched them they began momentarily to glow with a soft white light.

'What are you doing?' asked Harry, crouching down beside the Waymaster and gently rolling two of the glow-brights to join the others.

Denso hesitated to touch them, remembering all too well the loathsome crawling worms they had seemed to him in the Doorcrack. He stood back and watched the others line up twenty of the small round globes.

'We must drive the gradaurs back into the swamps,' Orun whispered forcefully, picking up the nearest ball and holding it tightly against his chest until it glowed bright white. Then he cast it down the steep slope.

It bounced and rolled across the rough rocky ground, its light inner core glowing brighter and brighter, ploughing a blazing trail of incandescence through the centre of the writhing mass of blue and orange creatures, causing them to twist and turn, snapping their claws before swarming after the light.

'Throw another quickly. Cast them all down the slope towards the swamps!' Orun cried, reaching for two more of the cold brittle balls and hurling them after the first.

The leading orb rose in two bouncing arcs with dozens of the crustaceans attached to it and it struck the slender trunk of one of the oakweeds that grew on the lip of the ledge. It shattered into a million shimmering splinters of light, destroying the clinging creatures and melting away into darkness. Harry shuddered as the glowbright exploded. It seemed so brutally cruel to hurl these harmless and beautiful things to their deaths on the ledge below, but Orun was shouting, urging him to gather the spheres. He clutched one in either hand and held them until their inner cores blazed white and then, gritting his teeth, he cast them down the slope where they shattered on the lower ledge in puffs of brilliance.

'More, more! It is the light that attracts them. If only we could make some of these glowbrights roll between the oakweed trunks and bounce over the lip of the ledge to roll down into the swamps they would follow.'

Denso thought of his skill for bowling and reached down for the nearest glowbright. He might get a lucky strike. He had to try. Taking careful aim for a gap between the trees he cast it down the slope. It crossed the rocky slope in three accelerating shallow arcs and bounced through the trees before flying out over the lip of the ledge where it bounded and rolled erratically down the scree and eventually landed with a splash in the inky waters of the swamp where it bobbed and floated. The brilliant whiteness of its light was stained with streaks of azure, stagnant yellow and bilious green from the waters of the swamp.

'They float! Look, they float!' Harry cried as another landed in a splash of turquoise bubbles.

'But they're too heavy to float, I don't understand. There's so much I don't understand about this place,' Denso muttered to himself, aiming for the same gap between the oakweeds. He hurled more glowing spheres down the slope and watched them drift out, reflecting the vivid colours of the swamps.

'No more,' Orun called making them both lower the glowbrights they had just picked up. 'Look carefully at the ledge below and you will see that the gradaurs have vanished. The last group of them is swarming along the edges of the swamps. Now it will be safe to return to our fire, rekindle it and sleep in its warmth until the new dawn breaks.'

'What will happen to those glowbrights? Will they drown in the swamps?' Harry asked.

Orun laughed as he shook his head. 'No, they will drift back to the edge and roll themselves up to the high ground before the sun sets tomorrow night.'

'Sleep!' Denso exploded, following the other two down the steep slope. 'Are you out of your mind? I'm not going to shut my eyes until I get out of this wilderness. I won't sleep until I am safely back home.'

Some time later Harry broke open the blue gradaur claw that Orun had been roasting over the fire and sucked out the flesh. He looked across the crackling flames into the Way-master's face and asked slowly, 'Tell us about the gradaurs. Why is it safe to light a fire now? I don't understand.'

Orun smiled and sighed. He indicated the edges of the marshes where the glowbrights still bobbed and drifted in the stagnant waters. 'Before the deluge there were no gradaurs and every village basked in the bright white light of the glowbrights during the hours of darkness.' He paused and tossed an empty claw aside. 'They fell in the deluge as a torrent of vicious snapping claws darkening the crystal rains that drowned our land of swamps and marshes. We soon discovered that we could eat the blue ones and at first we thought them a blessing, an endless supply of food, but they became a curse when they bred in their thousands in the shallow pools along the edges of the swamps. They devoured all the fish and other creatures and soon they began to emerge during the hours of darkness to hunt for light. They became an endless army that could decimate a village and leave it a desert of bleached bones before the sun rose.'

'Why do they look for light, surely they don't eat it?' Denso yawned, pushing into his top pocket the pencil stub that he had been using to jot down all that had happened to them in the small notebook he always carried. He was blinking to stay awake despite his earlier assertions.

Orun raised his hands. 'No-one knows. My people quickly learned to avoid the attacks of these creatures by using the light from the glowbrights. They set them to glow in the swamps and found that the gradaurs were lured away away from the villages by them.'

'You know it's funny, but I had a series of dreams about a place like this years ago,' Denso added thoughtfully. 'Lingering, penetrating dreams that stayed with me long after I had woken up but they weren't a patch on the real thing. What we've seen in the last few hours would make the bare bones of a fascinating story, much better than the one I wrote.'

'Perhaps the new one will sell another million copies,' Harry laughed, settling down drowsily beneath his coat.

Orun looked up at the sky and pointed up to the canopy of glittering stars. 'The stars are turning. Soon the sun will rise to cast morning shadows across the Weasand Fields.'

Denso stared at the Waymaster across the flickering flames and felt his spine run cold. It was the same name that he had given to a narrow throat of land that rose above the swamps. It seemed an uncanny coincidence.

'Where are the Weasand Fields?' he asked in a trembling voice.

Orun pointed first across the swamps to where the first hint of grey had touched the sky and then slowly moved his hand to the west to where night still covered the landscape with its shadowy blanket. 'It is the gateway to the City of Time – a narrow point of land that rises from these swamps to meet the Windrows of Thorn.'

CHAPTER FIVE

The Crystal Swamps

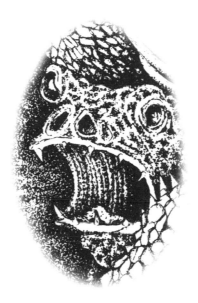

DENSO SHIFTED on the rough ground and started awake. He sat bolt upright, blinking with confusion. The morning sun felt hot upon his face and there were unfamiliar smells and distant sounds that he couldn't place. He could hear the chatter of birdsong and the grunt and roar of larger animals where he should have heard the morning hum of Manhattan traffic beneath Harry's apartment. He rubbed his eyes and stared at the litter of huge blue claws that lay split and broken in a careless circle around the ashes of the fire and the horror of the previous night's attack by the giant crustaceans came flooding back to him.

He cursed himself for falling asleep and tried to scramble to his feet only to collapse helplessly: his left leg must have been bent awkwardly beneath him and had gone numb while he slept. He moved it gently and pins and needles tingled savagely from hip to toe. His neck felt stiff and every joint and muscle in his body seemed to ache with cramp. He had always hated camping out and at that moment he longed for the comfort of his own bed. Soft voices behind him made him turn his head painfully to see Harry and the Waymaster standing close together on the lip of the ledge. Orun was pointing to something far away in the marshes and talking quickly.

Harry glanced back towards the burnt out fire as he heard the scrape of Denso's foot amongst the broken claw shells and he grinned, 'I thought you looked so comfortable there you were likely to sleep all day.'

Denso scowled irritably, climbed slowly to his feet and began to brush at the crumbs of earth and fragments of sticky blue shell that clung to his coat and trousers. His head ached, his mouth felt as if it was lined with dirty underwear and his hands were sticky. His fingernails were ruined with filth and he felt as wretched as if he had spent a fortnight in his favourite bar. Suddenly he began to scratch his arms and legs as he realised that he itched all over.

'Harry, I think I'm being eaten alive!' he cried tearing off his coat and jacket and frantically unbuttoning his shirt. 'Oh my God, will you look at this!' he screamed, clawing away at masses of tiny bright-red insects that were slowly crawling across his chest.

There were thousands of them all over him. It made Harry's skin itch and crawl just to see them and he began involuntarily to scratch at his own chest. 'Orun,' he implored turning to the Waymaster. 'Look, look at Denso. You've got to do something to stop these things from eating him alive.'

Orun smiled, 'They are only attags, gradaur mites. They lived on the shells of the creatures we killed last night. They are perfectly harmless fleas. They will all have died before sunset, the taste of human blood is poisonous to them.'

'I can't stand them crawling all over me until it gets dark! I'll go mad!' Denso shouted, stamping and spinning around and around as he tried to scratch everywhere at once.

Orun frowned, wondering why these people from Earth were so weak. He crossed to the fire and without another word scooped up two handfuls of the fine grey ash. 'Be still,' he hissed through clenched teeth and roughly smeared the ash across Denso's chest, back and arms.

Denso shivered with relief as he watched the tiny crawling insects contract and fall away from his skin leaving hundreds of small raw weals where they had bitten him clearly visible beneath the ash. Harry had stripped off his coat and shirt while Orun gathered up the ash and examined his own pale skin.

'No, not a single one,' he laughed, pulling his shirt back over his head. 'They obviously only have a taste for writers, Denso.'

'Clean skin attracts them,' Orun interrupted brushing the remains of the ash from his hands.

Denso paused from beating his clothes on an outcrop of rock and checked the folds and seams thoroughly for any sign of the live mites. He glanced up to the other two. 'Clean' the Waymaster had said – what a nightmare this place was becoming – he had never felt so filthy in his whole life and he felt a growing sympathy for some of the characters he had written into his books. 'If I ever get out of here alive I'm going to soak in a bath for a week. I'm going to burn these filthy bug-infested clothes and . . .' Denso's mutterings were cut short by the sound of Orun's voice.

'Dress quickly. The morning shadows are shortening toward noon and our journey's not yet begun. Hurry and follow, we have leagues to travel before the lurkbeasts begin to stir.'

'Come on, Denso,' Harry urged, his face softening into a smile as he picked up Denso's crumpled coat. 'I think our Waymaster is getting a little impatient.'

Denso took the coat and began to struggle into it as Orun, with Harry a step behind him, passed through the straggle of oakweeds and began to descend toward the swamps.

'Keep to the treadways and touch nothing,' he heard Orun's voice call up to him.

'Damn you, wait for me!' Denso cried, giving up on the

131

sleeve of his coat and throwing it over his shoulders as he hurried after them. He paused between the oakweeds to take one last quick look up at the thousands of black cave entrances on the hillside. He was damned if he could pick out the Doorcrack from amongst them. They all looked the same. He half-lifted his right hand in a gesture of farewell, knowing that the only sure road back to the real world was somewhere amongst them.

Turning back, he caught his breath as he gazed out across the shimmering landscape. The previous day's evening sunlight had given barely a glimpse of the mass of vibrant, shifting colours that now lay before him, or the maze of vivid aquamarine waterways that wound between what looked like long low tree-covered islands. The trees on the islands had strange, gnarled, complicated shapes, but what intrigued him most and held him spellbound to the spot was the way everything seemed to lie beneath a shroud of transparent crystal that distorted every line and contour and merged distance with perspective so completely that he felt he could almost reach out and touch anything he wanted.

'Denso, for Chrissake are you going to be all day?' Harry's voice, impatient and exasperated, floated up to him and immediately broke the spell.

'I'm right behind you!' he shouted back, hurrying down the track and following the clear footprints that they had left in the coarse, olive-dark grass.

Twenty feet below the ledge the track vanished beneath tall violet plants whose giant rhubarb-shaped leaves blocked out the sunlight. Denso stumbled blindly forwards following the track as best he could, blinking his eyes against the sudden indigo darkness. Thick plant-stems with a mass of spiralling spines crowded him on either side, brilliant luminous orchids trailed down across his path. He almost reached out to touch one when he saw eyes in the undergrowth and heard the rustle of movements beyond the silent shadows. Something was following them. He remembered the gradaurs and quickened his stride.

'Don't touch anything, Denso,' he heard Harry shout in a muffled and urgent voice. 'Orun says those plant spines and the luminous orchids are poisonous.'

Denso was sweating and breathing hard as he rounded a sharp bend in the path and came to an abrupt halt. The claustrophobic track had come to a sudden end and had widened out into a narrow grass bank that sloped down to the edge of the swamps. There was a glimpse of sky over-head. Tall indigo bullrushes and black-flagged reeds crow-ded along the lower edge of the bank, their brittle stems rubbing and clattering together in the hot stagnant breeze that drifted across the swamps. He caught sight of the end-less waste of mud-flats and wide, bubbling pools of slime between the swaying reed heads and shuddered at what might lurk beneath their frothing surfaces.

But it wasn't the swamps that had made him stop so abruptly and stare open-mouthed. It was the sight of the yellow straw boat that was moored fifteen paces ahead of him, tied to the bank at the end of a wide channel cut through the reeds. 'Boat' was a loose description for what looked like a cross between a high-sided, pot-bellied coracle and a Red Indian war canoe that tapered into a high bow and stern interwoven with sculptured animals. This strange structure was topped with a steep, thatched roof set on poles that overhung the sides of the craft by at least a foot. It looked precarious and temporary, and as if it would topple over onto its side at the slightest breath of wind. Denso could see through the narrow openings between the sides and the roof and could distinguish two shadowy figures inside adding to the craft's fragility as it rocked and dipped in time to their movements.

'Harry, Orun, is that you?' Denso called in surprise as he hurried forward.

'Look out! The edge of the bank is swarming with gradaurs!' Harry's face appeared in one of the openings.

The boat rocked violently as he shouted his warning and Denso hesitated, freezing to the spot as he searched the bank ahead.

'Where?' he shouted back, 'I can't see . . .' They were standing still, their front legs raised towards the sun, their gigantic claws wide open. Their shells had changed colour during the hours of daylight and they blended well with their surroundings.

'Thread your way carefully between them. Be quick before they wake and scent you,' Orun urged.

Denso felt beads of sweat begin to trickle down his forehead as he crossed the bank. The twenty feet of lush grass seemed more like a mile. The monstrous creatures were barely a footstep apart and they twitched and snapped their claws, almost snagging his trouser bottoms as he held his breath and cautiously picked his way between their ridged and armoured bodies. Gradually he crossed the bank, aware that his silent shadow passing over them made them blink their bulbous eyelids and turn their open claws towards him.

'Grasp my hands,' Orun whispered as Denso reached the edge of the bank.

Orun had opened a small hatchway in the side of the craft and Denso gripped his strong outstretched hands through it and felt himself lifted up across the narrow gap and into the boat. It rocked and swayed violently and Denso almost lost his balance as the Waymaster put him down on the springy straw deck. He heard Harry laugh behind him and turned, steadying himself on the ornately-woven gunwale in time to see a tide of sluggish marsh-slime stirred up by the movement of the boat rise up and wash over the lip of the bank, swamping dozens of the hideous crustaceans. They snapped their pincers and collided with each other as they scuttled noiselessly higher up the bank.

'That serves the bastards right,' Harry grinned. 'We would have walked right into them if we had been any later reaching this boat. They had just finished crawling out of the swamps to sunbathe when you emerged from the track. Apparently they are blind in sunlight or you would never have never made it across the bank.'

Denso swallowed and looked down at the thousands of swaying snapping claws. It was a living, breathing nightmare. Orun shrugged his shoulders and frowned at the gradaurs as he cast off from the bank, pushing the boat out into the channel with a long pole.

'Oh, my God!' Harry gasped as he watched the Waymaster delve into deep woven baskets strapped to the side of the craft and withdraw a dozen huge crabs just like the ones he had used to silence Kate. Then he hurried along on the edge of the deck pulling on twisted cords that hung down and using the crabs to secure them to the side of the boat. In this method he raised sections of the roof so that they acted as sails. The craft turned gently as the stagnant breeze caught in the rectangular straw sails and began to skim across the bubbling swamps.

'I've never seen anything like this boat. It's not at all how I had imagined boats of straw to be,' Denso murmured, craning his neck to peer up at the rows of strange rigging that the crabs rotated expertly to catch every breath of wind by shortening or lengthening the mass of cords that they held in their front claws while clinging onto the gunwales of the boat.

Orun laughed, 'Pinchquiets have many uses but this craft is very different from those early boats that our people built to weather the deluge. They were only crude shelters woven from wild straw.'

'But why straw? And why build them with such a wide roof?' Harry asked looking up. 'Surely ordinary sails would be easier to handle?'

'Because boats made of straw were the only craft light enough to float on the crystal rains that fell for forty days and forty nights and drowned our world. The sails are easily transformed into steeply-pitched roofs to protect us from a sudden crystal deluge or hide us from the sharp eyes of the soaring wrathwa beasts.'

'You mean that these swamps we are crossing are made of millions and millions of tiny fragments of crystal? You mean they're not filled with stagnating water and mud and . . .'

Harry frowned as the Waymaster nodded and busied himself with steering the boat. Obviously the substance of the swamps was of no importance to Orun: it was commonplace. Harry fell silent and gazed out across the shimmering incandescent surface of the swamps and allowed his thoughts to fall into place. So that was why the landscape had such a transparent look: he was seeing it through layers of crystal. But if it only rained fragments of crystal what did these people drink? Where did they get their water?

'Harry, come here!' The urgency in Denso's voice made Harry jump and he quickly followed him to the bow of the boat. Denso glanced around to check that they were alone before speaking in a whisper.

'Jesus Christ, Harry, this place excites and terrifies me. I thought I had dreamed it up, invented it, but look at it, it's as real and as vital as Manhattan or . . .'

He paused and leaned over the side of the boat, cupped his hands, scooped up some of the crystal liquid and held it out towards Harry. It shimmered and flashed in the sunlight and quickly drained through the cracks between his fingers, melting away and leaving his hand completely dry except for a few tiny flakes of crystal that clung to his palms.

'I know I based my ideas for *Swamps of Glass* on dreams but this is nothing like the dreams. This place is dangerously different and I think we'll have to tread carefully if we want to get out of here alive.'

Harry nodded in agreement, glancing darkly at the rows of pinchquiets clinging to the sail cords, 'I think we'd be much safer if we could wake up in my office in five minutes' time with an empty bottle of bourbon on the table between us and a big enough hangover to warrant inventing a place like this.'

'No, I don't want it to end, not yet. I want to see this City of Time,' Denso hissed. 'But I just have this uneasy feeling that without Orun's help we wouldn't last five minutes, not on our own.'

'Yes, we had better be careful and stick really close to him,' Harry agreed before Denso moved back to the centre of the craft where Orun was trimming the two main sails.

He talked easily with the Waymaster, asking him about the low islands and the groves of gnarled chameleon-like trees, jotting down everything he said about the shimmering landscape they were skimming past. Harry stayed at the bow looking out at the brilliantly coloured swamps. He could hear the other two talking and laughing and he felt alone, isolated and vulnerable. The sky ahead suddenly began to darken. Low thunderclouds boiled on the horizon, the bullrush stems clattered and bent and the straw boat rocked and spun as a gust of cold wind caught in its sails and sent it scudding sideways across the swamps, ploughing up an iridescent wave as it raced dangerously close to the groves of twisted trees.

Orun gave a sharp warning shout. 'Deluge!'

The pinchquiets let the cords slip through their claws to release the sails which fell back with a snap into their places, sealing the thatched roof against the downpour. The boat spun once more and came to a shuddering stop. There was a moment's silence when the drone of insects and the sounds of the swamps disappeared completely.

'What is it? What's happening?' Harry called, leaving the bow and hurrying to where Denso stood.

'Deluge!' Orun shouted again, throwing himself flat on the straw deck.

The landscape was rapidly vanishing, blotted out by an advancing wall of shimmering colour. A hissing sound grew into a thunderous roar and the boat shook violently from end to end, buckling and twisting sideways as the crystal deluge swept over it. Denso and Harry cried out as the deck leapt and danced beneath their feet and both of them threw themselves down beside the Waymaster, clutching at the shifting floor as purple granules covered everything. The roar of the falling crystal grew louder and louder. The air inside the boat was thick with shifting particles of crystal. They covered the deck and piled up against the sides in ice-cold incandescent drifts.

'Cover your mouths!' Orun shouted against the storm bringing his sleeve up over his mouth to show them.

The deluge subsided as quickly as it began, the sky brightened and the dark thunderclouds passed on to blacken the horizon behind them. Orun was the first to his feet and he moved quickly along the length of the boat opening small hatchways set flush with the deck into its sides. Gradually the piles of crystals that had drifted in beneath the roof began to subside as they poured out through the openings and into the swamps.

'I would never have believed it could possibly happen if I hadn't seen it!' Denso exclaimed as he climbed to his feet, blinking at the sore, gritty particles that had gathered in the corners of his eyes and rubbing them from his face and hands.

'Look, everything's changed,' Harry called out as he pointed out across the swamps.

The reeds and bullrushes, the low islands, everything had vanished beneath a blanket of shimmering crystal. All that could be seen were the tops of the trees. It was almost like snow.

'The boat will travel quickly after the deluge. We will reach the Windrows of Thorn before nightfall,' Orun interrupted as he pulled up all the sails. 'Help me to set them to the west,' he ordered.

The boat of straw gathered speed as it skimmed across the fresh layer of crystals leaving a wake of dancing iridescent waves behind it. Harry and Denso hesitated to press the cords into the pinchquiets' outstretched claws but Orun shouted that they would never be able to hold the sails steady on their own against the strengthening breeze.

'How do your people survive these deluges?' Harry called across the deck to the Waymaster as he mastered his fear of the crabs.

Orun nodded his head towards distant hills that rose above some higher ground that showed as a dark smudge along the horizon-line. 'My people abandoned their marsh-dwellings after the first great storm and built new villages in the hills. Now they only venture into the swamps to hunt the blue-shelled gradaurs.'

'But what about those huts that I saw last night on some of the larger islands?' Harry interrupted.

'Drowned beneath layers of crystal and unsafe for our people because no-one knows when the next great tempest will occur,' Orun answered flatly before adding, 'This recent shower will have drained away before morning and the swamps will look as they did when the sun rose.'

'Shower? You call that a shower?' Denso, cried in astonishment, but Orun only laughed and indicated that they should lower the sails. He glanced across the swamps at the dark windswept hills of Bendran and the laughter dissolved into a troubled frown. 'Mauders!' he muttered under his breath, turning the craft and slowing it as he prepared to beach it.

Aloud, he called out, 'Look, look there, ahead of us, there lie the Weasand Fields.'

Jothnar, the Asiri of Krak, Lord Mauder of Bendran, cursed the huge armoured dragma he was sitting astride and raked his spurs brutally across its scaly flanks.

'Be still!' he hissed as he steadied the watching glass to his right eye and followed the passage of the tiny straw boat which skimmed across the swamps.

Jothnar watched its progress until it eventually broke free of the last grove of chameleon-trees and reached the bleak, stony edge of the Weasand Fields. He lowered the glass and stroked his beard thoughtfully. His piercing black eyes narrowed and his sour, cruel mouth wrinkled into the shadow of a smile. He leaned down to his right and thrust the glass into his brother, Kys', waiting hand.

'So the great gathering has begun,' he murmured, watching the three figures disembark from the boat.

His brother rode a slightly smaller beast as befitted his lesser standing and he had to stand on tiptoe in his stirrups to take the glass. 'There are two strangers with the Waymaster. They are dressed in the strangest clothes I have ever seen. Shall we take them, kill them and strip them of their robes?' he asked, his voice rising with the anticipation of the chase, his mind already tasting the blood and the thrill of the capture.

Jothnar took back the glass and watched the three figures begin their long climb up the narrow archway of rock that would lead them to the Windrows of Thorn, a barren landscape of wind-blown rock and earth, ridged and furrowed with desolation, the perfect empty place to stage a taking, to murder and despoil the travellers.

'No, brother,' he answered softly, lowering the glass. His smile still hovered on his lips, 'There is more to these strangers than a handspan of pretty cloth and a goblet of blood.'

Kys scowled and gripped the pommel of his saddle so tightly that his knuckles whitened and he silently swallowed the reprimand that his brother had publicly given him in front of their company of Mauders. He added it to the thousand of other snubs that Jothnar had so easily and cruelly bestowed upon him while he had grown in his shadow, and secretly used it to feed the hatred, to strengthen his soul for the moment when he would strangle him with his bare hands and seize all Bendran for his own. His flesh would taste all the sweeter for the waiting but he wouldn't touch the bones, those he would give as an offering to the wrathwa to pick clean.

'You forget, brother, we hunt the rumour of Paradise and the one wrathwa in all Bendran that I can tame, not a handful of fabric.'

Jothnar's voice was soft, almost a whisper, and it cut through Kys' silent thoughts. He jumped, his spurs catching the dragma's flanks, making it start forward. Snatching at the reins to still the beast, he looked up into his brother's eyes. They were hooded, mere slits of liquid shadow that seemed to mock him, and his mouth hardened back into its familiar sour scowl.

'You will never find a wrathwa to tame,' Kys scoffed, 'unless it is so old that all its teeth have fallen out and its fire turned to fossilised dribble. Anyway, the people of the citadel are whispering that your wits are addled with all the talk of Paradise and I don't see what those travellers have to do with your hunt.'

Jothnar signalled to the company of Mauders to ride ahead and lead them back towards the gates of the citadel.

'Ride with me, brother,' he commanded, cracking his long silver tailed whip across the flanks of his dragma, making it rear up before it settled into a trot.

'I'll swear those strange travellers must know something of the way of Paradise,' Jothnar answered thoughtfully after the company of Mauders had ridden a length or two ahead of them and they were almost concealed by the haze of red dust that the dragmas' claws were churning up.

Kys twisted in his saddle and stared across at his brother, the look of surprise at his answer dissolving into a sneer of ridicule.

'If all you wanted was the secrets of their road then you were a fool to allow them to escape,' he snapped, reining in his dragma with a brutal tug and turning him on the spur.

'Come, there is still time to take them before they reach the end of the Weasand Fields. Perhaps then we can end this senseless wandering.'

'No!' Jothnar shouted angrily as he pirouetted his beast and cut in front of him sharply. 'We would be fools to act too quickly. I have heard the whispers of Paradise and there is more to this riddle than meets the eye. The great gathering of the wise could tell us so much more than those two strangers possibly can. No, I will not have you torture them.'

'Riddles and whispers! You think of nothing else.' Kys sneered, keeping a watchful eye on the long thin whip in his brother's hand as he goaded him. 'I don't know where you get them all from. Flying through the sky upon a wrathwa's back and all this talk of a great gathering of elders in a City of Time, I don't believe there's a thread of truth woven into it.'

Kys' voice rose in peals of laughter as he spurred his dragma beyond the reach of his brother's whip. 'And as for this Paradise filled with wonders beyond imagination that you hunger so much to see, that you squander our time searching for . . .' Kys paused, his breath coming in short gasps. He had never dared to say so much in all his growing: he felt heady and reckless and he glanced quickly around to make sure there were no witnesses, then he stabbed a dirty finger ringed with precious stones and bands of white gold towards the Crystal Swamps and then slowly swept it out across the whole horizon-line in a trembling arc.

'Paradise is here, brother. We, no, you as the elder, rule it all, from the Wrathendall Spires to the last, bubbling pool of slime in the Crystal Swamps. There is nowhere else, nothing but what you see.'

For a moment anger boiled in Jothnar's eyes. He began to raise the whip to slash it across his brother's face, started to turn his spurs into his dragma's flanks to drive him forward and make the cutting stroke, but the moment passed. He laughed and slowly lowered the whip to rest across his knees. Softly he said, 'Would you take the high office of Asiri, brother, if I were to offer it to you? Would you take it here, now, before the gates of the Citadel of Krak?'

Kys almost dropped his own bone handled whip in surprise as Jothnar's words echoed in his head. 'What?' he gasped, riding closer to his brother, forgetting to fear him in his surprise. He listened intently to every word as Jothnar slowly repeated his offer until the words 'Citadel of Krak' faded into silence. He knew there must be a catch, a hidden trick, somewhere in those clever words. An Asiri held his power right up to the moment of his death. His word was law, his punishment absolute, until his very last breath was expired.

Jothnar watched Kys wrestle with his offer for a long moment before he spoke again. 'Yes, brother, you guessed correctly, there is a high price to the title of Asiri. Nothing is ever free. I would offer you my rule of Bendran and all you can see for the whole of Paradise.'

Kys stared open-mouthed at his brother. He wanted to laugh, to call him a madman, because everyone knew that these rumours of Paradise were nothing more than the mumblings of old women. They were the rag ends of legends, fair stories passed down by rote. It was only the Journeymen and the Waymasters that had kept them alive as they entertained around the camp fires. Kys swallowed before he spoke.

'You would give me everything? You would proclaim me Asiri before the Mauders? I don't believe you would barter everything just for Paradise, there must be a trick.'

Jothnar smiled and nodded, 'Yes, brother, every Mauder will help me find this road to Paradise and fight at my side to win it.'

'Is that all?' Kys replied, struggling to suppress his laughter.

Jothnar spat thickly onto the palm of his right hand and held it out towards Kys. 'The barter shall be struck now, here upon the causeway, and you will be proclaimed Asiri between the great gates of the citadel before this failing sun sets.'

Kys laughed, overwhelmed by this turn of fortune. His plots against his brother were forgotten as he spat into the palm of his right hand and spurred his beast forwards to strike the palm of his hand forcefully against his brother's and seal the barter. For a moment his eyes clouded with doubt as he searched his brother's face, fearing that he might change his mind or break his word. Then he snatched at the reins with his left hand and wheeled his beast after the Mauders, cupping his hand to protect the drying spittle until he had shown it to them.

He called back over his shoulder before he had taken five paces, 'I will ride ahead and make all the preparations for a naming feast. I will await you in the shadow of the gateway.'

Jothnar smiled to himself. He was well satisfied with the barter he had struck and was content as he saw Kys vanish in a cloud of red swirling dust. He had known everything of the plots and intrigues Kys had begun to set against him, plots that would weaken the Asiri and divide his army in the coming battle to seize Paradise.

'You are a fool, brother, to have snatched so readily at the crumbs that I offer,' he murmured softly as he glanced at the bleak featureless landscape in the setting sun.

'To want so little when there is so much hidden out there beyond the edges of our sight.'

His mouth hardened into its familiar sour line and he gave a mean laugh as he drove his spurs hard into his dragma's flanks. He had never intended to share it anyway. He had only stumbled on the proof by accident. He knew now that there was a thread of truth running through all the rumours and fireside tales that told of wondrous things and peoples who existed beyond the world he knew. While spying on his brother's murderous plots he had gone astray and had stumbled into a dark and secret passageway that ran beside a disused maze of forgotten chambers on the north side of the citadel. Whispered voices and flickering pools of candle-light in the darkness had made him stop and find a spy hole in the crumbling walls. He had crouched down to watch and listen.

At first the mumblings and fervent whisperings of the group of withered elders had meant little to him. They were gathered in a close knot peering down at something that lay on an oakwood table. Then he saw the tallest of the group, a white haired man in a cloak of grey rags, pick up a leatherbound object and split it open. He began to chant and pace slowly around the table amongst the others. Jothnar had caught a glimpse of the signs and symbols that the elder was tracing with his finger. There had been words mixed in amongst the old men's mumblings, words and snatches of their chanting that had conjured up images in the candlelight. He had seen transparent pictures of things and places that must exist far beyond his wildest imaginings.

Jothnar had crouched there in the darkness, his imagination ablaze, his brother's murderous plots forgotten. Suddenly his breath had quickened as he remembered fragments of a Waymaster's fireside story. He remembered the tale of a city where time itself was made, where all the wonders of the world were written down in things they called 'books' and nothing was ever forgotten. He had leaned forward, pressing his eye to the spy-hole and stared at the leatherbound object that the tallest of the withereds was holding. He realised that it must be a *book*, a thing of mystery that invoked magical images and he knew then that he must have it. He had risen to his feet intending to stride into the chamber and seize it. As Asiri and Lord Mauder his power was terrible, his judgements absolute, but he had hesitated, fearing the book, sensing that it must be steeped in a magic far greater and far older than his own power if it had the ability to evoke such images.

He had shrunk back and at that moment, as he waited for the chanting to die away and the disused chamber to empty of the gathering of the withereds, he had begun to scheme. During the following days he had had his most trusted

Mauders hunt down the old men, take them to a high chamber and imprison them. Each time he had expected the magic to strike the Mauders down but it had not and he had grown bolder until he had, himself, seized the last tall, stooping figure, the one who had led the chanting.

Now the ancient, leather book was in his hands and all the images that lay hidden between its heavy covers were his alone to explore. Using the blade of his longest dagger he had gingerly prised it open and stood back waiting and watching, but nothing happened. In the brooding, lengthening silence he had moved closer to the book and stared down at its yellowing fragile pages which were marked with neat, black furrows of unintelligible signs and symbols. He had turned the pages one by one, pausing to examine the tiny spider-fine drawings that filled the margins. He could see fearsome creatures and men in strange armour who rode upon the beasts of the air, crafts with oars and wind-driven boats with sails of cloth. He had turned impatiently to one of the Mauders and sent him to bring the group of elders before him and when they had assembled he had demanded that they show him the secrets of the magic that lay hidden within the book.

The knot of withered figures had shuffled their feet, wrung their hands and looked anxiously at one another before the tallest of the old men had dared to speak for them. He told Jothnar in halting words that he, the Asiri, the Lord of everything that could be seen and touched, could not read. He could not know the meanings of what lay upon the pages of the book. Only the guardians of truth, the diviners of wisdom, could be taught. All others, even the Asiri, were forbidden such knowledge.

Jothnar shivered as he remembered the rage that had possessed him as the old man fell silent. He recollected how he had torn open his robes and clutched at the dry, wrinkled flesh and bones that covered the old man's heart and had threatened to tear it out. He had brutally tortured and terrorised every one of the elders in an attempt to force them to divulge the forbidden knowledge hidden in the book, to teach him to read, to understand the letters on each page. But nothing would move them. Nothing, until, in a fit of bitter anger, he had struck a spark and held it so close to the fragile pages that the yellowing parchment began to blacken and curl in the heat. With one cry of despair they had revoked their vows of guardianship and had promised to reveal the secrets of the book and teach him to read. In return he had promised not to destroy it. Laughing at the withereds he had crushed the spark beneath the book before he had held it open toward them. That was the start of the moment when his whole life had changed.

The thunder of dragmas' claws made him turn in the saddle towards the Wrathendall Spires. A lone figure was galloping towards him, spurring and whipping his dragma and leaving a gale of dust in his wake.

'Lord Asiri!' the rider cried, 'we have snared the most fearsome wrathwa. There are two hundred Mauders fighting to restrain him in iron chains. You must come quickly, quell his wildness, put a name to him and make him your beast of the air.'

Jothnar laughed with delight. 'Now I shall have everything I desire.' He paused: there were figures riding out of the great gates toward him, raising a storm of choking, red dust.

Jothnar frowned, reined his beast to a halt and commanded the messenger to wait and bind his tongue. He raised his whip for silence as the company of his most trusted Mauders galloped to meet him, their voices rising in a clamour as they milled in confusion all around him.

'Kys has proclaimed himself Asiri,' a dozen voices

shouted in dismay despite Jothnar's signal for silence.

'He is saying that you have bartered the rule of Bendran, Lord Asiri. He says that you have bequeathed to him everything as far as the horizon stretches in exchange for Paradise!' cried other frightened voices.

Jothnar laughed at their fears and cracked his whip against his boot in demand for quiet. 'Yes, yes, his words are true. I have given him everything.'

A sudden, startled silence swept through the ranks, their eyes widening with the shock of his words and the colour draining from their skin at the thought of Kys as their master, their Asiri.

'But we are your Mauders, your most trusted followers. Kys will murder us all,' cried a single voice amongst the crowd.

Anger kindled in Jothnar's eyes. 'Be silent, fool,' he hissed, stabbing the handle of his whip brutally at the company. 'It is to prevent my brother's murderous thrust for power that I have bartered this miserable wilderness.'

He paused for a moment and beckoned the riders to draw closer, 'He grows more impatient daily: the canker of hatred is swelling in his heart, he longs to take my place and to murder you all while darkness holds the hour, but he shall neither raise a hand nor lay one finger on your throats because his fear of the beast that I shall tame and ride upon will make him quail. You will vanish now, before the proclamation is made. My last command as Asiri is to dispatch you into the shadows of the Wrathendall Spires to help me to tame the wrathwa.'

The company of Mauders shifted uncomfortably in their saddles, fear of the beast showed in their eyes, but they raised their whips and turned their spurs against their dragmas' flanks for none dare to turn against the Asiri. Their huge beasts lumbered forwards, stirring up thick clouds of choking dust as they streamed out into the rolling grasslands.

'Wait!' he shouted, making them halt. 'Half of the company shall scour the lands of Bendran for sign of the withereds or their Waymasters: they cannot vanish completely without trace.'

He bitterly regretted not keeping a closer guard on the group of withereds: he had long sensed that they were keeping something from him, some vital link between what lay in the visions the book unfolded and his ability to, one day, reach out and touch them. At the turn of the moon he had seen, by chance, a Waymaster in their midst. He had been whispering urgently to them and he had caught the tail-end of their conversation as he came amongst them – something about a Grand Council of elders in the City of Time – no more than that. Less words than would cause a ripple on a still, moonlit pond yet it had been enough to cause a storm of waves clashing in his mind.

The Waymaster had vanished taking with him the withereds and their ancient book before Jothnar had the time to draw breath or to lay his hands upon him but those whispered words that he had left behind, 'Grand Council in the City of Time', had conjured up such images. He was sure it must, somehow, be bound up with this Paradise that he sought.

'Search the Windrows of Thorn! Find the tracks of that Waymaster and the two strangely-dressed figures who disembarked from the boat of straw. They will lead us to the great gathering, I am sure of it! Find the Waymaster's footprints and follow them, mark out the way that they have taken.'

'But there is nothing in that direction save barren and wind-blown ridges of rock and earth. No-one in their right mind would tread that path. I should know, I have travelled further than anyone in my search for wrathwa teeth,' called out a weatherbeaten Mauder shaking his head.

Jothnar laughed, 'Then you have never ventured far enough. Go, follow this Waymaster, but do not allow yourselves to be seen. I will swear that he is leading those strangers to this Grand Council, whatever that should mean.'

CHAPTER SIX

The Verge of Drasatt

DAWN GREYED THE SKY and with it arose a cold wind to blow mournfully across the barren landscape, rustling the brittle branches of the dwarf oakweeds and tangleheads that grew in serrated and bent ranks on the sheltered sides of each steep ridge. Dead leaves rustled and spun in the tracery of black branches which were skeletally etched against the chilling silver sky. Harry shivered, his teeth chattering from the cold. He sat up, pulled his coat-collar higher about his ears, and edged in closer to the dying embers of the fire. He stirred the glowing coals with the toe of his shoe. He had lost count of the days they had spent on this seemingly endless journey across the wasteland, living on trapped rodents that the Waymaster caught and then cooked on their fire. Denso snored fitfully on the ground beside him, his hands twitching frantically in his overcoat pockets. He mumbled incoherently and let out a sudden cry, his body stiffening, then he fell silent as the dream passed.

'There's no need to conjure up nightmares in your sleep,' Harry muttered, feeding dead branches into the embers. 'We're caught up in a real enough one here . . .'

He paused, frowning as he realised that the Waymaster wasn't in his sleeping place on the opposite side of the fire. He half-rose, anxiety mounting at the thought that they might have been abandoned in the wilderness, and quickly scanned the top of the wind-blown ridge of earth. A breath of relief escaped his lips as he spotted Orun standing statue-still between the oakweeds only about twenty paces away. He was staring out towards the dark side of the dawn scanning the trail they had already travelled.

Orun's tattooed face was drawn into a troubled frown. He turned his head slowly and then froze, his lips moving silently. Harry climbed to his feet and scaled the side of the ridge to see that he seemed to be watching something or someone, a shadow in the distance, that was moving toward them.

'What is it?' Harry began, only to have Orun hiss him into silence.

'It is a Journeyman,' he answered softly, drawing Harry back down the ridge until only their heads were visible above the level of the bare earth.

'A Journeyman? How can you tell from this distance? He's only a dot on the horizon.'

Orun smiled but there was a shadow of fear in his eyes as he glanced back towards the darkness.

'It is a part of our craft to have far sight.'

'But to see that far . . .'

Orun blinked and looked at the distant figure once more before adding, 'He rides upon a dragma, a beast of Bendran, and . . .' he paused, his eyes narrowing, 'there is a second person, a . . . a . . . a woman, riding upon the beast, sitting behind him.'

'What's happening? What's going on?' Denso's voice sounded loud and demanding, echoing along the bottom of the gully. He was standing, dirty and dishevelled, awoken by their whispering as they stood on the ridge directly above him.

'Quiet,' Orun hissed. 'Your voice will travel for leagues through these gullies in the Windrows if you shout so loudly.'

'Orun says there is a Journeyman travelling towards us,' Harry whispered, offering a hand to Denso as he scrambled up the steep bank and looked out across the desolate landscape.

It took him long moments to find and focus his eyes on the tiny moving dot. A crackle of burning wood and the smell of smoke made all three of them turn their heads and stare down at the bright flames as a plume of yellow smoke rose from the ashes of their fire in the bottom of the gully.

Orun cursed. 'Which fool would tell the Asiri where we are?'

'It was so cold when I woke up I ... I'll put it out immediately,' Harry cried scrambling back down the bank but Orun reached it before him and scattered the fire, trampling it roughly underfoot.

'It's too late. I think your Journeyman has seen the smoke, he's changed direction slightly. He's coming towards us,' Denso called down across his shoulder.

'It's not the Journeyman that I fear,' Orun muttered angrily, kicking loose earth over the smouldering branches.

'Do you think there's somebody else following us, then?' Denso frowned, searching the dark, desolate ruin of the horizon; but he could see nothing move save the withered branches of the oakweeds in the wind.

Orun laughed harshly and nodded as he scrambled back up the steep bank. 'The Asiri riders have been shadowing us since we reached the Weasand Fields. I caught a glimpse of the setting sun reflecting from a watching glass while we were on the plains of Bendran close to the Citadel of Krak. I'm sure it was a great company of Mauders who surround the Asiri. There were so many they shadowed the hillside as they stirred up a thick red cloud of dust but they were too far away for me to see more clearly or to count their numbers.'

'I don't know how you do it, Orun. All I could see was a hazy blur where the horizon should have been. But ...' Denso paused and then asked, 'Who the hell are these Mauders and the Asiri who are following us? And where do they come from?'

'The Mauders are the Asiri's sword-arm, his ruthless army of riders. The Asiri is the Lord of Bendran, but in truth he rules everything.' Orun hesitated before adding, 'Well, almost everything. He rules all you can see and his power is absolute because none dare contest it.'

'Well, as far as I'm concerned he can keep the lot,' Harry muttered in disgust, turning his back against the biting wind.

'No, there's more I think. Our Waymaster has held something back in the telling.'

Denso spoke quickly, holding Orun's gaze. He had noticed the Waymaster's hesitation and his eyes demanded the truth. Orun squirmed visibly and wrung his hands. The pledge of silence that he had given to Tholocus, the secrets that he carried in his head weighed heavily. At last he blurted it out in one breathless rush of words. 'The Asiri knows nothing of the City of Time. It is hidden in a veil of secrets and shrouded from his sight but there is word amongst the Waymasters that he has guessed that such a place exists and we fear that he has heard rumours of the great gathering and set his Mauders to snare a Waymaster or a Journeyman to discover the way. Tholocus warned me to guard every footstep that I took and bring you in secrecy to his door.'

'So that is why we are being followed,' Harry said with concern.

Orun nodded gravely. 'It is said that the Asiri is consumed with a madness to have the things that he cannot see or touch. That he builds castles in the air out of rumours and old wives' tales and that he talks of nothing but a

Paradise – a place where men ride upon flying beasts or have feather-wings so that they can fly higher than the wrathwa; although he says that if they fly too near the sun the wax that binds their feathers melts and they fall helpless back to earth.'

'That sounds familiar: I wonder where he got that story from?' Harry murmured thoughtfully.

'We must leave no trace, not a single footstep, behind us now,' the Waymaster warned, breaking into Harry's train of thought. 'I fear the Mauders have been following us for days. They are probably spread out in an unbroken line in the Windrows many leagues behind us. They will be searching for a sign, a footstep, to mark our passing, and they cannot have failed to see the smoke.'

'Why don't we get going now? What are we waiting for?' Denso urged.

'We must wait,' Orun shook his head and pointed toward the rapidly approaching rider.

'It is the rule of the road that binds all travellers to share the knowledge of any dangers that may lie in wait or tread hard upon their heels. We cannot move on until I have warned that Journeyman of the Mauders' presence in the Windrows.'

'But he may be one of them, an outrider,' Denso warned.

Orun smiled, 'It is true that he is a Journeyman of Bendran but he doesn't serve the Asiri. The Guild of Travellers belong to no master save Tholocus and the gathering of Diviners.'

Harry, who had been idly watching the approaching rider while Orun spoke, suddenly clutched at Denso's arm, panic hissing through his teeth. 'Look, just look at that monster coming towards us. It's not a horse your Journeyman's riding, it's . . . it's . . . it's a bloody dragon!' Harry paused a moment, his grip tightening on Denso's arm. 'I don't believe what I'm seeing: it's not possible. Nothing like that really exists. Pinch me, Denso, for Christ's sake make me wake up from this nightmare.'

Denso stared at the huge oncoming creature, transfixed. It could have stepped straight out of a book of myths and legends, it was so real in every detail. Its armoured scales shimmered with a porraceous glow in the silver light of dawn, clouds of vaporous steam boiled out of its nostrils and hung in streaming misty trails from the corners of its cavernous mouth. There were rows of prickly spines ridged along its powerful neck and down its long sinuous tail. It even had wings of shiny scales stretched tightly between skeletal ribs and set high upon its shoulders that flapped and clacked each time it moved with its strange reptilian gait. It stood almost upright on its hind legs, its back arched beneath the weight of its saddle and two riders. The high-backed saddle was held just behind the shoulders by a thick leather girth entwined with silver bindings. Sparks danced in the shadows between its long curved claws, struck up from the bare rocks and stones as it strode across the barren earth.

When it drew closer Denso heard the rattle of its breath and smelt the sulphurous steam that issued from its mouth. It looked and smelled real enough to him, so dangerously real that he took a hasty, involuntary step backwards, fearing that it would smother him at any moment with scalding tongues of fire.

Orun laughed softly at Denso's and Harry's apprehension and took a step forward, raising his hand in a greeting and calling out his name as the huge creature came to a halt in a roar of billowing steam on the ridge of rock and earth directly in front of him.

'This creature you call a dragon is, in truth, a dragma, a harmless beast of burden that the Journeymen of Bendran ride to ease the road. It will not harm you. Come, greet the travellers that it carries.'

' "Dragma", is that what you call it?' Denso muttered, scribbling down the name in his pad but hesitating to move.

'Come on, show a little backbone,' Harry hissed in his ear as he moved forward. 'If the Waymaster says it's OK then it must be.'

Denso pushed the pad back into his pocket and took a reluctant step only to stop abruptly as the creature turned its head toward him to stare with its cold, unblinking reptilian eyes and breathe thin streams of hot vapour at him. He fought down the impulse to scramble back down into the gully and run for his life, instead forcing a thin smile and looking up at the two figures perched in the high saddle on the creature's back. The Journeyman was dressed in different clothes to Orun, his jerkin was fashioned from darker skins and the weave of his breeches was much finer but his hair was the same colour, and his face, hands and arms were so heavily tattooed in the same way that he and Orun could have been brothers. But the woman sitting behind him was dressed completely differently. She was in ordinary clothes, slacks and a cardigan and a top coat, she could have stepped out of any house or shop in America, or England, and she was looking down at the three of them with uncertainty and apprehension in her eyes. Harry felt the stubble on his chin and looked at Denso's dishevelled appearance and wondered what she might think of them.

The Journeyman leaned forward, tapped the beast on its shoulder and called out a word of command. It lowered its head and bent its forelegs to allow them to dismount. The woman reluctantly followed the Journeyman to the ground but she stayed close to the dragma's side. Orun called to the Journeyman and gripped his arm, drawing him aside, his words blurring with haste as he stabbed a frantic finger back across the dark horizon line that morning had yet to touch. He was speaking too fast for Harry to understand what he said but he repeatedly caught the word 'Asiri' and 'Mauders' and saw fear in their eyes.

'I'm Denso, Denso Alburton.'

The sound of Denso's easy drawl made Harry turn to see him introducing himself to the woman. She had advanced a few steps towards him and stopped as she tried to prevent a bundle of papers she was holding from being blown away by the bitter wind. She looked up at the sound of his voice, her face breaking into a warm smile of relief. Harry saw she was young, perhaps in her early twenties, she was slim with hazel eyes and a classical English face framed by long strands of copper dark hair. He could have imagined her in those county magazines, the ones he kept in his outer office: she would be wearing a tweed jacket and there would be dogs, horses and a crumbling old country house in the background.

'You're Americans, aren't you?' she asked in a soft English accent that perfectly matched her looks.

'Yes,' Harry nodded. 'I'm Harry Murmers, I'm from New York and Denso is from California,' he explained offering her his hand as his face broke into a smile.

'I'm Mya, Mya Capthorne,' she replied, finally trapping her bundle of papers and fixing them more securely under her arm. She took his hand in hers, 'And I'm very glad to meet with some normal people in this wilderness. I thought I was the only person . . .' She paused and looked steadily at Denso. 'Are you Denso Alburton the author, the fantasy writer?'

Denso grinned and nodded, 'Yes.' He spread his hands out, helplessly indicating the huge dragma and the surrounding landscape of barren windblown furrows. 'But none of this is my doing. I didn't invent this place – my imagination would never stretch that far.'

'The Waymaster we are with, Orun, burst into my office in New York and more or less kidnapped us both,' Harry interrupted.

Mya frowned, glanced across at the two travellers and moved closer to Harry and Denso, lowering her voice before she spoke. 'One moment I was in England on my way to deliver a lecture on the environment and the next that Journeyman whose beast we were riding appeared out of the darkness and kidnapped me with some wild story about the City of Time. I tell you at times I have been terrified by some of the things I've seen on this journey.'

'Orun told us pretty much the same story,' Denso murmured as the two travellers turned and began to hurry towards them.

'I think we'll have to stick with these guides for the time being. There's no way we'd ever find our way back on our own,' Harry whispered before adding, 'You don't know the way back I suppose?'

'Oh, I'm not in any rush to get back to my research, I'm sort of looking forward to seeing this City of Time. This whole place fascinates me, doesn't it interest you? You know, it's like it's another existence in parallel with our own.'

'Yes, I'm getting enough material for a dozen books,' Denso answered with a laugh.

Orun and Kote burst in amongst them. 'Quickly, we must hurry. Look!'

'What on earth is that?' asked Mya, an edge of fear creeping into her voice as she turned and saw an ominous pall of dust boiling towards them over the dawn horizon-line. Faintly she heard the rumble of thunder and the earth trembled beneath her feet.

'Mauders!' Orun hissed, grabbing her wrist and roughly

pulling her down. He herded Denso and Harry after her into the gully so that their silhouettes were not exposed above the skyline.

'They must have seen the smoke,' Harry cursed.

Kote shouted quick commands to Lugg the dragma and then ran to join the others, following their path and brushing out all trace of their footprints as Orun led them along the floor of the gully.

'Why didn't we try to escape on Lugg?' Mya asked between gasping breaths, looking back over her shoulder to see the dragma trampling out any signs of where they had stood. He was thrashing the bare earth with his long tail before he fled away to their right, appearing and disappearing briefly before vanishing into the distance across the windblown furrows.

'The Mauders ride the fastest beasts in Bendran. If Lugg was carrying us they would overrun him before the sun had touched noon; but without our weight he will draw them away to the east and set the Asiri warriors on a false trail. Hopefully he will lose them in the drifting sand-mists of Chehung,' Kote told them in hushed whispers as they scrambled through a rocky break in the gully walls.

The sound of the Mauders' galloping beasts was getting louder and louder, the earth shook and loose stones and broken flakes of rock and soil began to tumble and cascade down the steep sides of the gullies all around them. Orun quickened his pace. They were running now at breakneck speed. He started to look desperately to left and right. With a cry of relief he stopped and grabbed at Denso's arm as soon as he reached him and pushed him towards a narrow overhang of rock.

'Quick, hide, lie flat against the rock. Do not move!' He snatched at Harry, thrust him toward another shallow overhang, catapulted Mya towards a third and sharply ordered them to lie still until the Mauders had ridden past.

With the speed of conjurors the two Journeymen took out their sticks of draweasy and drew an opaque veil of rocks, stones and dark earth across where they lay before pressing themselves into two shallow depressions. In the blink of an eye they had vanished completely beneath a tracery of scribbled stones and rocks.

'Lie still, perfectly still, don't make a breath of sound,' Kote whispered.

Mya shifted uncomfortably on the hard rocky ground. Dust and loose pebbles were showering down on to her in a steady trickle from the shallow overhang of rock above her head. She blinked and glanced up, lifting her hand to brush the debris away and froze. She was staring straight into the open claws of a black scorpion, armoured skin shining like polished glass: she could see each joint and knuckle on its legs and a cluster of minute baby scorpions clinging to its back. Its sting was arched forward over its back, hovering an inch from her face: the colour of death was reflected in its hard, smooth surface. She almost blinked, her eyelids barely moving, and the needle sharp sting tensed, drawing back slightly, as if to strike.

Terror knotted the muscles in her throat, paralysing and silencing the screaming shout that the shock of seeing the creature had triggered. The scream had already burst from her lungs and begun rushing up her throat but her mouth remained clamped shut and the cry echoed and filled her head. She felt an involuntary shudder of panic clutch at her bowels. The skin on her neck and face began to prickle and crawl as if a thousand hot needles were touching it. She wanted to hurl herself sideways in one wild movement away from the overhang and the stab of death that was now almost touching her cheek but she knew that her only hope was to fight down the primaeval terror that gripped her, to

165

stay still and calm. She tried to focus, to concentrate her whole being on the scorpion. She was a scientist: she had studied a lot of zoology, she had to try to see it scientifically. It was twice the size of any scorpion she had ever seen before, it was a female (she knew that by the cluster of young clinging to its back) but she could not remember if that made it all the more dangerous or not.

Suddenly the thunder of the Mauders' dragmas was almost on top of her. The overhang shook violently and out of the corner of her eye she saw their huge beasts descend and swarm into the gully. Scaly armoured legs milled about only a footstep from where she lay and curved claws scraped and churned up the loose rocks and earth around her. She heard loud voices shouting and cursing and the air was full of the cracking of whips. The thin curtain of draweasy that Kote had hastily drawn to hide her trembled and shook and a stone kicked up by a dragma's claw struck the curtain and began to tear it and reveal her.

Mya lay rigid. Her muscles cramped in terror as she continued to stare at the scorpion, willing it with all her mind not to strike. It opened its claws on either side of her nose. She could stand it no longer, she had to shut out the milling dragmas, the dust and the noise. She blinked her eyes tightly shut, her face contracting in anticipation of the searing pain. But nothing happened. The sounds and the shouts of the Mauders and their beasts in the gully grew fainter. Steeling her courage she opened her eyes the merest fraction. The roof of the overhang was empty. The scorpion had vanished.

'Mya, it is safe now. The Mauders have gone.'

Kote's voice close to her ear made her jump and broke the paralysis that had gripped her. In one desperate movement she threw herself away from the overhang. Tears of relief streamed down her face, she trembled from head to foot and beads of sweat oozed from between her clenched fingers. Slowly she climbed onto her knees and began to talk.

'There was a— ' Before she could finish Kote spun her round and struck her a violent glancing blow on her shoulder, knocking away the black scorpion that clung to her coat and sending it to the ground.

'Holy shit!' Denso gasped, leaping backwards as the scorpion turned towards him and then suddenly changed direction before scuttling away into the cover of the rocks.

'It's only a scorpion, Denso,' Harry mumbled, 'Arachnida Centruroides, but I've never seen one that large before. It must be the size of a crayfish,' he added as he watched it vanish amongst the rocks.

'I don't care what fancy names you give it: one stab from its sting and I'll bet you'd be as dead as mutton,' Denso snapped back.

'It's a female,' Mya answered flatly, recovering her composure, 'and there are ten baby scorpions on her back, but I don't think she'll attack you unless you provoke her.'

'How do you know that? How can you be so sure?' Denso demanded.

'Because she was sharing my hiding place with me,' Mya answered, looking up at Denso's stark white face as she brushed the dust from the sleeve of her coat.

'You . . . you were that close?' The words were barely a whisper, his lips trembling as he spoke.

Mya raised her right hand and opened her thumb and first finger until they were about two inches apart. 'Close enough to have asked her the names of all her young if I had wanted to.' She smiled at his obvious discomfort.

'Tread with care, all of you: they infest these barren lands. Only fools would jest about a scuttlebore sting.' Kote's gruff warning wiped the smile from Mya's face.

'Come, we have many leagues to travel if we are to reach

167

journey's end by nightfall,' Orun commanded, striking out due west. He led the way forward with the morning sun shining warmly on his back.

'I don't want to spend another night out in the open now I know it's crawling with scorpions,' Denso muttered, hurrying after the Waymaster.

'Will the Mauders come back looking for us?' Mya asked Kote, an edge of concern in her voice. 'Or will they keep following Lugg? Have we really given them the slip?'

Kote paused on the top of a furrow and looked round to watch the shrinking dustcloud vanishing towards the drifting sand-mists of Chehung. He wondered if the Mauders would be fool enough to follow Lugg's trail into the sand mists and shrugged. 'Nothing is certain, Mya, and yet everything is possible.'

'But Lugg,' she pressed. 'Will he be safe with those warriors on his heels? How will he ever find us again?'

Kote laughed and dropped back behind the others, brushing out their tracks as he followed. 'We have travelled ten thousand leagues together, he and I, and it is said that a dragma never forgets a footstep so he probably knows the way to everywhere far better than I do. But . . .' He paused, swallowing the fears that were crowding to the edge of his tongue.

He sensed that it would be better to keep from Mya the certain danger that Lugg would be in once he entered the sand-mists. The sand-dunes would be changed and Lugg, weary from his headlong rush across the Windrows of Thorn, would be likely to lose his way and perhaps stumble into a settlement. Or he might even be seen by one of the Chenos, the stone giants who wandered the Chehung, grinding the rocks and stone to a fine gritty powder that they mixed with the blood of living creatures to build their fragile towers. He had commanded Lugg to lead the

Mauders into the sand-mists so that they would become lost and blunder senselessly amongst the sand-towers, trampling them until the stone giants would raise such a storm of rage that the Asiri's men would never escape alive.

'But?' Mya frowned, glancing back to Kote, 'I heard doubt in your voice.'

Kote looked up, 'In all my journeyings, Mya Capthorne, I have never travelled such a dangerous road as this. I fear for all of us.'

Mya fell silent, then hurried forward to walk with Harry. He sensed her fall into step beside him and turned his head toward her, his eyes softening into a questioning smile.

'I don't know about you but I'm damned if I understand what this journey's all about. Did that Journeyman, the one with the dragon, tell you much? Did he give you any idea why he kidnapped you?' he asked in a quiet voice so that he didn't attract Kote's or Orun's attention.

'Yes, he told me a little,' she nodded moving closer and keeping her voice to a whisper as she answered. 'At first he kept repeating a wild story about some imminent disaster and said that Tholocus, Clockmaster of Eternity, needed my presence at a Grand Council in the City of Time. Of course I didn't believe a word of it then, what with the terror of being kidnapped and everything: all my thoughts were concentrated on trying to escape.'

'But what do you think now?' Harry asked. 'Now that you're here, wherever "here" is, now that you're on the wrong side of the walls of reality?'

Mya thought for a moment and then laughed softly, 'Right now I'd believe anything that appears in front of me, anything. Which for a scientist, I suppose, is a pretty rash statement ...' she paused, frowning, and brushed at the stray strands of hair that had fallen across her face. 'The thing is, everything here defies sense. It makes a nonsense of the environment we live in doesn't it? There are dragons that breathe fire, Journeymen with living maps tattooed on their skin, mountain spires that actually do touch the sky, and a land of drifting sand-mists. It's as if we have stepped into a place of living myths and legends yet it's all real enough to touch.'

'Yes, it's frighteningly real,' Harry echoed in agreement. 'It's the sort of world that Denso peoples in his imagination and so brilliantly describes in his novels. I tell you it was quite a shock arriving in the Crystal Swamps and some of the monstrous creatures we have encountered you just wouldn't believe! And we just don't know what's under the next footstep.'

Mya glanced up and smiled as she saw that Denso was keeping close to Orun's side and asking him a constant stream of questions, writing hurriedly as he stumbled along beside him.

Harry grinned. 'I think the real world sometimes frightens Denso a little: that's why his fantasies are so good – they're a place he can escape into from reality. He's not fond of creepy crawlies, but he knows that he's soaking up enough material through the soles of his shoes on this journey to write a whole new series of books.'

'I think we'll all be able to write a book at the end of this adventure,' Mya answered and they both trudged along in silence with the morning sun climbing stiflingly towards the zenith.

'You know, it's strange,' Mya murmured, swallowing to ease the dryness in her throat. She licked at her cracked lips before she could continue. 'I have been unofficially compiling a doomsday report for the last couple of years based on bizarre happenings, supernatural phenomena and animal behaviour, linking them with similar patterns that have occurred throughout history – the sort of things that have given people warning of impending disasters like famines and plagues. All my findings indicate that we are teetering on the edge of some enormous catastrophe. I wonder if all that research has anything to do with my being here?' Thoughtfully, she pushed the crumpled and creased bundle of papers more securely into her coat pocket.

'Is that the report?'

Mya nodded. 'I thought that Kote's face at my window was an omen, a warning that I should read the doomsday report in Masters' Hall rather than the official one that I had prepared on pollution, the one that my professor was expecting to hear.'

'Could I see it?' he asked quickly.

'Yes, of course, but it's only a rough draft.'

Harry smiled to himself. Listening to Mya had jogged his memory. Orun had said things about time running out and a huge catastrophe when he had first burst into his office. He wondered if there was a connection.

'Good God, my legs feel as though they're turning to jelly and I've got a splitting headache,' Mya muttered as they reached the crest of another ridge and began the long stumbling descent.

'If we don't stop soon we'll drop from exhaustion.' Harry called out to Orun, asking him when they were going to rest, but the Waymaster merely called back 'soon'.

He glanced down at his watch and shook it. The hands were pointing to 8.30 a.m. The harsh sun was almost directly overhead, shortening and intensifying their hurrying shadows. He followed the second hand as it travelled around the watch-face, then found his pulse and began to count as the second hand marked off the time. He frowned. It didn't make sense: this was the most expensive, reliable chronometer he had ever bought and it had never lost more than five seconds in all the years he had owned it: yet now it was running slowly. Either that or his heart was beating at twice its normal rate.

Orun stopped suddenly in the bottom of a gully and announced that they would now rest. Denso searched the ground minutely, gingerly turning over every loose stone and rock to check that there were no scorpions or any other crawling insects before he sank down to the ground. Mya sighed with relief and flopped down beside him, too weary to care what the rocks might conceal. Harry followed the Waymaster's climb to the next ridge where he stood watching the distant horizon shimmering with the noon-day heat, searching for any sign of the Mauders. Then he came slowly back to where they sat.

'Is time different here?' he asked.

'The sun and moon mark the travellers' time wherever we are,' Orun replied.

'No, I didn't mean that kind of time.' Harry tried to explain, lifting his arm close to their faces to show them the watch. 'It was evening in Manhattan when we climbed through that Doorcrack and evening when we arrived in the Crystal Swamps: in fact that journey only took about ten minutes. My watch corresponded with the sunrise this morning but since then it has been losing time and it has never done that before.' He paused and shook it vigorously.

Orun and Kote stared at the small flat dial with its black numerals and moving second hand. Orun's eyes narrowed and his breath hissed through his teeth in alarm as he examined the time-piece.

'By what magic do you wear this mark of mortality?' he cried, stepping backwards and raising his hand to shield his face.

Kote retreated with the Waymaster, his face paling beneath the mass of vivid tattoos that covered it. 'It is ill-luck to look upon a symbol of mortality,' he whispered.

'But ... but it's only a wristwatch,' Harry protested taking a step towards them. 'Look, it tells the time. It ...' He fell silent, letting his arm fall to his side, realising that neither Orun nor Kote had noticed his watch before as it lay hidden beneath his shirtsleeves and his heavy winter coat. Obviously it held a completely different, somehow sinister, significance for them, but what?

He tried again, drawing back his sleeve. 'In our world a watch or clock measures the hours and minutes, dividing the day into ...'

'You are wrong, Guardian: the sun's shadow divides the day,' Orun answered with conviction.

'Where have you seen these things before?' Harry asked. 'You must recognise this to fear it so much.'

Kote spoke in a hushed whisper. 'They are as numerous as wayside thistles in the City of Time, but you will never see them beyond the first Veil of Secrets and we are forbidden to look upon them or enter the Halls of Hours where they are kept.'

'No! You are a fool to utter such words lest they bring ill luck to our journey!' Orun cried, turning sharply on the Journeyman.

Denso and Mya had risen to their feet and moved closer at the sound of the heated voices from the top of the ridge. Harry glanced down to them and explained, 'All I did was ask Orun about the difference in the time here and show him my watch because it's running slow. He's acting as though I'm carrying some sort of evil talisman around my wrist ...'

Harry paused, indicated the other two and, raising his voice, said, 'In our world almost everyone wears a watch. It is how we tell the time.'

'They're nothing to be afraid of,' Mya smiled as she and

Denso both drew back their sleeves to reveal their wrist-watches.

Kote covered his eyes and Orun cried out before delving into one of the leather pouches that hung from his belt. He drew out a handful of reed-grass and tossed it into the air above his head to protect them against the ill-luck.

'Follow, follow, before bad omens overwhelm us all!' he shouted, hurrying forward across the barren landscape.

'Showing them your watch wasn't a clever move, was it?' Denso snapped between gasping breaths as he scrambled to keep up with the Waymaster who ignored his entreaties and strode silently ahead. 'See what you have done!' he cried. 'Orun won't reveal anything about his fears to me now.'

Harry shrugged, 'OK, it was a mistake, I'm sorry.' He dropped in line behind Denso. Any one of them could have made that simple mistake. Discovering that their guides were almost certainly illiterate had been fairly easy, but how could they possibly have known that they had a taboo about clocks and watches? He sighed, fell into step with Mya and they trudged on in silence.

The ground beneath their feet began to rise, the bleak featureless landscape of rock and earth changing gradually into undulating hills of coarse, dark grass. Wild flowers grew everywhere giving the swelling sweep of hills splashes of vibrant colour. There were trees in the distance, their tall solitary trunks etched against the skyline. The air grew still and hot and the sun vanished behind shrouds of grey mist which enfolded them in utter silence.

'Join hands or you will lose the way. We are passing through the first Veil of Secrets,' Orun cried, tearing up a handful of the coarse grass and winding it around his hand before he reluctantly grasped Denso's hand in his. 'To ward off the evil,' he muttered, striding forwards again.

'What is the Veil of Secrets?' Denso tried to ask, but the

Waymaster merely shrugged and hurried on, turning to left and right as though following a clearly-marked road through the mist.

Mya stumbled on an unseen outcrop of rock, lost Harry's hand and would have fallen had not Kote rescued her. He mumbled something beneath his breath and helped her back onto her feet, his dark eyes flashing a smile as they met hers. She felt her cheeks flush a little and thanked him quickly as she took a firmer grip on Harry's hand.

The ground became steeper and more difficult to climb. Huge boulders and jagged overhangs merged into a solid wall of cliffs that barred their way. Orun stopped, seeming lost and undecided as to which way to lead them. He twisted his head from side to side and pressed his ears against the cold, wet, mossy stone as if listening for something. He glared at Harry and muttered darkly about the power of evil omens. He had never once lost his way in all his previous journeys. He reached into his pouch and grasped another handful of reed grass, whispering magic rhymes over it before tossing it high into the air. He watched it drift away to the right and vanish in the mist. Turning, he skirted the rocks to the right with renewed purpose and uttered a cry of relief when he found a dark narrow, almost vertical, fissure in the rock-face.

'Quickly, follow me up Tholocus' stairs,' he called disappearing into the dark crack.

Denso hesitated, peering into the blackness.

'Here, let me lead the way,' Harry muttered impatiently edging past him. He stubbed the toe of his shoe on something in the gloom and sprawled forward striking his shins painfully on the sharp stone edges. 'Give me your lighter, I can't see a thing in here,' he called back to Denso.

He flicked it on. The long, thin flame danced around the wick illuminating a steep, narrow flight of stone steps that led upward, twisting and turning as they followed what looked like a natural fault in the rock.

'Stay close behind me,' Harry whispered, snapping the lighter shut and passing it back to Denso before feeling his way up the steps.

The worn stone stairway must have been built for giants, for each step was vast. It was also treacherously slippery, covered in thick layers of lichen and moss, and in places so narrow that he had to turn sideways to squeeze himself upward through the gaps. After counting twenty steps he paused and heard the muffled scraping and laboured breaths from the others below him. Satisfied that they were safe, he moved on and suddenly the stairway opened out into wide, rocky ledges. He climbed quickly across them toward Orun who was waiting impatiently and crouched on his haunches to catch his breath. Ahead the mist had vanished and the hot afternoon sun beat down fiercely. He glanced back to see that the Windrows of Thorn were still completely hidden in shrouds of mist.

Denso and Mya emerged from the stairway to join him and together they scrambled up onto the last ledge. None of them uttered a word as they stared open-mouthed at the eaves of the dark forest that stretched out in front of them as far as they could see in both directions.

'Look,' Mya whispered, finding her voice first. 'Look at those trees: I think they're moving.'

All three of them stared out at the impenetrable wall of trees. Tall elms and slender silver birch, rowan, pine and sycamore all grew so closely together that their trunks almost touched. They seemed to sway as if a sudden gust of wind had passed amongst them and their branches were moving, intertwining and rubbing noisily together. But it was impossible. The air was still – there hadn't been a breath of wind strong enough even to ruffle Mya's hair.

176

Orun watched fear of the trees grow large in their eyes and knew that he must give them courage. 'You stand before the second and final Veil on the Verge of Drasatt that shrouds the City of Time. It is a place of shadows and half-seen things, of whispers in the dark that search out the weaknesses in men's hearts. Stay close together and touch nothing. Do not stray from the path that I tread for you.'

'Are those trees alive? Will they hurt us?' Mya called out, but Orun turned away from them and disappeared through a gap that appeared between the trunks.

'Damn you, Waymaster, why don't you answer me?' she shouted angrily, taking a hurried step backward as the branches closest to her thrashed wildly against each other.

'Orun fears the symbol upon your arm: that is why he will not speak to you or look at you and why he hurries this journey to its end.'

Kote's voice made all three of them turn sharply towards him but he stepped away from them, quickly averting his eyes. Harry almost laughed out loud. A wristwatch as a powerful talisman – it was absurd, completely ridiculous. Mya saw his reaction and frowned, silencing him with a quick shake of her head.

'Do you fear us, Kote? Do you think we will cause this journey to fail?' she asked softly.

Kote swallowed and wrung his powerful hands together. 'Yes, no, my mind is in turmoil . . .' He looked up and for the merest second held Mya's gaze before looking away. 'You must follow quickly,' he ordered brusquely to cover his confusion. 'The trees will not harm you if you do not touch them.'

'It looks very dark and dangerous in there to me. I don't know whether to trust them,' Denso answered, hesitating to move forward.

'I don't think either of our guides would knowingly lead

us into danger after all they have gone through to deliver us to Tholocus and the City of Time, do you?' Mya retorted a little angrily. There had been something in Kote's eyes, some hidden spark, that made her leap to his defence.

'Come on, I'll lead the way,' Harry offered, breaking the tension and moving towards the gap between the trees where Orun had disappeared. He called over his shoulder as he walked on, 'There's no point in standing there all afternoon: we couldn't find our way back even if we wanted to.'

Denso muttered something under his breath and reluctantly followed him. Mya glanced at Kote and then slowly moved forward. Darkness and a whispering wall of silence enfolded her. The ground beneath her feet felt soft and springy for there was a thick carpet of pine needles and leaf mould that deadened the sound of her footsteps. Inside the edge of the forest the trees grew further apart, their massive trunks soaring upward as straight as cathedral columns to disappear amongst the tangle of leafy branches. Shadowy creatures moved between the trees: half-glimpsed stags, mountain-lions and bears twenty feet tall. She couldn't quite make them out and the more she tried to look at them the more they melted into the shadows. With a quickening stride she caught up with Harry and Denso. 'I think there are animals prowling all around us,' she hissed. 'Huge bears and . . .'

'What the hell . . .?' Denso cried suddenly, leaping forward and dropping to his knees, clutching at the top of his head.

'A branch . . . a branch reached down and tried to grab at me,' he stuttered hysterically, glancing fearfully upward at the dark mass of whispering wood.

'Do not be alarmed,' Kote called out softly from a few footsteps behind them. 'The trees are merely feeling, touching the truth that lies within you. Walk on, walk on.'

'I don't call that "touching the truth": they nearly tore my hair out!' Denso grumbled, raking his fingers through his hair.

'That's probably because they had to dig pretty deep,' Harry murmured, masking a grin as he helped him up. The trees frightened Harry but he was damned if he was going to show it.

'I thought I saw huge beasts hiding amongst the trees. There! Look over there!' Mya whispered fearfully to the Journeyman as she pointed away to the right.

Kote smiled, averting his eyes as he shook his head. 'You glimpsed your own fears, Mya. The shadows in this forest reflect the things you hide within your heart.'

Denso suddenly cried out and spun round, his eyes wide with terror as he tightened his grip on Harry's arm. 'Harry, Harry, for God's sake. We're going to be crushed to death!'

'What do you see? Where is it?' Harry hissed, staring into the empty shadowy darkness between the tree-trunks.

'There are crowds of people, shadowy figures swarming all around us, closing in. Can't you see them?' Denso's voice was shrill with panic and he raised his arm as if to ward them off.

'There's nothing there,' Harry whispered. 'Nothing but the swaying trees.'

Denso lowered his arm and blinked before slowly turning his head.

'It must be an illusion. Our imaginations are playing tricks,' Mya murmured, moving closer to the other two. 'Kote says the shadows reflect our innermost fears but they look real enough to me.'

'Look, there's light in that gap between the trees. Let's get out of here as quickly as we can,' Denso strode off in the direction that the Waymaster had taken.

'I don't see any light ahead, do you?' Harry frowned, hurrying after him.

'No,' Mya answered. 'But at least we're going in the right direction. I can see the Waymaster a few paces ahead of Denso.'

'Yes, and he must be real, he can't be an illusion, I can see him too.'

They quickly caught up with Denso and walked on in silence, focusing on the ground in front of them and following a broad well-trodden path through the trees. They shivered a little and shrank away from the fingery touch of the branches that reached down for them.

'What did *you* see in the shadows?' Mya asked quietly.

'Nothing,' Harry answered with an edge of misery in his voice. 'There was nothing between the trees but an endless emptiness.'

Mya glanced up into his eyes and saw the misery of his vision etched there. 'You fear being alone. Is that what your vision meant?'

Harry nodded bleakly, hunching his shoulders as he trudged on.

The land rose more steeply. Ferns and bracken grew in thick profusion on either side of the path, shafts of sunlight filtering down to break up the gloom.

'Listen,' Mya whispered against the stifling silence. 'I think I can hear rushing water somewhere ahead. Can you hear it?'

Harry and Denso both lifted their heads to listen.

'Ah, yes,' breathed Denso as he caught the faint tumbling roar of water.

'Yes, I can hear it too,' Harry added.

'Oh good,' Mya smiled, running her tongue over her dry and cracked lips. 'It must be real if we can all hear it. I am so thirsty and I was afraid it might be only in my imagination.'

The path began to twist and turn. The banks on either side were speckled with primroses and they could glimpse sheer craggy spires of rock between the straight pine trees.

The air was lighter and heady with the scent of resin and wild flowers. The sounds of rushing water grew louder and louder, a cold mist dampened their faces and rainbows shimmered in the shafts of sunlight. The path entered a dark and narrow gully and the roar of cascading water and their hurrying footsteps echoed all around them. They rounded a sharp corner and stopped abruptly. Before them Orun stood waiting, his hands on his hips. Behind him a narrow stone bridge stretched out in a single span across the great white wall of water that thundered and boiled down into a bottomless chasm to be lost in clouds of spray. The surface of the bridge was barely two footsteps wide and it looked slippery and treacherous. They could see through the haze of mist and spray that there was no handrail to guide or check the fall of a light-headed traveller.

'Oh no, I couldn't. I hate heights, I will never be able to cross that bridge.' Denso was shaking his head and retreating even before Orun had opened his mouth.

Kote checked him with strong hands. 'The way is safe. Watch carefully.'

Orun untied the fastening from two of the heavy leather pouches that hung from his belt and withdrew two long silken cords. These he attached to two iron rings screwed into posts at the foot of the bridge. Holding one in either hand he walked out, trailing the cords behind him and vanished into the mist and spray. Moments later, the cords were pulled as taut as bowstrings and the Waymaster re-appeared. He stopped in the centre of the bridge and waved, then he grasped the cord on the left with both hands and threw his weight against it.

Mya cried out in terror and covered her eyes. Harry gasped, a cold shiver tingling down his spine as he waited for the Waymaster to plunge to his death. Denso stared open-mouthed, his voice paralysed with the horror of it all. The cord gave a little, then tightened, pushing Orun into the centre of the bridge. He laughed and then threw his weight to the right. The cord still refused to let him fall. He shouted eagerly to the others and beckoned for them to follow.

'It is safe. You will not fall if you grasp the rope with each hand and follow me.'

All three of them hesitated. The bridge looked far too dangerously narrow. Mya turned and glanced anxiously back towards Kote. For once he held her gaze and shouted against the roar of the waterfall. 'Go, I would never let you set a footstep into danger.'

She knew from his eyes that he spoke the truth. She smiled, turned back and grasped a rope in either hand, swallowing gingerly as she felt her way out, step by step across the chasm. The taut ropes vibrated in the drifting mist and seemed to sing a whispering, haunted melody that guided her, although her eyes were tightly shut. She felt Harry and Denso as they grasped the cords behind her and heard Orun's voice above the roar of the water urging them on.

Her feet skidded and slipped. She cried out but forced down the dizziness that almost overwhelmed her and kept moving. Strong hands suddenly grasped her wrists and pulled her forward. The ground beneath her feet was rough: she blinked and opened her eyes and saw that she had safely crossed the bridge. Breathing a sigh of relief, she turned to see Harry and Denso reach the end of the bridge with Kote following them. Orun unknotted the cords and gave them a sharp tug. They flew toward his hands in neat, coiled loops which he easily stowed away in the pouches on his belt. Moving between them, he climbed a dozen stone steps and beckoned them to follow.

'You have crossed the Verge of Drasatt and reached journey's end,' he called, sweeping his hand out across the City of Time that lay in evening shadows below them.

CHAPTER SEVEN

The Halls of Hours

MYA SHADED HER EYES with her hand to protect against the rays of the sunset and slowly followed the sweep of the Waymaster's fingers.

'It's so beautiful,' she sighed softly, a smile touching her lips as her gaze took in the crowded roofs of bleached tiles, the high archways and classical porticos.

The City of Time lay below, wrapped in soft misty shadows and touched by the crimson colours of the dying sun. There was such a profusion of angles, curves and shadows to assault the eye but somehow they blended into perfect architectural harmony.

'It's as though we are looking down on fragments of everything ever created by man,' Denso exclaimed, breaking into Mya's thoughts. 'Look: there's parts of the Parthenon, the Colossus, Roman arenas. There's a temple from an Incan city, some pyramids and it's . . .' Denso paused, searching for words.

'It's as if all antiquity is crowded together down there,' Harry offered.

'Yes, yes, of course,' Denso frowned. 'But it's more than that: look across to the furthest rim of the city, look, there, I think there are some modern buildings. Can you see?'

'Why, yes,' Mya answered slowly. 'You're right, there's a cluster of skyscrapers and what looks like Sydney Opera House: and look, there's a castle and a cathedral almost lost in their shadows.'

'It feels really odd standing here looking down on a living blueprint of history,' Denso murmured.

'It doesn't look very alive to me. The streets are completely deserted,' Harry laughed uneasily.

'What do you think those towers are?' Mya wondered aloud, pointing to a series of soaring, white, pencil-thin spires that stood on the rim of the city.

'They're completely different to everything else down there.'

'Those are the Towers of Time where the Diviners dwell,' Orun muttered darkly, in a barely-heard whisper, his eyes clouding with fear. 'And the tallest, the one shadowed against the sunset, is the spire of Tholocus, Clockmaster of Eternity.'

As the Waymaster said 'Clockmaster of Eternity' Harry's head snapped up and he swung sharply around toward him.

'Clockmaster. Tholocus the Clockmaster. What do you mean by that?'

Orun held Harry's gaze for a long moment as he turned the question over and over in his head. Finally he shrugged. 'It is his title, just as I am a Waymaster and Kote is a Journeyman.'

'But what do you *mean* by the word "Clockmaster"?' Harry pressed.

Mya stood close to Harry and before Orun could gather his breath to find an answer she interrupted, 'What does the word mean here in the City of Time? What is a clock?'

Orun looked blankly at her and Kote spoke for him. 'Legends say that the clock is the windspring that measures lives and that it lies in the very centre of the City of Time in a squat circular tower, but none save Tholocus and the councils of the wise have ever seen it.' Kote fell silent, his lips trembling, his face showing deadly white in the gathering darkness.

Mya had a thousand questions on the tip of her tongue but she hesitated, sensing that he had already said more than he should. Instead she thanked him with a smile before turning thoughtful eyes to the lengthening shadows that were swallowing up the City of Time, advancing as silently and relentlessly as a flood tide across barren mudflats. Why, she wondered, had this Clockmaster woven such a web of mysteries around these magical lands? Why had he kept the people so ignorant? There was no literature, only myth and legend to nourish their histories. It seemed that their past was kept alive in travellers' tales at the fireside and even time itself was only understood at its most rudimentary level by the shortening of a shadow.

'Come, you must hurry, Tholocus awaits you in his high tower!' Orun's rasping voice broke into her speculations.

Denso called out, 'How long will it take us to get to this tower?'

'It is a swift night's journey away,' Orun replied impatiently. He edged toward the road that led down to the city.

'But we've been marching all day and my head's splitting with this terrible headache. Why can't we rest here and finish the journey in the morning?' Denso insisted, planting his hands firmly on his hips.

'I don't feel too good either,' Harry agreed.

Mya nodded too, 'I don't think any of us feel up to carrying on.'

Orun's eyes narrowed with anger and frustration. His fists clenched and unclenched as he tried to riddle out a way to make them follow him. Then he shrugged and turned away from them, calling across his shoulder as he left, 'From here your road is easy and plain to see. Rest and sleep well, I will go ahead and inform Tholocus that you are resting with a nest of scuttlebores as a pillow.'

'Scuttlebores?' Denso cried, stamping his feet and looking all about him, the colour draining from his face. The memory of the scorpion that had shared Mya's hiding place was still vivid in his mind. 'Wait! Wait a minute!' he shouted making the Waymaster pause and turn back with a triumphant grin on his face. 'Come on you two, the Waymaster's right, it's probably best to finish the journey now rather than hang around here all night.'

Denso hurried to where Orun was stooping on the verge of the road, searching for something in the unkempt undergrowth. The Waymaster rose with a grunt of triumph clutching a glowbright sphere in both hands. He tapped the lefthand one and as it began to glow he passed it across to Denso. 'Tread with care, avert your eyes from the symbols of mortality that litter the wayside on the outer edges of the city, and do not disturb them,' he warned, lifting his own glowbright to illuminate the road as he moved forward.

Harry pressed the palms of his hands against his temples but nothing seemed to relieve the band of tightening pain. 'Well, I suppose we had better get this journey finished,' he sighed.

'Wait,' Harry said, stopping suddenly and turning his head to catch at the persistent murmuring sound rising up from the darkened city on the night wind. 'Do you know what that sound reminds me of? It's as though we are hearing the tick tick tick of millions of clocks, all marking out their own rhythm of time.'

Mya paused beside him and listened. 'Yes, that's exactly what it sounds like and . . . and . . . in the background, can you hear, the sound of all the tiny grains of sand trickling through endless hour-glasses? Now that you've focused my attention on it how could I not have heard it before?' After a moment's pause she laughed. 'I can just imagine this Clockmaster we are going to meet – he'll be constantly running round and round the City of Time, his coat tails flying, as he tries to keep all those clocks wound up!'

Harry started to laugh with her and then stopped, a frown darkening his forehead. 'But why so many clocks? What are they all for?'

Mya shrugged: the picture of all those clocks seemed so far-fetched. 'I don't know, perhaps he just hates being late.'

Harry was about to answer when Kote stepped in front of them and turned, holding up his clenched fists. Soft light appeared shining out between each finger as he thrust them towards them. 'Light for your road,' he said, opening his hands to reveal a mass of brilliantly glowing creatures.

'What the hell?' Harry exclaimed, stepping backwards in shock.

'They are only glow-worms, they won't hurt you,' Mya smiled, taking some from Kote's right hand and closing her own hand around them gently.

'Ugh, they feel hot and they look like enormous caterpillars.' Harry's face tightened with revulsion as he watched the glow-worms wriggle outwards across his hands.

'Close your hand around them: don't let them escape, or they will metamorphose into lethal glow-wasps. This place is full of surprises, isn't it?' Mya exclaimed.

'No, thanks.' Harry answered, quickly passing the glow-worms back to Kote. 'I'd rather carry a glowbright if I can find one.' He searched the undergrowth, quickly found one and made it glow with white light before he fell into step with Mya.

They lengthened their stride to catch up with Denso and began the long, winding descent to the city. Mya glanced to left and right and kept looking towards the dark overhanging trees, straggling bushes and unkempt undergrowth. She frowned. 'I don't know if my eyes are deceiving me but I think there are the oddest things hanging up around us: they look like clocks, sundials, pendulums – all sorts of time-pieces hanging from every twig and branch. There are others scattered all across the ground and the sound we heard from the rim of the valley is getting louder, can you hear it?'

'It's unbelievable,' Harry gasped, almost stumbling and falling as he stared about him. He moved to the edge of the road and peered into the undergrowth. 'I don't believe it, just look at all these clocks and watches! Denso, Denso, come here and look at what we have found.'

'What? What is it?' Denso hissed in alarm and he stopped and turned towards the other two.

'No! You must not look upon the symbols of mortality!'

The Waymaster turned in panic and clutched at Denso's arm. 'Your fate might be mirrored in any one of their pale faces. Look only ahead. Look to the high tower silhouetted against the stars. Look towards your journey's end!'

Denso hesitated and pulled against the Waymaster's strong grip, then laughed out loud as he caught sight of the clock dials, pendulums and other artefacts of time that adorned the trees and undergrowth around them. 'But they are only timepieces. They cannot possibly harm you,' he laughed.

'You are a fool to look upon them. Don't you realise that it is death to glimpse your own reflection?' Orun's voice boiled with fear and anger and his grip tightened on Denso's arm, forcefully pulling him forward.

'Mya, the Waymaster is right. It is madness to tempt fate. Please do not look upon the glistening faces,' Kote spoke urgently, his voice pleading with her to move on.

Harry hesitated. There was something about the litter of timepieces beyond the verge that made him want to take a closer look. He glanced after the others as they moved away and he heard Kote shout to him to hurry but his voice lacked any real concern. Harry knew that he was only there by accident and that neither of the guides really gave a damn for his welfare. 'I'm coming!' he shouted after them, deliberately turning his back on the road and carefully picking his way between the profusion of artefacts that filled the undergrowth.

He stopped abruptly when he came to a broad area strewn with discarded hourglasses and broken sundials lying in careless heaps. He crouched down, held up the glowbright to cast a better light across the jumbled scene and began to examine the sundials. They were covered in a fine layer of white dust that shrouded the letters and numbers carved on the stone dials beneath. Harry brushed at the flat face of the closest dial with his fingertips and found a thin, black shadow had been etched deeply into the surface precisely dissecting an hour and a minute. Strangely, this dial cast no shadow however carefully Harry held the light from the glowbright. He looked at the rows of letters and numerals beneath the etched shadow and realised that they were written in ancient Greek, a language he had studied at school. He stared at the jumble of script: it had been years since he had translated any Greek and the cogs in his mind were rusted with disuse. He blinked and concentrated and he traced the letters as he read, 'Carperius', followed by the numerals for the year 823. Beneath the name and date there were small letters that were eroded and badly defaced as though the stonemason had tried to alter them and he couldn't decipher more than 'R' 'H' and 'O'.

Harry rose to his feet, looking over at the other broken sundials in the pile, saw that each one had a name, a date and a place engraved upon it. He cast his eyes slowly across the careless heaps of stone that stretched away into the darkness and his breath whistled between his teeth. 'There must be thousands, hundreds of thousands, of them,' he murmured, moving back toward the road.

He paused for a while on the edge of a field of forgotten hourglasses. Some were tall, some squat and others were beautiful pieces that encompassed all a glassblower's skill. He put the glowbright on the ground and picked up one of the hourglasses. He discovered that, for some reason, the sand had never finished trickling through the slender neck and almost two thirds of it remained trapped in the top section of the glass. Harry shook it and turned it over but the sand was petrified and he could not dislodge a single grain. He cleaned the dusty glass with his sleeve and found a strange set of hieroglyphics that he assumed must be a name and a date etched across the line of sand. Harry frowned, thoughtfully replaced the glass in exactly the place he had picked it from and examined another and another. He found that they were all slightly different, some with a little more and some a little less sand in the top half of the glass, but every one of them had a name and a date engraved across the moment the sand had stopped flowing.

Somewhere on the road deeper in the valley Denso was shouting, calling to Harry to hurry and look at something that Mya had just discovered. He took one last thoughtful glance at the mass of sundials and hourglasses and picked up the glowbright before retracing his footsteps back to the road. Beside a withered whipwood tree he paused for a moment and peered at a broken pendulum that swung and twisted in the breeze. He caught hold of it and found that it had 'Ebeneezer Doods, 1101' engraved across it. Harry shivered and let it go. A sudden thought struck him: he was standing on the edge of a gigantic graveyard of time. Gasping, he hurried to catch up with the others where they stood amongst a suburb of ruined and deserted buildings on the outskirts of the City of Time.

Denso and Mya were waiting in the shadow of a doorway in an enormous stone building whilst Orun and Kote were hurrying away from them toward the centre of the city.

'Harry, come quickly. Come here and see what we've found. We've been waiting for you for ages: where have you been?' Denso's voice was edged with excitement and he strode into the entrance of the building holding his glowbright aloft.

'Just look at this!'

Harry passed into the darkened entrance. Here he stopped abruptly and almost let his glowbright slip forgotten through his fingers as his eyes tried to take in the sight that lay before him. Everywhere he looked there were millions and millions of clocks and watches and every other mechanism that could possibly exist to measure time. They were stacked and piled carefully, one on top of another, in soaring, swaying towers and between rows of fluted stone columns that rose into the shadows overhead and marched away in diminishing perspective into the gloomy silent interior.

'It's fantastic isn't it?' Denso cried, breaking the eerie silence. 'I could never have imagined this, not in a million years,' making a note in his pad.

'Do you think this is one of those Halls of Hours that Kote mentioned?' Mya asked quietly.

Denso moved closer, edging his way between two of the tottering towers to take a closer look. 'I don't think it could be,' he called back over his shoulder.

'Be careful, that swaying mass of mechanisms doesn't look too safe. If you catch your sleeve on any of those sharp edges you'll bring the lot crashing down on top of us,' Mya warned.

Denso hesitated and carefully worked his way back out from between the two mounds. 'None of them are working, are they? And I'll bet there's a name and a date scratched or painted on every one of them,' Harry called, making Denso stop and look more closely as he retreated.

'You're right,' he replied after a moment. 'And all the dates are very close together. They're all between 1423 and 1430. But how did you know that?'

'There were names on the sundial and the hourglass, I guessed these would be the same.'

'They're much later over here,' Mya called, leaving the safety of the doorway and moving deeper into the building despite her warning to Denso.

Harry watched the soaring towers sway and tremble and called out an urgent warning as he backed towards the entrance. 'Your presence seems to be affecting the equilibrium of the building. I think both of you had better come out of there before the whole lot collapses.'

Denso glanced up, gave a cry of horror and staggered back. The colossus of clocks that he had been examining was swaying so violently that as it moved it overshadowed him completely. He turned and fled with Mya only a foot-step behind him. Sharp objects began to fall. Mainsprings, fragments of casing, pendulums and weighted chimes rained down noisily from the darkness of the roof into the narrow aisle where they had been standing only moments before.

'Jesus! That was a lucky escape!' Denso exclaimed, stumbling as he tried to glance over his shoulder at the clattering din inside the building. He stopped, regained his balance, straightened his coat, took out a soiled handkerchief and dabbed furiously at his dirty forehead, visibly shaken by his narrow escape.

'Now I understand why Orun was so against us venturing in there,' he muttered, frowning as he looked over to where Orun and Kote had stopped and were waiting for them. As

195

they reappeared the guides hurried on again and disappeared from sight.

'Now we're really lost. We'll never find that tower without the Waymaster's help.'

'What? What did you say?' Harry asked, momentarily distracted from the rain of clocks and watches gradually filling the aisles.

'Orun and Kote are getting a long way ahead of us. Perhaps we should catch them up,' Denso frowned.

The clatter of falling objects was lessening. The eerie breathless silence that they had disturbed was gradually re-establishing itself throughout the gloomy building.

'Yes, sure,' Harry agreed. 'Let's catch up with them: the only way we're going to get any answers about what is going on here is by asking this Clockmaster.' He hunched his shoulders and thrust his hands deep into his pockets.

Mya swept her hand out over the darkened city that spread across the valley to the furthest ring of slender spires pencilled against the star-strewn sky. 'I wonder if all those buildings are also crammed full of clocks and watches.'

Harry spoke thoughtfully, 'I wonder why they are here at all. What's their purpose?'

Mya paused and looked back into the dark entrance. 'You're probably going to think this is silly but going in there made me feel that I was trespassing, invading a tomb or . . .' She fell silent and threw up her hands. 'Oh I don't know, it's impossible to describe. I've been on hundreds of archaeological digs and I've helped to strip back the shrouds on hallowed ground to uncover the bare bones of history. Sometimes on those digs there is a feeling of awe at what we have found, or a great sadness or anger that the robbers had got there first, often centuries earlier. But I've never experienced this feeling before.'

'I think we had better get going or we'll never catch up with Orun,' Denso muttered.

'Yes, yes, we're coming,' Harry answered dismissively, turning his attention back to Mya.

'Earlier, while I was looking at those sundials and hourglasses higher up in the valley I had the distinct feeling that I was standing on the edge of a huge graveyard of time. I felt that each of these clocks or dials is the measure of a life that once existed. Perhaps that building we entered is a tomb. Perhaps here, in this reality, we are trespassing.'

Mya stared at him for a moment and let her gaze focus on the dark buildings all around them. 'Do you think that time is stored here? I mean each lifetime of days, hours and minutes?' Suddenly her mind rushed ahead of her, her thoughts in a blur. 'That would explain the utter silence inside that cavernous hall. In there time no longer exists. And if that is the case . . .'

Harry nodded, following the same track of thought, 'I must have been right when I thought that the sound we could hear from the rim of the valley was like the ticking of millions of clocks all measuring out their own rhythm of time.'

'Yes, yes you were,' Mya agreed. 'But I think that the sound we can hear is doing more than just measuring or recording time. Listen to the sudden surges and the relentless rise and fall of the rhythm: it's always the same but never constant. A clock is a mechanism for measuring, you wind it and set it to record the present and reflect the past but that sound isn't mechanical. Listen to it, really listen to it, it's more like . . .' She shrugged helplessly as she strove to find the words. 'It's more like a living, breathing existence.'

Denso's voice, trembling with breathless excitement, made them both turn toward him. 'Perhaps we have always misunderstood time. It's as if we have studied it through the wrong end of a telescope. Perhaps it's a gigantic heart-beat, a life-force, created by all the millions and millions of separate human existences here and in Bendran and in our own world. Perhaps the relentlessly-changing rhythm is generated by the thousands and thousands of births and deaths, the unending cycle of life throughout the universe.' Mya and Harry stared at Denso as the enormity of the canvas that he had just painted sunk in.

'But why the clocks, the sundials? Why all this?' Harry asked throwing his arms out to encompass the shadowy city as they all walked slowly forward.

Denso frowned and shrugged. 'I don't know all the answers, I've only just started to think about it. Perhaps because our life spans are individually so short they needed measuring and storing somewhere when they are over. Or perhaps it's to do with quotas, who knows?'

'The timepieces we've seen stretch back to the dawn of civilisation,' Mya began.

'Tholocus will answer all your questions. Now hurry please. We must reach the tower before the dawn brightens the sky again. I beg you do not trespass again beyond the edge of the road: it is forbidden to enter the Halls of Hours.'

Orun's voice made them jump.

'Questions, oh yes, there's an endless stream of questions that we want to ask this Clockmaster,' Denso observed, but Orun was not listening, having already strode on, his eyes fixed on the pencil-thin tower that rose above all the others on the skyline ahead.

Kote momentarily fell into step with Mya. His face was drawn and pale but his eyes burned with a fierce intensity as he held her gaze. 'I feared for your life when you trespassed inside that Hall of Hours. You must promise me that you will not do it again. I cannot protect you if you venture from the road.'

'But it was only a building stuffed with thousands of old clocks. Why, why do you fear them so much?'

Kote shook his head angrily, pressing his finger to his lips. 'You will bring ill luck to us all and bring Tholocus' anger down on us if you trespass in the Halls of Hours. Remember, it is forbidden.' He hesitated and then hurried to walk beside the Waymaster.

Mya studied his strong shoulders as he walked away from her and thought carefully about the fears and irrationalities he had expressed. She moved closer to Harry and Denso and asked quietly, 'I wonder if there's a clock hidden away in this place for each one of us.'

Harry glanced up at the tall, silent, overshadowing buildings and let his breath whistle out between his teeth. 'Well, if you find one for me and it's got a time and a date to show when I'm going to step off into eternity please keep it a secret.'

'Denso, would you want to see yours?' Mya asked.

He thought for a moment, then grinned, 'Authors are sort of immortal through their work, aren't they? But hell no, of course I don't want to know when I'm going to die. But what made you ask? What are you getting at?'

'I'm trying to fathom out what it is that our guides fear so much about this place. Kote certainly gives me the feeling that we are the first, probably the only, people they have ever brought here. And why are they so terrified of clocks? They are both virtually illiterate and they have no concept of measuring time as we know it, yet the clock-face is an awesome talisman to them and they walk in mortal terror of seeing one that relates to their fate.'

'But that's ridiculous,' retorted Denso, his voice edged with laughter. 'If they stumbled on one that belonged to them they are hardly likely to recognise it, are they? They can't even tell the time, let alone read their own names.'

'Perhaps their vision of fate is more primitive,' Harry offered. 'Perhaps to their simple logic just to see their own reflections superimposed on the glass face of any one of these millions of clock faces would link it to them.'

'You mean something like a tribal belief in sympathetic magic where they think you will die if the witch doctor points his magic bone or stick at you?' Mya murmured thoughtfully.

'I'll bet it's all a ruse, a crock of lies put about by the Clockmaster to keep them strictly on the road and stop them wandering into any of these buildings.'

'Yes, you're probably right.' Mya pursued the idea. 'But there must be a grain of truth in what they believe. There has to be if the names and dates engraved and scratched on all those countless clock-faces mean anything at all.'

They had been moving rapidly forward as they spoke, travelling deeper into the heart of the city, the voice of time getting louder and louder, reverberating all around them. Harry suddenly looked up and stopped them with a warning shout. 'Look, look over there, ahead and to the right: there's a steady stream of figures hurrying in and out of that huge modern building, the one constructed in spirals and curves. And there's lights on inside it!'

'There's more activity further up the street!' Denso called out. 'What a racket! It's so loud it's setting my teeth on edge and making my head pound. What the hell is it?'

'It sounds as though somebody is winding up thousands and thousands of clocks and setting them in motion,' Mya frowned.

A shout came from beyond the lighted doorway and shadowy grey-robed figures started hurrying in and out of it. Harry peered forward. He caught sight of Orun frantically signalling with his glowbright and realised that he was gesticulating at them, trying to make them run past the door and keep as far away from it as they possibly could.

'I don't know about you but I don't altogether subscribe to our guides' taboos. I want to take a closer look at what goes on inside one of these Halls of Hours.'

'Oh yes, you bet!' Denso replied, his curiosity fired up, but after a moment's pause he added, 'but I don't want to go blundering in there and have the lot come crashing down on my head: remember what happened last time.'

'You're right,' Mya agreed. 'It would be safer to stand in the road and watch from there.'

Harry slowed and stopped as they drew level with the huge open door. 'Jesus Christ, the light . . . the noise.' He blinked and screwed up his eyes before clamping his hands over his ears and staggering back a pace. The light that spilt through the doorway was blinding and intensified by the myriad of reflections from the countless polished clock-faces that magnified its brilliance. Apart from the clock-faces there were optical lenses and milled metal surfaces piled up in neat, well-ordered rows all around this Hall of Hours.

Mya shielded her eyes and studied the continuous stream of hurrying figures moving in and out of the entrance. They were stooping as if burdened beneath a great load, their serious age-lined faces set in determination. They seemed so intent on whatever it was they were doing that they barely gave Mya and the two men a second glance. She threw caution to the winds and shuffled a few tentative steps closer to the silent procession of grey-robed figures despite Harry's warning whisper. Each one of them was carrying something in outstretched hands and she wanted to see what it was they held so reverently.

'Clocks!' she gasped, retreating back to the other two. 'Between them they're carrying every kind of imaginable modern mechanism for measuring time. But the oddest thing is, none of them are working. Listen: they're making less noise than a funeral procession: all the sound we can hear is coming from within the building. I wonder what's going on in there.'

'Well, let's take a closer look.'

They followed Denso closer to the entrance and peered in, shielding their eyes against the glare.

'It's fantastic. I would never have been able to imagine this: it's a brilliant beginning for a story,' Denso whispered in awe.

Mya smiled, her eyes ghosted with tears. The air inside this Hall of Hours was alive with whispers. The stooping figures hurried past them through the doors to spread out along the narrow avenues between the piles of clocks until they reached some pre-destined place where they stopped and tilted their heads in statue stillness. Each one seemed to be listening for the first whisper of life before they set time in motion and carefully placed the clock or digital counter amongst the countless millions already lying there.

'Welcome, travellers. You are the first to have witnessed this mystery of the universe, the creation of time itself.'

The deep, resonant voice that came out of the darkness behind them made all three of them jump and spin round in guilt and fear. The voice laughed softly and a tall slender figure with shining white hair and a flowing robe of silk emerged from the shadows. His face was long and angular, etched with deep lines and wrinkles. His eyes were azure blue, glittering in the light that poured out of the open doorway. He held them still with a piercing gaze that stripped away all pretence and falsehood. Suddenly he held out his hands toward them.

'Welcome, Mya Capthorne and Denso Alburton, architects of the future. Welcome to the City of Time. Tholocus, the Clockmaster, thanks you for coming so hastily in his hour of need.' He paused and turned curious eyes to Harry. For a moment he seemed to be puzzled, a smile hovering in his eyes. In a moment his smile broadened and he clasped Harry's hands in his. 'You are an unexpected guest, Harry Murmers, but a most welcome one. Orun has told me of you. Come, come all of you, there is food set ready upon the table: it will ward off your hunger, and there are crystal goblets brimming with nectar to wash away the dust. Afterwards there are featherbeds in which to dream away the rigours of your journey and refresh you before the Grand Council gathers to debate the prophecies of catastrophe. Come now, follow me.'

'This is a most interesting place you have here,' Denso exclaimed, falling into step with the Clockmaster.

Tholocus smiled and slowly nodded his head, 'Yes, it is the birthplace of eternity. It is the eye of the morning in which the mystery of life unfolds.'

He paused, his smile crumbling into dark shadows that haunted his eyes. 'But I will not speak further of it here: there will be time enough to dwell on all facets of eternity when the Grand Council meets.'

Mya coughed and cleared her throat as she gathered up the courage to ask the question that was poised on the tip of her tongue. She sensed that Tholocus had wisdom a thousand times greater than the professors at her university and she felt awe at his obvious power. He turned his gaze towards her, his eyebrows raised in enquiring arches.

'Why did our guides fear those darkened buildings that we have passed on our way through the city?'

Tholocus frowned at her, darkening the haunting shadows in his face. 'We had to plant a fear of what lies within the Halls of Hours to keep the Waymasters from straying from their road and unbalancing the rhythm of time. I chose wisely in calling you to the Council meeting,

Mya Capthorne. You miss little in your search for answers. You see the purpose of the Halls of Hours: they are not there merely to record what has passed but to create the present and the future too. They hold all the triumphs and the catastrophes, the joys and the tears, the very tapestry of eternity.'

'So it was wrong of us to trespass,' Mya asked slowly as they passed the last of the huge buildings and moved towards the tallest of the towers.

Tholocus nodded gravely as grey-robed figures started to come out to greet them. The sky was lightening and the bright rim of the sun was edging its way above the horizon. Harry yawned, the promise of rest and food making him realise just how weary he felt.

CHAPTER EIGHT

The Grand Council of Disaster

MYA SHIFTED UNCOMFORTABLY in her high-backed chair of black ebony inlaid with gold and silver and fixed her attention on the twentieth Diviner as Tholocus called him forward to speak. The Diviner rose from his chair to address the Grand Council and read from an ancient, dusty manuscript lying on the table top before him, as all the other Diviners had done. He spoke softly, his words filling the chamber as musically as wind-bells touched by a gentle breeze, and emphasised the astrologer Berossus' predictions of catastrophe with flowing gestures of his long, fragile fingers.

Mya straightened her back, lifted her hands from the silky-smooth scales of the carved dragon's-head arm-rests of her chair and leaned forward, straining her ears to catch at the importance of the Diviner's words. She rested her elbows on the cool, curving marble table-top that swept away on either side of her in a huge oval to fill the centre of the circular tower where the Council had gathered. Her gaze flickered over the other members of the Council, from the serious faced, grey-robed Diviners to the handful of wrinkled, pale-skinned withereds who had fled from the Citadel of Krak in fear of the Asiri. Her glance took in the two tall, haughty Wizards of Thorn whose fingertips crack-led fire and who spoke repeatedly of the wrathwas' breath burning up the skies in Heaven; and the tiny figures from Chricaun who needed six cushions so that they could see above the table-top. She was constantly aware of the Elder of Gavati who wandered persistently around the huge table and never kept still. Oddly enough almost every one of them had, in some way or another, touched on Paradise in one breath: but each had linked it with a different phenomenon or unnatural happening that mirrored the ones she had so laboriously gathered into the crumpled Doomsday manuscript that now lay on the table before her. She could not fathom the connection but clearly, in this auspicious Council, she realised that no-one would mock her research or deride her findings. This was where time itself was created: here each voice echoed with deadly earnest as they foretold of a terrible, as yet unknown, fate that overshadowed Paradise, and it hadn't taken her long before she realised that they meant Earth.

For a moment her gaze rested on Harry and Denso and a smile touched the corners of her mouth. Harry looked as though he was witnessing the negotiation of the contract of a lifetime. His eyes had narrowed with shrewdness: although outwardly impassive he was attentive and watchful as he listened carefully to each word and measured what every speaker had to offer. Denso was completely fascinated by the impending catastrophe and the lengthening shadow that the Council feared was stretching over Earth. He was absorbing the idea as the foundation of a new work, perhaps a climax of achievement, and he devoured the words and scribbled down everything that was said.

Mya swallowed nervously. Soon it would be her turn to stand and unfold her thesis showing the signs of an impending catastrophe that she had monitored so meticulously. She let her eyes wander away from the Grand Council and the Diviner's voice momentarily faded in her head as she looked up across the millions and millions of books, manuscripts, scrolls and stone tablets that lined the wall of the tower and rose in lofty tiers to vanish somewhere above them amongst the rafter beams. She felt her skin prickle as if someone was watching her, sensing her lack of attention. She blinked and the Diviner's voice came back into focus. Looking around the huge table anxiously she saw Tholocus smiling at her. Her cheeks flushed as she fumbled with the crumpled edges of her manuscript to mask her embarrassment. Tholocus' smile briefly broadened with warmth and then his eyebrows creased with concern as he returned his attention to the speaker's soft voice.

Mya smiled as she remembered how Tholocus had taken her hand and led her into the tower on that first misty morning as sunlight painted the new day. She had stood staring in, transfixed by the climbing tiers of knowledge that lined the tower walls. Tholocus had dismissed it all with a sweep of his hand, telling her that no word or thought that had ever been written down, no matter how great or how small, had been wasted. Nothing had been casually thrown away, everything created by mankind from those first humble stone scratchings in the caves of glass to the splitting of the atom was recorded in the Towers of Time that stood upon the outer rim of the city.

She had paled at the implication of what she saw and behind her she had heard Denso gasp in awe. Tholocus had turned toward him with laughter in his azure eyes as he said, 'This is the fountainhead of all knowledge where the sharp grains of truth that lie in the heart of every myth are formed. This is where every story has its beginning.'

Harry had stared up at the endless rows of books and scrolls before asking quietly, 'How long have you been gathering all this knowledge?'

Tholocus looked at Harry and held his gaze for many silent moments before he answered. 'Let it be enough for you to know that I am Tholocus, the Clockmaster, the wind-spring of life. I am as old as time itself and as enduring as eternity. I am all-seeing and all-knowing and yet I am as ignorant as I am wise for I have touched a million, million fates, yet I passed through the temples of Baalbeck without leaving a single footprint. All my knowledge was but a whisper on the wind to Homer and a single teardrop to Sophocles.'

Tholocus paused and then clapped his hands together, 'But enough of philosophy, the Grand Council will unravel all the answers you need.'

Silence spread in widening ripples around the marble table broken only by the rub of the wind on the crystal windows of the tower and the murmuring beat of time that echoed throughout the city. The Diviner had finished speaking and this last word 'catastrophe' still hung in the air as he resumed his chair. One by one the Council members turned their heads towards Mya, their eyes following Tholocus' beckoning hand as he called her name and summoned her to stand and read aloud from the Doomsday report that she had compiled.

She blinked and felt the colour draining from her cheeks as she became aware that the eyes of the whole Council were upon her as they awaited her thesis. She pushed back her heavy chair and rose uncertainly to her feet, gathering up the crumpled manuscript in both hands. Public speaking and debate had always overawed her and she now felt too terrified to open her mouth. At the edge of her sight Harry moved, catching her attention, and he smiled and gave her an almost imperceptible wink of encouragement before nudging Denso who glanced up from his untidy sheaf of notes and quickly removed his glasses. He polished them slowly and pulled them back on as he realised that she was about to speak. 'Good luck, Mya,' he whispered, before burrowing back into his notebook.

She swallowed and tried to concentrate hard enough to bring the printed words on the page in front of her back into focus but a movement through a low stone archway on her right distracted her. She stuttered and looked up to see Orun and Kote crowding the doorway, watching and waiting for her to speak. The shafts of sunlight that streamed down through the high windows cast deep shadows across their vividly tattooed faces. Kote smiled at her, his eyes revealing such an intensity of feeling that Mya completely forgot what she was saying.

'Ca . . . ca . . . catastrophe,' she blurted out, searching for her place on the page and brushing at the stray strands of hair that had fallen across her forehead. She found a moment to think and saw the place where she should begin. Slowly she pushed away her embarrassment and began to force out to the brink of consciousness all her thoughts of the Journeyman or what the awaiting Grand Council would make of her work, then spoke in a clear, measured voice, unburdening all her thoughts on the prophecies that were pressed between the pages of her manuscript on environmental disaster.

She talked on, barely drawing breath. She told of the hordes of white hares, the ringing bells and plagues of mice. As she spoke the prevailing shadow of doom that had spread itself across the Earth became almost tangible, and as she reached the final page she paused and closed the manuscript, clutched it to her breast, and took a deep breath. Her eyes searched the serious silent faces for the verdict on her findings.

'And . . . and I think there's something wrong with the clocks on Earth,' she added quickly as Tholocus rose to his feet. 'I've noticed that in many of the local villages across the countryside the old church clocks have stopped working altogether.'

She fell silent abruptly and sat down heavily in her chair.

The Clockmaster stared thoughtfully at her, his azure eyes opaque with speculation. He interlaced his long thin fingers absently before he spoke. 'There are signs written large across the sky. Hundreds, no, thousands of them fore-tell of this disaster. Mya has warned us that in Paradise the shadow of catastrophe dwells. But . . .' he paused, spinning around and spreading his arms to encompass the whole of the Grand Council, his robes of silk fanning out behind him. 'But what is this disaster? What is this doom that the astrologer, Berossus, foretold 2,300 years ago would over-shadow Paradise? What is this catastrophe that Heraclitus the Greek illuminated and Nostradamus echoed when he walked the Earth?'

'There are clear indications of the nature of this disaster in their writings,' one of the Council members ventured, half rising from his chair and struggling to unroll an ancient scroll. 'They wrote that fire and flood will consume the land-scape and from the sky shall come a great King of terror.'

Another chair scraped back and a voice added heatedly, 'Yes, yes it is written, I remember the scroll: it said "their flesh shall consume away while they stand upon their feet and their eyes shall consume away in their holes".'

Voices had suddenly erupted all around the table.

'Paradise will burn!'

'Flood and famine will destroy the people!'

'Enough, enough! This is not a market-place where people haggle over the fate of Paradise!' Tholocus' voice rose in anger above the others and at a sharp clap of his hands the members of the Grand Council began to settle back into their chairs muttering and mumbling amongst themselves.

'How can you link Paradise with the earth we come from?' Harry asked in his Brooklyn drawl. The question made the Clockmaster spin around to face him.

A heavy silence enveloped the Council. Harry frowned. He had never expected his question to have such a startling effect. He glanced around the circle of faces and saw the Diviners' features freeze as his gaze passed over them. None of them would meet his eye.

'You have the advantage over us,' he continued slowly. 'I don't think Denso or I, or perhaps even Mya, really understand why we are here or what this talk of disaster is all about. One thing that has stuck out as clearly as the Statue of Liberty is that almost every one of your Council members has mentioned 'Paradise' and some of them have used the word 'Earth', but you can't be talking about the same place because where we come from 'Paradise' is a mythical place or somewhere that you end up after you are dead depending on your beliefs, but these guys have talked about it as if it were a reality.' Harry paused for breath and fiddled with his jacket buttons in the pressing silence. 'You see,' he added hesitantly, 'before the Waymaster burst into my office and dragged us here I would have called this whole thing crazy and if someone had told me about it I would have dismissed it as the ravings of a lunatic! But after our journey and the things we have already seen I would believe anything can exist. So tell me what connection there is between the Earth and Paradise? Where is this place that you are afraid is about to go up in a puff of smoke?'

Tholocus seemed clearly shaken for the first time since their arrival. He paced slowly around the outer circumference of the Council-table lost in thought, his lips moving silently as though he wrestled within himself for the words. He paused at each of the tall crystal windows and gazed out across the City of Time before returning to his place at the head of the Council. He rested his fragile hands upon the marble of the table and leant on them wearily before he spoke. 'Your world, this place you call Earth: that is Paradise.'

Denso's head snapped up at the Clockmaster's words as though somebody had tugged at strings on the back of his neck. His pencil slipped unnoticed through his fingers as he rose to his feet and sent his chair toppling over noisily behind him. 'Paradise?' he cried. 'You would call Earth a Paradise, a Garden of Eden? But that's ridiculous: it's little more than a cesspit of violence, famine and disease. Haven't you noticed the industrial pollution that is slowly choking it to death? You would do better to call it a living hell from the daily catalogue of murder, poverty and deprivation that goes on there. It's a million miles away from being anything like . . . like . . .' He threw his hands up in a helpless gesture and then bent down to retrieve his chair.

Tholocus' reference to Earth as Utopia hadn't come as quite the shock to Mya as it had to Denso. She had sensed throughout the grand debate that they were viewing Earth's reality very differently from Bendran, Thorn and all the others, but the way the Diviners flinched as Denso reached the height of his outburst disturbed her. The bewildered looks in the withereds' eyes as Denso fell silent set her mind racing: there were secrets here, deep secrets.

'Perhaps the Council would like to elaborate a little on this Paradise for us, for it doesn't ring true with all we have learned on Earth. And maybe they would also tell us why we are really here.'

Harry's voice cut the silence in half. He sat slightly back in his chair, the faintest smile picking at the corners of his mouth but his eyes were narrowed and glitter-hard as he held the Clockmaster's gaze. Tholocus frowned and at first shook his head as he stared back at Harry but gradually his shoulders sagged and he sighed.

'Yes, yes, perhaps we must lay bare the bones of the truth about Paradise before . . .'

'No, it would be madness!' Several voices interrupted from around the table and a cry of dismay erupted throughout the Council.

'Time would be destroyed!' one of the members gasped half-rising from his chair.

'The great clock in the sky will collapse if the truth is known. The zodiacal threat that we have woven so carefully through the universe will snap!' shouted a man who slammed his fist heavily down upon the table.

'Darkness will smother eternity. Claustrophobic silence will cover everything we have striven so tirelessly to keep in motion!' cried a frightened voice.

'We can't even guess at the repercussions if the truth were spoken!' wailed one of the Diviners, clutching his head in his hands. 'Remember our vows of silence!'

'Be silent, all of you!' Tholocus thundered, clapping his hands loudly twice before he was able to restore order to the High Tower. 'I am the Clockmaster, the divine head of this Council, and I am persuaded that the very perpetuation of our secret may be what threatens eternity. Those lies and half-truths that we in our wisdom used to seal up the walls of reality may be at the root of this impending catastrophe. And . . .' he added in a softer, more persuasive, voice, 'what we now divulge need go no further than the circumference of this tower. They could swear an oath of silence.'

'Oh yes, there must be a vote. The Council must have a voice before you embark on such recklessness,' a voice interrupted harshly.

Tholocus laughed and wearily nodded his head in agreement. 'You may vote until the last clock stops if you so desire but half the secret has been told already. I doubt if

Mya will need many moments to piece the rest together.'

He swept his hand out towards where she sat as if summoning her to rise or speak.

Mya rose to her feet, her mind reeling with thousands of images that the heated arguments of the Council had set loose. 'Earth is totally different. It is as though it has been kept apart from the other worlds we have journeyed through to get here. But I don't really understand . . .'

'There! I said that Mya would touch at the heart of this matter in no time at all!' Tholocus cried, cutting across her doubts before they revealed to the Council the shallowness of her understanding. He didn't want the vote of the Council to silence him. Deep down he had always sensed a flaw in creating a Paradise, a world apart, but the Grand Council of Diviners had overruled him long ago in the dawn of civilisation. Ever since that moment when they had sealed the walls of reality the fear that they had sown the seeds of some far-off but eventual catastrophe had gnawed away at him and he knew that many other members of the Council shared his worries. For tens of thousands of years it had troubled him enough to whisper his fears to the wind so that philosophers and prophets might riddle out the mystery as they trod the footsteps of their lives on Earth. They mirrored his fears as each one foretold that all life would be destroyed and all their calculations pointed to a distant future time and date that was now drawing closer by the hour.

'In the beginning there was fire and light,' Tholocus spoke quickly before a single voice could oppose him. 'Violent storms tore at the shadows. The wind roared and the rocks cracked. Earthquakes threw up mountains of boiling lava and sulphurous ashes rained down for millennia. It was an age of darkness when a bitter rain fell and the seas rose to drown the landscape, when the waters swallowed the molten rocks and the mists of time were formed. In the cooling silence civilisation was born – but not as you know it,' he added hastily. 'Mankind evolved in a thousand different guises. Some swam and lived beneath the sea while some could gallop on all fours or fly with the birds and beasts of the air.' Tholocus paused for breath but before he could continue pandemonium erupted. It was as though he had lifted the lid of a boiling cauldron and before he could speak again another member of the Council rose and cried out, wringing his hands.

'It was a violent and unpredictable time that defied the laws of logic and order that we, the Guardians of Eternity, had so laboriously compiled. There were those within the circle who sought perfection despite all argument and they insisted that there must be a world in harmony, one that did not defile Nature, and Paradise was created.'

'Your laws of Nature, your harmony, they were unnatural. You excluded the people who lived beneath the sea and the winged ones!' shouted the angry, red-faced figure who had spoken earlier of the unrest in the lands of Bendran.

'Not all the Council were for such an unnatural creation nor should any one of us forget that the debate to seal up the walls of reality raged on for more than ten thousand of their years.'

'The motion, however, was carried even though the Clockmaster voted against it!' shouted another grey-robed figure, rising angrily from his chair. 'And it is preposterous to think that such a tranquil place of beauty and perfect harmony could spread such a shadow of doom. I do not believe that this malady emanates from Paradise.'

'Enough!' Tholocus cried, crashing his fist so firmly down upon the table-top that the marble cracked, fracturing outward from where he stood, zig-zagging crazily in spidery-fine lines. Every member of the Council gasped and sat rock-still as he spoke.

'The dust of countless centuries lies heavily on our decision to create a separate Paradise and it is long beyond another word of debate, just as the repercussions that it caused to ripple throughout the universe are irreversible. This Council was summoned to seek a remedy to the shadow of doom that stretches over us, not to pick at old sores. Mya Capthorne the scientist and philosopher, Denso Alburton, the visionary and great thinker, and Harry the Guardian of the Wise, were brought here to share their knowledge of their world with us in the hope that it would help us to understand the nature of the disaster that I fear now threatens us all.'

Mya stared at the Clockmaster. The brief arguments that had raged across the huge marble table between the Diviners had momentarily left her bemused. The implications of what they had revealed were enormous, throwing everything she had ever believed in upside-down and turning every scientific theory of the universe, every thought of religion, of history on its head. Denso was the first to break the lengthening silence.

'Do you mean that Earth was once a part of all these places that we have just travelled through? Do you mean that it wasn't, no, isn't, the separate planet that we believe it to be? That it is not a part of the solar system revolving around the sun, that . . .?' he hesitated: there were too many terrifying questions crowding his mind. Lost for words, his mouth opened and closed soundlessly.

'What you are implying is crazy.' Harry leaned forward and spoke into a void. 'We have had spaceships leaving Earth's atmosphere: we have been exploring space for years and we have never seen any of these worlds. They have never shown up on the photographs that these satellites have taken.' Harry paused and scratched at his chin as though he doubted his own certainty. 'But on the other hand I have seen the Crystal Swamps and I have walked through the Windrows of Thorn and I know they are real even though they have never been seen on Earth before.' He shrugged. 'None of this is making any sense to me.'

Tholocus smiled and asked softly, 'What exactly is reality, Harry? Is it something you can only experience with the senses or can it exist in parallel to them?'

Harry frowned. 'I don't know, I'm no philosopher. I have never given it that much thought. I imagined the world I lived in was real enough, it covered all the angles I have ever worried about before.'

'What about God and evolution? What about the laws of physics and the splitting of the atom: what about relativity and astronomy?' Mya asked slowly.

Tholocus studied her bewilderment for a moment before he answered. 'Of course our revelations will shake the foundations of your beliefs. The development of your civilisation is a rich tapestry of experience and a profusion of gods and religions were seeded into it to mask the truth.'

'But the universe, the solar system, is it real or just an illusion?'

Tholocus sighed and spread his hands, his silken sleeves sweeping across the cracked surface of the table as he strove for the words to explain to her. 'The sun, the moon and the stars are real,' he began slowly. 'They are set there as a vast cosmic clock, a great revolving wheel of twelve constellations that fills the sky and measures out the rhythm for all forms of life. It completes its full circle every 25,920 years of time as you measure it. What you see, Mya, as you stand and look up into a dark, starlit sky at night is no illusion: it is the very ticking of time.

'Your world, the place you call Earth, was shrouded,

hidden in a vale of secrets and nurtured and fostered above all the other realities that we watch over. It became a haven in which civilisation could grow and flourish. But it took many thousands of years before our work was completed: too long, we fear, to create and seal up the walls of reality, and during that time of flux peoples and creatures trespassed across the boundaries. Wandering giants and dragma roamed your earth, bouglin and wrathwa beasts flocked in your skies striking terror wherever they shadowed the sun. These creatures almost became a part of your world but we wanted no place for them and we denied them their existence. The dragons were slain, the giants banished, until only their bare bones were left in your myths and legends and with the spread of time and our carefully planted untruths they became no more than the fabric of fantasy and fairy tales.'

'Of course!' Mya suddenly cried. 'These other worlds or realities have been staring me in the face all the time. Images and descriptions of them fill those ancient manuscripts. The mermaids and sea monsters, the centaurs and unicorns, they weren't just figments of their imaginations, they were peoples and creatures that actually existed!'

Tholocus nodded gravely. 'Yes, they were as real as the two Waymasters and the dragma that brought you here.'

'So everything from folklore, all the myths and legends, they really did happen?' Denso asked. 'Are they as much a part of history as the building of the pyramids and the plagues that swept across Europe in the Middle Ages?'

'Yes.' The Clockmaster frowned, glancing darkly at the huddle of Diviners on the far side of the table. Denso had accidentally touched a raw nerve in the Council. 'And many catastrophes that have blackened your history need never have happened if the walls of reality had been more stable and had not torn or fractured. Wars need not have started nor diseases like the bubonic plague spread unchecked. The plague was caused by rats from Yakk who brought it with them when they swarmed through the Doorcracks that suddenly broke apart in your twelfth century.'

'These Doorcracks or tears – can we accidentally pass through them even if we don't know where they are? Even if we have no-one to guide us?' Harry asked suddenly. 'I'm thinking about the Bermuda Triangle and such places. It would explain away a lot of strange disappearances.'

'Yes, yes, of course. The walls of reality are very unpredictable, anything is possible,' Tholocus answered, an air of impatience creeping into his voice.

He had opened the floodgates of curiosity and now he feared a tide of questions would overwhelm him. He glanced anxiously around the circle of Diviners but they sat still and impassive, waiting for him to finish. The darkening shadows of evening lengthened across their faces. He lifted his right hand towards the rising tiers of books and scrolls that lined the tower. 'All you seek to know is stored here, but now I must press you to return your minds to the impending doom that stretches out to engulf us all.'

'One last question, please,' Mya called before the Clockmaster could start again.

'Why are the Journeymen who brought us here and the peoples of these other realities illiterate when you have such a fountainhead of knowledge stored in the City of Time?'

Tholocus took a deep breath and Mya could see by the thunderous glare in his eyes that her question had angered him. 'This city grew up out of the need to record and watch over the world we had created. In the beginning there was only the central tower where we dwell. It was in a vale of trees and soft meadows, a place of peace and eternal silence, not the vast sprawl of buildings that now fills the landscape with the hum of time. Because the people from your civilisation grew and flourished so the Halls of Hours were built to store the windsprings of each individual life. Gradually the outer ring of slender spires were also erected to accommodate the wealth of wisdom and in our haste ignorance seemed the safest way to keep the knowledge of Paradise a secret. Only a handful of learned men in each world was allowed the gift of literacy.' The Clockmaster paused, the frown that lined his forehead deepening as an ancient withered slowly rose from his chair and began to speak in a crackling dry voice.

'Jothnar, the Asiri, Lord Mauder of Bendran, searches for Paradise. He came secretly upon our reading chamber in the Citadel of Krak and made us his prisoners. He tortured us into teaching him to understand the symbols that belonged to the illustrations of the men with wings. We were lucky to escape with our lives.'

The whole Council let out a cry of dismay. Grey-robed figures rose, gripping the table in their anguish, their chairs crashing and toppling behind them.

'You fools! It would have been better if you had died dumb rather than reveal the knowledge that was entrusted to your safe-keeping!' Tholocus cursed, advancing toward the cowering withereds. He stabbed a quivering, accusing finger at them.

'But the knowledge he stole is of little use to him. It is only dead words and a picture of a place that has vanished into obscurity long ago. And much as we were forced by torture to divulge it, some good has come of our teaching. The Asiri no longer murders for pleasure, nor does he ransack and plunder his people to swell his power. His pursuit of a way to Paradise has brought a measure of peace to the lands of Bendran.'

The Clockmaster towered over them, his fist clenched, his face white with anger. 'It is the hunger that scrap of knowledge has created that is the danger!' He paused, almost incoherent with rage.

'The Asiri's Mauders have been trying to snare a Journeyman in the lands of Bendran for an age of days but there are none quick enough to catch us,' Kote cried, taking a step into the chamber from the dark stone archway where he and Orun sheltered, only to hesitate and then hastily withdraw.

'No, no, enter, come both of you,' Tholocus called, beckoning Orun and Kote through the archway. 'The time of secrets is drawing to a close. Forewarned is forearmed.'

'I don't get it,' Denso frowned. 'Where we come from knowledge is considered a basic requirement. Why is it so awful for the Asiri to know about us?'

'You have seen and almost been trampled by the might of the company of Mauders: surely you would fear them overrunning your world?' Orun ventured.

Harry laughed, 'Is that all you're worried about? Jesus, you don't know much about how we have advanced. If this library really contains everything we have ever achieved you haven't grasped modern technology. Those galloping dragons and riders wouldn't last five minutes against a battalion of Sherman tanks or a squadron of Tornadoes.'

The pandemonium and panic that had swept around the table at the withered's revelation stopped abruptly. Heads turned and eyebrows arched in speculation as Harry finished. Chairs were righted hastily and one by one the Diviners and the elders resumed their places with a whisper of excited anticipation sighing through them, which melted away to a breathless quiet as Tholocus raised his hand for silence.

'We, the Council, are forbidden to dwell or set foot upon your Earth. We are not allowed to meddle in its affairs: that was the price and forfeit we had to endure for creating

Paradise. We are cursed never to see the triumphs of our labours.'

Tholocus' voice faltered and Mya had the distinct impression that something, some noise from beyond the chamber, had distracted him. For a moment she wondered if he feared a greater power was eavesdropping, but his distraction deepened. A frown of anxiety wrinkled his forehead as he turned his gaze towards the tall crystal windows. He pushed his chair back and took two hesitating strides forward, fingers clutching at the throat of his gown. Suddenly a huge winged shape enveloped in smoke and fire soared past the tall windows and spiralled down to land. The members of the Council leapt to their feet in disarray.

'A wrathwa beast has violated the sanctity of the City of Time!'

Mya could see Orun and Kote tensed, their heads tilted to one side as if straining to catch at some far-off sound.

'Dragmas!' Kote hissed. 'There is the sound of dragmas on the high ground above the city, hurrying towards us.'

Tholocus turned sharply towards the Journeyman. 'Did anyone follow you here?'

'No, master, we were most careful!' Orun cried. 'The Mauders pressed us deep into the Windrows of Thorn but Kote's dragma, Lugg, lured them away into the sand-mists of Chehung. No-one witnessed our passing through the Verge of Drasatt.'

Mya had half-risen, listening intently while Orun spoke, waiting for the sound they all feared, beyond the rub of the wind against the tower and the persistent, mumbling rhythm of time that hummed throughout the city. A roaring thunder shook the tower: books and scrolls began to tumble from the collapsing shelves. One by one the tall crystal windows shattered, followed by the crash of splintering wood and a rush of cruel shouts around the base of the tower.

'Go, Journeyman!' Tholocus shouted as panic seized him. 'Go, Waymaster, and defend the doors against whoever has violated our sanctity!' The Clockmaster strode back to the table in a frenzy, fear etched across his face. He spoke with urgency directly to Mya, Denso and Harry. 'There is still so much to unravel, centuries of warnings and prophecies that point as straight as an arrow to the destruction of Paradise, but I fear we are too late to seek a remedy or avert the catastrophe. You must escape. You must return to Earth and use whatever time is left to prepare against this disaster. We must erase all evidence of Paradise!' He stared wildly around the circumference of the tower at the tiers of books, scrolls and tablets of stone. His gaze soared up, up into the shadowy darkness of the rafters and he opened his mouth to shout commands at the Diviners.

'No! It would be a monumental crime to destroy them!' cried Mya, leaping to her feet.

'We must! We must!' Tholocus replied as the thunder of armoured boots drew closer to the door. He raked his fingers through his hair in desperation. 'Only the members of this Council, the withereds, elders and a handful of the most trustworthy Waymasters and Journeymen know of this city. Our only defence has been secrecy: there are no guards or armies to defend us. Now that we are being invaded we must destroy all trace of Paradise. They must never know of it!' He slapped his hand against his forehead, 'Of course! That is what all these prophecies were pointing toward. They were forewarning us to erase the knowledge of its existence. Only then could it go on forever, hidden by the walls of reality!'

'No, that is madness!'

Mya shouted out, trying to make herself heard against the pandemonium in the chamber and the clatter of armoured boots and wild cries rising from the stone spiral staircase that led up into the tower. Something Harry had said about Earth's technology a few moments ago had set her thoughts racing.

'Wait!' she cried as Tholocus began to crackle sparks between his fingertips in preparation to light the tinder dry manuscripts on the lowest shelves. 'Perhaps all of those predictions of catastrophe that I collected in our world were echoes of those ancient prophecies: highlighting the fact that you wouldn't be able to keep your paradise a secret forever: that at one disastrous moment in time it would come to an abrupt end.'

Tholocus and the whole Council froze as the awful implications that lay within her words engulfed them. She had cut straight through to the heart of the matter and exposed the seed of their own destruction, the canker of the catastrophe. They had fashioned it themselves as they wove the walls of reality. They had done it with their own hands. The door of the chamber shook and burst open, its hinges splintering as a dozen Mauders dressed in the armour of the Asiri swarmed into the chamber. They dragged Orun and Kote bound helplessly in thick iron chains between them.

A dark shadow filled the shattered window and shrouded the evening sunlight. A roaring scream shook the slender tower and clouds of steam and sulphurous fire scorched the outer walls. Mya spun round and looked up through the window to see a hideous wrathwa beast hovering and beating the air into a gale of stinking fumes beneath its leathery wings as it gradually settled in wreaths of smoke and flames on the ground before the door-arch of the tower. A tall, angular figure in armour of hammered gold alighted from a black saddle high upon the beast's back and threw the reins of linked iron to a waiting warrior before striding toward the doorway.

' "From the sky shall come a great King of terror". The

prophecies are already coming true: look, it is Jothnar, the Asiri of Krak, and he has tamed a wrathwa!' cried one of the withereds and all the elders who had managed to escape from the citadel fled to the furthest corner of the chamber and cast their hands over their heads as their voices rose in a wail of terror and his armoured footsteps echoed on the stairwell.

As he strode into the chamber, he seemed to fill it with raw power, the light reflecting from the thousands of engraved pictures on his armour telling the story of his conquests. He stopped, a triumphant smile thinning his lips, and let his eyes sweep over the countless rising shelves of books. He saw Tholocus crouching, a flame flickering between his fingers beside a shelf of manuscripts; he saw the grey-robed diviners; and a cowering huddle of withereds on the far side of the room; but what held his gaze were the three strangers whom his Mauders had followed into the Windrows of Thorn. He took a menacing step toward Harry and raised his clenched fist. 'You shall give me the road to Paradise!'

Harry stumbled backward, putting the table between himself and the Asiri. 'No, no, you shall have nothing,' he stuttered. 'I . . . I can't give you anything.'

The terror in Harry's voice broke the trance that had bound Tholocus. 'You shall have nothing! You have violated the sanctity of the City of Time!' he cried, thrusting his flaming fingers toward the piles of manuscripts but Jothnar spun round, crossed the chamber in three giant strides and grasped the Clockmaster's fragile fingers in his armoured fist. A sneer of pleasure pin-pointed the pupils of his eyes as he crushed out the flame and heard the brittle bones begin to crack.

'No-one dares defy the Asiri,' he hissed, but a spark escaped from Tholocus' index finger and fell amongst the pages at his feet. It spread hungrily, burrowing into and blackening the parchment, leaping up in sheets of orange flame to crack the stone tables and melt the heavy gold and silver bindings on the books. The sudden roar of flames and billowing choking smoke swallowed the outer walls of the tower and rows of burning books came crashing down. Scrolls unwound in ribbons of fire and threw the chamber into chaos.

Jothnar screamed with rage and rent and tore at the bindings of his armour as the metal heated and scorched his skin. His Mauders fought one another to escape from the burning chamber. Thick smoke began to fill the room. Mya scrambled backward and collided with Harry and Denso in the smoke as they looked desperately for a way to escape the fires that were now encircling the chamber.

'We're trapped!' she shouted in anguish.

'Follow! Follow!'

Mya felt a pluck at her sleeve and glimpsed Tholocus through the smoke, beckoning them urgently to follow him. Figures bumped, barged and pushed against them as the Clockmaster led them toward the solid wall of flame on the right-hand side of the chamber furthest away from the spiral stairway and the way out. Mya hesitated, choking as she inhaled the smoke.

'There is another stairway!' Tholocus shouted against the roar of flames.

'Kote – Orun, you can't leave them behind . . .' she cried as a wall of flame seemed to rear up and Tholocus pushed them forcefully through it.

Mya screwed her eyes tightly shut, covering her head with her hands as she stumbled through the searing flames. She heard her hair crackle and felt the heat blister her skin. She blinked and opened her eyes. Ahead of her there was an arched doorway and hands were reaching out to grasp at her arms. They pulled her forward down a dark stairwell. She had to fight down the rising panic and the will to scream. It was pitch-black and the air stank of scorched flesh and hair and the reek of burned cloth. She was being jostled and carried helplessly forward by a crush of unseen bodies. The surge of the crowd bumped her against a rough stone wall on her left and she tried to reach out and touch it when she missed her footing and stumbled heavily against the figure in front of her.

'Take care,' one of the diviners hissed close to her right elbow. 'We are descending the Windsmith's Stair.'

She felt him grip her arm and steady her as she felt cautiously for the next worn step. Gradually her eyes grew accustomed to the darkness and she could make out the vague shapes of moving heads ahead of her and the walls of the narrow arched stairway. She could easily have reached out with both hands and brushed her fingertips on the rough stonework if it had not been for the press of people hurrying her forward. She realised, as she almost lost her balance on the uneven stairs, that the steps must have been hollowed out of the wall of the tower as an escape route thousands of years ago.

They could not have descended more than twenty of the uneven steps when from somewhere above she heard Harry curse as he lost his footing. Tensely Denso called out her name in the darkness and begged to know if she was safe.

'Yes, don't worry, I'm down here ahead of you,' she answered, coughing as she drew in the acrid smoky air.

'But where is the Clockmaster? One moment he was pushing me through the flames and the next he was gone. Did he escape? And what about . . .?' She gasped and gave a startled cry, twisting her head to look upward across the sea of moving heads and shoulders and heard the sound of splintering timber. She saw a dozen doors that opened into the outer stairway burst open, riven from their hinges. Bright orange tongues of flame licked at the low vaulted roof and illuminated the stairwell, throwing hideous shadows from the armoured figures that now swarmed after them through the broken doors. Jothnar was the first to breach the stairhead, his screams and snarls of rage piercing and loud enough to splinter stone as he leapt down the steps. His armour reflected the flickering flames, smoke and the stench of scorched flesh issued through every one of his joints and seams as he raised a double-headed mace and swept it in a blazing arc of sparks at the fleeing crowd. He had torn off his helmet to reveal the hideously peeling and burned and blackened skin on his face. He was shouting now, hurling venom at the fleeing diviners. 'I am the Asiri. Fire cannot harm me. You will not escape. I shall have the road to Paradise if I have to strangle it out of every one of you!' He shouted, bringing the blazing mace down to strike the Diviner almost directly behind Harry.

The man fell, his skull crushed to pulp, and he landed on the uneven stone steps, pushed and trampled by the sudden surge of panic that filled the stairway.

Tholocus' voice echoed around them. 'The Asiri must not capture Mya Capthorne or Denso Alburton, nor must they take the Guardian, Murmers. Quickly, let them pass by and escape.'

Strong hands suddenly grasped at Mya's arms and waist and despite her violent struggles and cries of protest she was raised above the jostling throng until she almost brushed against the vaulted ceiling. Then she was passed forward, hand over hand, over the heads of the crowd. Mya twisted her head and looked back and saw Harry and Denso being lifted as she had been and shuffled forward. Beyond the curve of the stairs she heard the Asiri bellow with rage and redouble the ferocity of his attack.

'Quickly, quickly, there isn't a moment to lose.'

She heard Tholocus urging his Diviners from just ahead of her. She turned her head back and saw him gesticulating with his arms outstretched to someone in a narrow doorway before he turned and waited to lift her down and hurry her through.

'Quickly, follow me, we must hide. Give me your coat. The Diviners and the Journeymen will lay a false trail to lure the Asiri away.'

'Kote, Orun, you're safe!' Mya cried as she regained her feet. She ran toward the doorway where the two men were crouching on the threshold, rubbing at the raw weals on their wrists from where the Mauders had bound them in iron chains.

'The Clockmaster rescued us,' Kote muttered quickly.

'Beware the wrathwa. Keep to the shadow of the tower and follow me to the closest of the Halls of Hours. You will find shelter amongst the clocks,' Tholocus urged as he broke in between them and the Journeymen.

'But we will disturb the rhythm of time!' Mya cried.

'There is no other choice,' Tholocus commanded grimly.

The crowd upon the stairway surged frantically forward and they could clearly hear Jothnar's voice cursing and screaming for their blood.

'All of you, follow me.'

He moved soundlessly around the base of the tower using the thickening pall of smoke to hide them as it billowed out of every door and window and slipped past the waiting wrathwa beast and into the thin shadows that stretched away to touch the nearest of the vast buildings. Harry and Denso, with Orun close on their heels, followed the others through the doorway and began to skirt the base of the tower and head toward the Halls of Hours. Behind them, the clamour of pursuit sounded loudly in the entrance. The remnants of the Council, those who had escaped death on the stairway, were fleeing, scattering in every direction to draw the Mauders off their scent.

'This smoke makes it difficult to see which of the halls Tholocus is leading us to,' Denso whispered, slowing and peering through the drifting smoke.

Orun hissed him into silence. Something moved away to their left, they could see it through the haze of smoke. There was a roaring snarl and a sudden clatter of leathery armoured scales. Then the reek of sulphurous death and corruption drifted over them. Denso stumbled to a halt and stared up at the towering bulk of the wrathwa that was moving toward them through the haze. Its black leathery wings were lazily opening and closing, stirring the drifting smoke into dancing whirlpools of shadow. Its monstrous reptilian head began to turn slowly toward them as it hunted for the sound of their whispering voices and scoured the ground with its hot unblinking eyes.

Harry was staring up so intently at the creature that he almost collided with Denso and fell away from the shelter of the tower in an effort to avoid him. 'Damn!' he cursed, regretting it the moment he heard himself speak.

He scrambled backward, searching for cover, but it was too late, the beast had seen him. It opened its cavernous mouth and bellowed, sending clouds of scalding steam down upon them as it advanced with giant strides. The Mauder holding its iron-linked reins was pulled wildly off-balance. He cursed and fought to keep the wrathwa still in the place where Jothnar had commanded him to wait. At that very moment the Asiri's voice cut through the shouts of the fleeing Diviners and rose above the wrathwa's snarls as he emerged from the tower and caught sight of Harry just as the boiling clouds of steam enveloped him. Orun grabbed at Harry's collar, dragged him roughly from beneath the wrathwa's huge armoured claws, set him on his feet and pushed him with Denso toward the brightly-lit entrance of the closest Hall of Hours.

'Run, run for your lives!' he cried, springing after them.

Denso fled, his head flung backwards, his mouth gulping lungfuls of air. His hands were clenched into white-knuckled fists of terror and his feet pounded the ground. Harry overtook him in three strides, head down, arms pumping as fast as steam hammers as he raced towards the lighted entrance. Tholocus appeared in the huge doorway urging them on. The sound of the clocks that noisily numbered the millions of lifetimes within the hall grew louder and louder as they drew closer, but always a step behind them and relentlessly gaining was the clanking scrape of the Asiri's armour and the roaring fetid breath of the wrathwa scorching their heels.

Tholocus snatched at Harry's arm as he leapt up the last stone step of the brilliantly-lit portico and propelled him into the narrow central aisle between the soaring, swaying walls of cloaks.

'Keep going until you meet Mya and Kote!' he shouted, his voice straining against the continual throb and echo of time.

Denso was only a pace behind him, gasping and staggering. The raw terror of Jothnar's armoured fingers clawing at his back and the huge wrathwa's feet threatening to crush his bones to powder made him throw himself across the threshold and sprint after Harry and he quickly vanished into the bowels of the cavernous building. Behind him he heard Orun scream, afraid to enter the building, and a great shout of triumph rent the air. He heard Tholocus' voice rise against Jothnar's as he urged the Waymaster to cross the threshold. Denso stopped and turned as Harry, Mya and

Kote cautiously retraced their steps until they could see the entrance.

Orun crouched on the broad top step looking desperately to left and right for another way of escape. He would not enter the Hall of Hours despite their urgings. The Asiri was immediately behind him, his armoured hands reaching out for Orun's neck. Fire and steam from the wrathwa's jaws boiled across the entrance, cracking the stone and blackening the columns as it singed the Waymaster's orange hair.

'No, I dare not enter. I cannot look upon the faces of mortality!' he shrieked as Tholocus risked the wrathwa's breath and ran out to grasp his wrists and try to drag him in across the threshold.

Jothnar purposefully crossed the last footsteps that divided them. His burnt cheeks were hideously disfigured and victory lit his murderous eyes as he closed his armoured fingers around Orun's throat. 'Now I shall have the road to Paradise and everything I desire.'

He began to pull and drag the Waymaster away from the Hall of Hours, making the Clockmaster stagger and lose his fragile grip. Orun fought to break free, his arms flailing as he tore at the vice-tight grip on his throat.

'Be still,' Jothnar snarled, raising his free hand and bringing it down with vicious force on the back of Orun's head.

The Waymaster gasped, his eyes bulged momentarily, his backbone arched and his vivid, tattooed cheeks blackened as the fist crushed the back of his skull and he slumped forward limply. Jothnar paused to release his murderous grip on the Waymaster's throat and let him slip through his fingers to slump to the ground between his feet.

'None of you will escape!' he snarled, stepping over the unconscious body and reaching out an armoured hand to snatch at Tholocus' wrist.

But his hand snapped shut on empty air. The wrathwa

roared and sent out a cloud of sulphurous fire and steam and a blaze of hot sparks crackled between Jothnar's fingers as they met. He cursed as the elusive figure, who had twice now dared to thwart him, melted away at his touch only to reappear further back upon the portico, silhouetted in the lighted doorway of the vast echoing hall.

'I will kill you all,' Jothnar hissed as he unsheathed a scimitar that hung from his belt and strode forward.

'You cannot enter the Halls of Hours. I, Tholocus, Clockmaster of Eternity, forbid it.' Tholocus stood defiantly, arms raised to block the way.

'You'll never stop him, he'll kill you!' Mya cried.

Jothnar heard her and a blistered sneer split his face. 'No-one can stop me. I am the Asiri, I take what I desire.'

He brought the curved blade down with a brutal scything stroke to decapitate the Clockmaster but as the blade touched his skin it shattered into a blinding rain of sparkling splinters leaving Tholocus completely unharmed. The hilt of the scimitar glowed white hot and forged itself into Jothnar's clenched fist. The Asiri screamed and staggered backward, falling to his knees and clawing desperately at the gauntlet with his other hand until he managed to tear it off. Tears of uncontrollable rage streaked his blackened cheeks and his teeth ground together as he climbed back to his feet and again advanced towards the doorway.

'You must not enter. You cannot conceive of the harm you will do to the rhythm of time!' Tholocus cried again even more urgently from where he had retreated a dozen paces inside the hall.

'Time?' Jothnar sneered, letting his narrowing gaze sweep over the swaying, towering aisles of the millions of clocks and timepieces that were piled and stacked one on top of the other until they vanished into the gloom amongst the rafters or diminished away in receding rows and alleyways into the heart of the building. 'This place has nothing to do with time,' he laughed harshly, 'The sun and the moon, daylight and darkness, the changing seasons – they are time, not this echoing chamber of noise, this vault of trinkets!' He took a huge stride over the threshold into the hall.

'You tamper with things you know nothing of. I order you to keep out!' Tholocus shouted as the tiers of clocks that flanked the doorway began to tremble and sway more violently.

The rhythm of time suddenly changed. It grew in volume, becoming frantic and uneven. Lenses began to crack and shatter, hands began to melt and wither and clock-faces began to fracture. A single clock crashed to the ground, its complex springs and cogs exploding into fragments. Another, then another crashed down beside it at the Asiri's feet. In moments whole tiers were collapsing in a roaring crash of splintering glass, wood and metal as hundreds and then thousands of clocks cascaded down to fill the narrow alleyways close to the entrance.

Jothnar cried out and stumbled as the deluge struck and rebounded off his armour. He threw himself out of the hall over the threshold. Bruised and visibly shaken he crouched on the portico, hands over his ears, as the roar of destruction reached a crescendo. The strings of lamps that lit the first part of the vast hall began to flicker and one by one they went out.

He rose to his feet as the rhythm of time resumed and shook his fists at the darkening entrance, shouting, 'You won't escape from me by blocking the entrance with a magic avalanche of broken trinkets! I'll order my wrathwa to trample this and every other hovel within your city into ruins. I'll order him to breathe fire over the broken stones and roast you alive . . .'

To prove his words Jothnar turned, raised his scorched

hand and shouted to the creature, summoning it forward in its wreaths of boiling steam and fire.

'We've got to get out of here fast before we're crushed to death!' Denso cried, retreating along the narrow, swaying alleyway and seeking desperately for a way to escape.

'There must be a door or something at the back. But hadn't we better wait for the Clockmaster?' Mya answered quietly. She was huddled close to Kote who crouched trembling with terror, his head buried in his hands. It had taken every ounce of his courage to venture through the doorway.

'Stay still and completely silent, all of you. Do not disrupt the rhythm of time.' Tholocus' voice came to them, a whisper out of the mountainous ruins that blocked the darkened entrance. He gathered up the hems of his robes, scrambled up and over the mounds of broken clocks and burst out on to the portico. 'No!' he cried out. 'Whatever destruction your anger causes here it will bring untold devastation to the Paradise that you seek.'

The urgency in Tholocus' voice made Jothnar hesitate and spin round, shocked to find the Clockmaster standing close to his elbow.

'So there is truth in what I seek. Paradise really does exist?' he asked.

Tholocus stared at him then nodded reluctantly and although Jothnar's eyes narrowed into suspicious slits slowly he lowered his beckoning hand and the wrathwa sunk back to its haunches in clouds of hissing steam.

'Now tell me, what does this vast hall of hidden echoes have to do with the place that I seek to find?' he demanded.

Tholocus lifted his frail hand and gestured back to the piles of ruined clocks, springs, cogs and wheels that had spilled out through the doorway behind him. 'By invading this City of Time, by trespassing into this Hall of Hours, you have disrupted the rhythm of thousands, perhaps millions, of lives on Earth. Your careless actions have brought about their deaths. Those clocks, or trinkets as you called them in your ignorance, those timepieces that your presence in this hall caused to shatter and come tumbling down were the windsprings for the people who dwell in Paradise. They measured the years, days, hours and minutes of their lives. But now they lie in ruins, prematurely destroyed, and who knows what mayhem, what disasters you have caused to sweep across the surface of the Paradise you seek. What plagues or floods, what famines or earthquakes now stain its tranquillity?'

Jothnar stared past the Clockmaster in awe at the mass of broken mechanisms that spilled out of the doorway. He stirred the closest with the toe of his armoured boot and watched closely as the bright metal cogs rolled away from him. He hadn't understood the implications of the Clockmaster's words, nor did he care. Paradise, or Earth as the withered old man had called it, really did exist and he knew that here within this secret city he would find the knowledge of the road that would lead him to it. He kicked out savagely at the broken springs and clock faces, revelling in the power over life and death he had unwittingly discovered by trespassing within this vast building. Laughing softly, he turned and with an echoing shout summoned his Mauders to bring the captured Diviners and withereds so that they could bear witness to his final triumph.

As he turned back, a sneer of triumph lit his eyes. He could never have imagined that when he glimpsed those two travellers crossing the Crystal Swamps or followed the riderless dragma to the gates of this city that they would lead him so easily to what he had sought for so long.

'I am the Asiri, the Lord Mauder of Bendran and all the lands that touch each horizon. I hold the power of life and death over all my peoples and others. Now give me the knowledge of the road to Paradise.'

'No, I cannot. There are no clear ways through the walls of reality. Earth is a secret place, a world set apart from all others. Give up this passion of yours before you cause untold damage. Go before . . .'

'Silence, fool! I know that millions may die so that I may achieve what I desire. That is the price of conquest!' Jothnar screamed in rage, froths of white spittle clogging the corners of his mouth.

'I would rather die than reveal anything to you,' Tholocus answered defiantly.

'You will deny me nothing,' the Asiri hissed, taking a threatening step toward the Clockmaster. But as he reached out to strike him he remembered how easily the frail, withered figure had evaded him before and hesitated. Then he stabbed a quivering finger back to where the wrathwa crouched on its haunches breathing sulphurous clouds of smoke and steam. 'No-one in all your legends or tales of long ago has ever dared to harness such a savage beast of fire and tame its wildness, yet I name it Graksha and ride upon its back. I, the Asiri, the greatest to have lived, have done this to aid my search amongst the clouds. But I grow impatient: such feats of bravery are not enough. I hunger to conquer this land where men have wings fashioned from feathers of eagles and soar above an azure sea. Tell me of the road now or I will summon Graksha and he will pour smoke and fire through this doorway.'

'I speak the truth,' Tholocus cried, his determination turning to anguish as the great beast began to rise and climb the broad stone steps. The Asiri was so blindly obsessed that he cared nothing for the destruction he would cause.

'Bring out those travellers you are hiding within the hall!'

239

Jothnar snapped suddenly, 'They must know of the way. They must know better than anyone else. Bring them to me before Graksha burns them to cinders.'

'They know nothing. There are no clear roads, you must believe me!' Tholocus cried in vain as the shadow of the monstrous wrathwa spread across him. 'The walls of reality were sealed up thousands of years ago. But there have always been cracks and tears within their fabric. Dark, dangerous, unpredictable Doorcracks that may open up or fold shut at any moment.' Tholocus sucked in a shallow breath and carried on recklessly in an effort to halt the advancing wrathwa and extinguish the plume of flames that were issuing from its cavernous mouth.

'Doorcracks! Dark dangerous roads that few would dare to travel?' Jothnar hissed, glancing down at the Waymaster's body, his eyes narrowing to cunning, calculating slits. He stilled his beast with a shout and for a single moment held the Clockmaster's gaze.

'There is a clear path to follow. Paradise will be mine!' he laughed, the gloating words splitting the moment's silence. He stepped back over Orun's unconscious body, reached down and hooked the fingers of his gloved hand into his collar. With his other hand he tore open the Waymaster's jerkin and began to study the mass of tattoos that covered his chest and arms. Frowning and muttering he turned him over and held him up by a handful of orange hair. Suddenly he gave a cry of triumph and hurled the limp body high into the air. He turned to give the Clockmaster one last threatening gesture as the old man tried to rescue his faithful servant and then he shouted to the gathering of Mauders who stood on the steps below him. 'Drive the Clockmaster and his friends back into the hall, make sure none escape and then erect a skinning frame on this portico.'

'What the hell is going on out there?' Denso asked as

Tholocus climbed back over the pile of clocks wringing his hands in anguish and hurried back into the hall.

'The Asiri has realised that Orun's journey-lines must lead him to a Doorcrack.' And he walked back into the hall with his head bowed.

Almost immediately they could all hear the rattle of hammers and the rasp of bow-saws. Kote looked up from where he crouched in the shadows next to Mya. His face was deadly pale beneath its covering of tattooes and his lips trembled as he spoke.

'The Asiri has commanded his Mauders to skin Orun alive. It is the only way he can preserve the journey-lines that are tattooed on to his skin.'

'Jesus, that's barbaric! We have to do something!' Harry cried.

'Oh, my God, we have to try to save him,' Mya gasped, jumping to her feet as she felt the bile rising in her throat.

'It is impossible. The Mauders have already encircled this building. We will never get out of here or even get close enough to cut his throat,' Kote answered, shaking his head in despair.

'Good God, you call slitting his throat helping him? You're no better than those barbarians out there!' Denso cried in horror. The thought of what Kote was suggesting made him forget the headache that had been eating away at the inside of his skull ever since they had plunged through the Doorcrack above the Crystal Swamps. It also made him forget to keep his voice to a whisper.

'Quiet! Your voices will disturb the rhythm of time.' Tholocus hissed as he turned sharply towards Denso.

'Real life and death, the values and morals of existence, are totally different here. To slit Orun's throat would give him a high, noble traveller's death. It would also deny the

Asiri all knowledge of the journey-lines tattooed upon his body.'

'Do you mean that those monsters will literally skin him alive?' Mya stuttered, shuddering in revulsion and gripping tightly to Kote's arm.

'Oh yes, they must,' Tholocus answered in a hushed whisper. 'They must remove the skin carefully to ensure that the thousands of veins that feed it are unharmed. They will tease and stretch the veins without breaking them leaving the skin joined to his body only where the jugular runs closest to the surface in his neck. The skin will then be stretched out beside him upon the frame and oiled constantly with essences of myrrh and sap from the blackthorn tree, thus rendering it transparent and heightening the colours of the journey-lines that live within it. But . . .' Tholocus paused and glanced anxiously at the mounds of ruined mechanisms that clogged the doorway. Beyond it he caught the sound of the scrape and crunch of the Mauders' armoured boots and their shouts as they worked upon the skinning frame that they were building on the portico. He drew the others closer to him with a whisper. 'But to sever the flow of a Waymaster's life blood will make his skin wither and die and the tattooes will fade away to nothing. You see, these travellers that I sent out to search for a way through the walls of reality and bring you all here to the Grand Council are not ordinary mortals. They are wayfarers who spring from an ancient lineage that keeps alive the knowledge of thousands of far-flung places. They have the arts of elusiveness, stealth and speed and their skins are enchanted, their blood enriched, to record in vivid detail living illustrations of every journey they undertake. Only in a violent and bloody death are those memories erased forever. The Asiri must keep Orun alive for his skin is the only map of the road through the walls of reality that exists apart from the one Kote carries tattooed upon his body.'

'But why must they skin him? Why can't the Asiri just tie him onto the frame? Why do they need to do anything so horrible and brutal?' Mya cried, clutching even tighter to Kote's arm.

Tholocus hunched his shoulders, brushed his hand through his head of flowing, white hair and crouched even closer to them so that they could hear the dry breath rattling in his ancient chest. 'What you can see tattooed upon the outer surface of the Waymaster's skin is only one view of the journeys that he has undertaken. Once stretched and oiled into a transparent membrane those journey-lines become a three-dimensional map, revealing every landmark the traveller has glimpsed as he passed upon his journey.'

'We've got to do something, and quickly,' Harry muttered, frowning and turning his head toward the entrance as he realised that the hammering and sawing outside had stopped. Now nothing broke the silence but the persistent rhythm of time. 'But what can we do? he added, pressing his hands against his temples. 'I suppose rushing those Mauders is out of the question?' he muttered.

'Impossible. They are trained warriors.'

'If Kote can become almost invisible like Orun did in New York why can't he slip between the Mauders and use that dagger that hangs from his belt?' Denso asked.

'Oh no,' hissed Mya in alarm. The words were out of her mouth almost before she realised it.

'No, I forbid it!' Tholocus hissed, gripping Kote's dagger- hand firmly. 'He would see you the moment you leave the shadow of the doorway. If the Asiri catches you he will have the only other journey-line that can lead him to the walls of reality. No, it would be madness to risk such a venture.'

A scream of agony tore through the rhythm of time,

quickly followed by the Asiri's triumphant laughter as he called the Clockmaster to come out and witness his victory.

'It has begun. There is nothing we can do,' Tholocus cried as he turned and scrambled to the top of the mound of broken clocks with the others at his heels.

Denso stopped abruptly as he reached the top, his knees and hands sinking into the pile of broken mechanisms and retched, his stomach heaving in violent contractions at the sight that lay before him. Mya sobbed uncontrollably, her head buried in her hands, her fingers pressed in her ears to shut out the Waymaster's screams. Harry felt hot tears of rage wet the corners of his eyes and he ground his teeth in bitter helplessness and clenched his fists so tightly that his nails cut into the palms of his hands and the blood trickled out between his fingers.

'You'll pay for this, you bastard!' he shouted, raising a bleeding fist at the Asiri.

Jothnar merely laughed at the idle threats and beckoned him to come forward. 'Come on, Earthian, come and break bread at my table and unfold the secrets of Paradise while my Mauders unravel the road we shall take.'

CHAPTER NINE

Journey-lines

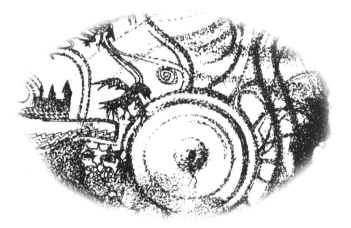

'GOD, WHAT I'D GIVE for a Smith and Wesson automatic with a bagful of ammunition clips right now,' Harry muttered bitterly as he let his clenched fist fall uselessly to his side. He stared across the portico over the heads of the guards who barred the doorway.

The area had been set with a ring of flickering rush-lamps that clearly illuminated the pitiful sight of the Waymaster strung up upon the skinning frame. He had been stripped naked and the mass of tattooes that covered his body were vividly reflected in the lamplight. He had fought with every ounce of his massive strength but he couldn't stop his arms and legs from being brutally stretched apart into a star shape and tied with black, fibrous ropes that had been knotted around his wrists and ankles. He had been fixed securely to the ring-heads of long, thick iron bolts threaded through the main structure of the frame. Four swarthy Mauders were tightening the bolts with long iron keys, cursing at him and shouting for him to be still as he tried desperately to escape. He was twisting and turning, making the tightening ropes burn and damage his skin. His head was being pulled upwards by dozens of thin cords that had been knotted into his orange hair which then fanned out up and over the top and upper edges of the frame through oiled grooves. Three muscular warriors, stripped to the waist, were throwing their weight upon those cords, laughing and cursing at

Orun as their brutal strength stretched his neck, making his veins show up as clearly as gnarled tree-trunks. The pressure distorted his face, twisting and flattening his nose, mouth and cheeks into a hideous agonising leer. His bones creaked and groaned as the keys turned. His muscles bunched and convulsed and sweat oozed out of every tortured pore making the tattooes seem to ripple and melt together.

The keys turned and he screamed again, a wailing, choking scream of helplessness and despair that burst out of his throat and echoed across the city touching each of the vast Halls of Hours as it stretched away into the darkness.

Jothnar's cruel laughter cut through the Waymaster's scream as he raised a razor-sharp curved, skinning-knife and made the first incision into the skin in the hollow of Orun's armpit. 'Now I will find the journey-line that leads to the Doorcrack. It shall signal the beginning of a new age of conquest when I shall rule Paradise!'

The curved blade pierced Orun's skin and the tension of the wires and ropes that held him taut upon the frame caused his skin to split along the soft underside of his arm revealing raw glistening flesh and darker bundles of sinews and muscles. His elbow burst through as the split widened and travelled down his forearm.

'All my dreams, everything I desire, will soon be mine!' Jothnar shouted, puncturing Orun's other armpit and motioning to the figures holding the keys to tighten the ropes again.

Then he stopped to allow the six waiting Mauders, their skinning-knives ready, to close in on either side of the Waymaster and begin with skilful paring cuts to peel back his skin. They carefully dissected out the forest of arteries that fed it, cursing as their knives slipped and they pricked and punctured tiny vessels causing droplets of blood to splatter onto their arms and faces while minute portions of the tattoos faded.

'Take care, you fools,' Jothnar hissed, 'I want to see every footstep that he has ever taken. I want his skin.'

Orun's body contracted into violent spasms as their knives stripped away at his nerves and one wailing shriek of pain tore through his lips and followed the first scream into the darkness.

'You are wrong, Asiri!' Tholocus cried angrily, suddenly leaping to his feet and scrambling down across the mound of broken clocks. 'You cannot begin to grasp at the catastrophes your conquest will unleash.'

Jothnar hesitated and for a moment his eyes clouded with doubt as he watched the Clockmaster try to reach the skinning-frame and deny him the knowledge of the road to Paradise. He shouted to his guards who crowded forward and barred the way, forcing Tholocus back at spear point. The desire to conquer Earth overwhelmed the Asiri. 'Stay back, you old fool, or I will summon Graksha and render you all to ashes,' he sneered. 'What you are witnessing is the birth of a new age.'

Tholocus hesitated and retreated, thwarted, back to the entrance of the hall. In triumph Jothnar turned his back on the Clockmaster and snapped his fingers at the bloody warriors gathered around the skinning-frame, urging them to cut and tear faster.

'I can't stand another moment of just kneeling here and watching this butchery!' Mya shouted, tears of anger and disgust coursing down her cheeks.

She grabbed a handful of the sharp clock wheels from where she knelt and hurled them with all her might across the portico. The ring of guards ducked in surprise as the whirring metal discs flew over their heads and before their warning shouts could alert the butchers at the frame one of the serrated wheels skimmed in a curving arc towards them and struck the bare shoulder of the Mauder carefully paring the skin away from the right side of Orun's chest. His blood-sticky hand and razor-sharp knife were three inches inside the loose fold of hanging skin around the nipple, dissecting out the intercostal arteries. The mass of tattoos wobbled and moved as the blade worked its way along the underside of each rib towards the sternum and stripped away the arteries and nerves that lay in the chest wall. The Mauder cried out as the cog hit him and his knife jerked downwards, its needle-point puncturing a hidden artery. A fountain of bright blood gushed hotly over his hand and spurted through the torn nipple to splash onto his face. It spread in a dark, widening stain across the loose folds of hanging skin.

Jothnar spun round at the Mauder's cry and saw the tattoos within the spreading stain fade, the details becoming blurred and merging together. He screamed with rage and snatched the warrior away. With his armoured hand he crushed the larynx with one violent contraction of his fingers and threw him carelessly aside. He plunged his other hand into the bleeding mass of flesh and muscles, found the pulsating artery beneath the skin and brutally pinched the wound to stem the flow of blood.

'It worked. Look, those tattoos on his chest have already vanished!' Denso shouted, grabbing handfuls of clock-wheels, springs and pendulums and hurling them through the portico.

Jothnar snarled with anger and shouted at his guards to bring forward one of the iron-linked nets they used to snare wild dragmas and stretch it across the doorway. Orun raised his bloodshot eyes and stared at him through a veil of pain and agony. The Asiri's face slowly swam into focus.

'You shall have nothing . . .' he tried to say. The cords knotted into his hair were pulled so tight that he could do

no more than gargle, but the look of defiance was clear for Jothnar to see. Orun raised his eyes a fraction more and through a film of blood and searing pain he saw Denso hurl dozens of shining metal discs at the raised net and then advance on the solid wall of guards wielding a long metal pendulum in both hands.

He whispered Denso's name before the agony overwhelmed him and he sank into a black pit of unconsciousness. Mercifully he felt nothing of the last moments of his torture as the layers of tattoos were stripped from his back and shoulders and the left side of his chest before being stretched out flat upon the frame beside him. At a signal from the Asiri a waiting Mauder, balancing on a rickety scaffold of bleached dragma bones behind Orun's head, carefully pierced the skin above his jugular and cut a precise incision along the angle of his jaw and up around each ear. He drew his blade up along the back of his neck, through his thick orange hair and over the crown of his head, stopping only when the blade reached the vivid tattoos upon his forehead.

The two bloody butchers at the front of the frame reached around Orun's head and with careful cuts stripped free the temporal artery before probing with their sticky fingers into the widening gash and tearing his scalp free, pulling it brutally over the top of his head. The thin cords that had been knotted into his hair to hold his head rigid were slackened off and before his head could slump forwards in a senseless stupor his hair and skin were ripped free and dragged down over his forehead, tearing away from the bridge of his nose and cheeks, taking his eyelids and lips off in one vicious tug.

The outline of his face collapsed and formed a hideously distorted mask in the hands of the two Mauders as they stretched it, kneading the skin between their bloody fingers, teasing out the torture lines before they hung it up upon a single black iron hook at the top of the frame.

The Mauders stepped back, the skinning complete. Orun's body now hung in unconscious wretchedness. His raw, glistening nakedness of trembling flesh, sinews and muscles was exposed to the cold night air. A forest of arteries and minute veins that the Mauders had meticulously dissected out criss-crossed the narrow gap still linking him to his skin, feeding and nourishing the thousands of vivid illustrations portrayed there.

Jothnar laughed, a cruel pitiless sound of triumphant delight. He signalled to the Mauders who held the iron keys to tighten them gently and stretch the skin without distorting the journey-lines. Two anointers dipped soft bouglin-feather brushes into deep silver vessels of oil of myrrh and sap from the blackthorn that hung on either side of the frame and began to wet the skin with sweeping strokes. It quickly became translucent and the tattoos glowed with an intense richness. Jothnar impatiently pushed the anointers aside and began to pore over the thousands of intricate pictures, muttering and mumbling to himself as he briefly traced the line of a journey only to disregard it and pursue another.

'More oil. Be quick,' he hissed, stepping back to watch the anointers' soft brushes send a rippling curtain of oils over the skin.

'We have completely failed,' Mya sobbed as she saw Orun's head move as the veils of unconsciousness began to lift. She heard a wailing scream issue from the bloody hole where his mouth and cheeks should have been.

'I will find a way to put an end . . .' Kote began when a shout from the Asiri made him stop speaking and rise to his feet. He moved forward to the mound of clocks that blocked the doorway and peered out. Jothnar had moved back to examine the skin and was pointing excitedly to an area on the left shoulder.

'The Crystal Swamps! I knew the road would be somewhere in those shimmering wastes. Look! Look!'

The Mauders crowded round, craning their necks to follow the Asiri's pointing finger.

'Look at those forests of towers: there must be millions of lamps,' a voice gasped.

'But it's a place of strange monsters with blazing lights set in their heads!' cried another fearfully.

'Those soaring towers must be the citadels in Paradise,' Jothnar whispered, ignoring the timid voices. He turned impatiently to where Graksha crouched below the first step of the portico and summoned it to ascend the steps. As the monstrous wrathwa towered over the translucent skin and followed the Asiri's movements with its red-hot eyes, Jothnar tried to trace the secret road that Orun had travelled through the Crystal Swamps.

'It's there somewhere. It has to be there!' he shouted impatiently. He leapt into the wrathwa's saddle and urged it forward. Suddenly he halted and issued a string of orders to the milling Mauders.

'Bind the skinning-frame securely between the anointers on the two strongest dragmas. Keep that Waymaster alive and ride toward the Crystal Swamps. I will study those journey-lines and discover where the Doorcrack lies long before we reach journey's end.'

His eyes travelled over the rings of guards to pause for a moment on the mound of ruined clocks and the group of figures in the doorway of the vast echoing hall. He spurred Graksha a pace toward them and his blackened face split into a victorious leer.

'Soon I will have the knowledge of the road that I seek; nothing can prevent me from discovering it. The Waymaster's journey-lines are mine now, do you hear me old fool? Your threats and denials are empty husks of hot air.'

He laughed and raked his spurs across the wrathwa's armoured flanks and wheeled the great beast away from the entrance. In one giant leap they descended from the portico scattering and trampling on the crowd of watching Diviners, crushing the slowest into the dust as Graksha spread his wings, beating the air into a gale of stinking fumes as he rose above the Hall of Hours.

'Lord Asiri,' the Captain of the Mauders cried as he ran to the edge of the portico. 'What shall we do with the Diviners? What shall we do with the withereds and the Earthians who are hiding in the hall? Shall we bind them in chains and bring them with us?'

Jothnar leaned forward, gripping the high pommel of his saddle and looked down, his eyes narrowing into murderous slits. 'Kill them all for daring to defy me. Kill every one of them and reduce this ... this ... this city of hidden echoes into a wasteland of silence. And be quick, for once I have discovered the Doorcrack I will not wait long for you upon the threshold of Paradise.'

He laughed cruelly and turned the monstrous wrathwa toward the Crystal Swamps, promising that he would be lord of the skies in Paradise, and then flew low across the city.

The remainder of the Mauders, full of fear that they were to be left behind, rushed to the edge of the portico and leapt upon their dragmas. They streamed out of the city after the Asiri, leaving only a dozen guards to take heed of Jothnar's last command. These drew their curved swords in preparation to slaughter the remains of the Grand Council. Screams and shouts of terror rang out across the portico as the Mauders' swords rose and fell.

'Quickly, get back into the hall!' Tholocus cried as the

guards let the last of the withereds fall lifeless to the ground and began to advance toward them.

Harry stared at the carnage and shouted toward the Asiri as he vanished into the lifting dawn, 'You're going to pay for all this you soulless, murdering bastard!'

'Come on Harry, for Christ's sake,' Denso hissed, grabbing at his sleeve and physically dragging him back into the hall as the closest Mauder lunged at him.

Running at the Clockmaster's heels they followed him through a maze of twists and turns into the cavernous building.

'How the hell are we going to escape now?' Denso gasped, hearing the scrape and clatter of pursuit that filled the entrance behind them.

Tholocus stopped and held up his hand to halt and silence the others. 'The rhythm of time in this hall is your time on Earth, that is why your presence does not affect it but the Mauders dare not trespass too far in here. Listen: their presence is already affecting the rhythm of time. If they try to venture any further in the clocks will start to tumble down.'

At that moment the Mauders stopped and their voices rose in heated argument. Tholocus smiled grimly as he listened to them, then he turned to the others and whispered, 'They fear the rhythm too much to pursue us any further, and the lure of Paradise is far too strong.'

The Mauders' voices faded through the doorway. There was a sudden rush of armoured boots across the entrance, whistles and shouts as the Mauders summoned their dragmas and then the sounds of galloping claws receded into the distance. Tholocus waited until nothing but the stumbling rhythm of the clocks was to be heard before beckoning the others to follow him as he slowly retraced his steps back through the doorway and on to the wide portico.

Harry hesitated for a moment, glancing darkly at the mountainous rows of clocks. 'Somewhere there's one ticking for each one of us here,' he whispered.

Denso shivered and hunched his shoulders. 'I don't want to see mine,' he answered as he hurried after the Clockmaster.

Tholocus stood on the portico perfectly still, the dawn breeze ruffling his hair and spreading out his silken robes as he surveyed the carnage. 'We were wrong. The catastrophe – the dark shadow that we feared threatened Paradise foretold our own doom – it was of our own making. We sowed its seeds with our own hands in the dawn of time. We . . .' His voice crackled and faltered and he would have fallen, bowed down with despair, had not Harry been close enough behind to catch and hold him.

Anger rose as thick as bile to choke Harry's throat when he saw the senseless destruction, the brutal butchery that they had been powerless to stop. He helped the Clockmaster across the portico, guiding him through the litter of bodies that lay where the Mauders had cut them down and were now surrounded by widening pools of blood. Gently he lowered Tholocus to sit upon the top step, his head bowed forwards in his hands, his frail body trembling, as he repeated himself over and over. 'Time is at an end. The shadow of death is spreading beneath the wrathwa's wings as he flies across Paradise.'

Mya listened to his mumblings for a moment and then knelt down beside him and clasped his hands tightly, drawing them away from his face. 'Tholocus, what is going to happen now? What will happen now that the Diviners are dead and your tower is burnt to ashes? How will time come to an end?'

Tholocus' shoulders stopped trembling as her voice penetrated his consciousness. The tragedy had briefly overwhelmed him. He looked up past her to the black pall of smoke drifting in the dawn breeze above his gutted tower.

'He hasn't found that Doorcrack yet, perhaps he never will,' Harry offered.

Tholocus shook his head. 'The Asiri is no fool, he will find it and lay waste the Earth. The wrathwa's fire will scorch Paradise to a cinder!' he cried. 'Soon the rhythm of time will be silent and the eternal darkness of death will cover these halls.'

'But what if that doesn't happen?' Denso asked. 'What if the wrathwa and the butcher riding on his back are shot out of the sky?'

'But you don't understand ...' Tholocus cried in anguish. 'Nothing can stand against the wrathwa's breath and it isn't only one beast that your people will have to destroy. The Mauders who witnessed the skinning will carry the word of Paradise throughout all the lands of Bendran, Thorn, Chricaun and the Crystal Swamps. Hordes of creatures, large and small, and wild ruthless peoples will try to overrun your world. Once they hear word of your Earth they will assault the walls of reality where they are weakest. The walls will crumble and soon there will be a thousand pathways to invade Earth. You will not be able to stop them no matter what weapons you have.'

'And once we are all dead time will stop completely?' Harry frowned.

'I ... I ... don't really know,' Tholocus hesitated. 'Yesterday my answer would have been "yes", it would have fulfilled the prophecies. But today they have come true in the most unexpected way. The immortals have been destroyed and eternity has come to an end for the Diviners.'

Tholocus stopped and stared wildly at the bodies that lay all around him.

'Yes, but you haven't answered my question. What if we destroy the Asiri with our modern technology? Would this tower of time still go on creating life without the Diviners to watch over it?'

Tholocus frowned and for a moment he listened to the persistent echo of the millions and millions of clocks. The rhythm had changed radically when the Asiri violated the sanctity of the city and tore Orun's skin from his body. It had become more frantic, more uneven, but it hadn't altered again with the death of the Diviners.

'Perhaps it will continue, yes, I can hear it now,' he cried leaping to his feet. 'Perhaps the disaster the prophets fore-told was the ending of the Diviners' immortality, not the fall of Paradise. We misread the warnings. Quickly, you must return to your Earth and warn your people to prepare against the Asiri's conquest. Perhaps you can avert it.'

'If we could end Orun's torture, kill him before the Mauders reach the Crystal Swamps, we would deny his journey-lines to the Asiri and then he would never find that Doorcrack no matter how hard he looks.' The determina-tion in Kote's voice made them all turn towards him.

Tholocus looked up sharply and nodded his head. 'Yes, we must do everything to delay the Asiri but his Mauders have at least an hour's start and I fear you would never catch them. You must realise yours are the only other journey-lines that show a clear way through the walls of reality. It would be madness to risk them falling into the Mauders' hands. The rumour of Paradise will draw thousands of creatures who will be swarming through the Crystal Swamps. No, it would be far too dangerous.'

'If we could only catch up with those murdering bastards before they reach the Crystal Swamps you wouldn't need to

259

let Kote get anywhere near them – I would put Orun out of his misery myself,' Harry interrupted hotly.

'Then we shall do it together!' Kote cried, gripping Harry's hand. 'And we shall overhaul them before they reach the Weasand Fields where you shall make the dagger thrust.' This said he put his two little fingers to his lips and whistled twice before adding, 'I think I glimpsed Lugg through the window of the tower before the Asiri attacked but I feared to call him because they would have killed him if he had tried to rescue us.'

The sound of the dragma's claws broke through the rhythm of time and then Lugg appeared out of the morning shadows. There was blood on his flanks, his armoured scales were burnt and shrivelled from the wrathwa's breath, the saddle was scorched black and gouged with savage cuts and spear-thrusts and one of his wings lay broken at his side, the leathery feathers torn away.

'Lugg, oh, Lugg!' Mya cried, rushing down the steps as the wounded dragma came to a halt and lowered his head for her to caress his scaly neck.

'Fear not, Mya, Lugg will heal quickly,' Tholocus called out softly to her.

'I want to come with you,' she turned to Kote, her eyes flashing with anger.

'No, it is far too dangerous,' Kote replied, adding quickly to appease her anger, 'too many of us would burden Lugg and we would never be able to overhaul the Mauders.'

Denso moved closer to Harry and whispered, 'You must be off your head, Harry. Why do you want to go chasing after those Mauders? Look what they've done to this dragma. Jesus! What sort of chance do you think you'd stand? Anyway you'd never get close enough to kill Orun: those guys are warriors, they're really sharp.'

'I know,' Harry muttered testily, looking around him.

'What I really need is a high powered hunting rifle. Or . . .' he fell silent, moved back to the mound of broken mechanisms and began to sift through it as an idea began to form in his mind.

'What is it you seek?' Tholocus asked, following him back to the entrance of the hall.

Harry shrugged, 'I don't really know. I was looking for something to make a weapon, maybe a bow or a spear, but there's nothing here that's any good.'

'A bow?' Tholocus murmured thoughtfully. 'Ah yes, I have seen drawings of such a weapon in the tower. The lifesmiths who make the windspring of each life within the Towers of Time could forge you such a device.' He turned toward the burnt-out tower, his shoulders sagging. 'But I forgot, all knowledge of such a weapon has been destroyed. I couldn't show them what you want.'

'But I could draw it for you,' Denso offered, feeling in his pocket for his pencil before realising that he must have lost it when they fled from the burning tower. 'If you could find me a pencil and paper.'

Tholocus vanished in a rustle of silk and reappeared, breathless from his haste, with a scroll of ivory parchment, quill pens and ink that he had found somewhere inside the hall. Mya and Harry knelt and held the scroll unfurled and flat upon the ground while Denso carefully sketched a long bow and an arrow shaft with a barbed blade.

'Come quickly, follow me, but do not try to venture too close to the Towers of Time,' Tholocus instructed them as he rolled up the scroll and hurried into the heart of the city towards a squat, round tower veiled in clouds of steam.

As they drew closer the beat of time grew louder until it filled their heads and almost burst their ear-drums. The ground beneath their feet trembled and shook, the force of it making them stagger. It was as if they were hurrying

261

toward the heart of a monstrous living beast. The throb of it overwhelmed them and made them stop long before they reached the tower where the air grew darker and the ground around it was strewn with thousands of different sized clocks. Tholocus threw his hands up in despair. 'What are we to do with all these windsprings now that the Diviners are all dead?'

Then he hurried ahead of them and left them standing amidst the debris.

'The noise is going to split my head in two!' Denso shouted, turning to Harry and clapping his hands over his ears.

'Look inside the tower: Tholocus has opened a door!' Mya shouted, taking a pace forward.

Denso stared over her shoulder at the open doorway. He saw furnaces of molten fire sending up fountains of white-hot sparks. The walls themselves seemed to pulse with life. He glimpsed cogs, wheels, clock-springs and hands, chains and huge crucibles amongst the vats of molten fire, and everywhere giant shadowy figures moved to and fro. The door swung shut and the vision was gone. He blinked and for a moment allowed his mind to re-capture the creation of life. He had seen human shapes being moulded in the flames, thousands of tiny infant faces. The giant, shadowy figures seemed to be hammering out the mechanisms that would control the span of their lives, they were winding the mainsprings and setting the hands. He had heard the wail and scream of new life echo amongst the thunderous roar of this Tower of Time as each new clock was set in motion.

The door opened and Tholocus emerged with a bow and six arrows in his right hand, but now the figures within the tower were shrouded in darkness as if a great cloud of doubt hung over all inside. The Clockmaster hurried toward them. He seemed thinner, his skin almost transparent, as though he had been purged by the cauldrons of fire. His eyes shone with a brilliant intensity. Harry took a step toward him and the ground shook violently, plumes of boiling steam issuing from hidden vents in the side of the tower and threatened to envelop them all.

'Keep back!' Tholocus shouted, gathering them to him, and hurried them back through the city to where Kote and the dragma waited. He drew in a shallow breath and spoke urgently. 'You must hurry and do all you can to stop the Asiri from invading Paradise. The litesmiths in the tower fear a wholesale destruction will sweep your Earth.' He paused to hand the bow and the six arrows across to Harry.

The heat of the furnaces still lingered on its polished surface but it felt light and fitted well into his hand. From the tension on the bow-string it felt immensely powerful.

'They must have strung this for one of those giants to use. I don't think I'll even be able to draw the string back, let alone loose an arrow,' he murmured in dismay, passing the bow to Denso.

'Perhaps you had better try to use it before you go chasing after those butchers,' Denso frowned, quickly handing it back.

'Yes, sure,' Harry nodded, choosing one of the arrows and nocking it onto the bow.

He hooked his first two fingers onto the string, one on either side of the feathered flight and began to draw it back. The bow creaked and bent as the flight touched his cheek.

'Aim at the keystone of the door-arch on that far tower, the one on the right. Think of nothing else but where you want the arrow to fly,' Tholocus instructed him.

'But that's over five hundred yards away. He'll never be able to hit that!' Denso cried.

'Aim,' Tholocus insisted as Harry brought the bow up and steadied it.

He held his breath. His eyes narrowed as he concentrated

263

on the target. The tiny key-stone swam into focus and he loosed the arrow. It rose in a shrieking, spinning arc across the city and struck the centre of the stone, sending up a shower of chippings and burying itself deep in the top of the archway.

'I would never have believed that was possible!' Denso exclaimed.

'Now you must ride with the speed of the wind if you are going to catch up with the company of Mauders,' Tholocus urged.

Mya gripped Kote's hand as he prepared to clamber up into Lugg's saddle. 'Take care,' she whispered, feeling the colour rising to her cheeks.

Kote smiled as he held her gaze and tightened his fingers around hers, 'I promise you this, Mya, we will return with tomorrow's dawn.'

He let go of her hand without a backward glance and sprang up into the saddle.

'You be careful now, I'd hate anything to happen to you,' Denso muttered, trying to suppress his emotion as Harry climbed up and slipped into the dragma's saddle behind Kote.

'Sure thing,' Harry laughed, waving the bow above his head and clinging onto Kote's waist with his other hand as Lugg surged forwards to follow the clear trail that the Mauders had left.

Mya and Denso stood silently watching them climb up the side of the valley, growing smaller and smaller until they were mere specks in the distance. Then they vanished from sight.

Harry thrust the bow over his shoulder and clung desperately to Kote's waist as Lugg stretched out his neck and began to gather speed. The dragma ran with a swaying, rolling gait, covering the ground with huge, leaping strides and it felt as precarious and unstable as trying to sit astride a giant ostrich at full gallop. Soon the city lay spread out below them in the floor of the valley, its beautiful roofs and spires bathed in a hazy morning sunlight. Lugg followed the Mauder's trail along the high rim of the valley and Harry sought a glimpse of the Windrows of Thorn, the soaring spires of rock and the dense spreading crowns of the dark forest that guarded the City of Time from curious eyes.

'There were shrouds of mist hiding this place before but now they're gone. I can see the Crystal Swamps shimmering on the horizon,' Harry shouted against the wind as Lugg suddenly slowed and turned, leaving the trail he was following.

They began to descend a dark, narrow, twisting gorge that surrounded them with echoes and the sound of rushing water.

'The Asiri's presence must have torn the secret shrouds apart. Hold tightly, this path is dangerously narrow!' Kote shouted back as the sheer, overhanging walls of the gorge drew in on either side of them and shut out the daylight.

The descent became a blur of shadows and roaring sound as ice-cold mists and stinging sheets of rain swept over them. Lugg's claws slipped and skidded over mossy rocks and they splashed through deep pools of black shadows. White water cascaded down the glistening rock-face, filling the narrow gorge with boiling clouds of spray. Harry gritted his teeth and clung on so hard that his fingers burned as the spray became a roaring deluge that threatened to sweep him out of the saddle. Lugg had to scrabble to keep his balance against the force of the water in the darkness.

Harry opened his eyes and thought he could see a glimmer of light some way ahead through the thunderous

265

curtain of water. The gully was waist-deep in swirling foam but Lugg regained his footing and surged forward, taking them through the waterfall and out onto a ledge of rock. Kote touched Harry's hand where it gripped him and shouted against the roar to tell him that they were safe. Suddenly he pointed to something above and behind them. Harry blinked, shook the water out of his eyes and narrowed them against the misty shafts of rainbow colours that seemed to fill the air all around them. He turned his head and gasped. They were standing on a narrow ledge only yards away from a great white waterfall that boiled and thundered down behind them. He felt his stomach tighten and his head spin.

'Get me out of here before I black out!' he cried, screwing his eyes tightly shut.

Kote laughed, 'You have nothing to fear. Lugg will not slip nor will I let you fall. We have merely taken a quicker, though more dangerous, road through the eye of the waterfall. It is shorter than the one we used on our journey into the city.'

Harry half-opened his eyes, looked up through the shimmering rainbows in the waterfall's spray and saw the narrow arch of rock that spanned the falls hundreds of feet above them. 'I think I'm going to be sick,' he gasped as dizziness swept over him.

Kote laughed again and spurred Lugg forward along the ledge to where it opened out onto a well-defined rock-path that fell away steeply towards the edge of a forest. Lugg quickened his stride as they descended through the trees. The scent of resin, oak and sycamore filled Harry's nose and he opened his eyes and let out a breath of relief to see that they were on solid ground once again, surrounded by the leafy darkness of the Verge of Drasatt. The trees grew threateningly close on either side of the track and nothing moved or broke the stifling silence. Harry shivered and a gnawing doubt began to eat away at his heart as he wondered if he would be able to complete the task that lay ahead. He glimpsed shadowy figures, bowmen and archers amongst the trees. He felt a compulsion to call out and the words rose to his lips.

'Keep silent,' Kote hissed suddenly. 'The Forest of Drasatt is enchanted and shows the weakness and doubts that fills men's hearts in order to lure them from their path. Look ahead and to the left and you will see that even the Mauders were not immune to its power.'

Harry turned his head to the left and stifled a cry of horror. Three Mauders were hanging by their necks amongst a lattice-work of strangling branches. Their blackened, crow-pecked faces and frantic bulging eyes stared back at him. The Mauders' armoured fingers were frozen onto the tightening twigs as they had fought for that last choking gasp before their purple, swollen tongues had choked them to death. Harry shuddered and buried his face between Kote's shoulderblades.

'Fill your mind with only the purpose of our journey. Leave no room for doubt. Your thoughts will protect you.'

They rode on in silence, each one focusing on the task ahead. The trees gradually began to thin out, the air grew lighter and there was birdsong in the branches. Wild flowers splashed vivid colours in the brambles beside the track. Lugg broke free of the edge of the dark forest and as they left the last of the rocky ground he began to lengthen his stride to cross the rolling ochre grasslands and follow the clear path that the Mauders' dragmas had trampled. Kote watched the ground ahead and twice pulled Lugg to a sudden halt, leaping down to examine the trampled grasses.

'There they are: I can see their dustcloud in the Windrows of Thorn!' Kote cried.

The second time he stopped beside a muddy waterhole and looked up bleakly, holding up his hand, glistening with blood and oil. 'Orun is still alive. The company stopped here so that the anointers could wet his skin with more of their filthy oils.'

'How far ahead do you think they are?' Harry asked, fingering the arrows thrust through his belt.

Kote offered him a drink from a leather flask as Lugg drank from the waterhole and slowly unbuckled a pouch from the pommel of the saddle to retrieve a hunk of blackened waybread. He shrugged before answering. 'They are not far.' He glanced up at the noonday sun. 'We might overtake them before they reach the Crystal Swamps but . . .' he hesitated, strode away from the waterhole and shaded his eyes against the glare before studying the barren Windrows that lay before them.

'The rumour of Paradise has travelled faster than fire through a thicket of dead oakweeds. There are bands of travelling warriors and hordes of beasts everywhere. They are hurrying towards the Weasand Fields. And look, the Asiri is flying backward and forward on his wrathwa scouring the swamps for the Doorcrack. It will be impossible for us to travel that way.'

Harry shielded his eyes and saw the moving specks converging on the swamps. 'What the hell are we going to do now?' he cried angrily, his thoughts jumping around a thundering headache that was threatening to burst out of his skull. 'We can't just turn back and leave Orun strung up in agony on that hideous skinning frame.'

Kote watched the wrathwa for a moment and then turned to gaze back thoughtfully towards the dark line of hills. 'If the Asiri continues to search towards the centre of the swamps there is a way we can reach the far side before the Mauders,' he answered, slowly opening his jerkin to reveal the mass of vivid journey-lines that covered his chest.

He singled out a line of tattoos that showed a winding tortuous road that skirted the swamps and ran through dark valleys and over narrow, barren ridges. It traversed the hills that surrounded the horizon and disappeared into the wilder lands beyond. Harry examined the tiny illustrations and the closer he looked into them the more details that seemed to come alive. He blinked and rubbed his eyes before looking up past the Journeyman to the line of distant hills and saw that the tattoos were a perfect mirror-image.

'But it must be miles out of our way to go around the swamps,' he frowned. 'And how can you be sure we'll get ahead of them, let alone know if we will ever find those Mauders again once we leave their trail?'

'We must try, it is our only chance. Now, can you remember where that Doorcrack through the walls of reality brought you into the Crystal Swamps?' Kote asked.

'No, I don't know at all. No ... wait ...' Harry muttered. He closed his eyes and pressed his fingers against his temples. The throbbing headache made it difficult to concentrate on anything. 'Yes!' he called as a hazy picture began to form in his mind's eye. 'There was a ledge with thousands of caves that pockmarked the steep hillside above it, and ... and ... away to the left I remember a break in the hills. There was a sort of bare saddleback ridge without any trees growing on it.'

Kote examined the journey-line on his chest for some moments before asking, 'Is this what it looked like?' as he pointed to a dip in the line of hills.

Harry bent so close to Kote that he could smell the sweat on his body and almost hear his heartbeat. 'Yes, I'm sure that the doorway was just there.' He indicated a minute tangled line of oakweeds and a mass of pinpricks of dark colour that represented the caves in the hill.

'Are you sure?' Kote asked.

Harry looked again and nodded: there was no mistake.

Kote wet a finger and held it up. 'The east wind blows in our favour. The Mauders are bad boatmen and it will take them all day to cross the swamps. We can reach that saddleback in the hills before the Asiri's men step out of their straw crafts.' He gathered up Lugg's reins, clambered up into the saddle and reached a hand down to Harry. 'Now we ride without stopping,' he muttered grimly.

Harry made sure that the bow was slung securely across his shoulder and clung on tightly to Kote's waist as Lugg surged forward. They followed the Mauders' clear trail to where the rolling ochre grasslands met the Windrows of Thorn. Here Kote turned the dragma toward the line of hills and all day Lugg ran at a tireless, bone-jarring pace that made Harry's teeth rattle and his headache hammer mercilessly inside his skull. But gradually the hills drew closer and what had looked like dark, indistinct smudges on their steep slopes became clumps of brambleheads and blackthorn bushes or dense wooded areas of ebony and oakweed. Patches of wild flowers, ferns and orange grass splashed bright colours amongst the sombre woodlands while sheer craggy ravines and broken spires of rock edged the skyline and in places fell away into secret shadowy valleys.

They left the barren rock and sparse soil of Thorn behind as the sun was sinking toward evening and began to climb, skirting the Crystal Swamps and following a narrow stony track up across the wooded slopes.

'Look, there are the Mauders!' Kote shouted back to Harry, gesturing down toward the swamps as they passed out of a dark, airless copse of ebonies.

Harry followed the Journeyman's pointing hand and caught a glimpse of a line of straw boats moments before a squall of crystal rain drifted across and obliterated them from sight.

'We were right to come this way: we're ahead of them now!' Harry shouted back as they entered a grove of oakweeds.

'Yes, and we would never have managed to cross the swamps on our own, the swamps are alive with creatures following the Mauders to Paradise!' Kote shouted back.

Harry looked down again as they galloped clear of the oakweeds and he saw that the shimmering surface of the swamps was everywhere broken by monstrous hump-backed animals of every shape and size, all following in the wake of the straw boats; and behind them he could see all manner of strange craft overloaded with hundreds, perhaps thousands of different peoples. The air was thick with winged beasts all following the rumour of Paradise. This was merely the beginning, the first trickles of the flood that would surely follow and fear of the imminent invasion gripped Harry's heart with ice-cold fingers. What if Earth's modern technology couldn't cope with such an avalanche, such a deluge of the absurd?

Lugg's rolling gait altered suddenly as he slowed and Kote's urgent voice cut through Harry's nightmare speculation.

'The Mauders' straw boats are drawing close to the shoreline. We must set our ambush quickly. Do you recognise anything yet? Are we drawing close to the Doorcrack?'

Harry blinked, looked up the steep, sloping hillside and shook his head. Evening was drawing long misty shadows from rock and branch and nothing looked familiar.

'No,' he muttered anxiously, turning his head and looking down across the swamps.

The setting sun had lit their surface with shimmering

waves of crimson and indigo fire and he caught sight of the line of straw boats as they sailed in beneath the overhanging trees at the edge of the swamps.

'Christ, we're going to be too late!' he cried, looking wildly up across the darkening hillside for the gaping black entrances to the caves.

'There is the saddleback ridge that breaks the line of the hills,' Kote hissed as Lugg took them round a bare promontory of rock and the track rose steeply toward a dense grove of oakweeds.

'And there are the caves ahead of us – and the ledge below it!' Harry cried with relief.

The sound of the Mauders' dragmas crushing and trampling their way through the undergrowth, their curses and shouts and the crack of the iron-tailed whips as they drove their beasts forward floated up to them on the evening breeze which rose gently from the shimmering swamps. Kote whispered Lugg to a halt in the copse of oakweeds, quickly dismounted and crawled through to the edge of the thicket. Harry followed and frowned as he looked through the parted branches.

'Jesus, it must be well over five hundred yards to the centre of the ledge. It's going to be too dark for me even to see that skinning frame. I'll never hit it from this distance anyway. It's impossible.'

Harry fell silent and drew back as the first of the Mauders' dragmas reached the ledge and crashed through the thin line of oakweeds and brambleheads that grew along its edge. The air suddenly darkened overhead. The first evening stars were blotted out and a gale of stinking fumes and the rattle and clatter of wrathwas' wings blew across the steep hillside. The oakweeds' branches bent and swirling eddies of dust billowed up across the ledge as Graksha settled in a cloud of reeking smoke and fire. Jothnar's voice, harsh and demanding, cut through the gathering darkness as he dismounted from the wrathwa's back and strode toward the arriving warriors.

'Bring that wretched Waymaster's skin before me,' he demanded impatiently. 'I've scoured these foul swamps all day to no avail. That Doorcrack is hidden somewhere in this line of hills, it has to be. Hurry, your Asiri awaits!' he snarled, turning savagely on the closest warrior and cracking his iron-tailed whip across his face, cutting a bloody weal deep into his cheek.

'Our Mauders are widening the path up through the undergrowth, Lord Asiri, lest the overhanging branches snag or tear the Waymaster's skin. The anointers are insistent upon it,' the warrior cried, staggering backward, the blood from the gash oozing between his fingers.

Jothnar turned, cursing impatiently under his breath, and stared up at the thousands of black, gaping entrances to the caves that speckled the hillside. He had explored hundreds of them during his fruitless search but there had not been enough time to search them all. The sound of the anointers' dragmas as they breasted the rim of the ledge and trampled through the screen of brambleheads made him turn back. The Mauders swarmed around them as they stopped and untied the skinning frame, carefully lowering and setting it upright upon the ground.

'You're setting it down too far away, you bastards!' Harry muttered to himself as torches were lit and set about it in a tight flickering circle.

The anointers liberally washed their oils over the transparent skin, cleaning it of the thousands of tiny insects that clung to it and making the tattoos glow with rich colours. Harry felt his stomach retch as the lamplight illuminated Orun's shivering body.

'Oh my God, he's conscious,' he hissed to Kote in horror.

273

The Journeyman shook his head sadly. 'No, his flesh is crawling with insects. They are eating him alive.'

Jothnar strode across to the skinning frame, a flaming torch in his right hand. He examined Orun long and hard. 'The Doorcrack must be amongst these cave entrances.'

Suddenly he shouted at his warriors and pointed to an illustration of a dark tunnel that led towards a forest of glittering towers beyond. A sneer of triumph thinned his lips but it quickly dissolved into a shadow of doubt. 'But which of these caves is the Doorcrack?' he cried in desperation.

'Now! Loose the arrow now!' Kote hissed, holding back the thin curtain of branches to give Harry a clear view.

Harry blinked at the trickle of sweat that was stinging the corners of his eyes and blurring his focus. He knew that he would only get one shot and that he had to pierce Orun's heart to end his torture. At this range, in flickering lamp-light, it would be almost impossible.

Jothnar straightened his back and turned to stare up at the mass of gaping, black holes in the hillside. He was lifting his arm and pointing. It was now or never. Harry blinked again and concentrated his whole mind as Tholocus had instructed him. He thought of the left side of Orun's chest and it swam sharply into focus, so sharply that he could see the swarms of insects feeding and burrowing into Orun's raw flesh. Rage at what the Asiri had done stilled his trembling fingers as they tightened on the bow-string. He drew it back until the feathered flight lightly touched his cheek, then sucked in a shallow breath and held it before sending the arrow spinning out of the cover of the oakweeds and across the darkened ledge.

Jothnar heard the shriek of the arrow and spun round and leapt toward the frame, but the arrow struck Orun's chest a finger's span to the left of his sternum, tearing through muscle and flesh, splintering bone before piercing his heart. The Waymaster's head jerked up and for an instant he regained consciousness, his eyes opened and held the Asiri's gaze as their light faded and a bright fountain of blood gushed out, splattering across the anointers' faces. Jothnar tore at the arrow shaft, hurling it aside before thrusting his hand deep into the wound in an attempt to stem the flow of blood, but it was too late. One by one the brilliantly-coloured tattoos began to fade and vanish as they melted away to nothing.

The Mauders were milling in confusion. Jothnar's voice rose in a terrible scream of rage. Graksha snarled and roared as he beat his wings in response to the uproar and extinguished the ring of torches. Harry had begun to reach back for another arrow when Kote grabbed his arm and pulled him back to where Lugg waited. He threw Harry up into Lugg's saddle and leapt after him, spurring the dragma away into the covering darkness.

The sounds of uproar rose from the ledge behind them as Lugg broke cover from the grove of oakweeds and fled. He ran along the track for about a hundred yards before Kote headed him up through dense blackthorn thickets and rode him into a narrow rock-strewn gully. Lugg turned awkwardly around and pressed himself into the shadows of the overhanging rocks while Kote delved into a pouch which hung from his belt and found a stick of draweasy. With rapid strokes he drew leaves and bramble branches across the entrance and over the top of their hiding place.

'Not a movement. Not a sound,' he whispered bringing his middle finger to his lips.

Below them and to their left beyond the thicket of trees lights sprang up as the lamps were quickly rekindled and enraged Mauders, already mounted on their dragmas, snatched them up and streamed out through the oakweeds. They began thrashing at the undergrowth, criss-crossing one another's tracks, in their search. Graksha roared and sent out a plume of fire and, with Jothnar again on his back, rose into the air and swept low across the hillside, backward and forward, his scorching breath igniting a trail of destruction as he tried to flush out the Waymaster's assassin.

Harry crouched low, his hands clasped over his head, as the wrathwa's searing tongue of fire burned up the clump of bushes only yards in front of their hiding place. He heard Jothnar scream and curse with raw fury at having the Waymaster's journey-lines destroyed a foot in front of him and feared that the next time the wrathwa passed over them they would be burnt to death. The beast was hovering above them, darkening the stars; suddenly they heard the Asiri give a shouted command as he called the Mauders back to begin searching for the cave entrance. In a loud voice he shouted across the swamps to them. 'We have no further need of the Waymaster. His journey-lines have already shown me that the Doorcrack is hidden somewhere on this hillside. Now we will search until we find it.'

Graksha stooped down at his command, flew across the ledge and hooked his armoured talons around the top of the skinning frame where Orun still hung, his body torn to ribbons. His transparent skin was as white and as empty as it was before he took his first step. The wrathwa lifted it up and flew out across the swamps where he let it fall and vanish forever with a dull splash. It disappeared in a widening circle of sluggish, incandescant ripples. A Mauder high above the ledge gave a shout of discovery and Graksha turned in a slow arc, following the voice, and flew toward the dark hillside. He hovered for a moment above the gesticulating Mauder and then descended into the echoing entrance. Jothnar turned in the saddle to shout to his

Mauders, commanding them to follow. Then the beast folded back his wings with a leathery clatter and extinguished the plumes of fire until they became a single flickering flame which licked around his lips and lit their way in the darkness. In a moment Graksha and Jothnar disappeared through the walls of reality in a cloud of steam.

Kote and Harry crept silently out of the narrow gully and watched the company of Mauders reassemble on the ledge and begin the steep climb up to the gaping black entrance which would lead them to Paradise. For a moment they milled around uncertainly, worried about crossing the dark threshold, but Jothnar's voice, shouting with excitement, telling of all the wonders that he had found, came back to them, a muffled, luring echo floating out of the darkness. The warriors heard his cry and poured after him in a swelling roar of eager shouts and the thundering of their dragmas' claws.

Harry opened his mouth to speak and let out a cry of fear as primaeval creatures of every shape and size began to swarm up over the perimeter of the ledge, snarling and growling, trampling the brambleheads and oakweeds as they passed through the ring of guttering torches. They cast monstrous shadows across the ground as they clambered up the steep rocky hillside and vanished through the Doorcrack. Angry shouts, whinnies and what sounded like the neighing of horses rose from the swamps. Moments later, a herd of centaurs, unicorns and winged horses appeared upon the ledge, rearing, plunging and fighting one another as they galloped forwards, each one striving to be the first across the dark threshold. Behind them other swarthy figures, some with two heads or a crest of horns, began to rush for the ledge.

'We have failed, utterly failed!' Harry cursed in despair as he watched a huge six-handed giant barge his way through the crowds of creatures, crushing their heads with three clubs the size of tree-trunks.

The giant reached the Doorcrack, stopped and then amidst the sound of splintering rock and angry curses forced his way through the walls of reality.

'No, we did all we could,' Kote answered fiercely. 'There were too many whispers, too many rumours of a Paradise for one arrow strike to deny its existence or halt the exodus of creatures that would swarm into it once it had been discovered. Your arrow gave Orun an honourable Waymaster's death and erased all the secrets that his journey-lines showed. You ended his suffering.'

'Yes, but if only we had killed him before they reached . . .'

'No,' Kote hissed, stabbing a finger at the huge gaping Doorcrack on the hillside and cutting him short. 'The shrouds of secrecy that hid your world are tearing apart. Look, another is already opening up beside it.'

Harry heard the boom of thunder as a new Doorcrack tore open. He put his hands over his ears, his headache was turning into a tightening band of pain that was crushing at his temples. 'It's hopeless,' he cried. 'Every freak of nature will soon be able to swarm through. We might just as well nail up a signpost.'

Kote shook his head. 'All three of you must return to your Earth and warn your people. You must go now: there is no time to lose.'

He scrambled up onto Lugg's back and reached down for Harry's hand. Harry slipped into the saddle behind him and pointed down at a new wave of beasts who were already swarming across the ledge. 'We'll never get back through that Doorcrack. Those creatures will devour us, tear us limb from limb if we try. It's all hopeless: we are never going to be able to return to our world.'

'There is another doorway that I know of,' Kote whispered, spurring Lugg away into the darkness toward the City of Time. 'There is a Doorcrack where the Wrathendall Spires touch the sky.'

Harry yawned and clung tightly to Kote's waist. Waves of tiredness swept over him as the dragma's rolling gait ate up the leagues. Dimly he felt Kote tie his wrist to his belt to prevent him from falling as he drifted into sleep. He awoke once or twice during the long night's journey and saw the shimmering Crystal Swamps in the moonlight and the rush of dark, overhanging branches above his head. Once, he saw the broad sweep of empty downland and then he was awoken by voices to find that they had stopped in a small village of reed huts where figures in a tight circle stared up at him in the flickering torchlight.

The people's faces were a mass of tattoos just like the Journeyman's. Kote spoke quickly in a soft, musical language that Harry couldn't understand and the circle of figures pressed closer, their voices rising in whispers of curiosity. One by one they reached up and gently touched the material of his trousers and the leather uppers and soles of his shoes. Kote felt Harry stir as he woke up and shrank away in alarm. Quickly he released Harry's wrists, turned to him and whispered. 'Do not fear them. These are my people, they will not harm you. They are all Journeymen by birth and are curious to know the feel of someone from such a distant land as yours. We have stopped here so that I may ask to borrow Gyma, Lugg's sister. She will carry you and Denso to the Wrathendall Spires.'

As Kote spoke the circle broke apart and an elder, dressed in pale satin robes, strode forward leading a huge dragma that was already saddled and bridled in exactly the same way as Lugg. The elder stopped and bowed to Harry as he offered him the silver-braided reins.

'Well thank you, thank you very much,' Harry smiled awkwardly down at the elder, not quite sure what he should do next. He looked to Kote with raised eyebrows asking for help.

'Dismount,' Kote whispered. 'Bow to my father and say "kendus" – it is the word for thank you in our language – and then climb up into Gyma's saddle. Ride beside me. Be quick: dawn will soon herald the new day.'

'I'll never be able to ride that beast on my own,' Harry exclaimed, looking up at Kote in dismay.

Kote laughed softly and spoke rapidly to the circle of villagers who then smiled broadly at Harry and murmured amongst themselves.

'Gyma will not let you fall,' Kote laughed as Harry climbed cautiously into the saddle. 'Now gather up your reins and follow me.'

Kote shouted a farewell to the villagers and spun Lugg round, spurring him forward. Gyma leapt after him and Harry only managed to stay where he was by hanging on grimly to the saddle. Behind them the villagers shouted parting wishes and their flickering circle of torches rapidly dwindled to a single point of light in the vast darkened landscape.

Riding Gyma was easier than Harry had imagined as long as he held on to the pommel of the saddle tightly and he quickly drew level with Kote. 'What did you say back there that made everyone laugh?' he asked.

'I said that your courage greatly outmatches your skill as a rider!'

'I'm doing the best I can, dammit!' Harry answered crossly.

'Yes,' Kote smiled against the rush of wind that their speed had stirred up. 'And my people and all the Way-masters and Journeymen across the length and breadth of

Bendran, Thorn and the Crystal Swamps will honour the name of Murmers, the Guardian, whenever they gather. They will remember you for your great feat of marksmanship with the bow of Tholocus and they will tell the story of how you ended Orun's torment and weave it into every fireside legend.'

'Jesus!' Harry muttered under his breath. 'It was just a lucky shot. If I hadn't been so angry at what the Asiri had done, if . . .' and then he fell silent as they rode up onto the higher ground toward the lightening dawn.

CHAPTER TEN

Paradise

MYA WAS BUSY WORKING in a Diviner's tower when she heard the faint clatter of dragmas' claws descending from the rim of the valley toward the city. She looked up from the mountainous piles of books and manuscripts that she was trying to catalogue into some sort of order for Tholocus and picked her way through the litter of forgotten knowledge to look out of the tall, curved, crystal window. She caught sight of Lugg cantering down the side of the valley and a smile of relief tugged at the corners of her lips. But the smile dissolved into a frown as she saw the second dragma travelling a pace behind him. She ran to the doorway and descended the narrow spiral stone stairs two steps at a time. She shouted a warning to Tholocus and Denso, telling them that Kote and Lugg had returned with a strange dragma on their heels.

Denso appeared at a run when he heard her warning shout, his arms loaded down with clocks and watches of every shape and size. He stopped in the centre of the main broad avenue as Kote reined Lugg to a halt in a cloud of dust in front of them.

'Who the hell is that following you?' Denso asked, his eyes searching for Harry who should have been seated behind Kote.

Harry reined Gyma to a haphazard halt in front of him.

'Harry! You're safe, thank God, but what happened?' Denso cried, staggering backward and staring up at the dragma's labouring sweating flanks. Harry stretched and patted Gyma's scaly neck before climbing stiffly out of the saddle and sliding slowly to the ground.

'We failed to stop the Asiri from discovering the Door-crack,' he said grimly before telling them everything about Orun's death and the hideous rush of creatures that had fled through the walls of reality.

Harry paused and looked quizzically at the armful of noisy clocks that Denso was clutching to his chest.

'We've been helping Tholocus. He's in a complete muddle: this place is chaos now that the Diviners are all dead. You should see the mounds of clocks piling up around that Tower of Time. We are trying to move as many of them as we can while Mya is beginning to catalogue all copies of the knowledge stored in the towers. I can assure you that running about with armfuls of clocks is doing nothing for the headache that is hammering away inside my head but I wonder what the hell is happening back home now that all those creatures are swarming through the walls of reality,' Denso muttered. He stooped down to lay his burden of ticking clocks in a neat row upon the ground.

'Where is the Clockmaster? We ought to tell him what happened,' Harry frowned.

At that moment Tholocus appeared from a tower away to the right, a bundle of papers tucked untidily beneath his arm. 'Yes, I know, the Asiri has broken through the walls of reality. There is no time to lose, you must return to your Earth,' he called out breathlessly. As soon as he reached them he thrust the papers into their hands.

'There was nothing we could do to stop him,' Harry muttered, taking one of the pieces of paper and smoothing it out.

He narrowed his eyes and tried to focus on the tiny lines of print and small photographs that were printed on it. At first glance he thought it was the front page of a newspaper but on closer examination he realised that it was the whole of the *Daily Mail* condensed down to one page. He scanned the date and the headlines – February 21st 1993. 'Invasion from Outer Space' 'Fairy-tales Come to Life' written in bold banner headlines. He read on through the leader article and learned of the trail of chaos and destruction that Graksha had left in its wake as it had flown over southern England. He read the varying eye-witness reports that ranged from people who believed that they had seen a spaceship to others who insisted it was a flying dragon that breathed smoke and fire. The paper was full of reports of sightings of centaurs and flying horses and stories of sea monsters causing havoc to shipping in the Atlantic.

' "New York has been invaded by Fairies" – hey, where did you get this newspaper?' Denso cried.

Tholocus waved a hand vaguely towards the circle of spires. 'Over there is Illundus' tower. There is a lens in his high chamber that can record everything that is written on Earth.'

'If the Asiri went through that Doorcrack above the Crystal Swamps close to where we came through he should have come out in Manhattan, not England, shouldn't he?'

Tholocus frowned and put his hands together thoughtfully. 'Yes, you are right, Denso,' he answered in time. 'But the fabric in the walls of reality was not woven to follow logic but to mask and shroud distance and time. A thousand leagues or a hair's breadth can lie side by side, a stride apart, for those who pass through them.'

'So those monsters could appear anywhere?' Harry exclaimed, 'and as fast as we try to stop them they'll simply burst through some place else. Jesus, this is hopeless, we'll never be able to stop them.'

Tholocus took his time, then answered slowly,

'Normally the tears or Doorcracks have occurred where the seams of the walls overlap. It took a lot of collective thought from the Diviners in the Council to create a Doorcrack amongst the City of Towers for Orun to travel through.'

Mya suddenly remembered the location of the doorway that Kote had taken her through and asked, 'These seams in the walls of reality, could they correspond to the ancient ley-lines that exist in our world?'

'Yes, yes, it is possible that we left some trace of our labours in the dawn of time,' Tholocus agreed.

'Ley-lines?' Denso interrupted. 'I've read somewhere that they are supposed to be the sites of supernatural occurrences but I don't see how it's going to help us stop those creatures from breaking through.'

'Wait, let me think,' Mya answered, holding her fingers against her temples to ease her pounding headache as she tried to remember the fragments of articles that she had read and recall the lectures she had attended that had touched on the subject of ley-lines.

'Yes, I borrowed some maps and charts from a retired school teacher called Jenkins,' she spoke slowly, teasing the memories out. 'I attended a lecture he gave – "Footprints of Antiquity". He said that people have recorded specific surges of energy, fluctuations of magnetism, that link up ancient monuments, prehistoric routes, the sites of pagan temples and things like that. His talk was fascinating and afterwards he lent me the maps he had compiled. They show the whole network of ley-lines crossing each other. I found them very useful when I was gathering material for my research, only I didn't grasp the significance of it all then.'

Harry quickly caught the thread of Mya's idea. 'So you think where these ley-lines cross are where the walls of reality are likely to tear apart?'

'I can't say for sure,' she answered uncertainly, 'but if

they do I think we could pinpoint exact locations where the invasions are most likely to occur.'

'And what good do you think that will do?' Denso asked hotly, thrusting a couple of the broadsheets he had been reading toward the others and stabbing a finger at the various articles that highlighted what was happening.

'They're breaking through everywhere. Those monstrous flying dragons, the Mauders, giants, they're causing chaos, laying waste to towns and cities everywhere.'

'Well at least we can warn the governments. We can tell them what's happening and where these things, these beasts are coming from and where they're likely to appear next,' Mya answered defensively.

Denso laughed harshly, screwing up the newspapers he was holding into a tight ball which he threw into the air. 'Do you really think that anyone is going to believe us, Mya? What do you think they'll say when we try to tell them about what we have seen? Do you think they'll listen when we describe Tholocus, the ageless Clockmaster and his Council of Diviners who, thousands of years ago, devised "walls of reality" to shroud the Earth from the other worlds that lie in parallel to it? Jesus! They'll think we're stark staring crazy! They'll probably tell us to join the queue of doom freaks who are already trying to report what they can see is happening.' Denso paused for breath, then snatched the newspaper that Harry was holding and thrust it towards her. 'If you don't believe me read through those reports again and you'll see that every paragraph is loaded with scepticism and denial. Creatures from outer space they say, fairy-tales come to life!'

'It is our fault,' Tholocus cried, wringing his hands together. 'From the dawn of civilisation we have buried truth, we have not allowed you to see that other worlds exist. Of course no-one is going to believe what is happening.'

289

'But we have to do something.'

The determination in Mya's voice made the others turn toward her. 'We can't just stand around here lamenting our fate and letting them overrun our world. We should be back on Earth where those ley-lines intersect, we should be organising some sort of resistance against the creatures who are even now swarming through.'

'Yes, yes of course, you must try to do everything possible to stop this invasion of your earth,' Tholocus cried.

'Let's get going right now,' Harry urged, turning towards Gyma and scrambling up into the dragma's saddle before reaching down with his right hand to help Denso climb up behind him.

Mya hurried to where Lugg stood and reached up to grasp Kote's hand. He swung her up into the saddle behind him.

'What do you think will happen to our world?' she asked, looking down at the Clockmaster. 'What will happen if the people and creatures of those other worlds do manage to overrun us despite our modern weapons?'

Tholocus bowed his head and was lost in thought for a moment; but when he looked up again his face had lightened and banished the shadows that had haunted his eyes. 'Once I would have feared that your civilisation was too fragile to exist side by side with the tyrants who would roam Earth should they breach the walls of reality, but now I know you have the spirit to survive whatever happens. My only fears are that your Earth will be laid to waste in the struggle for victory.'

'We'll beat the bastards long before that!' Denso muttered with determination.

Harry waved his hand to salute Tholocus and dug his heels into Gyma's flanks, wheeling the beast around.

'Will you come with us? We could use your knowledge,' Mya called out to the Clockmaster as Lugg surged forward.

Tholocus shook his head and spread his hands out to encompass the city. 'I dare not leave this place now that all the Diviners are dead. If there is to be a future the burden of time will weigh heavily on my shoulders. There will be so much here for me to do, so many lives to watch over. Now, ride on the edge of the wind to the Wrathendall Spires: I shall wait in the tower of Illundus for news of the fate of Paradise.'

Mya clung to Kote's waist as Lugg gathered speed and felt tears trickle down her cheeks as she looked back at the diminishing figure standing in the centre of the broad empty avenue.

'How the hell are we going to get word back to the Clockmaster if we do find a way to stop the Asiri's invasion and conquest? The newspapers will just deny there ever was such a thing,' Denso called out to Harry, but the rush of wind tugged his words away.

Tholocus' voice could almost be heard answering him but it was mingled with the thunder of the dragmas' claws. 'You, Denso Alburton, shall weave all you have witnessed into one great enduring tapestry. It will be the crowning triumph of all your works, a masterpiece of the truth.'

'For God's sake don't lose your grip and fall,' Denso hissed in terror through clenched teeth as he screwed his eyes tightly shut against the bottomless drop that lay below them.

He locked his hands together around Harry's waist and buried his face between his shoulderblades as Gyma snarled and scrabbled for purchase, her long tail thrashing at the rocks and her claws skidding as she slipped on the

291

treacherous surface of the crumbling granite chimney that rose sheer above them to the top of the Wrathendall Spires.

'Keep still, Denso!' Harry cursed. 'Every time you shift your weight Gyma loses her claw-hold.'

Harry shuddered and fought down the wave of dizziness that was drenching him in ice-cold sweat. He hated heights and this sheer ascent of the Wrathendall Spires was churning his stomach into a jelly. He was clutching so hard at the pommel of the saddle that his fingers burned and to make it worse he was sure that one of the thick leather straps that Kote had bound around their legs and then buckled onto the dragma's girth to stop them toppling out of the saddle and plunging to their deaths was working loose, but he couldn't summon up the courage to take his hands off the pommel to check it.

Gyma lurched sideways, her claws tearing at the crumbling rocks, dislodging a cascade of loose shale before she found new purchase and began to climb, zig-zagging upwards. She swept her tail against broken storm ruts and narrow gullies to gain extra balance and her laboured breaths billowed out across the glistening slippery rocks in clouds of vaporous steam. Above them and to the right Harry could hear the clatter of falling stones and could just see the outline of Lugg's shoulders against a dark chimney of rock with Kote hunched forward, gripping the pommel of his saddle with Mya hanging onto his back like a limpet. He was about to call out and ask how much further it was to the top when he heard Kote's warning echo down to them across the weathered rocks and gullies.

'Keep quiet, there are wrathwas soaring above the spires.'

The two dragmas continued their traversing in silence, zig-zagging over the sheer rock face, keeping in the shadows of the towering chimneys as best they could as they climbed toward the ultramarine sky. Night was gathering shrouds of darkness across the Wrathendall Spires and glistening sheets of ice were forming on the rocks. A cold wind began to howl and moan in the ravines, making Mya shiver as its icy fingers sought every crease and fold in her coat and tugged and ruffled at her hair. She clung more tightly to Kote and whispered, 'Tholocus told me that the wrathwa beasts are older than time itself. Are all life-spans so long here?'

Kote half-turned his head and smiled. 'I'm not sure. I have never thought to measure my own life before. For the Journeymen of Bendran life is a time of journeys and all the days of it are tattooed upon our skin. It is only complete when there is no room for another journey.'

Lugg suddenly froze and pressed himself into the shadows of a gully. Kote fell silent and tensed as he glanced up anxiously at the shadow of a wrathwa gliding silently across the rock-face only yards above them. Mya looked up and felt her blood run to ice as she smelt the sulphurous stench of decay and saw the creature's bilious yellow under-belly and armoured claws descending rapidly toward them. Its outstretched leathery wings blocked out the last of the failing daylight.

'Keep still!' commanded Kote as the monstrous dragon began to beat its wings, stirring up a gale of acrid smoke and boiling steam as it slowed its descent and hovered, hunting the storm runs and deep crevices twenty feet above them.

Suddenly with a clatter of its wings and a snarling fountain of flame from its open jaws, the beast scorched the rock-face, enveloping them in a downdraught of choking fumes as it swooped past and then gathered speed before rising in a widening, soaring arc toward the top of the spires. Kote drew his eyebrows into a frown as he watched the wrathwa spiral upward to become a tiny speck in the darkening evening sky. He couldn't understand why it

293

hadn't attacked. Why had it hunted only the gullies and broken chimneys, behaving more like a glow-wasp hovering in search of the entrance to its nest?

Mya broke his troubled silence with a sigh of relief as she whispered, 'We were lucky that monster didn't spot us.'

Kote almost shook his head in disagreement and was about to explain that the wrathwa could see a grassland hare from twenty leagues and smell it from even further, but he hesitated: they were so close to the top and the Doorcrack back into her world and he didn't want to frighten her.

'Yes,' he murmured. 'Very lucky,' and he urged Lugg to begin climbing again.

Glancing down he picked out the shape of Gyma emerging from a dark crevice just below them and called out softly to warn Harry and Denso of the wrathwa and to tell them to move with extreme caution.

At last Gyma drew level with them. 'We have almost reached the roof of the world,' Kote breathed with relief.

Both dragmas scrabbled up the near-vertical rock-face, scraping gouges in it with their front claws and pulling themselves up over the crumbling rim of the Wrathendall Spires. At last they slithered forward on to the summit of jagged, snow-covered rocks.

'Wait. Be still,' Kote hissed, pulling savagely on the reins. Everything had changed: the deep windblown snowdrifts were blackened and trampled with countless wrathwa clawscrapes. The towering ice sculptures that had once crowded the white landscape had been melted by the beasts' breath and had then refrozen into hideous liquid pools and strata of purple, luteous ice.

'The wrathwas have trampled the snow but I don't understand why . . .' He began to call out to the others when a snarling roar and a clatter of wrathwa wings drowned out his voice. He looked around wildly to see that the beast that had hovered above them while they climbed the spires was swooping down toward them and this time it was going to attack. It was approaching in a wide, sweeping arc that would bring it across the summit of the spires directly to where they stood. 'Get down, Gyma!' Kote shouted desperately as he drove his right spur hard into Lugg's flank. Both dragmas threw themselves sideways into the deep ridges of trampled snow only moments before the creature overflew the rim of the spires.

Mya cried out as a huge armoured claw ripped through the fabric of her sleeve. She was dragged helplessly upward but the leg-straps bound around her thighs held, biting painfully into her legs as the claw tore free and she fell back into the saddle. She had a brief terrifying glimpse of the beast's cavernous mouth as the claw held her. She had seen a white-hot cauldron of fire and the monstrous black silhouette of its body that blotted out the evening sky as it passed over them. Then it vanished suddenly by diving into the snow, its roar becoming a muffling echo as it left behind nothing but a thickening ribbon of smoke and crackling sparks.

'Up! Up!' Kote cried, looking around desperately to see from which direction the beast would attack next, and also searching for somewhere for them to hide as Lugg and Gyma thrashed their tails, creating a cloud of snowflakes. He knew they wouldn't be able to escape the wrathwa's second pass if they stayed where they were.

'Where the hell did that creature go?' Harry gasped.

'Over there: it flew straight into the ground,' Mya whispered, visibly shaken by the attack. Her lips were trembling from the shock as she gingerly probed her fingers into the long tear in her sleeve.

'It did what?' Kote asked as he stilled Lugg with a touch on the reins and turned to stare at her for a startled moment before following her pointing hand towards an area ahead of them where bare spires and gullies of rock showed as a wide blackened patch against the trampled snow. A pool of yellowing smoke hung in the air above it.

'The Doorcrack! Of course, that explains why the beast didn't bother to attack us earlier. It was searching for a way through the walls of reality.'

'But that's crazy, you're the only one who knew about this entrance. How could that monstrous creature have found out about it?' Denso frowned.

Kote shrugged and looked at the thousands of claw-scrapes that marred the wilderness of ice and snow for as far as the eye could see. With chilling clarity he remembered the wrathwa that had followed him through the Doorcrack when he had first discovered it. Bleakly he lifted his head, spurred Lugg closer to the bare, black rocks and listened to the bitter wind that was rising in mournful eddies through the Doorcrack. He could hear the hidden echoes of the world that lay beyond the walls. He rode closer and caught the choking stench of the huge beast in the air but beyond its gagging odour he smelt a waft of Paradise in the breeze and he knew it must be luring the wrathwas through. He turned in the saddle, his face drawn and pale beneath its vivid layers of tattoos, and whispered to the others, telling them what he feared had happened.

'You mean those monstrous, fire-breathing creatures are going to keep pouring through that Doorcrack?' Denso gasped as he looked up from the dark hole in the rock to the star-strewn sky for more of the winged creatures.

'I don't understand how those huge beasts can squeeze through.' Harry exclaimed peering towards the dark entrance in the rock. 'Each one of them is larger than a warehouse.'

'They can distort and stretch their bodies to hunt the

storm rills and rock chimneys for food, forcing their way through the narrowest of gaps. They are not herd creatures but they have the scent of one of their kind, the one that followed me through when I entered your world. That and the rich, heady scent of Paradise will draw every wrathwa that lives to the top of the Wrathendall Spires in search of the Doorcrack.'

Denso exploded, 'Now we're really stuck! We can't get home this way because at any moment one of these wrathwa beasts will be slithering and clawing its way through the Doorcrack with us, and we can't go back because the other way is swarming with . . .' he threw up his hands helplessly.

'When do you think the next beast will appear?' Mya asked, anxiously scanning the night sky.

Kote looked up at the millions of stars sewn across the void and said, 'Wrathwas do not usually fly at night unless they are disturbed in their roosts.' He paused and stared thoughtfully at the black entrance before adding, 'I think it would be safe to use the Doorcrack now under the cover of darkness.'

'You must be crazy!' Denso cried. 'That wrathwa has only just flown into that black hole: look, you can still see the smoke trail it left drifting across the entrance. Anyway, how do you know it won't return?'

Anger flashed in Kote's eyes, 'I do not: no-one can predict what these creatures will do, but I can promise you that more wrathwas will fly across the roof of the world when sunlight brings the new dawn. They will be hunting for the entrance. What will you do then? Where will you hide when they begin to scour the snow with their fiery breath and turn this white wilderness into pools of boiling slush and cause the rocks that lie hidden beneath it to turn red and crack with the heat?'

'Kote's right, we must try to get through now!' Mya urged impatiently.

'Oh no, I'm not risking meeting that monster head on. I'd rather go back to the City of Time and find another way,' Denso insisted, twisting around in the saddle and leaning back as far as the leg straps would allow.

He could just see over the rim of the spires and down into the sheer, dark, bottomless drop and his head began to swim. 'Harry, Harry, what do you think we should do?' he gasped, pulling himself upright and trying to shut out the terrifying drop that lay a yard behind them.

Kote knew they must break through the walls of reality while darkness covered the roof of the world and he had edged Lugg closer to Gyma during Denso's show of resistance. They could not go back: he had promised Tholocus to return them and he waited, watching Harry's eyes for the moment when he would turn to answer Denso.

'I don't know . . .' Harry glanced back toward the sheer drop, but Kote suddenly snatched Gyma's reins out of his hands and spurred Lugg forward into the doorway.

'There is no other choice!' he shouted as he rode Lugg recklessly over the bare, burned rocks, dragging Gyma with him through the yawning black entrance.

'No, no, no!' Denso wailed, struggling helplessly as the darkness swallowed them up.

The ground vanished abruptly and both dragmas snarled and thrashed their tails as they tumbled over and over. Gyma's reins snapped through Kote's fingers and they drifted apart only to collide roughly before spinning away from each other, rubbing and brushing against a myriad of indistinct shapes. The stench of the wrathwas and the smell of burning wood and bracken enveloped them, making them choke and causing their eyes to smart and stream in the darkness. The sound of rushing wind grew louder, sucking painfully at their eardrums. They were tumbling faster and faster, their plunging descent knotting their stomachs with convulsions, waves of nauseous blackness sweeping over them.

Suddenly they landed with a bump and slid sideways down a steep, wet slope through a tangle of charred branches and burned undergrowth. Mya blinked and regained consciousness as Lugg scrambled to his feet. It was pitch-dark and raining hard. She could feel the cold raindrops stinging her face and she smelt the burnt wetness of the undergrowth. She knew they were back on Earth. Beyond the dense circle of blackened trees she could see long trails of fire burning unchecked.

'Kote, we've made it,' she called out softly, touching his shoulder.

He stirred and suddenly put his hands up to his temples and groaned. 'Kote, are you all right?' she asked, her voice loaded with concern.

'Yes, but my head burns with pain. What about the others, have they survived?' he mumbled, reaching down to release the leg-straps.

Mya searched the undergrowth and picked out the shape of Gyma against the skyline. 'Harry, Denso, we're back on Earth. Are you two all right?'

'Yes, I think so,' Harry grumbled, unbuckling his leg-straps as Denso slowly regained consciousness behind him.

Suddenly he sat up and gave a startled cry. 'Jesus, these wrathwa beasts are making one hell of a mess if they started all those fires!'

Before another moment passed the ground shook violently, and with a grinding thud the Doorcrack that they had just passed through squeezed shut. The way through the walls of reality had closed. Kote cried out in dismay and urged Lugg down through the burnt tree-stumps and charred branches. He searched in vain for the void of moving shadows and listened hard for the shriek of wind being sucked along the dark road back to the summit of the Wrathendall Spires, but he could only hear the driving rain beating on the undergrowth. He stopped beside Gyma in despair.

'Oh, my God,' Mya gasped, forgetting the Doorcrack as she looked out across the broad expanse of countryside below them.

Single clumps of trees and acres of forest, vast tracts of wild undergrowth and heathland were ablaze. Miles and miles of ancient hedgerow were alight, sending up ribbons of crackling sparks and billowing clouds of thick, choking smoke into the darkness. Isolated houses and villages for as far as the eye could see stood out as bright as fire-beacons.

'It's the end of the world,' Mya whispered, blinking at the rain on her eyelashes. She cried out as a lorry about half a mile away exploded with a dull thud. It was etched briefly against the dark skyline as a sheet of flame engulfed it.

'Dante's *Inferno*,' Harry commented bleakly.

'It isn't only the wrathwas that have created all this destruction,' Kote spoke slowly, shielding his eyes against the driving rain as he surveyed the burning landscape. 'There are many beasts and peoples from beyond the walls of reality. There are Mauders and monsters silhouetted against the flames. I can see manditaurs . . .' he paused, rubbing his eyes quickly. 'My vision blurs. I cannot see them clearly.'

'Hush, listen,' Harry hissed, holding his hand up as a different sound began to make itself heard amongst the distant crackle and roar of the thousand fires. He turned in his saddle, following the sound as it grew louder. 'Choppers!' he cried, recognising the hum of their rotor-blades only moments before four Lynx helicopters thundered overhead, their downdraught scattering the undergrowth and sending the charred twigs and branches up in a blizzard of debris all around them. The dragmas snarled and reared in alarm as the gale of wet air tore at their wings and almost caused them to stampede.

In seconds the helicopters had swept over them in a tight battle formation, their searchlights missing them by yards as they scanned the burning countryside. Shifting beams of white light slid over the burnt-out shell of an isolated farmhouse, briefly illuminating the glistening green scales of at least three huge hump-backed creatures that were swarming through the ruins. The note from the helicopters changed as they swung back, their searchlights fixed on to the creatures and sporadic bursts of tracer preceded the flash of rockets. The beasts reared up, clawing and snarling, disturbed by the lights, before they scattered in all directions, howling and screaming as a hail of bullets tore into their hides.

Most of the rockets exploded harmlessly amongst the ruins but the last found its target. It pierced the armoured flank of a fleeing creature, bowling it over and over. They heard the dull explosion and watched in awe as the monster's armoured scales swelled in brilliance and changed colour through porraceous greens to sapphire hues until it became white hot before exploding into a gushing fountain of livid sparks that rose hundreds of feet into the dark night sky.

'That will teach those murdering bastards a lesson!' Harry shouted, thrusting a clenched fist triumphantly into the air above his head as the crackling sparks of colour began to die away.

'Wrathwa!' Kote suddenly cried, stabbing a warning finger up towards a faint, flickering, orange light travelling at tremendous speed in a tightening arc through the low clouds toward the formation of helicopters.

'Look up! Look up for Chrissake!' Denso cried helplessly

301

at the helicopter pilot against the lashing rain as the huge creature, wreathed in smoke and fire, broke through the cloud base directly above the central helicopter and enveloped it in a roaring orange blowtorch of death.

The stricken machine lurched violently sideways, its rotors screaming in a desperate bid to escape, but the wrathwa closed its jaws, crushing and trapping its tail-fin. The body of the helicopter glowed white-hot, its windows cracked and melted as its rotors smashed themselves to pieces against the wrathwa's teeth. Frantic figures trapped in the cockpit fought to jump free, their clothes bursting into flames as they plunged like burning candles to earth. Moments later the machine exploded into a fireball, the blazing fragments spinning away into the rainy darkness.

'Oh my God, what a horrible death,' Mya gasped, clutching Kote's sleeve as they watched the aerial battle unfold.

The three remaining helicopters dived low, keeping close to the ground. They veered away in different directions and began firing at the wrathwa as it rose in a slow, spiralling circle above them and vanished back into the clouds.

'It just seems hopeless,' Harry groaned.

Denso muttered as the roar of the rotors faded into the night. 'The bullets and rockets just seem to explode harmlessly against their armoured hide: they'll need to attack them with proper missiles.'

'Well they'd better get on with it pretty quickly!' Harry growled through clenched teeth.

Resting her left hand on Lugg's wing, Mya leaned forwards and shielded her eyes against the rain as she looked out across the desolate, burning countryside towards a distant blur of light on the horizon. 'We could at least tell the authorities the exact spots where these creatures are breaking through,' she said quietly, making the three men look toward her.

'I know it's not much, but do you remember that newspaper cutting we saw from the *Daily Mail*, reporting that the creatures were wreaking havoc in a broad band across the eastern part of England. Perhaps . . .' She broke off, snatching her hand away from Lugg's wing. His scaly skin and feathers had grown so hot that it had scorched her left hand and fingers badly.

Kote twisted around in the saddle at her cry, his face lined with concern as he saw her nursing her hand. He muttered harshly at the dragma in a language that Mya couldn't understand and Lugg shuffled forwards a pace and folded his wings down tightly against his flanks.

'I'm all right, it's not Lugg's fault,' she muttered, gingerly rubbing at her sore fingertips. She was more worried that the dragma's body temperature appeared to have rocketed up the moment they had journeyed back through the walls of reality. His scales had been ice-cold to touch the other side of the Doorcrack. Lightly she touched his flank, then quickly drew her fingers away, her concern deepening. If he grew any hotter, if . . .

Harry's voice broke sharply through the shadows of dread that were gathering on the edge of her consciousness. 'You mean you really want to tell your government and your army about your ley-line theory?'

Mya shook the rain from her eyes and blinked. 'Yes, that's right. It would at least give the pilots some idea where they're breaking through and where their next attack is likely to be coming from,' she replied, firmly ignoring the hint of derision in Harry's voice. 'I'm pretty sure that there is a mass of ley-lines crossing the countryside around here. If I can get to that set of detailed maps in my rooms in Cathedral Close, I can check the co-ordinates first and see if they do match with the fires we can see. I know for sure that the Beechwell Stone Circle and the Giants' Chairs are in that direction, over there where the fires are brightest. If I'm right then I am going to inform the government and try to get someone to listen to me.'

Harry shook his head, scattering raindrops away from a disbelieving scowl. Mya saw his expression and added, 'Well at least it's got to be better than doing nothing. Better than sitting here getting soaked to the skin and being passive spectators to the end of the world.'

Denso shivered and pulled his coat collar up tighter to try to stop the rain from trickling down the back of his neck. 'She's got a point, Harry,' he said in a flat expressionless voice. 'We ought to give every angle a try, no matter how fanciful – unless you've got any better ideas.'

Harry glanced round angrily at Denso and was about to open his mouth in disagreement but he hesitated, swallowing his words with a shrug. 'Is this Cathedral Close far?' he muttered without looking at her.

'No, it's only a few miles, in that direction,' Mya swept her hand out across the burning countryside toward a belt of trees on higher ground beyond which a brighter glow lit the sky.

Kote was hunched forward over Lugg's neck pressing the palms of his hands against his temples.

'Kote, is there something wrong? What's the matter?' she called, anxiously gripping his arm.

He stirred and straightened his back and slowly turned towards her stifling a groan. 'My head is full of the sound of thunder and feels as if it is on fire.'

She reached up and placed her hand on his forehead, brushing away the tangle of orange hair. His skin was so hot it was as if he was burning with a raging fever. 'We have to get you to a doctor!'

'No,' Kote stuttered, drawing back from her. 'It is the same pain that I suffered when I broke through the wall of reality to search for you. It will pass.' He dug his spurs into Lugg's flanks and the dragma surged forward through the last of the burned trees. Kote let him have his head as they crossed the sodden ploughed fields and wide ditches. The dragmas' claws sank deep into the heavy clay making them grunt and snarl as they laboured over the rising ground toward a dark line of trees.

All around them the low scudding clouds reflected a dull orange glow. Explosions sporadically rocked the ground and brilliant flashes of light lit up the sky.

'It looks as though there is one hell of a blaze getting going beyond those trees,' Denso muttered, then raised his voice to shout into Harry's ear. 'It looks like we might be too late to get to those maps!'

Harry was about to turn his head to shout an answer when they reached the dark line of trees and passed under its eaves. 'Jesus, look out!' he cried, flinging his arm up to protect his face as Gyma ploughed relentlessly through the dense undergrowth, snapping off stout branches and rushing them through a tangle of sharp, scratching twigs, cutting a straight path through the wood.

'Oh my God, the Cathedral ... the University!' Mya cried as Lugg halted just inside the trees on the far side of the wood above the main road.

She stared down at the burning town, trying to pick out the familiar landmarks that she knew ought to be there through the leaping flames and the drifting pall of thick smoke. The roof of the great hall of the University had collapsed, St. Swithin's church and the public house that stood beside it lay in ruins and the surrounding streets leading towards the Cathedral had vanished beneath mounds of rubble, broken beams and fallen masonry. She could see figures illuminated by the flames running for their lives, driven by panic, fleeing heedlessly in all directions, unable to comprehend the disaster that had befallen them. Fire tenders, police cars and ambulances were trying to force a passage through the chaos and, directly below the wood, tanks and armoured vehicles were rumbling slowly along the road with units of heavily-armed troops interspersed amongst them. They were heading towards the north west corner of the town.

'What a mess. It looks as though the whole town has been trampled by those beasts and then set alight.' Denso fell silent as his gaze swept over the desolation below.

'Those savage beasts did not do all of this!' Kote cried. 'Look, look over there where the flames are still burning at their brightest. I can see the Asiri and his Mauders through the smoke.'

The others crowded forward and tried to see where he was pointing.

'There, over there,' Kote repeated, following them with his eyes. His voice faltered as he hunted for breath and raised his arm, his hand trembling with effort as he pointed out across the glistening, rain-swept roof-tops.

The thick pall of smoke seemed to move and split apart, torn by a changing wind and the rising currents of hot air from the countless fires. The icy rain-squalls hit them with renewed force making them retreat beneath the overhanging branches.

'Yes, yes, I can see them!' Denso called out, 'Where that line of long, low roofs are on fire – to the right.'

The others followed his directions and saw the huge winged shape of Graksha with Jothnar silhouetted against the leaping flames. The wrathwa was slowly circling across the roof tops and leaving a spiralling trail of smoke and fire in its wake. Drifting columns of smoke began to obliterate the desolate scene but as it disappeared they caught a glimpse of the Mauders swarming amongst the ruins.

'I think Graksha is seeking a place to roost,' Kote muttered, pressing his hands against his temples.

'I'd like to get my hands on that murdering bastard's throat,' Harry growled through clenched teeth.

'Not a chance,' Denso answered him in despair. 'You'd never get within a mile of him while he is surrounded by all those Mauders.'

Mya continued to stare down at the drifting smoke for a long moment after it had shrouded the scene before she spoke. 'I wouldn't be so sure, Denso,' she muttered slowly. 'I think there is something wrong with the Mauders' dragmas.'

'What?' cried Harry turning sharply towards her. 'What do you think is wrong with them?'

'I don't know for sure,' she added hesitantly. 'It's difficult to see much, but they seem to be moving with faltering steps. They look listless, and sick, not at all like they did when they overran the City of Time.'

Kote suddenly swayed and clutched dizzily to her arm, 'Graksha will rise up with the dawn to fly again. You must find those maps quickly and warn your people.' His breath came in shortening gasps. 'Help me, help me Mya, I cannot breathe.'

'Oh my God!' she cried, putting her arm around him and gently lowering him so that his back rested against the gnarled oak tree.

'Mya,' he whispered through tightening lips, his eyes wild with panic as they implored her to help.

She gripped his hands in hers. 'Breathe slowly,' she whispered, 'I'll get help.'

She untangled her fingers from his and pulled open the collar of his jerkin to hear his breaths come a little easier before she rose to her feet. His panic dissolved into a smile. 'Lie still, rest,' she said with concern before turning and quietly drawing away to follow the other two.

'What is the matter with Kote?' Denso asked in a worried voice as soon as they were out of his hearing.

'I don't know,' Mya replied, glancing back at him. 'But ever since we emerged into our reality his physical condition has been deteriorating. It's as if he has a raging fever, his throat's constricted and he's so dizzy he can barely stand.'

'Perhaps it's something he caught while we were pursuing the Asiri around the Crystal Swamps. I saw some horrific insects while we were there,' Harry offered.

'But you haven't caught it. You don't feel ill in any way do you?'

'Well, no,' Harry answered thoughtfully. 'In fact, quite the opposite. I felt as though I was running a fever most of the time we were on the other side but the moment we got back I felt fine.'

'My headache's gone too,' Denso agreed.

Mya bit her lip and frowned, 'We had better get someone to look at him pretty quickly. We'll try to find a doctor when we get these maps.'

'Are you crazy? There are savage beasts running around down there. There's probably nothing left to salvage in those ruins anyway and I should think there is little chance we can find anyone who can help Kote. Remember, he is not from our world.'

The bare truth in Denso's words cut deep. Mya glanced back to where Kote sat huddled and shivering in the shadows of the gnarled oak and bright teardrops ghosted the corners of her eyes as the awful realisation that he might not be able to survive here on Earth struck home.

'I know,' she whispered bleakly turning to look down to where the ruined walls of the Cathedral showed through the drifting smoke like so many blackened and broken teeth.

Two huge hump-backed creatures were moving through

the ruins, bellowing and snarling as they went. She blinked away her tears and lifted her chin, knowing that if she couldn't find anyone to help him somehow she would have to get Kote back into his own world. She brushed fiercely at the stray strands of wet hair that clung to her forehead as she remembered the maps. If her theory was right those ley-lines would reveal dozens, perhaps hundreds, of openings.

'I must find those maps. It is more important now than anything else,' she whispered urgently to Harry and Denso, hurrying back to where Kote sat. She crouched down beside him. 'Stay hidden until I get back.' She pressed her lips against his cheek and, gripping his hand tightly in hers before she rose, she left the cover of the trees and ran down the steep slope of bracken and hummocks of wet grass toward the town.

'You can't go down there on your own. Those ruins are crawling with beasts!' cried Harry, sprinting after her. 'Wait, wait a damn minute!'

The convoy of military vehicles had moved into the distance and the road was deserted except for the litter of burnt-out cars and lorries. They crossed quickly and made their way through the outskirts of the town, scrambling over mounds of rubble, ducking down and hiding in dark, broken doorways as huge manditaurs and lurkbeasts lumbered aimlessly past them. Twice they met patrols of soldiers who shouted to them and told them to get out of town and head for one of the civilian reception centres that had been set up on Hadout Heath, but the patrols were too busy shadowing the manditaurs and lumbering lurkbeasts that were roaming through the town to bother to escort them. As they worked their way toward the Cathedral they found that the streets were littered with the bloody carcasses of fallen creatures.

Harry paused to examine some of them, frowning as he

straightened up. 'It's very strange. A lot of these beasts seem to have just collapsed and died long before the army started shooting at them.'

Mya stopped beside him and stared down at the rigid body of a centaur lying in the gutter. She shuddered and fought to disperse the horror that was crowding at the edges of her mind. Perhaps it was Earth's atmosphere that was killing these beasts from beyond the walls of reality. Perhaps time was running out for Kote. 'We must hurry!' she cried, splashing heedlessly on through the puddles.

Mya eventually found the ruined entrance to Cathedral Close and they crouched behind a pile of debris to survey the vast expanse of lawns and buildings that surrounded it.

At the far end the Cathedral had been reduced to a gigantic mound of rubble. Here and there the remnants of the stone windowframes rose twenty feet into the air, fragments of the stained glass still clinging to them. The spire had collapsed, toppling across the lawn as if some giant's hand had pushed it over. Its huge blocks of stone looked like the ribbed bones of a mammoth, stark white against the backdrop of billowing smoke and leaping flames. The shapes of huge beasts moved backward and forward through the fires.

Mya scanned the low buildings that flanked the lawns. 'God, what a mess!' She sighed, eventually picking out the house she lived in. Its roof and a part of the top floor had collapsed and most of its windows were shattered but it didn't look as if it had been set alight.

'Come on,' she whispered, rising to her feet and cautiously skirting the enormous blocks of masonry strewn across the lawn. Keeping a wary eye on the creatures prowling in the rubble, she led the other two to her rooms.

She felt her way along the corridor until she found her doorway. It was still locked and it took Harry several attempts to kick it open. It smelt of damp and the light-switch didn't work.

'Wait,' she whispered, feeling her way to a cupboard beneath the sink where she kept matches and a box of candles.

With a lighted candle she surveyed her study. Rain had blown in through the broken window soaking the carpet, there were boxes and papers scattered everywhere: otherwise it looked much as she had left it. Mya searched through the bottom drawer of her desk where she knew she had left the maps.

'Thank God,' she sighed as she found and lifted out the heavy bundle, safe in its blue plastic wallet. She cleaned the desk-top with a determined sweep of her hand and withdrew the map of the town and surrounding countryside. It showed the land as far as the Beechingwell stone circle and the Giants' Chairs. She spread it out and bent over to examine the ley-lines.

'Keep an eye on those beasts,' Harry whispered to Denso, nodding his head toward the window before peering down over Mya's shoulder in the soft, dancing pool of candlelight to look at the mass of intersecting coloured lines drawn on the map.

'It looks a complete jumble. What do all those colours mean?'

'They represent different historical and archaelogical periods,' Mya answered without looking up. 'The earliest are red, then blue . . .' She paused and slowly traced her finger along one of the red lines that crossed the town until it merged with a dozen others causing a small red blob to obliterate the symbol of the Cathedral.

'Of course,' she murmured, pulling open the top drawer and sifting through the untidy contents for her magnifying glass. When she had found it she bent over the map again and brought the Cathedral sharply into focus. 'It must mean that my theory's right. And it does explain the utter devastation of the Cathedral doesn't it, if one of those doorways opened up right in the middle of the place?'

Denso laughed grimly from the window. 'Jesus, I would have hated to have been in there saying my prayers when it happened. I'll bet the archbishop thought the Devil himself had come to claim him when all those monsters suddenly appeared.'

Mya moved the magnifying glass slowly backward and forth across the town.

'The red lines seem to cross wherever there is a church or one of those symbols for an ancient site,' Harry observed looking down across her shoulder at the map.

'Yes, at a glance I can see at least another ten sites where the walls of reality could have opened within the town and dozens more stretching out across the countryside toward the Beechingwell stone circle and the Giants' Chairs. That would certainly explain all . . .'

The rumble of two Challenger tanks entering the Close drowned out her voice as they growled across the rubble. They came to a halt and searchlights mounted on their turrets sprang on, illuminating the buildings. The beams slowly swept across the ruins of the Cathedral, throwing it into stark relief and finding and freezing the huge shape of a manditaur. Mya and Harry ran to the window and watched as the tanks fired in rapid succession. The ear-splitting explosions made the buildings in the Close tremble. Mya saw the beast rear up and surge forward and then a wave of acrid cordite smoke obliterated the scene. When it had drifted away the manditaur had vanished. The tank-engines roared and then they began to turn slowly toward the entrance of the Close.

'Wait! Wait!' Mya suddenly shouted, rushing across the

room and grabbing the map from her desk, sending the guttering candle toppling to the floor as she headed out of the room and along the corridor towards the lawn and the departing tanks.

Harry and Denso sprinted after her, the full force of the torrential rainstorm hitting them in the face as they caught up. Harry grasped her arm and stopped her from running under the tracks of the second tank.

'What the hell do you think you're doing?' he shouted at her over the thunder of the tanks' engines.

'The gunfire must have driven that creature in the ruins back through the doorway!' she answered breathlessly. 'If I can only get one of these tank commanders to see the doorway through the walls of reality and show him how it corresponds to the ley-lines he will have to believe us. He would have to, wouldn't he?'

She waved the map in the air, broke free from Harry's grip and ran out in front of the tank. The huge machine swerved violently to avoid her and came to a grinding slithering halt. The hatch on the top of the turret swung open and an angry face appeared, but before the officer could speak Mya shouted to him, frantically waving the map and stabbing her finger at it. 'We know where these creatures are coming from. There's a doorway to another reality in the Cathedral! There's at least a dozen smaller ones in the town.'

'You're in a restricted area. You'll get yourself killed if you carry on like that. Now get out of here before I radio for a patrol to take you away!' the tank commander shouted back.

'I'm sure there are bigger Doorcracks out at the Beeching-well stone circle, and perhaps some at the Giants' Chairs,' Mya carried on, ignoring his warning.

'The map's getting ruined in the rain and he's not listening to you,' Harry said from just behind her, reaching up and taking the map out of her hand. Quietly he folded it up and pushed it into his coat pocket. 'What have you got to lose by taking a look in the ruins? You'll see that the creatures have disappeared!' Harry shouted.

The figure in the turret looked down at him. His anger dissolved into a weary scowl and he raised a hand to his head and pushed back his headset. 'Look, mister, I've heard a thousand theories of where these creatures come from. I've had it from scientists, doomsday fanatics, seventh day adventists and even my commanding officer; and on top of that the airwaves are full of reported sightings around the world. *Grimms' Fairy Tales* and every myth and legend you have ever heard of has come to life – from mermaids in the Serpentine to winged horses flying over Tokyo – but all I care about right now is that the bastard things keep dying or disappearing when we attack.'

'But listen to what I'm trying to tell you. From the ley-lines drawn on this map you will know exactly where these creatures are going to appear. Don't you see the significance in that?' Mya cried in frustration. 'Don't you understand that with this information you will be ready and waiting in a position to drive these creatures back into their own reality the moment the Doorcracks open?'

The tank commander stiffened and closed his mind against Mya's protest as he reached up to pull the headset back down over his ears.

'You would be a complete fool to ignore Dr. Capthorne's advice, Major. How can you so quickly push aside what years of research here at the University have revealed?' Harry called up to the officer in his most persuasive voice. 'It won't take you more than a minute to take a look for yourself in the ruins of the Cathedral, will it?'

The commander hesitated and looked down more closely

at the bedraggled woman. 'What sort of research do you do?' he asked guardedly.

'Environmental research. I monitor and collect information on external agents that influence our existence – pollutants, acid rain, that sort of thing,' she answered quickly.

The officer thought over her answer for a moment, then spoke briefly as he issued a string of rapid orders into the mouthpiece of his headset. 'All right, I'll take one quick look inside the ruins of that Cathedral, but that's all!' he called down to them, pulling off his headset and passing it to another member of his crew. He gathered up a powerful flashlight and slung a Sterling sub-machine gun across his shoulder before scrambling to the ground. 'OK miss, I mean Doctor, if you'll lead the way.'

Mya took the wallet of maps from Harry, extracted the one she wanted and folded it to show the Cathedral as she walked beside the soldier across the lawn. She pointed out to him where the ley-lines crossed at the nave and explained their significance. She also showed him how they met at the Beechingwell stone circle and the Giants' Chairs, explaining that from the mass of lines they might be longer Door-cracks. As they reached the outer wall she folded away her maps and quickly asked, 'When you have seen the doorway, the opening into another reality, for yourself you will report it to your commanding officer won't you?'

The tank commander nodded brusquely, 'Yes, if it's there I'll report it. Now be quiet, please, in case any of those creatures are lying in wait.'

Silently they worked their way along the main outer wall, picking a path between the corpses of fallen beasts and over the piles of slippery, rain-soaked rubble, until they reached a massive breach where mounds of granite blocks had been hurled out across the lawns. One by one they clambered through the breach and stopped to stare in awe at the devastation that lay before them. Hundreds of splintered rafter beams, pews and collapsed galleries protruded like blackened, broken bones from the mountains of rubble that choked the interior of the Cathedral. The soldier switched on his flashlight bringing the litter of carcasses and destruction into stark relief as he swept the light slowly across the debris.

'My God, what a mess, what an . . .' Denso began when Mya hissed at him.

'Stop, look over there!' She gripped the soldier's arm so abruptly that it made the beam of light waver wildly and chase the shadows up across the shattered remnants of a stained-glass window, making the glass glow with all the colours of the rainbow.

'What did you see?' Harry whispered urgently as the soldier steadied the light.

'I think I saw the doorway over to your right, close to that solitary standing stone column. There was a black shape, a hole in the darkness. But . . .' Mya hesitated. 'But I'm not really sure, it's so difficult to see anything clearly.'

The tank commander brought the beam of light down, following her directions and swept it obliquely across the petrified chaos. Suddenly he froze and each gave a cry of alarm as the beam revealed the huge, menacing shape of a manditaur rising out of the ruins less than ten yards from where they stood. In one swift movement the soldier had swung the machine gun from his shoulder, flicked the safety catch and cocked it ready to fire.

'Wait!' Harry called, peering forward. 'It's lying half on its side. I think it might be dead already like the rest of them in the ruins. Here, give me the light for a moment and I'll take a close look.'

With the flashlight in his hand he picked his way cautiously forward, shuddering as he climbed over the slippery scales of the dead beast until he reached its head. He played the beam of light across the creature's huge flanks and underbelly and along its serrated tail. He illuminated the layers of glistening iridescent scales and rows of razor-spines covering the humps and wrinkles of the beast's leathery hide.

'It's dead!' he called out flatly, moving the light so that they could see the massive prehistoric head thrown tortuously backward, the savage jaws gaping open in a last snarling roar. The opaque, red eyes stared blindly into the middle distance and its huge forelegs and claws were stretched out, locked in rigor mortis.

'There are hundreds of them, half-buried in this gigantic wall of rubble!' Harry cried, sweeping the flashlight up across the bodies before he scrambled up and over the piles of splintered pews and beams and broken stone archways to get a closer look. 'Yes, I was right,' he called out, shining the light to reveal a mass of hind legs and tails sticking out from amongst the blocks of granite.

'The doorway must have been where that wall of rubble cuts the Cathedral in two,' Mya added, unfolding and pointing to the map as she hurried forward. 'It must have closed, trapping those creatures and . . .'

'No!' the soldier interrupted firmly, his mouth tightening with anger. 'There are no doorways to anywhere except in your imagination: you've been wasting my time. Those monsters probably brought the lantern of the tower and the vaulted roof crashing down whilst trying to escape from our guns. You'd better get out of here before my patience snaps and I have you arrested.' He turned away from them and began to hurry back toward the breach in the wall.

'But the roof had already collapsed before you fired on those creatures. You've got to believe us!' Mya cried out in desperation. 'You've got to understand. These Doorcracks exist and thousands more of these beasts will swarm through the Beechingwell stone circle and the Giants' Chairs.'

'Get out of here now, and fast, that's an order!' the soldier shouted, his eyes narrowing as he raised the machine-gun menacingly at them.

'Come on, we had better do as he says,' Denso urged, tugging at Mya's sleeve. 'This guy's not going to believe another word we say.'

The tank commander escorted them through the ruins and across the lawn to the entrance of the Close, maintaining a rigid silence. He watched them until they had vanished in the drifting smoke towards the civilian reception centre at Hadout Heath. For a moment he stared back at the ruined Cathedral. Sighing, he reached for his headset and wearily pulled it on to report to GHQ Mya's crazy theories of a doorway into other worlds.

Once they were out of sight of the Close they doubled back, ducking down and hiding from passing patrols as they worked their way slowly through the outskirts of the town toward the edge of the wood where Kote was waiting for them.

'There's no point in trying to get any medical help for Kote: that tank commander probably reported our presence in the Close and if we stop any of the patrols they'll arrest us.' Mya's voice was worried. She walked on in silence for a while before speaking again. 'There was a doorway in that Cathedral: the damage to the building, the beasts, everything that happened, even the map pointed to it. I know it was there. But because the bloody thing had closed and trapped those creatures we couldn't show it to that soldier. Now nobody is ever going to take us seriously again, not once he has filed his report. That means this orgy of destruction will go on and on.'

'We'll find a way to convince someone, I'm sure of it,' Denso offered, but his voice sounded tired and lacked any real conviction. He hunched his shoulders against the rain.

Harry merely shrugged and trudged along a pace behind them, splashing through the puddles and picking his way around the fallen beasts and over the piles of rubble that littered the pavements. His face was drawn into a frown as he tried to get a hold on the dozen or so loose ends to this affair. Mya was right: there had been a way through the walls of reality in that Cathedral and it must have closed only moments before the tanks had stopped firing because the blocks of fallen masonry that formed the centre of that gigantic wall of rubble were hardly wet from the pouring rain. Most of the creatures he had scrambled over inside the Cathedral had been dead long enough to grow stone-cold before the tanks arrived. He was sure something else was killing them faster than the military, but what? He also remembered what a sorry sight Jothnar and his Mauders had looked when they spotted them earlier through the smoke and Kote's sudden sickness: it made him wonder if this invasion of Paradise was turning out to be everything that the Asiri and his Mauders had expected it to be.

Dawn was beginning to grey the sky as they reached the main road. Low clouds were brushing across the roof tops and drenching the fires. They paused to check for passing patrols before Harry broke his silence.

'Perhaps it doesn't matter if they know where the doorways are going to open or close. Perhaps this invasion will peter out all by itself if it's given the time.'

'What do you mean?' Mya frowned, his words began to crystallise ideas that were already forming on the edge of her mind, ideas that she would rather have dismissed and thrown aside. She gripped his wet sleeve and searched his face as he strove to find the right words to explain.

'I . . . I don't know for sure. I just have this gut-feeling after seeing all those dead creatures in the cathedral that they were trying to get back to where they came from, rather than invade us, when the doorway closed against them and trapped them there. I think our atmosphere killed them.'

Harry was about to explain how he came to that conclusion when he felt Mya's grip on his sleeve tighten and saw the colour bleed out of her face in the faint dawn light.

'Kote!' she whispered, her lips trembling. 'We have to get him back, if it's not already too late.'

She fled across the road and up the hill toward the woods calling out his name.

'Well you did that pretty tactlessly didn't you?' Denso snapped at Harry as they chased after her.

Mya reached the gnarled oak ahead of the others and found the spot where she had made him sit and wait. It was empty. She searched frantically along the gloomy trees, tears scouring her cheeks as she called his name. A sudden movement from inside the wood, a faint snarling sound, brought her to a halt.

'Lugg, Gyma!' she shouted remembering the two dragmas as she ran among the trees.

She found Kote half-kneeling, his hand stretched up and clinging to Lugg's stirrup as if he was trying to mount.

'Kote, Kote, thank God you are still alive!' she cried, scrambling through the dense undergrowth of bracken and brambles that separated them.

She threw her arms around him to support him and cradled his head in her arms. She blinked back tears as he slowly looked up into her eyes. The skin on his face was stretched taut with the pain he was suffering and it was paper-white beneath the mass of vivid tattoos. His eyes had become deep pools of shadows, reflecting his inner agonies.

Thin trickles of blood seeped out of his ears and ran down his neck to spread in a widening stain across his collar. He shivered and smiled weakly as he gathered his breath to speak.

'I . . . I . . . I cannot share the beauty of your world, Mya,' he whispered, linking his fingers with hers.

'We must get you back to Bendran as fast as we can,' she whispered back, fighting down the new tears that had welled up in her eyes.

The other two broke through the undergrowth and ran to help her as Kote slowly shook his head. 'The way is closed. I cannot go back: I must die here.'

'The maps!' Denso cried, linking his arms around Kote to support him. 'Get out the maps and use those ley-lines to find the closest doorway. There must be hundreds around here.'

Kote frowned and slowly looked up into Denso's eyes, 'The maps? You found them?'

Denso grinned and nodded. 'Yes, hang on there, Kote, we'll have you home in no time.'

'No,' the Journeyman whispered, trying to move. 'You must warn your people. My life is nothing . . .'

'I've tried to warn them already and they wouldn't listen, so now they can wait,' Mya interrupted, trying to keep the emotion out of her voice without looking up from the map that she had opened beside him.

Harry bent forward and peered over her shoulder, doing his best to shield the map from the driving rain that was blurring the coloured lines, feathering their edges into soft rainbows. 'You mentioned the Beechingwell stones and the Giants' Chairs earlier: perhaps we should go for them if they are where the majority of the ley-lines intersect,' he suggested, pointing to the Beechingwell stone circle.

Mya nodded, 'Yes, I think you're right. The two ancient

sites are next to one another. I'm sure there are more likely to be major pathways there even if we can't guarantee that they will remain open. But . . .' she hesitated, quickly calculating the distance. 'The stone circle is almost six miles away as the crow flies.' She looked up at the two bedraggled dragmas and caught her breath as she saw how much their condition had deteriorated since they had emerged through the walls of reality. Their heads hung low as they stood with dilated nostrils and gaping jaws, sucking in shallow, laboured, rattling breaths. They were swaying, staggering slightly from side to side, constantly shuffling their splayed claws to keep their balance as they stared down at her with dull and cloudy eyes.

'Lugg and Gyma will never be able to cover that distance. I'll have to find somewhere closer,' she admitted, returning her attention to the map.

'Well you had better find that "somewhere" quickly. Kote's getting weaker,' Denso warned as the Journeyman sunk lower in his arms.

'There isn't anywhere else with as many ley-lines crossing it!' she cried bleakly, looking up from the map. 'It's got to be the Giants' Chairs at Wicklewood: but at least it's straight across country to the north-east. If we follow the line of electricity pylons running parallel to this wood they will lead us right to it. Now let us hope that we don't meet any patrols on the way and that the doorway is still open when we get there.' She rose to her feet, folded the map into a sodden triangle and thrust it into her pocket. 'I'll mount first, then you can pass Kote up to me.'

At that moment the crash and snap of branches and a bellowing shout from the edge of the wood made her spin round. A huge giant and a herd of frantic unicorns burst through the undergrowth and blundered past them. Following them and climbing the hill towards the woods they could hear the roar of powerful diesel engines. Harry took a hesitant step towards the edge of the wood and saw more of the creatures scrambling through the trees. Behind them, silhouetted against the dawn sky, the drab, bulky shapes of tanks and personnel carriers loomed into view.

'Jesus! We've got to get out of here right now!' he shouted to the others.

Mya caught a glimpse of the advancing tanks and gathered Lugg's reins into her left hand as she scrambled up into the saddle. 'Lugg,' she whispered urgently as she reached down for Kote's hand, 'those bastards will kill us if they catch up. You must run faster than the wind if you are to reach the Giants' Chairs and the Doorcrack ahead of them.'

Lugg roared, his voice growing stronger, and he staggered forward, arching his neck as Harry and Denso lifted Kote up across the saddle and laid him in Mya's arms.

'Now run! Run for your life and keep well inside these trees until we reach the north-east corner of the wood. After that we must follow the pylons!' she cried as Lugg surged forward, his rolling gait veering wildly from side to side as they cut a haphazard path through the mass of fleeing creatures that now filled the undergrowth in the edge of the wood. Harry and Denso scrambled up into Gyma's saddle and quickly followed.

Behind them the roar of the tank engines changed and became softer and then they faded completely. There seemed to be a moment's silence broken only by Lugg's laboured breaths and the wet, crackling hum of static from the line of pylons. Then the world exploded all around them as the tanks fired through the trees: creatures screamed and howled as the shrapnel tore into their bodies.

'Run! Run for your life!' Mya shouted, driving her heels into Lugg's flanks as a huge elm tree crashed to the ground beside them.

The firing stopped as suddenly as it had begun as the tank engines roared into life. 'I think they're going to move round to the outside of the wood and try to cut us off!' Harry shouted as Gyma drew level.

'We'll never outrun them. We haven't got a hope,' Denso shouted in despair.

'We must. We must!' Mya shouted back, urging Lugg toward the edge of the wood.

Lugg burst out of the trees and into the rough, unploughed fields twenty yards from where the pylon-heads were lost in low cloud. They turned away from the wood and marched straight across the broad, bleak and empty landscape of burnt fields and hedgerows, deep dykes and ditches that stretched away to the north-east.

Harry looked back. 'The tanks haven't reached the corner of the wood yet: we've got a chance of staying ahead of them.'

Kote stirred in Mya's arms and reached slowly for her hand, entwining his fingers with hers as he tried to whisper something to her but his head sank against her breast as he passed out of consciousness. Fresh tears of despair blurred her sight, running down her cheeks as she tightened her grip on his hand.

The sudden roar of jet engines behind them made Mya pause and twist her head to scan the dark line of trees that crowned the hill. 'Lugg, for God's sake run! Run!' she cried, snatching her hand free and desperately digging her heels hard into his flanks as she saw a line of Tornado fighters appear above the wood.

The roar of their engines became a rush of thunder that deafened her and shook the ground, scattering the hordes of fleeing creatures that were streaming out of the trees behind them. There was a brief flicker of bright orange flame around the nose-cone of each of the planes and then she heard the sharp clatter of machine guns before the exploding cannon shells tore up the rough, unploughed ground all around them. A centaur screamed as its body exploded into a mass of splintered bone and bloody flesh. Manditaurs and lurkbeasts reared up, howling and bellowing, as the cannon shells tore into their armoured hides as easily as sharpened pencils tear through tissue paper. The beasts clawed helplessly at the air and then sprawled forward, their incandescent scales splitting and tearing apart as they collapsed in bloody heaps.

Gyma staggered and almost fell as a shower of wet, black earth was thrown up by the murderous hail of cannon fire and hit her side. Harry clung on grimly as the roar of engines faded and he watched the formation of Tornadoes shrink into the distance until they became black, menacing dots against the horizon. He let out a gasp of relief but swallowed it when he saw the fighters climb and bank sharply as they began to turn back towards them for a second attack.

'They're coming back! The bastards are coming back! They'll cut us to pieces if we don't find some cover!' Denso cried, looking at the carcass-strewn ground on either side of them.

Mya looked ahead before shouting back, 'I think there's a dyke behind that burnt-out hedge at the bottom of this field!'

'Jesus, it's too far, we'll never make it!' Denso hissed through clenched teeth as Gyma surged forward.

The formation of Tornadoes had levelled out. They were coming in fast and low, hugging the terrain, the thunder of their engines getting louder and louder. Harry saw the bright orange flashes of their guns as they opened fire. They were sitting targets and there wasn't a damn thing they could do about it.

Mya's lips trembled as she shouted desperately to Lugg. 'Gallop, Lugg. Go faster!'

The ground around them erupted in smoke and fire. She had wanted to save Kote's life but instead, it seemed, she had led him into a death trap. Lugg ran on, his reptilian head weaving from side to side with exhaustion. Together, the two dragmas burst through the burned hedgerow and threw themselves down into the deep, water-filled dyke.

Denso gave a wailing shout as they slithered down the steep earth bank and plunged into the stagnant, murky water. They sank in a swirling mass of green bubbles. The roar of the attack abruptly vanished as the dark water closed over their heads, the shock of it driving the breath from their lungs. The dragmas felt their claws sinking into the soft oozing mud at the bottom of the dyke and frantically beat their wings as they scrabbled up for air. Gasping and choking they reached the surface as the formation of Tornadoes thundered ovehead, white hot flames pouring out of their afterburners.

Harry spat out a mouthful of brackish slime and shouted at the others. 'Keep your heads down as low as you can and stay still. Perfectly still. It's our only chance if they make another attack.'

The roar of the jet engines changed as they climbed above the dark line of trees that crowned the hill and began to turn back. Mya tightened her grip on Kote's limp body and put her hand under his chin to lift his mouth above the water. Forcefully she shook him and called out his name. His shoulders convulsed as he coughed violently and thick dribbles of the greenish water ran out of the corners of his mouth and from his nose.

'Keep still!' Harry cursed.

Mya shivered in the icy water that was chilling her bones. She didn't know how long they could survive in this temperature, but at least it had cooled Kote's fever and Lugg's scales were no longer burning hot. The tanks had moved around the edge of the wood and she could see that they had positioned themselves beneath the trees and that dozens of armoured personnel carriers were lined up behind them and disgorging hundreds of heavily-armed troops. The thunder of the jet turbines was getting louder as the Tornadoes levelled out to strafe the remaining creatures fleeing across the fields on either side of the line of pylons. Mya was about to look up at the fighters when the officer standing in the turret of the tank in the centre of the line caught her attention. There was something familiar about him. He was studying a crumpled map and speaking rapidly into his headset, dividing his tanks and troops into two columns and directing them north-east along the line of pylons towards the Beechingwell stone circle and the Giants' Chairs. The tanks and troops were edging slowly forward, waiting for the Tornadoes to complete their attack before they began to advance.

Mya suddenly remembered where she had seen him before. He was the major she had tried to convince about the Doorcrack in the ruins of the Cathedral. 'Damn!' she muttered bitterly as she tightened her grip on Kote's hand. She realised that the major must have listened to her theories after all and he was focusing all his forces towards the very Doorcrack they were trying to reach. Now she was sure they would never make it.

'Wrathwas!' Denso cried, lifting a freezing, dripping hand out of the water to point up into the sky. 'There are two of them almost directly above those jets. They've just broken through the clouds from the direction of the stone circle. Jesus, look at the speed of those monsters!' he gasped.

'Look up! Look up, you fools!' Harry shouted,

327

gesticulating wildly with his arms as the wrathwas descended, long tongues of fire pouring out of their gaping jaws.

One of the navigators must have glanced up because at the last possible moment, just as the wrathwas' breath was about to scorch their wings, the formation broke up. The Tornadoes banked violently to left and right, climbing on full power, their afterburners white hot and their engines reaching an ear-splitting roar.

'Those guys must be pulling some Gs,' Harry muttered as they reformed into two groups and climbed vertically, looping and spiralling to get the winged monsters in their sights.

'Nothing can harm a wrathwa beast. They are the strongest creatures beyond the walls of reality and they are as old as time itself!' Kote called out, his voice sounding stronger.

'Well, those pilots are certainly going to try an attack!' Denso shouted back as rapid machine-gun fire and the whoosh of launching rockets drowned out his voice.

Moments later the boom of an explosion overhead shook the ground and sent a sluggish ripple along the surface of the water in the dyke. 'It's a direct hit!' Harry shouted, clapping his hands as the larger and slower of the two winged monsters was enveloped in a sheet of blue-green flame after the rockets exploded against its side.

The huge beast bellowed and arched its back in convulsions of rage as it emerged unharmed through the flames. It snaked around, turning in its own length, spitting out a column of white fire two hundred feet long as it flew head-on toward the Tornado that had attacked it. The pilot must have hauled desperately at his controls in those last seconds before the beast's gaping jaws enveloped him but it was too late to pull away. The nose-cone vanished, the canopy blackened and shattered, the markings on the fuselage

bubbled, shrivelled and then burst into flame and the wings and tail momentarily glowed a dull red as the fire engulfed it. The wrathwa snapped its jaws shut, shearing through the nose-cone, before it soared away as the Tornado exploded in a ball of orange flame and black smoke that darkened the sky.

Harry balled his hands into fists of rage, shouting angrily, 'Get the bastard! Shoot it out of the sky!'

The surviving Tornadoes pursued the beast, attacking as ferociously as angry wasps, banking and diving as they fired their rockets into the wrathwa's sides.

'I tell you, nothing can harm the wrathwas,' Kote insisted.

Then another wave of rockets struck the monstrous winged creature. They exploded against its armoured hide, this time shattering the glistening layers of armoured scales that protected it. Pieces of shrapnel ripped through its sinuous body, cutting through the thick leathery membranes that were stretched across its skeletal wings, penetrating deep inside its rib cage and piercing its ancient heart. Harry gave a triumphant shout as the wrathwa shuddered and convulsed, beating its torn wings frantically and spitting out blasts of fire as it plunged in a spiralling arc towards the ground. Fountains of bright sparks and ribbons of bilious, yellow smoke gushed out of the ragged wounds along its sides leaving a sulphurous stain low across the morning sky pointing to its crash, a blazing pyre of flesh and bones about a mile away from the line of pylons.

The Tornadoes thundered low across the dyke and reformed into a tight formation as they climbed steeply to chase the other wrathwas up through the clouds. The thunder of their engines grew fainter and fainter. Suddenly the roar of the tanks filled the silence.

'The tanks are starting to move. We've got to get out of

here!' Harry cried, urging Gyma to scramble up the slippery bank as the tanks fired their first salvo of shells which screamed over their heads to explode about a quarter of a mile away amongst a mass of fleeing creatures.

Dark fountains of earth, bushes, trees and the bodies of manditaurs and lurkbeasts were hurled high into the air. 'We're never going to make it!' Denso shouted, instinctively hunching his shoulders and clinging to Harry as the thunder of guns echoed across the hillside behind them.

This time the barrage of shells exploded even closer to them, sending up black plumes of smoke, earth and mangled corpses.

'Keep close to the pylons!' Harry shouted to Mya over the clatter of machine guns and the boom of exploding shells as Lugg drew level. 'If we're lucky they won't aim directly at the pylons.'

The two dragmas ran on. All around them huge creatures were fleeing towards the Doorcrack. They appeared and disappeared through the thickening haze of smoke caused by the exploding shells. They stumbled blindly over the blackened carcasses of thousands of previously mythical beasts that had collapsed and died and now littered the ground. Swarms of gradaurs filled the ditches with their brilliant orange and turquoise shells split open wherever they were submerged beneath the murky waters. A monstrous two-headed, horned creature appeared beside Lugg and almost blundered into him before it staggered and fell onto its knees, clutching a clawed hand to each of its heads. Blood was oozing out of its ears and eyes and trickling out of its mouth. It howled and fell forwards, clawing at the wet earth as it died. Mya looked back at the creature as they surged forwards. She knew it hadn't been hit by a bullet, it had just keeled over.

'I'm sure you're right about those creatures in the

Cathedral!' she shouted across to Harry. 'Our atmosphere is killing them faster than all the weapons we're using against them.'

'Yes, but you try telling that to the military!' Denso shouted back.

The sound of gunfire was getting closer and an exploding shell showered them with earth. The tanks were catching them. Suddenly the firing changed direction, the shells began exploding away to their left. The smoke was thinning. Ahead of them there were clumps of trees as the flat, featureless landscape rose into low, undulating hills crowded with the exodus of fleeing beasts. Mya knew they were nearing the stone circle and the Giants' Chairs.

'Hold on, we're nearly there,' she whispered to Kote as she held him tightly against her and urged Lugg forward, scattering a herd of centaurs in his path.

Gyma kept level with them, her breath bursting through her nostrils in clouds of steam, her flanks white and dripping with sweat.

'Mya!' Harry shouted against the rumble and crash of gunfire and the baying, howling cries of the fleeing beasts all around them. He pointed urgently away to his left. 'There are thousands of the Asiri's Mauders swarming across our path. If they don't change direction they're going to overrun us before we reach the Doorcrack.'

Denso glanced quickly back at the two lines of advancing tanks and the mass of troops spread out behind them. 'What the hell are they doing? They're going in the wrong direction for the Doorcrack. Don't they realise that they'll be slaughtered if they attack those tanks? Look, dozens of them are collapsing even before the shells hit them.'

'The Mauders are warriors. They must fulfil their pledge to the Asiri and conquer Paradise. There is nothing but death that will stop them,' Kote said wearily.

'We must keep going, we must try to reach the Doorcrack before the Mauders overrun us. We're so close now.' Mya urged them all onward. 'The stone circle and the Giants' Chairs are just beyond that second pylon where the ground rises into a small hillock. They're directly ahead of us.'

They drew closer, shortening the distance in long, exhausting strides.

'I can see two circles of huge stones that ring the top of it. There are creatures swarming between the stones trying to get back through the Doorcrack!' Harry shouted back as they passed the last pylon and the ground began to rise.

'That's it! The outer ring is the stone circle, the inner one is the Giants' Chairs. We've made it! We've got to get there before the Mauders!' Mya cried with relief, but a shadow suddenly swooped across them.

'What the hell?' Denso cried, looking up to see the monstrous, winged shape of Graksha, with Jothnar sitting on his back, pass low over them. They were heading towards the line of tanks.

'Don't you realise when you're beaten, you crazy bastard?' Harry shouted.

The Asiri gave a scream of rage as he recognised Harry's voice. He shook his fist and turned the enormous wrathwa slowly toward them. Graksha scorched the ground with a blazing column of fire a hundred feet long. The leading rank of Mauders reached the rising ground and began to close in, their dragmas staggering and stumbling.

'Damn!' Harry murmured grimly.

'We got so close!' Denso hissed in anger as the ring of Mauders tightened around them.

Graksha landed in a blaze of sparks a hundred yards from the granite chairs but he had descended too fast. His talons snagged on the carcasses that littered the ground, he slewed sideways and clawed desperately at the soft, wet earth. His right wing-tip touched a staggering lurkbeast and made him stumble: he emitted a roaring gush of flames and threw Jothnar high into the air out of the saddle. He landed sprawling on the ground between them and the Giants' Chairs. The great winged beast slid on past Lugg and Gyma, its claws tearing deep weals in the soft earth before it crashed into the closing ranks of Mauders, crushing a dozen stricken dragmas beneath its huge underbelly. With a thunderous roar it thrashed its tail and toppled helplessly forward, snapping its huge jaw shut. A convulsive shudder rippled through its body as it gulped, swallowing its own fire.

'Ride for the doorway now: it's your only chance!' Harry shouted at Mya as the wrathwa frantically beat its wings, trying to rise and sending the Mauders and their dragmas crashing into each other as they milled in confusion.

Jothnar struggled to his knees. Blood was oozing from his mouth, his ears and his eye sockets. He cursed and grabbed wildly at Lugg as Mya spurred him up the grassy slope, forcing a path through the crush of creatures who were surging towards the Doorcrack. The Asiri's armoured glove caught on the edge of one of the dragma's scales and he was dragged almost to the summit before the scale tore free and he fell backward, tumbling over and over to the bottom of the mound. The thunderous roar of gunfire, the howls of fleeing beasts and the screams and shouts of the Mauders struggling to escape from Graksha's crushing wings boiled across the Doorcrack. Kote struggled forward out of Mya's arms, keeping one hand entwined with hers as he clasped the other around the pommel of the saddle. Lugg squeezed through a gap and entered the ring of stones. Before them waves of limping, bleeding creatures were vanishing into a black, echoing void of moving shadow that filled the centre of the hill. A wind was moaning past the standing stones, rising to a howling shriek as the sounds of death and destruction were sucked through the open Doorcrack.

'I will always love you as long as I live!' Mya cried, unable to stop the rush of tears as she kicked her feet out of the stirrups, leaping to the ground before she clung onto one of the standing stones seconds before Lugg plunged through the opening. Her fingers briefly locked with Kote's before they slipped apart, their eyes meeting in an endless parting moment.

'I will find a way to come back one day!' he called, the echo of his voice growing fainter and fainter as the darkness swallowed him up.

Gyma, riderless, staggered past her and plunged into the dark echoing void. Angry shouts from the bottom of the slope made Mya turn around and force her way back between the standing stones to see Harry and Denso hurriedly backing away from the Asiri.

'Don't you understand?' Harry was shouting. 'You can't survive here. Our atmosphere is killing you. Your only chance of escape is to go back through the Doorcrack. You cannot conquer Paradise!'

Jothnar staggered back to his stricken wrathwa and screamed as he climbed back into the saddle. 'I shall have it all! Paradise shall be mine!' And he cursed and shouted at his Mauders, commanding them to attack the advancing tanks.

'Get down behind one of those stones!' Harry shouted breathlessly as a barrage of shells exploded amongst the Mauders.

Graksha beat his wings frantically on the ground and lurched forward, gathering speed as a shell exploded against his flank. His armoured scales began to crackle and grow red-hot as he rose above the ground. His body began to swell, splitting apart between his scales. Sheets of blue and gold flames gushed out, totally enveloping him and his screaming rider in fire. Graksha's armoured scales buckled and bent seconds before he exploded with a thundercrack that made the ground tremble, showering the advancing Mauders with a spreading rain of fire. The Mauders screamed and fought one another to escape as the fire consumed them, leaping from warrior to warrior, beast to beast.

Mya shuddered and buried her head in Harry's protecting arms, but Denso stood his ground. His face was grim and determined, knowing that he must watch everything and remember it so that he could write it all down for Tholocus. A thick pall of smoke rose from the burning corpses making them cough and cover their faces as it swirled across the stone circle, staining the sky before a freshening wind blew it away.

'Listen,' Harry whispered softly as he helped Mya to her feet. 'The guns have stopped firing. The invasion of Paradise is over.'

Denso nodded, remembering the biblical prophecies that he had heard at the Grand Council. 'From the sky shall come a great King of Terror', and 'Their flesh shall consume away while they stand upon their feet and their eyes shall consume away into their holes'. He smiled, looking down to where the Mauders' bones had turned to ash. Those ancient prophecies whispered thousands of years ago in the City of Time had come true at last.

'Can you remember exactly how all this began?' he asked Harry, reaching into his pocket for his sodden notebook and pencil stub and carefully writing the words 'Hidden Echoes' at the top of the blank page.

Limited edition T-shirts and sweatshirts with illustrations taken from *Hidden Echoes* are available in black or white, sized medium and large.

T-shirts £12 (plus £1.20 postage and packing)
Sweatshirts £17.50 (plus £1.50 postage and packing)

Please make cheques payable to Mike Jefferies, and send your orders to:

Nicola Willis
HarperCollins Publishers
77–85 Fulham Palace Road
London
W6 8JB